BAD BOSS CHICKS

PERK THIRTY

Cole Hart
SIGNATURE NOVELS

Bad Boss Chicks

Published in the United States of America.

Published by Cole Hart Signature, LLC.

Mailing List

To stay up to date on new releases, plus get information on contests, sneak peeks, and more,

Go To The Website Below...

WWW.COLEHARTSIGNATURE.COM

PROLOGUE

The Honey Bee colony was broken down into three groups: Queens, workers, and drones. All have specific jobs and ranks within the Bee organization. The drones were male bees who didn't have stingers, but they did have what it takes to "sting" and fertilize a Queen. Sadly, they died right after mating. But as most males would agree, at least the drones went out in some sweet pussy.

The worker bees were the females who weren't capable of reproducing. They did all the work in the hive. They did housekeeping, collected pollen and nectar, made wax, and last but not least, they were responsible for feeding the Queen.

The Queen Bee was the heart and soul of the colony. Her job was to regulate shit and to lay lots of eggs. However, there could typically only be one "Queen Bee" in a hive, so when new queens hatch, they killed their competitors. A newly hatched queen would sting her unhatched rivals, killing them while they are still in their cells. If two queens hatch at once, they fought to the death. This was called "A Royal Death Match." It was kill or be killed in the honey game.

Bees were one of the few animals that attacked yo

knowing they might die. That was the true definition of a ride or die character. Putting one's life on the line for the cause you believed in and rode for. It's what soldiers did every day. It's what many people from the streets did, every day.

When you have a smooth running, loyal hive, the finest honey would drip forth, and everyone associated would be happy. That's always been the goal of the Bad Bitchez Click. But just because a few honeys were Queens, didn't mean they are restricted to only one kind of **Bee.**

You could be a **B**ad **B**itch, **B**eauty, **B**illionaire in the making, **B**reezy, **B**o$$, **B**opper, **B**ugaboo, **B**ooster, **B**usser, **B**aker, **B**artender, **B**ookkeeper, or whatever the fuck! There were tons of **B** words that one could claim, that one was immersed in. It's all about who you were and what you represented that made you a **Bad B.** But whatever it was, claim it wholeheartedly, without shame, and be the best **Bee** that you motherfucking can be! **B**zzzzzz.

PART I

THE HU$TLE

1

SUMMER

"Damn baby, you freaky as a muthafucka," Young Racks moaned as he looked down at the pretty redbone kneeling between his legs. She looked up at him and smiled with her honey colored eyes. Her mouth was occupied at the moment as it held both of Young Racks' testicles on each side of her jaws like a chipmunk. She was performing her trademark "Alvin, Simon, Theodore" trick, where she sucked on both balls simultaneously while sticking her tongue out and licking the sensitive area right by the asshole. This move made men's toes curl! Young Racks, Atlanta's hottest new rapper, was going crazy at the moment.

"Shit, shit, shit!" He shouted as Summer put her hands under his knees and pushed them up to his chest. When she tongued his puckered hole, she knew he was on the verge of losing it. But Summer didn't want him to blow his load just yet. She had other plans for this fool. If only his punk ass girlfriend would hurry up. The bitch was fucking late!

Young Racks was in heaven. *This bitch is a BEAST,* he thought to himself as she turned his ass out. Seeing her iced out BBC medallion bling between his legs turned him on even more. He liked his bitches icy *and* light-skinned. And this redbone sucking him off was one of the baddest he'd ever had. Almost as bad as Tasha...

"What the fuck is this ho ass shit?" His girlfriend of 18 months said, storming into the living room.

"Ta-Ta... Tasha? Whatchu– "

"Bitch ass nigga, I ***LIVE*** here! Remember?" she said, cutting him off.

"But you was supposed to be in Jamaica with your sister," Young Racks said, standing up and reaching for his pants. Tasha grabbed them and flung them to the other side of the room.

"*WAS*. I came back early because I called myself missing yo dog ass. And I come home to this?" Tasha said, walking up on him. "I can't believe you Racks. This is fucked up. Uh-uh nigga. You got caught with your pants down for the *LAST* mutha-fuckin' time," she said, pointing her finger in his face. "Nigga, didn't I tell you if you cheated on me again, I was gonna pop your ass? Huh, didn't I?"

"Baby look. It ain't what chu think. It ain't even like that ma," he whined to her.

"What? It ain't what it ***LOOK*** like?! Fool, I walk into ***OUR*** home, and this ho got your legs in the air like a bitch, spread eagle, eatin' your ass! So how isn't it ***LIKE*** that?" Tasha said as she reached into her Prada purse and pulled put a chrome .380. Everybody got bug-eyed.

"Oh shit!" Summer said, putting her hands in the air. Young Racks did the same thing as he slowly backed up, naked from the waist down.

"Shut up bitch!" Tasha told Summer. "I'm gonna shoot this nigga, then I'm gon' pop you too hoe!"

"Look ma, I ain't know. For real for real, the nigga told me he ain't have no girl," Summer said.

"Oh yeah?" Tasha said, returning her attention back to her man. "You ain't got no girl huh?"

Rarr! Rarr! Tasha pulled the trigger two times. The shots echoed loudly in the living room as a slug was put into each of the rapper's thighs. He collapsed on the couch, yelling hysterically as he clutched each bloody hole in pain.

"You still ain't got no chick, Racks? Huh? I ***TOLD*** you don't fuck wit me nigga. I ain't no punk ho!" Tasha yelled, standing over him and waving the still smoking gun around as she talked.

"I know, I know! Damn mami. I'm sorry. Fuck! Aaggghh. Look baby. Pleeeease baby, please..." he begged.

"Please what Racks? Huh nigga? I'm gonna shoot cho dick off since you wanna stick it in everybody and they mama!" Tasha grabbed Summer's long hair and dragged her in front of the wounded rapper. When she put the hot barrel to Summer's temple, Young Racks looked at a real live hood bitch in action. He underestimated her thoroughness, until now.

"You love this bitch Racks? You think she badder than me?" Tasha asked him as a single tear rolled down her smooth cheek. She looked into his eyes, hatred clouding her own pretty brown ones. "I'll paint this whole room with this bitch's brains nigga. Don't play with me! Do you love this bitch?"

"NO! NO! Baby... I love you," he pleaded.

"Is she badder than me?"

"Oh God.... Tasha please..."

Rarr! She shot him in his foot.

"No! You the baddest chick mami!" Young Racks screamed as the burning of the lead traveled through his body.

"Yeah, I thought so," Tasha said as she pushed Summer to the floor and kicked her in the back with a pointy 4-inch stiletto heel.

"P-p-please Tasha. I'll give you anything. ANY fuckin' thing! Just...don't..."

"Shoot your dick off?" Tasha finished his sentence with an evil smile on her face. "Hmm, well let's see. What is you cheating on me worth?"

"Anything ma. You can have whatever!" Young Racks doubled over in pain as his blood pooled on the floor.

"Alright, where the dope at?"

"Huh?"

"The dope, nigga. You know. *DRUGS?!* You think I don't know you ain't still out here moving that shit? Nigga, you ain't even go *gold*! And you sho' ain't doing numbers like that. So, I know you gots to be holding. Where it's at?" Tasha said, pointing the .380 at his crotch.

Young Racks was in pain and started to go into shock. Without even realizing it, he told Tasha that he kept a rented U-Haul storage garage on the other side of town. And when she asked about the safe behind the Tupac painting (that he *ALSO* thought that she knew nothing about), he spilled the digits ASAP.

"Alright nigga. You bet not be lying to me, or I'm coming back for dat ass," Tasha said, waving the pistol in his face. "I'll call 911, but you don't know *who* shot you. Got it?"

All he could do was nod. Tasha put the barrel inside of the entrance wound in his left thigh and twisted the gun slowly. He yelped in agony.

"Got it?" She said between clinched teeth inches from his face. She could smell his fear.

"Y-y-yes! I got it!" He stuttered.

"GOOD, NOW FOR *YOU*," Tasha said, pointing the .380 at Summer. "Ho, get the fuck up outta here! Breathe a word of this and I'm at your ass too!" Summer hurriedly gathered her things and headed for the front door. Before she turned the doorknob, she looked back at the woman holding the gun and winked at her. Tasha smiled and headed for the safe.

"DAMN BITCH, you paying for my next massage," Summer said to Tasha later that night. The two women were at Young Racks' storage garage loading a red Chevy Tahoe with the contents the cheating rapper had stored away.

"Putting your motherfucking heel all in my spine and shit. Damn bitch, that shit hurt!" Summer emphasized, rubbing her back where Tasha's Jimmy Choo had been a couple of hours ago.

"Yeah, yeah, yeah. My bad. You know I had to make it look real. I couldn't go too easy on you. Shit, you see I even turned on the waterworks," Tasha said, referring to the emotional tears she shed during the whole fiasco.

"Yeah girl, you coulda won an Oscar for that shit! When we start producing films, I'm putting your ass in a movie," Summer said, and they both laughed.

"Mmhm. Well, with all this shit we getting, your ass should be straight. You can pay for your own damn massage," Tasha said.

She was right. Their "set-up" had hit the jackpot. Racks had 40 bricks of coke, 15 bricks of heroin, and 27 pounds of Loud in the U-Haul garage. Not to mention the Infinity G37X with $250,000 cash stuffed in a Nike duffle bag in the trunk. Indeed, Young Racks was definitely "holding" like a muthafucka!

Tasha also pulled another half mill out of his wall safe, along with several watches, chains, and rings. There was also a Desert Eagle with a laser beam on it and a Glock with a silencer.

Ever since BBC got word that Racks was a big-time drug dealer in the ATL, who was in the process of transitioning into the rap game, they'd been plotting their move. This was two years in the making.

Summer, a model, video vixen, and a multi-faceted hustler, was a prestigious member of The Bad Bitchez Click (BBC) out of Milwaukee, WI. BBC had an alliance with Tryfe Lyfe Bitchez (TLB), a cut-throat goon squad of women from various parts of the Midwest that specialize in armed robberies and contract killings. Tasha, whose real name was Lyza Williams, was TLB.

"Tasha," as she went by for the Young Racks' assignment, was trained by the BBC in the art of seduction and mind games for this job because all TLB knew was straight gutter shit. Stick-ups and gunplay were TLB's specialty. Whereas BBC were sophisticated "finessers." They were so smooth and enticing, they could talk a polar bear out of his fur in a snowstorm, and the damn thing wouldn't even know it! True hustlers, The Bad Bitchez Click could sell water to a well.

For this job, Tasha went undercover to become Racks' wifey and waited until his music career began bubbling before, she pulled the ultimate betrayal. He never saw it coming. And to this day, he still thought it was just the emotions of a woman scorned that made him take an L and hand over all his work and bread. When in all actuality, it was an elaborate plan from the get go.

"Damn girl, this weed stank!" Summer said as she threw the tightly wrapped blocks of green into the truck.

"Bitch... that's why it's called **LOUD**! Duh," Tasha said.

"Yeah, I know. But this shit saran wrapped da fuck up and it's *still* bangin'! I'mma have to sample dis shit. Mmhm, yes I is," Summer said, holding a pound up to her nose and inhaling it.

"Shiiid, you ain't wrong girl. Come on ma, that's it. Let's ride," Tasha said as she put the last of their take into the Tahoe.

"Are we gonna leave the Infinity?" Summer asked.

"Hell naw! You know TLB's motto: "Everything must go!" I'll

have Nee-Nee come scoop it. This muthafucka phat! We can get 20 for this *easily.*"

"That's what's up!" Summer said, high fiving Tasha and getting into her white on white 300 Touring. She followed Tasha back to the hotel, where they divvied up their take. Once they took care of that business, Summer made the several hour drive back to Wisconsin with a big ol' smile on her face. Another successful mission complete.

2

GG

"Bounce that ass bitch!" "Wooo she killing it!" "Throw that muthfucka!"* The customers at the Solid Gold strip club were yelling as they showered the stage with dollar bills. The headline stripper "Gushy" was on stage contracting her booty cheeks, making them go up and down like a 6-4 with switches. At 5'6" and 168 pounds, Gushy (aka GG) was super thick! But none of her weight was sloppy. She worked out at Anytime Fitness four days a week. She also did Yoga and Pilates regularly.

Her stomach was flat, her chocolaty breasts were a firm 36 C cup (and 100% real), and she had no kids, so there were no stretch marks or saggy parts on her fine brown body. At 36-26-48, her coke bottle figure was **MADE** for showcasing. And being the exhibitionist that she was, GG was proud to show it off.

She loved performing to the "U Ain't Even Know It" remix because when 2 Chainz rapped, "Throw it...tho' that ass!" she'd slang her big butt cheeks like a boomerang, making dudes throw money like confetti at her fantastic twerking skills. Plus, the song had a hidden meaning for her. All the "so-called" players, pimps, and ballers were really trickin' their hard earned dough they were taking penitentiary chances on, just to give it to her, making GG rich, and they ain't even know it.

After she finished her set, she gathered all her tips off the floor, wrapped a couple of rubber bands around the wad of cash, and exited the stage. A flock of men surrounded her. *"How much for a sample of that?" "Let me be your sponsor." "Giiirl, I'd drink your bathwater!" "Baby, I got a few hun for a lap dance." "What up wit that gushy stuff?"* She'd heard it all before and paid them no mind. GG smiled politely and sashayed past them as she went to the bar to get herself a vodka-cranberry.

Usually, she didn't drink on the job because she had to drive home, but her girl Summer was back in town and doing bottle service tonight and was the designated driver once they got off work. GG gave Nadia, the 6'3" Amazon Russian bartender, a ten for the drink and a $20 tip. The tall sexy tatted up blonde smiled and thanked GG for her generosity; she was always known for big gracious tips. GG took a sip of her cocktail and sauntered off to go and find Summer.

"Hey baby girl, let me holler at you for a sec," a slim-built guy said, grabbing her arm. GG hated being grabbed. But in her profession, one had to tolerate it. She politely removed his hand and told him her time was money and that she had things to do. He slipped a hundred-dollar bill in her bra strap.

"Just for a sec?" he said, smiling.

"What's good Daddy?" GG said, turning on the seduction as she batted her long fake mink eyelashes.

"Shit ma, you was handling yo bidness up there. I was wondering if you do private shows?"

"What's your name Daddy?" she cooed in his ear.

"T-dub."

"Well, T-dub, my answers ain't free either. So..." He peeled off another hundred from his bankroll and slipped it next to the Benjamin Franklin in her bra strap.

"What kind of private show you talkin'? Group or solo dolo?" GG asked him.

"Just me babygirl," he said, licking his lips. She looked at him for a second, sizing him up. Nicely kept shoulder-length dreads with a crisp taper. True Religion'd out. Clean cream-colored suede Saint Laurent boots. Icey Movado watch on his wrist and 4 carat "boogers" in his ears. *Yeah, homeboy's definitely holding*, GG thought to herself.

"Twenty-five hundred... an ***HOUR***," she said, looking him in the eye.

T-dub let out a long whistle. Looked her up and down, from head to toe. Feet were pretty. Skin was smooth. Ass was stupid fat! Nice titties. **REAL** titties (he hated fake ones). Gorgeous face. Had that Taraji P-kinda look to her. Twenty-five hundred? Yeah, she was worth it. Why not? Hell, it ain't trickin' if you got it!

"Bet. Let's set something up then," he said, pulling out his iPhone.

"You give me ***your*** number," she told him. He looked her up and down like um, *do you got a phone in your thong or something?* She seen the quizzical eyebrow raised and she laughed. GG grabbed a Sharpie out of a nearby Bottles girl's pocket and handed it to him. He knew what to do. He peeled off another hundred-dollar bill and scribbled his digits on it. He then put the crispy Franklin in her bra.

"Shit, I hope you worth twenty-five ma," he said, putting the cap on the marker and handing it back to her. She took it, clipped it on her bra, grabbed his wrist, and shoved his hand down the front of her thong. The first thing he felt was a gooey wetness coating her fat puffy lips. Then he felt a hot metal ball.

"You know why they call me Gushy?" she asked, looking deep into his eyes. He shook his head, and she flexed her pussy muscles several times and moaned as she came all over his hand. His mouth dropped in awe. "Because I'm multi-orgasmic," she continued.

"I cum in the blink of an eye. And with this piercing in my clit,"– she made the silver ball move up and down against his fingers– "I cum just from **WALKING!** This is the tightest, hottest, gushiest pussy you'll *EVER* have," GG told him and removed his sopping wet hand from her underwear.

"Oh... and it's the tastiest too," she said, grabbing his wrist and licking her cream off his fingers.

T-dub was stuck. The bitch just blew his mind and had him pitching a serious tent in his True's. He was at a loss for words, dumbstruck and frozen with a lump in his throat. The throbbing in his crotch told him she'd be worth more than $2500. He ***had*** to have her!

"Babygirl... you can have everything I got. Here..." he said, handing her the entire bankroll he had in his pocket. *I knew you'd say that*, GG thought to herself knowingly. They all do! She smiled and said, "Aww, thank you Daddy. I'll be calling you soon." She gave him a light kiss on the cheek and sashayed away, making sure to put some extra swivel in her hips because she knew he was watching.

T-dub looked at all dat ass leave his presence. ***Mm!*** Looked like two WNBA basketballs bouncing up and down when she walked. He vowed to tear that ass up whenever he got the opportunity.

GG found Summer by the Aquarium stage. Dozens of rainbow-colored exotic fish swam in a 20x30 all glass raised platform under the dancers' feet. It was a sight to see.

"Girl, who was Mr. Dreads over there? He is ***fiiine***," Summer said in GG's ear. They both looked over at him. T-dub was still standing where she last left him, drooling with that stupid look on his face. Gets 'em every time!

"Oh, that's my new side project," GG told her.

"Yeah? Hmpf. He is sharp girl... anyway mami, we got one to go," Summer said.

"Yeah? Who?"

"See that white dude in the business suit over there," Summer said, pointing toward the stage.

"Well. He owns a Fortune 500 company. And his ultimate fantasy is to be with a black woman."

"Uhh, ok. So, why ain't *YOU* at him?" GG said.

"Bitch, cuz I'm yellow! He don't want no light skin. He wants some dark chocolate. Some Hershey kiss nipples. Some blackberry pie. Know what I mean?"

"Oh, yeah. I know exactly what you mean. Good lookin' ma," GG said as she adjusted her bra to make the "girls" sit up and pop out a little more.

"No prob. Now go get him girl," Summer said, smacking GG on her ass. Just that 'lil tap made that thang jiggle for like five seconds.

GG waited until Lemons was done dancing before she approached the white man and tapped him on the shoulder. When he turned around, she smiled her mega-watt beam at him. Perfectly straight white teeth set in a flawless, chocolaty, gorgeous face. For him, it was love at first sight.

"Would you like a complimentary lap dance sir?" GG asked him. His face turned beet red as he stared at the black Goddess. Her voluptuous curves shined with a metallic body glitter, and she smelled like some kind of exotic fruit. He swallowed hard and could only nod to her offer as he loosened his Brooks Brothers tie and began to sweat.

As the next song began to play, GG did her motherfuckin' thang! Seductively moving her hips to the music and slithering up and down his tailored suit. He was erect in no time. She smiled and gyrated against his penis.

"Wow... someone's packing. You got a conceal and carry license for that gun buddy?" she whispered in his ear, straddling him. She rested her forearms on top of his shoulders and wound her hips on him.

The white man looked to be in his early 50's with salt and pepper hair. He had that Richard Gere/George Clooney flair to him, but GG knew men, and this one had "kinky" written all over him. Summer said he owned a Fortune 500 company, but GG wouldn't be surprised if he was some kind of politician.

"So... what's your name sugar?" she asked him.

"Al-Al-Allen," he stuttered.

"Hmm. Allen, huh?" she placed his hands on her hips and said, "I've never seen you here before Allen. You don't even look like the Gentlemen club's type. Though I can tell you *are* a gentleman."

He smiled nervously as sweat began beading his upper lip. "Um... th-this is m-m-my first time. I'm going through... Oh God you're hot!" Allen lost his train of thought as he stared at the chocolate Goddess move and sway her sexy body back and forth. She put his face between her ample breasts and motor boated him.

She was very good at what she did. Stripping was an art form that she mastered to perfection. It was all about making the customer feel comfortable and relaxed. If an exotic dancer could make a man (or woman) feel desired and wanted, they'd be more likely to spend *more* money. And that was her one and only goal, to secure the bag and run up a check on motherfuckers.

"You're going through?"

"I'm going through a divorce right now. So, a colleague of mine suggested I attend one of these uh, places... to unwind, if you will."

"Aww sugar, I'm so sorry to hear about the big D. It's her loss though. You'll find better," GG said, pushing her titties practically in his mouth.

"I already have," he mumbled into her chest. She lifted his

chin up with a perfectly manicured finger and asked, "What cha say honey?" He looked up at her with big blue eyes, her body glitter all over his face, and through his thin lips he told her, "Um, I think I already have." She smiled that knowing smile of hers again. *Gotcha!*

When she shoved his hand down her panties and did the "waterfalls trick," Allen handed over his whole wallet. Driver's license, credit cards, and all.

"Take it. You can have EVERYTHING!" he told her. GG laughed and told him to wait for her while she changed so that they could leave together.

When she told Summer that she was leaving with Mr. Fortune 500, she said, "I better get my finder's fee bitch!"

"I gotchu ma," GG shouted back as she left the club arm in arm with Allen.

He opened the car door for her, and she sat her purse on the floor and adjusted the passenger seat. Before he even touched his push-start on his BMW 535 IX Drive, GG had his pants around his ankles and his five-inch pink dick in her mouth, sucking loudly on it like it was a *Blowpop*.

"Jesus Christ! My fuckin' God!" he shouted all sorts of blasphemous obscenities as he gripped the steering wheel until his knuckles turned white.

GG moved her mouth up and down on his pecker while her pierced tongue swirled around his tender glands. He came in 90 seconds flat! She hungrily swallowed his seed (because as she says, a lady ***never*** spits), and kept on sucking until he was limp and begging for mercy.

Allen took her to his mini mansion out in Mequon, where she fucked his brains out until the sun came up. And when she told him over breakfast that she didn't have a car (a lie), he signed the title to the Beemer over to Regina Gordon (her REAL name). He also told her to go shopping with his credit cards, which she did, spending a whopping 33 geez before she went home to prepare for later.

She called T-dub to set up their "private show," and he informed her he'd throw in an extra stack if she could come tonight. She said, "make it two since this was short notice," and he agreed.

He had an immaculate condo by the lakefront, and GG arrived there at 7p.m. sharp. On his 80-inch screen TV, he watched her arrive through the security cameras in the locked lobby. He popped a Molly and washed it down with Remy Martin. He took a deep pull on his kush blunt as he buzzed her in. He was trying to get Superman high cuz he was about to get his money's worth tonight!

T-dub answered his door in head to toe Gucci. All Brown and tan. Even his diamond trimmed shades were Gucci. His Gucci belt had the iced out G's on the buckle, and he wore a diamond necklace on his neck with a platinum and diamond T on the end of it. He blew kush smoke in the hallway as he let her in. She had to admit the nigga ***was*** sexy.

"What up ma? Welcome to me Casa," he said, stepping aside so she could enter the crib. He stared at her phat ass in the tight pink chiffon dress she wore as she switched past him. She sat her purse on the table, put her hands on her hips in a wide-legged stance, and stared at him.

"Damn you fine girl," T-dub said, licking his lips and rubbing his palms together. "Yo. You's a BAD bitch

"Sooo. We gonna talk or make shit happen? Cuz yo hour started two minutes ago," she said, looking at her rose gold Rolly with the pink face trimmed in crushed diamonds.

"Ok, ok. A woman 'bout her bidness. I can dig dat. I feel you mami. That's what's up. Shiid, what it do then?"

"You tell me. What chu wanna do? Look or play?"

"BOTH!" He said, running to the wrap around leather couch like a kid and plopping down on it. He grabbed the remote off the marble and glass table and hit a couple of buttons. The sultry voice of Sade came out of the speakers in the walls.

"Ohhh. Ok. You got some taste huh? What chu know about Sade boy?" GG said as she began slowly snaking her body to the sensual music. T-dub took three long pulls from his blunt and set it in the ashtray. He leaned back on the soft couch, holding the smoke in for what seemed like forever.

GG stood between his legs and let her hands roam all over her body, caressing her curves to the rhythm of the music. T-dub pulled a fat ass rubberband wad of bills out of his pocket. He counted twenty-five Franklins and placed them on the glass table top.

"*Now* we're cooking with fish grease," GG commented after seeing her fee. He then counted out another twenty Franklins, "for squeezing me in on such short notice," he said and sat them next to the other bills.

The money made her pussy wet, and she was ready to turn up like a muthafucka now! She spun around, and with her back to T-dub, she bent at the waist, giving him a view of that heart-shaped booty in his face.

"Soooo, T-dub. You ballin' pretty hard I see. What chu do for a living? I follow sports, so I know you ain't no ballplayer. You a rapper or something?" GG said conversationally, hiking up her dress and showing her thick brown thighs.

He laughed, finally exhaling the weed smoke. "Nah, I don't rap ma. I get money though. That's all that matters right?"

She grabbed her ankles and made her booty bounce up and down like two dribbling basketballs, but she did it in slow motion. Her hair dragged on his plush carpeting as she looked between her legs at him.

"Yeah Daddy, you right. Long as you getting it. It don't matter *how* or *where* you getting it from. Long as you *getting* that shit," she said. GG rocked side to side and T-dub stared at the pink panty-clad camel toe staring back at him. *Damn that muthafucka fat*, he thought to himself.

When she stood back up straight and faced him, the top of her dress was pulled down to her waist, revealing perfect cantaloupe titties with dark brown areoles and pointy hard black nipples!

"Damn ma, even yo nipples off da charts! Look at them muthafuckas... they like AK-47 bullets!" T-dub said, reaching out and brushing his fingertips across them. His touch was light and made her shudder. Her "bullets" grew even harder and she moaned.

GG got closer to him and removed his Gucci sunglasses so she could look into his eyes. They were bloodshot red and half-closed. That kush he was toking on must be that flame! She caressed his face and smiled. He smiled a big, goofy, high grin back at her.

When she placed his hands on her hips, he knew what was up. He pushed the rest of her Alexander Wang dress down until it pooled at her ankles. She stepped out of it and kicked it away, standing in only her Louboutin pumps and pink satin thong. Her body shone with a coconut-caramel body oil that she wore.

GG never stopped "dancing" as T-dub stuffed hundreds in her thong; he also casually tossed some in the air while she did her thing. He thoroughly enjoyed the show as Sade sung song after song.

The light pink thong had turned hot pink as the secretions stained the crotch and highlighted her thighs with glistening moisture. He didn't know it, but GG had cum seven times already. Every time she orgasmed, she bit down on her glossy lip to muffle her pleasure as her eyes closed to conceal them rolling in the back of her head. Sade's music was so erotic, it put her in an even ***hornier*** mood.

When she grabbed T-dub's hand and put it on her monkey for the "waterfall finale," he slipped his middle finger inside of her and stroked her G-spot. She came and collapsed in his lap. He held her until her climax subsided, and when she recovered, they tore into each other like animals possessed! They fucked all over his condo. From the couch to the kitchen. The balcony to the hallway walls until they ended up on his bedroom floor, rolling off the king-size Tempurpedic.

"Damn babygirl, you got that million dolla– "

"Ooh, ooh, ooh," she interrupted. They both laughed as they lay in heaps of sweat on his hardwood floor, trying to catch their breath.

"With a shot like that, and as fine as you is, I can't believe you ain't got no nigga," T-dub said.

"I told you. I don't do relationships. I'm on my grind. My hustle is my 'man'."

"Yo hustle huh? What chu know 'bout hustlin' girl?" T-dub said as he stroked her sweaty thigh up and down. Her skin was burning hot.

"More than you think I do nigga. I'm a Bad Bitch! And Bad Bitchez get money in MANY ways."

"Oh yeah? That's what this BBC tattoo stands for then? And here I thought you just loved Big Black Cock," he said and laughed as he rubbed the cursive ink tatted on her arm.

"Yup. Bad Bitchez Click. We do whateva for the dollar," GG said proudly.

"Mmhm. Whatever ma. Y'all ain't bout that life," he teased her. "Me and my niggas out her hustlin' for REAL! We eatin' like a muthafucka."

"Nigga please. The only thing you eatin' is this pussy," GG said, sitting on his chest. "All that jackin' like you out here doing numbers or something. Shit, for all I know, this could be your moms or pops crib or something. Trying to make it rain on me and stunt for a bitch. Nigga, you probably a trust fund baby or some shit," she said, standing up. She knew that'd get him.

He looked up at that swollen pussy. He could see it pulsating. He knew he just put it down, but this bitch was standing over him talking mad shit like she ain't respect his gangsta or something!

"What?! I ain't doing numbers? Bitch you got me FUCKED up! You better ask somebody," he said, sitting up.

"Well, I ain't heard yo name ringin' out here Daddy, so how am I supposed to ask about something don't nobody even know about?" She said, looking down at him with her hands on her hourglass hips.

T-dub stood up and pushed her leg out the way. He grabbed her arm and stormed out of the room with the full condom still on his piece, dick swangin' everywhere!

"Come here. I'm a show yo ass. I bet you ain't seen no nigga ballin like this", he huffed, dragging her into another bedroom. When he opened the door, she thought she had just entered the Build-A-Bear store. The room had floor to ceiling shelves on each wall....and they were filled with Teddy Bears!

GG bust out laughing. "Umm, what the fuck is this nigga, Toys 'R' Us or something?" She said, doubling over in laughter, slapping her thighs.

"Toys? Hell naw bitch," he said, getting angry. "Each Teddy Bear got shit stuffed in them," he said, trying to explain.

"Yeah. They got shit stuffed in 'em alright," GG said, laughing loudly. "Stuffed with cotton muthafucka!" Frustrated, T-dub pulled the nearest stuffed bear off a shelf and grabbed a pair of scissors out of a drawer. He stabbed the 20-inch bear and pulled out some cotton. He began tearing at the furry fabric and ripped it open further, dumping a cube shaped brick wrapped in duct tape on the floor.

"The white bears are filled with coke. The brown ones full of that boy. And the other colors are stuffed with money," T-dub bragged foolishly. He was so high he didn't even realize what his stupidity was actually revealing. GG had put that bomb ass gushy on him to let his guard down and weaken his defense.

Then she egged him on about his hustling status until his dumbass dropped dime on himself; and he ain't even know it!

GG looked at him. Then the bears. Then back at him again. "Damn Daddy, my bad, my bad. A thousand apologies. Ok, Ok. You da man," she said, kneeling in front of him. She pulled the slimy Magnum condom off his dick and turned it upside down. He watched as all of his cum dripped out of the condom and landed on her pierced tongue. She looked into his eyes and swallowed it all in one gulp before licking her lips.

"Mmmmmm, baby. Yo nut taste so fucking good. Sooooo, I was wondering, can I have one of those pink bears Daddy?" she said, smiling.

3

ROSE

"Get the fuck outta here chica!" Rose exclaimed as she listened to GG.

"No bullshit ma. The nigga got at least a hundred bears of ***each*** in that muthafucka! And he gave me this pink one," GG said, pointing to the bear she put on the table. "He said I owe him 20 mo' private shows. Shiiit, I said cool!"

They were at the "Titty Table," a mammoth breast-shaped oak table in a 14,612 square foot mansion in Fox Point. They called this spot "The Greenhouse." They were congregating. Every other week, GG, Summer, and Rose got together for a mandatory click meeting, where they broke bread at the "Titty Table."

BBC were independent feminists and didn't want your typical "round table" that men strategized at. No, they wanted something that symbolized their own female power in a unique form. So, they had the boob-shaped table custom made and sat it in the tastefully decorated den.

Every two weeks (when their schedules permitted it), they'd haul in the latest merch from whatever moves they had bust the weeks prior and spread it all out on the Titty Table. Jewelry, drugs, guns, credit cards, deeds, stocks, bonds, car keys, and cash. Mostly cash. Lots of motherfucking cash! They counted everything up in money machines, recorded the totals, and decided together what would be invested into their many other endeavors.

They were a team. And they had BIG dreams. So, no matter who's "take" was bigger every meeting, it all got put into the pot for the click anyway. Because ultimately, they were a family. And when one prospered, they *all* prospered. They were so well plugged in the streets, muthafuckas didn't even know how much power these Beez really had!

"So, you're saying, every color bear had something different in 'em?" Summer asked.

"Hell yeah girl. The white ones had coke. The brown ones had heroin. And the others were blue, red, green, purple, pink, all kinds of shit! They all got money in 'em," GG told her Beez.

"And it was fifty geez in this one?" Rose said, holding up the cute lil pink bear that was now gutted.

"Yup! Fifty motherfucking bands," GG replied. "But there were all different size bears in that bitch, so ain't no telling how much was in *those*. He had big ones, small ones, medium sized ones. Even those big dumb ass ones you can win at the Carnival. He had a few of them on the floor cuz they were too big for the shelves," GG said, eyes glowing with excitement while she told her homegirls what she saw.

"Hmpf. I'm gonna see if Nacho knows who this nigga is. Obviously, he's plugged and has a nice smuggling operation going on. We need to find out with ***who*** before we make our move," Rose said.

"Girl, you musta REALLY put it on that fool for him to expose his hands like that on the first date," Summer said.

"Mami, you know she do that waterslide trick and have them clowns' noses wide open!" Rose said.

"First of all, it ain't no water **slide**... it's a water***fall***. Cuz all it takes is one sample, and they *fall* head over heels and madly in love with this," GG corrected her.

"Well excuuuuse me. Waterfall, waterslide, it don't make no difference. Your weird pussy ass is still a freak! I still don't see how you can stand all them damn orgasms a day," Rose said.

"Shit, ain't no thang. I'm used to it now. But don't hate cuz my 'weird pussy ass' can cum and your dried up cooch can't even get moist," GG shot back.

"Whatever mami. Anyway, switching gears. I think I finally found our missing puzzle piece," Rose told them.

"Say whaaaat, you got a snow bunny?" Summer asked.

"Yeah. A white chick from Appleton. Her family is rich as hell. They own a tanning salon chain. Anyways, ol' girl buys a couple of pounds from Chula once a month like clockwork. I've been watching her for a minute now. Word is, she's moving major pills up north. She drives nothing but Benzes. Has like four or five of them."

"My kinda bitch!" GG said.

"Yeah well," Rose continued, "I told Chula to tell her the Plug wants to meet and talk business with her, so I'm going to meet her for lunch tomorrow."

"You sure about that mami? I mean, you don't even *know* this bitch," Summer warned.

"Yeah Rose, and you know how scary white hoes is. Them people threaten to take they pets away, and they'll tell on they own damn mama! Fuck they family, long as their damn cats and dogs straight!" GG said. They all laughed.

"Naw, you know I wouldn't go in if I wasn't sure about her. I told y'all I been watching her for a minute. I did my research. She got caught with a half pound and didn't rat. They gave her probation and an outpatient program for her first offense. Her parents are connected, so they got that expunged off her record."

"So, she's only moving two pounds of weed a month? That

ain't no money. How does that make her a Boss Bitch?" Summer asked.

Rose smacked her lips. "Bee, you ain't no ditzy blonde, so quit acting like one. That's her per-per. She smokes that a *month*."

"Ohhh. My bad," Summer blushed, feeling foolish.

"Anyway, she's been shopping with Chula for 3 years straight now. CONSISTENTLY. She has her conceal and carry license and goes to the gun range every Thursday morning. She only fucks with black dudes that hustle. Not no big-time heavy hitters, but not no nickel and dime wanna-be's either. And like I said, she's moving pills herself."

"What kind?" GG asked.

"Percs, Oxys, Adderall, Riddalin; all that stuff them white folks like. You know how they is," Rose said. GG and Summer nodded knowingly.

"And she slangs ex when she can get her hands on some. But the girl is doing STUPID numbers up there though."

"How much she getting?" Summer asked.

"Fifty a pill," Rose told them.

"A pill?!?" GG and Summer said in unison, eyes wide.

"Yup. But her supply is limited. She's paying off some senior citizens for a few scripts, and she's got some college dude up in Green Bay who gets her some jars of ex every now and then," Rose said.

"Damn, she sounds like a bad bitch. But is she ***BAD***?" Summer asked.

Rose pulled her Samsung Galaxy S10 smart phone out and brought up some pictures of Rebecca Slinkowski, aka "Becky." There was multiple pics of the 27-year-old blonde bombshell who was 5'4" and thick as a coleslaw sandwich! She looked a lot like the model CoCo, Ice-T's hot Caucasian wife.

Becky had an hourglass body and a tiny waist that sloped out to some wide hips with her 50" ass! Her long blonde hair came to the middle of her back and was perfectly cut so not a split-end was in sight.

Her big doe-like eyes were a vibrant sky blue, and she had deep dish dimples in her round blemish-free face. Her lips were a bit on the thinner side, but they still looked soft and supple. And with the red MAC lipstick that she always wore, they managed to look sexy and "fuller" than they actually were.

BBC needed some "snow" to infiltrate the clicks who had a thing for white women. It seemed everywhere you turned, white bitches were in high demand; they had become the hot new commodity to have, even for hood niggaz. But Rose, GG, and Summer grew up in the hood in Milwaukee. Wasn't no white bitches around, and none attended their schools either. Well, there may have been one or two, but they were poor trailer trash who couldn't afford to go to a better school, so they were forced to attend the inner-city MPS.

Over the years, as BBC migrated from the streets into the Corporate world, they began mingling with white women in various social settings but could never find one worthy enough to certify as a "Bad Bee." You had to have book and street smarts. Beauty *and* brains. Class *and* style. But most importantly, in order to be a true "Bad Bitch," you had to be an ultimate hustler, who would do whatever it takes to succeed. That was why the three of them thrived so fluently. They shared the same passion, and outside of BBC, they'd cross anybody and everybody to prosper.

The way they envisioned it; their goal was to have a multiethnic hustlers crew of Bad Beez that took over the world! GG was black. Summer was a caramely redbone (her grandmother was half white). And Rosalita "Rose" Jimenez was half Brazilian and half Puerto-Rican. If they had a pure Snow Bunny in the click, all they'd be missing was an Asian chick. Then maybe they could veer off and get a Jamaican and a few other foreign dimes, so they could truly be the Baskin Robbins of the Underworld. All flavors on deck!

The women looked at all the pics of Becky taken from different angles as Rose swiped through them. They nodded their heads in approval and commented on her tasteful choices in fashion.

"She rocks cute outfits," Summer said.

"Mmhm, and she's in heels in every pic," GG commented.

"Yeah. It's all she wears. She's like Mariah Carey or something. I never seen her in anything else. Even when she leaves the gym, she's in stilettos," Rose told them.

"Aight. Well, she ***looks*** like a bad bitch. Go interview her and see what's up. If she's cool, then we'll go from there," Summer said.

"No doubt. I'm gonna keep her on my hip for a few days, see how she rolls and shit before I bring her to y'all. Then after y'all meet her, y'all can vibe with her on an individual basis. We'll vote at the third meeting next month. That'll give us all enough time to feel her out," Rose told them as she put her gold-plated phone away. They all agreed and went back to feeding their money machines some more dead presidents.

Rose was feeling good. Her click was ballin' out of control, and they had some more moves lined up for the next couple of months. All of BBC's cash-fronted businesses, the Beauty salons, Barbershops, clothing stores, and restaurants, were all doing well. They were "washing" their dirty money efficiently and planning another trip to Switzerland next month to deposit some more millions into their Swiss bank accounts. Yeah, life was good. Well, except for the greedy maggots she had to deal with.

Rose whipped her gray Lexus RX450H SUV through traffic

with one hand while she dialed a 920-area code. After a few rings, a bubbly voice answered.

"Becky, hi, it's Rose."

"Oh, hi!"

"Hey, I was just calling to say I might be a couple minutes late for our meeting cuz I... uh, have to take the garbage out," Rose told her.

"Um, ok." Becky wasn't sure what Rose was talking about, but it was cool. "I'll just sip on me a little drinky poo until you get there."

"Alright mami. See you in a little bit."

"Ok, bye bye," Becky said.

Rose disconnected. *Drinky poo?* She laughed. *White girls, I tell ya*, she thought to herself.

Rose pulled up on a shabby block deep on the Southside. It wasn't even noon yet and the block was crackin'! Fiends went in and out of trap houses. Hustlers loitered in front of decrepit, boarded-up buildings with their leash-less pit bulls. Old school Chevys and Monte Carlos stormed up and down the block, beating Jeezy, Boosie, Yo Gotti, and other hood artists.

Yeah, business was booming. As it should. Seeing as how BBC were the ones flooding the streets with top quality cocaine and grade A heroin at the best prices in the Midwest. Perks of being plugged with the Colombian Cartel, which was ran by a distant relative of Rose's.

Rose parked on the side of Louie's Bar on Beecher street and walked into the laid-back establishment with her head held high. Her long, silky, jet black hair hung to her waist, and it swayed when she walked. It was fairly quiet inside the bar. The only sounds were the click-clacking of Rose's Jimmy Choo heels on the concrete floor.

Esperanza, a friend of hers who managed the bar, was putting glasses in the dishwasher. Rose waved to her as she walked to the back. She opened the door leading to the basement and closed it behind her. She walked down the dimly lit stairs and could smell the piss and fear in the air as she entered the dungeon-like setting. Rose nodded at her lieutenants, some Spanish mami's from THOT Gang, who were a branch of hood bitches off the BBC tree.

The women moved swiftly and removed the black bags that were over the heads of two people tied to chairs in the middle of the room. One man and one woman. The hostages blinked rapidly and looked up at Rose while their eyes tried to adjust to the light.

"So... you two *maggots* have sticky fingers huh?" Rose began as she walked circles around their chairs. "What, you thought you could steal from me and get away with it?"

"Wh-what are you talking about? We didn't steal ANYTHING!" the young Dominican woman said. Her name was Teresa. She'd been in charge of BBC's Mexican restaurant El Rubio's on National, which also doubled as a major cocaine trafficking spot.

After declining profits for the past 9 months, Rose had hidden cameras installed all over the restaurant. She saw that business was NOT declining, but rather Teresa and her coke sniffing boyfriend Joker were skimming off the top.

And although Teresa didn't "treat her nose," she did, however, look the other way while Joker continued to feed his habit with coke that didn't belong to him. They thought the 10 geez and couple ounces a week they were skimming would go unnoticed, but they thought wrong.

Rose was a certified accountant. And while there were no "official" titles within the Bad Bitchez Click, it was an un-said given that Rose was the delegated treasurer of their organization. She was a smart businesswoman, who was *extremely* good with money. Which also meant she monitored EVERY SINGLE DOLLAR that went through her domain. So, she knew when something wasn't quite right financially; it's called a Hustler's intuition.

Teresa and Joker didn't know they were working for Rose (or BBC for that matter) because she was a "behind the scenes" Boss. She had layers upon layers of lieutenants and generals who fronted as the "head honchos." Which is why Joker asked, "Stealing from ***you***? Bitch, who da fuck is you?!"

Pita, a short chubby THOT Gang member, whacked Joker in the forehead with the butt of her 9mm gun. Blood instantly gushed from the fresh wound.

"Watch your mouth nigga," Pita warned him in a heavy Spanish accent.

Rose stood in front of her two captors. The entire basement floor was covered in thick plastic so any evidence could be disposed of easily. She looked down at the dried blood already congealed at their feet. THOT Gang had already worked them over pretty good. They both had black eyes, pumpkin heads, busted lips, and broken limbs.

"All in all, you two have gotten me for at least a half a million. Maybe more. That's two Lamborghini's or a 3-bedroom house in West Allis. Do you have two Lambos for me Teresa?" Rose said, lifting the distraught girl's chin. Teresa shook her head in fear. Fresh tears made a trail through the dried blood on her battered face.

"Do you have a 3 bedroom in West Allis for me Joker?" He didn't answer out of defiance. He just mean-mugged her. *Men*, she thought to herself. *Always wanna be big and bad and macho.* Well, no one was as *bad* as her. Rose laughed shrewdly. "I didn't think so..."

BLAM! She punched him in his left eye, causing the chair to tip over backwards. His head hit the floor with a loud thud. In a matter of seconds, the girls sat him and the chair back upright. Rose shook the stinging feeling out of her hand.

"P-p-please... whoever you are boss lady. We'll pay you back. I promise," Teresa begged.

"Si? And how you gonna do that? Your coke head boyfriend here snorts up everything in sight! Y'all live in a pissy two-bedroom dump. And your bank account ain't got more than four figures in it. So, tell me mami, how the FUCK are you gonna pay me my money? Huh, puta?"

"I-I-I don't know. I'll think of something though. I'll do anything," Teresa sniveled.

"Tisk, tisk, tisk. You had so much potential. I picked you ya know? Yeah, you were a smart girl with a good head on your shoulders. A down ass bitch that I saw going places in life. That's why I had Jackie put you in charge of El Rubio's. Then you meet this clown ass bastard and he fucks your whole life up. Was the dick ***that*** good ma?"

"No. I just..."

"Fell in love. Young, dumb, and in love. Yeah, it'll getcha every time. Too bad. A real shame actually. Cuz when you bite the hand that feeds you, you get cha muthafuckin' mouth blown off. Sandra..." a slim Mexican chick that looked like Eva Longoria walked up to Joker and put .357 magnum to his jaw and squeezed the trigger. Half of his face splattered on Teresa as she screamed hysterically.

"See mami, now your boyfriend's big mouth is all over you. Slick talking *puta*. Muthafuckas nowadays have no respect," Rose said, circling Teresa's chair.

"Look, I-I'm sorry. Really, you don't have to do this. Please don't kill me. He made me– "

"You know what ma? I hate when muthafuckas blame the next person for their actions. Bitch, you're a grown ass woman! He didn't *make* you do shit. You *chose* to go along with him and his fuckboy ways. Accept it, own up to it, and change your ways."

“I will. I promise. Oh God, I’ll do anything. Please, I swear to God…” Teresa sobbed.

“Ah-ah. Don’t bring God into this with your blasphemous ass.”

“Oh, I’m sorry. Forgive me. I— ”

“Teresa, I don’t wanna hear your excuses and apologies no more. Sandra, kill this stupid bitch.”

“Nooooooo!” Teresa screamed.

Sandra put the .357 into the Dominican woman’s screaming mouth and pulled the trigger, silencing her forever.

Rose tip-toed around the gruesome mess and spit on the two bodies. They disrespected her and her team in life; she'd disrespect them in death. She reached into her purse and pulled out a small vial. She opened it and drizzled the contents over the two dead bodies. Soon, the plastic would have their honey covered corpses would be wrapped up in plastic, no longer to be seen or heard from again.

Tucking her hair behind her ears, Rose strode back upstairs. Now that the trash was disposed of, she could go and meet the missing piece to her empire puzzle.

4

BECKY

Becky was a nervous wreck. She had already smoked a dozen bowls that morning. The day had finally arrived when she'd meet Chula's connection. Ever since she was told 2 months ago that the lady behind the bomb ass kush she smoked wanted to meet her, she was super excited.

At first, she thought, *lady*? But then Chula informed her there were well-connected people in power who just so happened to be female also. And hell, Becky was a money getting chick herself who wanted to have the best in life, so it shouldn't have surprised her that "the plug" was a woman. Even though it did. But she thought it was pretty cool once that tidbit of information sunk in.

Her and Rose had been talking sporadically on the phone for the last week, getting to know one another. They never discussed anything incriminating, just your everyday "girl talk."

She could tell just by their conversations that Rose was a real *boss* chick. And she exuded class and intelligence like no other. Her Spanish accent was distinct yet sexy, and she seemed wise beyond her 28 years.

Unlike Becky, Rose didn't do the whole social media thing,

so Becky couldn't see pictures of her on Facebook or Instagram. She thought it was odd that a twenty-something year-old female didn't at least have a FB account, but then again, she wasn't dealing with any ol' female. Rose told her she'd have to wait for their face to face to see what she looked like. That whole mysterious aura in itself was appealing to Becky.

Everything was riding on this luncheon and she knew it. The door of endless opportunities was just an arm's length away. And no matter what, she could ***not*** fuck this up.

All the black guys she dated could never elevate her in the drug world. They were small-time suppliers themselves. Plus, they underestimated her hustle game because she was white *and* female. But what they didn't know was that "Snow Bunny" was a unique specimen like no other.

Becky Slinkowski was doing it stupid big up north. Making more money slangin' pills than they did on the coke and heroin tip *combined*! But it was cool, she wasn't tripping. She let them think what they wanted to think. While they figured she was some rich little spoiled brat who was born with a silver spoon in her mouth and moved "a few pills" here and there, she was really getting her bands up, using them for their big black cocks, and quietly soaking up game on the low.

Yeah, she was a suburbanite, but she wasn't no square bitch. She didn't "pretend" to be black or act like something that she wasn't. Becky was naturally a cool ass chick. She was hip and had mad flavor. She was proud of her German and Polish heritage, but she loved the black culture that accepted what her own people denounced.

Ever since the white boys and girls in middle school would tease her for having a big butt, calling her "fat pig" and "thunder thighs," she openly embraced the culture that celebrated women with curves and **FAT ASSES**!

Black guys had been flocking to her since she was ten years-old, complimenting her and making her feel pretty and appreciated. They accepted her for who she was. So, it was only natural that she'd get with those who were into her. And although the first boy to take her virginity when she was fifteen wasn't black (he was a nineteen-year-old Italian), she'd been with nothing but "brothers" ever since.

Her love for hip-hop, R&B, and bad boys had been immersed in her ever since she was a teenager. Her parents had no idea about the double life she led. Besides the couple of years she was hooked on pills, Gail and Tom Slinkowski thought their first born was a sober little miss goody-two-shoes. And around them, she was, but she was sober now. But as soon as they turned their backs, she was a care-free wild child that partied hard and stayed turnt up!

Becky wasn't sure if Rose scheduled their meeting for the first day of Spring on purpose or not, but she found it quite ironic that her Horoscope for the day said:

New avenues will present themselves to you. When cleaning house, choose wisely and you will be rewarded with GREAT success. There is no room in your life for love right now, you must focus on business because Cupid won't strike until you climb the corporate ladder.

She laughed at that little inside joke. *I have Cupid in my front yard, I see him every day,* she thought to herself.

Becky believed whole heartedly in horoscopes and astrology. She followed them religiously and always took heed to what they had to say.

Before she left her 3 bedroom cul-de-sac, she was dressed to perfection. You only get one chance to make a first impression, so she went all out. Liking to match her outfit to the car she'd be driving for the day, she chose a royal blue ensemble because she was gonna dip the royal blue CL563 Benz with the matching 24-inch Diablo Morpheus rims. The CL563 was her favorite car and her favorite color. Even the inside had custom royal blue alligator interior trimmed in white leather.

She chose to go braless since her all natural 34D size tits stood up nice and perky by themselves. She did, however, slip on a royal blue silk La Perla thong since she hated panty lines.

Her outfit of choice was a royal blue Louis Vuitton dress with sky blue LV signs all over it and a pair of 6-inch Gianvito Rossi lace up pumps. The dress was skintight and came up to mid-thigh, showing off her smooth, tan, beautiful thick legs.

All of Becky's jewelry was Tiffany & Co. A platinum and diamond Patek Philippe watch with a royal blue alligator-skin wrist band. A 10-carat sapphire diamond ring adorned her right hand. Huge diamond Vhernier teardrop earrings (the size of those 5 hour energy drink bottles) hung from her earlobes like chandeliers. She was blinging something serious!

She slung her matching Louie V bag over her shoulder, slid her Louie V sunglasses (with the diamond LV on the sides) on her oval face, kissed her poodle "Dior" goodbye, and went to meet the woman who would forever change her life.

BECKY PULLED into the Perkins Family Restaurant beating Beyonce's "Flawless" remix featuring Nicki Minaj. "*I woke up like this*!" She sang in the rearview mirror as she applied a fresh coat of lipstick to her puckers and checked her make-up.

After getting a booth by the window, she sipped lemon water while messing around on Facebook on her iPhone X. She saw Bucky was throwing a party at the Cold Shot Club in a few days. *Hmm, interesting*, she thought.

Twenty minutes after she sat down, a beautiful woman with green eyes and a creamy complexion stood over her with her arm extended. "Hi mami, I'm Rose. Nice to finally meet you," the stunning mamasita said.

Becky stood up and shook her hand. "Oh my God! It's so nice to meet you too... Wow, you're like soooo gorgeous," she said, looking her up and down. Rose was wearing a cream Donna Karen pantsuit with a push-up bra underneath the blazer, exposing *lots* of cleavage where an iced out BBC medallion dangled.

"Aww, thanks ma. You're easy on the eyes your damn self. Though I don't swing that way," Rose said, and they both giggled as they sat down opposite each other.

"What cha eating chica?" Rose asked, opening her menu up and scanning the items.

"Mmm, I was thinking about going with the biscuits and gravy with a side of bacon," Becky replied.

Rose nodded, "Good choice."

"You haven't eaten yet?" Becky asked her.

"No, but I'm starved."

"Oh."

"What?" Rose inquired.

"Um, I don't know. I thought maybe you had had a bite to eat or something already and spilled a little on you while you were driving." Becky said, looking at the tiny red drops on the front of Rose's blazer.

Rose looked down and swore under her breath. She didn't see the microscopic drops of dried blood before now. She was slippin', and she had to be more careful. She was glad her protégé had a good eye for detail.

"Oh this? Nah, the garbage got a little messier than usual when I took it out," Rose said, smiling. She removed the blazer and sat there in her black push-up bra. A few patrons turned and stared, especially the men, but Rose carried on like she wasn't even half naked in a diner.

"Waitress?" She said, raising her arm and calling over the thin woman who was serving them.

"Two biscuits and gravy please. One with a side of bacon, and the other with sausage patties. And two large orange juices please. That will be all," Rose said, handing her their menus.

"Jeez. You'd think these people never saw boobs before," Rose said, looking around at the people she felt eyeing her. "Anyway, tell me how you got into the skittles game," she said, cutting straight to the point.

"Well, when I was a cheerleader in high school, I had a real bad fall my sophomore year. Fucked up some disks in my back and the doctors had to prescribe me some pain meds. Well, I got addicted to them *fast*. It was real bad too. I was fucking popping twenty, thirty pills a day! My parents saw my downward spiral and put me in rehab. But that didn't do shit but make me bring out my inner-actress and pretend like I kicked my habit and was all better. But in reality, I was still getting high as a kite. All day every day. Hell, it was worse when I got *out* of rehab cuz I met other pill-heads in the program and made new connections through them. I also learned about all kinds of other pills that I'd never heard of before that can get a person high too. It wasn't until my senior year that I quit cold turkey after my BFF overdosed. That scared me straight..." Becky trailed off, eyes watering.

Rose reached over the table and put her hand on top of Becky's. "I'm so sorry sweetie. That musta been really hard for you." Becky nodded somberly.

"What was her name?" Rose asked

"Sharon," she said, turning her left arm over and rubbing her wrist where the cursive tattoo of her deceased friend's name was inked at.

Rose already knew all of this information. She had done a thorough background check already on Ms. Rebecca Marie Slinkowski. She knew that her and Sharon Josephson had been best friends since five-years-old, from kindergarten up until she died of a lethal overdose of oxycontin, morphine, and heroin at the age of 17.

She knew where Becky got her scripts from and who she sold pills to. She knew Becky's entire extended family. Their names, birthdates, addresses, social security numbers, even their secret fetishes. She also knew that Becky had a brown birth mark that looked like a cashew on her inner thigh, right next to her pussy.

The reason behind her questioning was to look into the beautiful blonde's eyes while she answered Rose. That way, she could tell how real the bitch was. Any deceit or fakeness would be exposed in the windows to the soul because those never lie.

“I haven't touched pills since,” Becky continued. “Well, besides some Ex every now and then. But I never liked coke, and I'm afraid to death of H. So that good ol' green has pretty much been my serenity.”

“But what made you want to sell pills? I mean, your family's rich right?” Rose asked. Just then, the waitress came with their orders and sat their plates down, trying not to look at Rose's big titties standing up in her wonder bra. Becky waited until she left before she answered.

“Yeah, they're loaded,” Becky shrugged. “They started a Tanning Salon when I was like nine or ten years-old. They began franchising in 2003, the same year 50 cent's *Get Rich Or Die Tryin'* came out. Now they own 28 chains and I co-own 4 of them.”

“But I was a thrill seeker. An adrenaline junkie. That's why I like to sky dive and bungee jump and all that crazy stuff. A boring vanilla lifestyle never appealed to me. I like living on the edge, driving fast, and doing shit that society says I'm not supposed to do, just for the fuck of it ya know? It's like, screw them. I'll do what the hell I want, when I want, and effin' live how I wanna frickin' live. Goddamn cocksuckers! If I wanna hook-up with black guys and listen to rap music then *damnit...*” she said, slapping the table and getting loud, “I'll get all the black cock I can stand and crank up Lil Wayne as loud as I damn well please!" She noticed she was getting worked up and looked around the restaurant. People were whispering and looking in her direction. "Oops, sorry," Becky giggled, covering her mouth with her fingertips. "Anyway, I started selling 'skittles' cuz I was already in the circle with all the addicts. A lot of them were my friends and I hated to see them jonesing cuz I knew what that felt like. So even though having a few of our friends OD wasn't enough to scare most of them straight, I figured I could at least be there for them and help them out when they needed it. At least they could trust me. A lot of people were getting beat. Cocksuckers would sell 'em aspirin and drywall and shit. So, I said fuck it. I could make some extra cash and make sure my friends don't keep getting ripped off ya know? Too many phonies doing fuck shit! I met a few old people at the nursing homes my parents volunteer at and found out a lot of them had relatives with all kinds of prescriptions, but they were strapped for cash. So, I started buying their scripts from them every month. And well, the rest is history."

ROSE NODDED as she ate her biscuits and gravy and sipped on cold orange juice.

"And besides, I was born with an independent spirit. Sunset Tanning is my *parents'* creation. I want my OWN shit! I want to earn my OWN way. Fuck some handouts. My passion is in hustling. There's nothing like counting some cold hard cash. That shit makes my pussy wet," Becky said and giggled.

"Si Mami. I can't disagree with you on that one," Rose stated.

"I'm doing pretty good for myself though. But I know I can go much bigger and way harder if I had the resources. I mean, I've lived up here my whole life, so I know who's straight and who the snitches are, so I don't mess with everybody."

"But the demand outweighs the supply up here because

let's face it, this is a rich white bread town, and it's a party city. So, all the neighboring towns come over here to kick it. Especially the College kids. We have like a kajillion bars, so they migrate to College Ave. every weekend like it's Spring Break! I have a few bartender friends who I have sell pills for me in the clubs they work at. I can't be everywhere at once, so I need a little help sometimes ya know? But with the right quantity, I could lower the price and eliminate my competition," Becky told her.

"Do you have a lot of competitors?" Rose asked.

"Well, yes and no. There's the J-Twins, Jessie and Julie. They're both nurses so they steal pills from their job. They only sell them for 30 a pop, but they're users too. So, they only have a certain amount they put on the market and the rest goes in their whore mouths or up their slut noses. When that happens, their customers shell out the extra 20 bucks to score from me since they can't cop from the twins. God, I hate those skinny little cunt bitches! They think their shit don't stink."

"Anyhoo, then there's Bucky's big-tooth ass. He's a really big-eared, overbite redneck that pretends like he's hard. He's such a poser. His *mommy* is a doctor, so he forges her signature on scripts for all of his friends. It's like 8 of those douchebags. They're these wannabe-black, white boys that think they're all gangster and shit. They swear they' re kingpins or something. But Bucky's posse has very loyal clientele. If they can't cop from them, they'll wait it out. They won't score from anyone else. No matter how good the price is.

Hell, we *were* cool, until he tried moving in on my territory. He started giving out free samples to my people in Menasha. Menasha is MINE! It's like the Beverly Hills of Appleton and he knows it. Cocksucker stepped on my toes and stole a few of my custys. Well, his homeboy Lincoln did, I should say. Bucky said he had nothing to do with it, but I know he did. He's the leader of that dimwit crew and they don't so much as *sneeze* without Bucky's permission first.

Other than them, the rest are out of towners from Oshkosh, Stevens Point, and Fond Du Lac that come in and get rid of some pills when they can. I'm not too worried about them though. They sell to any and everybody. And half the time, they end up delivering to narcs and get busted, so..."

Rose nodded as she digested all of Becky's information. Rose already knew about Bucky and his boys. They called themselves "Pill Mobb." Foolish and flashy young redneck punks that wanted to be black so bad. They were easy targets.

But Rose knew nothing about these "J-Twins." They were nurses and selling skittles at $30 a pop? Hmm, they could be a problem.

"Do you know who's selling coke, weed, and heroin up here?" Rose asked her.

"Yeah, that's a big melting pot. Mostly the black guys from Milwaukee, Green Bay, and Chicago come up here and try to turn Appleton into the next New Jack City cuz they can get $200 for a gram of good coke or H easily. Some of them get a good run in; maybe a solid year or two, if they're smart and low-key. But most of them get busted within months. And because they're black and from bigger cities, they end up getting slammed with a shitload of time. My mom's booty call is a sheriff whom I sell oxy's to, and he tells me everyone the cops are about to bust. He knows I date a lot of dealers, so he gives me a heads up so I'm nowhere around when shit hits the fan."

"YOUR MOM'S BOOTY CALL?" Rose asked.

"Yeah. She and my dad have an open marriage. They're like, swingers and shit. Anyhoo, they say it keeps their marriage 'alive'. So hey, whatever floats their boat," Becky shrugged.

"So, the dealers you date... do you give them money?" Rose asked her.

"I used to. Then I realized, why am I giving away ***my*** money *and* my kitty kat? I wasn't getting shit in return. Yeah, they have big cocks, but so what? Most of 'em don't know how to make a woman orgasm. It's like they never heard of the clitoris. So, I was feeling cheated and said to hell with y'all. Get some other bitch to give you money. I'm not no sugarmama!"

Rose laughed at Becky's candor. She had some "flavor", but she talked so proper and white, that it was so funny to hear her try and get sassy.

"Well, at least you wizened up. If anything, men should be giving *US* money. Not the other way around. Ya see, dick is easy to get. When you're a Bad Bitch, every man wants to get in your pants anyway. If a woman is really about her money, she should have no problem making those men's wish come true...as long as the price is right of course. Most bitches be like 'I ain't no whore. I don't sell my pussy! That's what prostitutes do.' But dumb ass bitch, you bussin' down with every Tom, Dick and Harry, fucking and sucking all kinds of dick anyway. And for what? For motherfucking free that's what! Like you said, the majority of the time, we ain't having orgasms wit these niggaz. They get to bust they nut *and* brag to their boys that they fucked a dime. But what did *we* get out of the deal? Shiiiiid, if anything, a bitch should feel like a used up *free* whore after that bullshit. At least if we get compensated for opening our legs, we'd at least walk away *with* something. Ya feel me?"

"Fuck yeah I do!" Becky said, high fiving Rose across the table.

"Then we can go home and let our 'rabbit' or 'bullet' finish what them non-fucking dudes couldn't finish," Rose said, smiling.

"You see this mami?" Rose said, grabbing the iced out BBC pendant on her gold necklace. "This stands for Bad Bitchez

Click, or Bad Boss Chicks, it's all the same" she turned her right shoulder and showed Becky the BBC tat on her upper-arm. A honey Bee was the dot on the I. "Our motto is 'We do whatever for the dollar.' It used to be 'We do whatever for the cheddar,' but cheddar is old, don't nobody say that shit no more."

"Anyway," Rose continued, "if financial gain can be obtained, then we all in! The only moral codes and loyalty we have are for each other. Cuz we family. And you don't cross family. Everyone else though? Fuck 'em. We hood bitchez. We grew up in a hostile cut-throat environment. We've all been raped, abused, and taken advantage of at some point in our lives. But instead of crying and being the 'victim', we found our inner-strength to rise above the bullshit and persevere," Rose took a few sips of her OJ and broke it down for Becky.

"We're not man haters or no shit like that. Nah, not by a long shot. We LOVE men. But we love us..." she paused to kiss the BBC ice, "even more. We're a family. 'Til death do us part. And if you get down with us Becky, you'll be pledging your life and loyalty to us... FOREVER. We ride or die for each other. I know you ain't no hood bitch, but I think you were born to be a **BAD BITCH**. And we gon' take over the world together," Rose said.

Becky sat there in wide-eyed amazement. She was mesmerized by the passion in Rose's voice as she spoke highly about a group of women Becky never knew existed, but she wanted so desperately to be a part of. Her heart was racing. Her palms were sweating. And her nipples were hard as hell! Meeting this beautiful Boss Bitch was hands down the best day of her life. She didn't care what she had to do in order to get in, she'd do it. Becky fixed Rose with a serious stare and said,

"I want in!"

"Good," Rose nodded, "take me to meet your parents."

Rose followed Becky in her Lex to the Slinkowski's biggest Sunset Tanning Salon in a strip mall on the west side. Rose threw a black V-neck blouse that she had in her truck on before they went in to meet Becky's mother.

Gail was a fifty-something year-old woman who looked good for her age, but she was *way* too orange. She had a slim, in shape figure from doing lots of Yoga and stood about five feet even. Becky got her big piercing blue eyes from her mother, but that's where the resemblance stopped.

Gail had a heavily botoxed face that didn't allow her eyebrows to move, which looked funny since she tended to talk so animatedly. She was very touchy feely and had a high-pitched bubbly voice. Mrs. Slinkowski was nice and friendly and glad to meet a new friend of her daughters, (especially an *"ethnic"* one). She gave Rose a big coupon booklet for discounted tan treatments, even though she wouldn't be using them. Rose was Hispanic and had a natural tan and told her she should come over for dinner sometime. Rose promised that she would, and they left.

"She doesn't ***look*** like a swinger," Rose commented on the way to their vehicles.

"Ha! Don't let the Real Housewives of Orange County look fool you. That woman is a FREAK! Like, super kinky," Becky said and laughed.

Next, they visited her father at one of their downtown locations. Tom Slinkowski was over 6 feet tall with short brown hair and brown eyes. He was casually dressed in Lacoste slacks, matching button down and boating shoes. Everything was color coordinated and sharp. Mr. S had some style.

He was younger than his wife; at 47 years-old, he was in great shape too. The Slinkowskis were big on health and fitness so he had a very nice build. With his square jaw and clean-shaven face, he looked a lot like the actor Jon Hamm.

Hmm, I wonder if he's a "Mad Man" himself, Rose thought, smiling after the introductions were made.

Her father sized up Rosalita and licked his lips lustfully.

The look in his bedroom eyes said "he wondered what it would be like to taste that Latino pie." Rose turned on the charm and sex appeal, flirting nonchalantly. She laughed at his jokes, even the corny ones, and lightly touched his muscular tan arms with her pretty French tip nails when she talked. By the time they left, she had him in the palm of her hand.

"Stop by anytime Rosalita," he said, stuffing six Sunset Tanning Salon coupon booklets in her hands as they left. "And if you ever need anything... ***anything,*** just let me know!"

"Your dad wants me... BAD," Rose told her in the parking lot.

"Like, I knoooow, right? He was sooo drooling over you. Holy fuck! He's embarrassing like that's sometimes. I'm so sorry about that. Has anyone ever told you that you look like Jennifer Lopez? You should be a model. I'd buy every magazine you were on the cover of,""

"Ah, it's cool. It wasn't so bad since he's kinda cute. But—"

"Eew. Please don't tell me. Nope, I do not wanna hear it," Becky said, covering her ears for effect. "But hey, if you wanna do him, go ahead! He's already banged two of my other friends."

"NAH MAMI, I wouldn't do that—"

"Rose, seriously I could care less. IDGAF. He *is* loaded. And he's not stingy. He took my friend Veronica to the Cayman Islands for a week and spent tons of moola on her. If the opportunity presents itself, go for it. You have my blessing," Becky told her.

"Mami, if I don't know any better, it sounds like you're tryin' to sic me on your pops!"

"Hey, sharing is caring right?" Becky said and they both laughed.

They drove to the Slinkowski's six-bedroom ranch off

Highway 41. Rose had seen pictures of the massive house Becky's family called home for over a decade, but to see it in person was another thing. It sat on so many acres of land that it looked like it was in the middle of a forest!

They pulled into a long double-entry driveway that curved around a neatly kept island of grass that had a statuette/fountain of a baby cupid shooting water out of its wee-wee. Rose shook her head and smiled in amusement as she got out of her truck.

She checked out a pineapple yellow '94 Caprice with 28-inch Stratus Hurricane rims and chrome spinners on it parked out front.

"That's my little sister's boyfriend's car," Becky said, referring to 17-year-old Deemontay James. A small-time crack peddler who went to her sister Britney's school and was her "first" everything: boyfriend/sexual partner/love.

Walking into the three-story modern house with the big picture glass windows, Rose couldn't help but admire the tasteful decal. She knew right away that an interior decorator had plushed them out. All of the furniture was earth toned and foreign made. They had crystal chandeliers hanging from the ceiling and a 100-gallon fish tank full of Tiger fish in their living room.

The paintings and sculptures that adorned the rooms were all classic pieces. The real McCoys. No imitations. Becky showed her around the whole house before she knocked on Britney's door.

"Oh shit, who is that?" Deemontay jumped, looking at the door, but asking Britney.

"I don't know... God!" she said, taking his 8-inch cock out of her mouth and wiping saliva from her lips before responding.

"Whaaaat?" Britney yelled.

"Brit-Brit, it's just me. I have a friend of mine here that I want you to meet," Becky told her 16-year-old sister from the other side of the door.

"I'm busy. Can't it wait til later?" She whined.

"Well, hurry it up. It's not like y'all really know what you're doing anyway," Becky teased.

"Whatevs," Britney said, putting the jet black tool back in her mouth and deep throating it.

"They're probably fucking. They'll be done soon. Come on," Becky told Rose as they walked off and went back to the living room.

"Don't know what I'm doing? I bet she wouldn't be saying that if I had my dick all up in her!" Deemontay said, palming Britney's head and fucking her face.

"Shut up! Don't say stuff like that," Britney mumbled around his penis and slurped him loudly.

"Fuck that! She think cuz I'm young that I can't handle my bidness? Take that shit off so I can pound your pussy out." Deemontay said, pulling his spit-drenched dick out of her mouth.

Even though Becky had her own room in the house, she hardly used it. She owned her own 3 bedroom "bachelorette pad" in Menasha. But she did come home often to eat with her family and kick it with her little sister.

Becky and Britney were very close. They told each other *everything*. Britney looked up to her big sis and wanted to be just like her someday. And even though there was an 11-year age difference between them, you could tell they were sisters. They were a spitting image of each other. The only difference was hair color.

Becky was a honey blonde and Britney was a brunette with long brown hair. She wanted to dye it blonde, but Becky told her to keep her originality and have her *own* look. Her own identity. So, she agreed... for now.

They both had those Katy Perry-looking, big sky-blue eyes

and striking facial features. She was a bit shorter than Becky, but she was still growing. And at sixteen, she already had the body of a full-grown woman. Big titties and an even bigger ass. Just like her BIG sister.

Becky and Rose kicked their feet up and flipped through the DIRECTV channels when all of a sudden, they heard a big crash, then a car alarm going off.

"Bring your bitch ass out here slut! You too, you cheating, cocksucking bastard!" A shrill voice yelled from outside.

Becky and Rose ran to the window and saw seven or eight cars in front of the house and about thirty teenagers standing on the front lawn. Some tall girl with long pink and purple hair was standing on the island where the cupid statuette peed water. She had a brick in her hand and a scowl on her long pale face.

Another brick was sticking out of Deemontay's front windshield. "What the fuck yo?!" he yelled, running down the spiral staircase, trying to pull up his pants and fumbling with his belt. Britney followed right behind him as they rushed out the front door.

"Ah-ha! I knew it. You cheating low-life scumbag. You *WERE* fucking that bitch. I caught you with your pants down motherfucker! You said you weren't messing with her cunt ass no more and here you are FUCKING the bitch?" pink/purple hair said, and then she threw the brick in her hand and shattered his back window.

"Hey, what the fuck man? Bitch you crazy," Deemontay said, pushing a button on his keychain and turning the annoying car alarm off. "What the fuck you busting my shit up for man? Damn, look at this shit," he said, surveying the damage and looking devastated. She also keyed the word **CHEATER** on both sides of his car in big letters. Deemontay looked like he was about to cry.

"Fuck you motherfucker. And that fat cunt!"

"Cunt? Cunt? I've got your cunt, you slut," Britney said, storming off the porch.

"How am I the slut when you're the one fucking another girl's man?" Pink/purple hair said.

Britney had been Deemontay's girlfriend for 16 months now. He took her virginity 5 months ago, and she didn't know him to screw around on her.

"Deemontay, what the fuck is she talking about? Are you fucking with her?" Britney asked, walking up on him.

He put his hands in his pockets and wouldn't look at her. "Shiid, I don't know. I *kinda* was. But not no more. Bitch done broke my shit and shit. Fuck that. How am I gon' pay for this Amber? I ain't got no insurance. You paying for my windows bitch. And a new paint job," he said.

"I'm not paying for SHIT! Get ***that*** bitch to pay for it, you dirty frickin' dog you. I can't believe you, you sonuvabitch. You played me. I'm the one who bought these fucking rims for you, Dee. You didn't tell her that did ya? Nah, I bet you didn't. Just like she didn't know we've been screwing for the past six weeks. Every... fucking... day! Yeah, that's right bitch. He comes and gets ***THIS*** pussy cuz he said your fat ass can't even fuck! You just lay there like a cold fish!"

"Oooh," the crowd said, egging her on.

"Awww, the little baby wanna cry? Huh? You're nothing but a big bootied slut Slinkowski. You fat whore!"

Britney bared her teeth like a lion and ran full speed ahead at the other girl. Amber charged her too and they collided like two wrestlers in the ring, pulling each other to the ground.

"Fight! Fight! Fight! Fight!" All the other teens chanted as they pulled their smart phones out and recorded the two girls going at it. Within minutes, the whole ordeal went viral all over YouTube and Snapchat and other social media sites under "cat-fight" and "white girls brawl."

Rose observed the whole spectacle from the porch. *These*

mothafuckas showed up mad deep, she thought to herself. She hoped they weren't gonna try to jump Britney cuz she really didn't wanna have to put the smack down on a bunch of teenagers.

Amber and Britney rolled around in the grass, pulling each other's hair and shouting obscenities. *Bitch, whore, slut, cunt* were repeated like a broken record. Britney was thicker, but Amber was stronger. The pink and purple haired girl ran track and played volleyball, so her stamina and endurance was greater than her rivals. Plus, she was lean and very disciplined in her attack.

When Amber finally managed to free her pink and purple locks from Britney's hands, she sat on her chest and began pummeling her with one-two punches. The crowd ooh'd, ahh'd and damn'd as Amber went ham on Britney's face. Becky made a move to intervene, but Rose grabbed her arm and said, "she has to learn to fight her own battles mami. Fall back."

Although Britney was getting her ass whooped, she didn't give up. She flung Amber off of her and landed 2 quick punches of her own to the girl's throat and ear.

"That's it Brit!" Becky yelled. "Kick her ass! Hit her in the chin!"

Britney swung wild haymakers and Amber side stepped and dodged them all. Rose could see Britney was fighting with her emotions while Amber remained focused and fought with calculated precision.

Amber hit her with a 1-2-3 in both of Britney's eyes and the crowd "ooh'd" and flinched. Britney tried to rush her again and Amber grabbed her hair and flung her to the ground. Britney kicked Amber in her knee, and she landed on top of Britney where they rolled around kicking, clawing, and punching for several more seconds. Amber punched Britney in her neck and chest, those blows got the feisty girl off of her.

They both got to their feet and squared off. Britney could

only see out one of her eyes because the right one was closed shut and more purple than Amber's hair. **Whack! Whack!** Amber caught her in the forehead and temple. That seemed to piss Britney off as she grabbed a handful of Amber's hair and punched her in the jaw. Amber rammed forward and head-butted Britney, causing her to stumble backwards.

"You bitch!" Amber yelled, kicking Britney in the vagina. The crowd cringed, and everyone grabbed their crotch, (girls and boys alike), as if *they* were the ones who just got kicked in their private parts. Britney couldn't believe the bitch just kicked her in her pussy! It was bad enough Deemontay had beat it up only minutes before. Now she was taking a foot to it?!

Britney stood up straight and put her dukes up. She was wobbly and seeing double, but she was not gonna back down for anything in the world. Britney fake jabbed and swung wide, trying to cold clock her, but she missed. Amber stepped in swiftly and delivered a hard punch to Britney's nose, making her neck snap back. The crowd "dammmned" instantly and flinched at the loud and sickening crunch of bone. Britney looked like a bobble-head doll the way her head jerked back and forth. Blood dripped into her mouth and she spit-sprayed some onto Amber. "That's all you got?... *Bitch*," Britney taunted.

Amber looked down at the blood that was just spit all over her ripped up Taylor Swift T-shirt and said, "You fucking cunt!" She uppercut Britney in the stomach, and as she doubled over, Amber brought down a sharp elbow to the back of Britney's head, making her fall flat on her face. Blood pooled in the grass.

"That's it," Becky said, shaking Rose's hand loose off her arm and storming into the house. While Britney was down, Amber took the opportunity to repeatedly kick her in the ribs and kidneys. Britney didn't curl up into the fetal position or ball up once though. She tried her best to dodge the swift kicks by rolling around left to right because she was obviously too winded to get to her feet.

When Amber let up on the kicks of fury, Britney rolled on to her back and looked up at the pink and purple monster snarling down at her.

"Bitch, I'll get you back. Mark my words ho, this shit isn't over," Britney said, spitting more blood out of her mouth.

Amber lifted her pink memory foam Sketchers foot in the air and paused for affect. Ready to give her one good stomp to the face to knock Britney out, she looked down and said, "Fuck you, you fat cunt. It *is* over..." Just as she was about to stomp Britney's lights out– ***Rarr! Rarr! Rarr!*** Gunshots rang in the air and teens screamed and scattered like roaches with the light on, hopping into their cars and smashing off. Amber slowly put her foot down and took a few steps backwards.

"Get the fuck off my property bitch!" Becky said, walking down the front steps holding a Glock in her hand.

"Whoa, whoa, whoa now," Amber began, putting her hands up and backing away.

Rarr! Rarr! Becky shot at the ground next to Amber's feet, making the young girl involuntarily dance like she was tip-toeing on hot charcoal.

"I said...get...the...fuck...off...my...PROPERTY!" ***Rarr! Rarr! Rarr! Rarr***! Becky squeezed four more rounds next to the terrified girl's feet, chunks of grass and dirt flew into the air.

AMBER WASTED NO TIME. She ran and jumped into the passenger side of her friend Kia's car, who already had the door open for her. They sped off and Becky pointed her Glock in the air and kept squeezing the trigger until the clip was empty. "All of you, get the fuck outta here. Shows over. Get off my fucking property!" she yelled.

There were a few "rubberneckers" who hadn't left with the

first bunch because they wanted to stay and record the "gangster" footage from a safe distance. But once they saw the hot blonde meant business, they all got the fuck out of dodge! Fishtailing it out of the Slinkowski's driveway and burning rubber in the process. Britney got to her feet as they were leaving.

"Yeah bitch! You better bounce," she yelled at the cars that made a fast getaway. "I'll see you again bitch. And I'ma– "

"Don't," Becky said, cutting her off. "Just... stop. Look at you... you let that bitch come to YOUR house and beat you on YOUR turf," she said, shaking her head in disappointment.

Becky rubbed Britney's back as she surveyed the damage to their yard.

"I hope he was worth it." Becky pointed towards the shattered glass in the driveway where Deemontay's car *was* parked. He was nowhere in sight now.

He got his nut and got ghost and didn't give a damn about having her back. It was Britney's first real life lesson she learned about men. They were dogs and didn't give a fuck about nothing but themselves.

5

BRITNEY

Becky cleaned up her little sister's wounds with peroxide and doctored her up as best as possible. After determining her nose wasn't broken, her and Rose got the glass out of the driveway and patched up the lawn. Then they all piled into Rose's SUV and rode to Becky's house.

"You're gonna stay here with me for a few days. Or until you completely heal up," Becky told her as they sat down in the living room.

"What about school?" Britney asked.

"I'll tell mom I'm taking you, and I'll call your school pretending to be her and say you'll be out for a week cuz you're sick," Becky said as she stuffed a weed pipe full of kush.

Britney nodded somberly. "I'm really sorry Becks. I know I let you down and– "

"Look. You win some, you lose some. Ok? Plus, I kinda have to blame myself for it. I taught you how to shoot guns but never taught you how to fight. That was ass backwards on my part," Becky said, lighting a bowl and taking a long drag.

"So, you know how to shoot guns mami?" Rose asked her.

"Yes. I'm pretty good at it too. Better than I am with my fists," Britney said.

"Yeah, well where *I'm* from, they don't even use these," Rose said, raising her balled fists.

"Really? Where are you from?" Britney asked.

"I was born in Brazil, but I grew up in Milwaukee."

"Ohhhh, wow. Yeah, we hear it's pretty rough in Milwaukee. There's like shootings everyday down there, isn't it?"

"Yup. Too many. Muthafuckas die every day in the Mil. It's like the Wild Wild West. Shoot first and ask questions later. Kinda like how the police have been lately. But yeah everyone has guns now. And usually when some beef pops off, them shots ring out. **BOOM! BOOM! BOOM!** And just like that, you could lose your life."

BECKY NODDED KNOWINGLY. Most of the black dudes she dated were from Milwaukee. She was with some of them down there when they got into some drama. She'd never been shot, but she witnessed a few of them get into shootouts and get hit themselves. Two of her exes even died. It wasn't a place where she wanted to live, but she admitted to herself that she did love the adrenaline rush that came from being in such dangerous situations. That's why she was so attracted to the "thug" type. Because Bad Boys made her pussy wet!

"Wasn't Milwaukee like the murder capital of the world before?" Britney asked, taking a hit of the weed pipe and passing it to Becky. Britney choked and started coughing loudly, "Holy shit! This is that bomb!"

Rose laughed. "Yeah a couple times we had the highest homicide rate in the country. It's not really nothing to be proud of, but sometimes a person has to do what they gotta do. If your back is against the wall, you gotta handle your business."

Britney looked at Rose's knuckles. "Is that why your hands are all swollen, cuz you had to handle your business?"

"Mm, something like that," Rose said, massaging her knuckles softly. Becky filled another bowl and offered the pipe to Rose.

"Nah mami, I'm good. I smoke, but I don't do the pipe thing. I smoke blunts."

"What's wrong with pipes?" Britney inquired.

"Makes me feel like a hype," Rose replied.

"A hype?"

"Yeah, you know... a fiend. A junkie. An addict. I know it's not crack or meth in the pipe but still. Where I'm from, you're considered "weak" if you smoke a pipe of **ANY** kind. You're looked at as a hype. We associate pipes with crackheads. And crackheads are deemed the lowest on the totem pole of all the drug users. So, we don't fuck wit dat shit. Plus, if you get sweated by the cops, how you gonna get rid of the evidence? You can't dispose of a pipe as easily as you can a blunt or joint. You can swallow that shit cuz they're paper. You can't swallow no damn pipe though," Rose said.

"Wow.... You know, I never thought about it like that. Damn, you're right," Becky said, looking at her pipe. "It's just you get *all* the weed this way— "

"I know. Bongs are cool at big parties and shit. Huge steam-rollers and whatnot, but we just got love for the bliggedys in my culture. Plus, you look so much ***cooler*** smoking a B or a joint ya know?" Rose said.

"Yeah, you're right. You do look cooler that way," Britney said, mimicking like she had a B between her fingertips. "Wow, you're pretty hip!" she said enthusiastically.

"Well, thank you chica. And ***you***, miss thang, have a lot of potential. I saw how you took those kicks and punches like a champ. Not once did you run, back down, or ball up like a bitch in the fetal position. You may have not been able to strike back, but you didn't tap out either. That was real soldier shit mami. You got heart. Your sister should be proud of you."

"I am," Becky responded.

Britney blushed, "Um, thanks. I mean, I'm no coward. Becks told me no matter WHO a person is, or how big they are, boy or girl, NEVER show fear. So, I try to be brave and stand my ground. She just got the best of me. And can you believe her? Bitch kicked me in the cooch!"

"Yeah, well, ain't no rules in street fighting. Anything goes. And you do whatever you have to do to win. But shit, I ain't seen no catfight in a minute! Y'all was some hair-pulling, shit talking bitches I tell ya! And you really took a molly whopping. I was amazed at how you hung in there. Even taunting her like, 'that's all you got ho?' I was like 'Wow, this girl has some BALLS!" Rose said, laughing.

"Yeah, my lil sis is one tough cookie," Becky said, ruffling her sister's hair.

"Ow," Britney said, taking the ice pack off her eye and putting it on the lump on her head. Just then, Becky's poodle Dior walked up and sniffed at her ankles. She scooped up her pet and sat it in her lap.

"Heyyy girl. How's mommy's wootle wootle cutie pie doin'? Hmm? Kiss kiss kiss," Becky said, rubbing her nose with the dog's.

"I think you should enroll her in some self-defense classes," Rose told Becky. "Karate, Judo, Tae-kwondo, Boxing, the whole nine. The girl needs to know how to fight *AND* protect herself. You said she can shoot already right?"

"Fuck yeah, she's almost as good a shot as I am," Becky told her.

"And Becks is *DAMN* good," Britney bragged.

"I saw that. The pink hair bitch looked like she was playing hopscotch or jumping rope when you was bussin' at her feet," Rose said, laughing.

"Yeah, I shoulda shot the bitch for what she did to Brit-Brit."

"Nah. Britney lost fair and square. She'll get her revenge though. 'Til then, we'll put her in some classes so she can get on her shit," Rose said, turning to Britney. "You're too pretty to be walking around with your face all hamburgered up chica. You look like mince meat. She gave you a serious pumpkin head," she said, tucking a loose strand of brown hair behind Britney's ear.

"I know," Britney said, lowering her head sadly. "I'll do better next time. I'm a fast learner so— "

"Hold your head up mami," Rose said, lifting Britney's chin gently. "**NEVER, EVER** look down! That's a sign of insecurity and weakness. You are NOT weak. You hold your head high wherever you go. No matter what happens to you or what you go through, you do NOT let the world see you in a vulnerable position. Shoulders back, chest out, stomach in... they teach you that in the military. We adopt a lot of their practices cuz like I said, we embody the whole soldier movement.

Soldiers are loyal, courageous people who fight for a cause; for something they believe in. They risk their lives for what they love most. *That*, is true loyalty. And if you want to be someone someday, I mean ***TRULY*** be somebody, you have to take inventory of your surroundings and decide what is most important to you and what's not.

We shouldn't be fighting over men. Let them fight over US! Why the fuck do we have to take the fall and consequences for them? You think they'll do that shit for us? Hell naw! You seen Deemontay. He didn't step in to break up the fight or try to haul his side bitch away. He coulda snatched her up and told the bitch to fall back. But nope. He ain't do shit! He just sat there and watched you get your ass beat. Then when the smoke cleared, he was in the wind. Nowhere to be found. That's pussy shit. He's a bitch. That ain't loyalty Britney. I'm telling you mami, you deserve better than that," Rose told the young girl.

Tears slid down Britney's face. She was so moved by what Rose said to her because it was the TRUTH. Every point she made hit home and registered deeply within her soul. She ***felt*** that shit to her very core.

Britney looked at the pretty Latina with the long silky hair and smiled. "I like you," she said and gave Rose a big hug.

"I like you too lil mami. What a first meeting!" Rose said and laughed.

"I know right? I bet you was like damn, these white motherfuckers are nuts!" Becky said.

"Yeah, I did. But it's all good. That shit was entertaining as fuck! You'll get your get back tho so don't trip. Now let's go get some Swishers and get high as research monkeys!"

6

GG

My bitch bad, looking like a bag of money, That bitch bad, looking like a bag of money. I go and get it and I let her count it for me, I fuck her good, and she always ride it for me.

GG slithered up and down the pole to the Maybach music group's tune, showing all the customers in Encore tonight why she was a real live bad bitch... that looked like a bag of money!

Oooh she bad, she bad bad bad, she bad bad bad...

GG had more tricks on the pole than a magician. She rarely used her hands. With vigorous leg strength and a rock-hard core, "Gushy" performed moves that made a person's eyes pop out of their head! And it was a lot of poppin' going on tonight.

Pussy poppin'. Bottle poppin'. Guns poppin'...

BOOM! BOOM! BOOM! The deafening sounds of a 12-gauge shotgun rang out over the music. Men and women screamed, running for cover, hitting the floor, crawling under tables.

Click-click BOOM! A 6'6" 300-pound security guard got blown halfway across the room. A hole the size of a softball was in his chest where his organs spilled out of.

Over a dozen ski-masked and bandana wearing women stormed the strip club with heavy artillery. P89's, Mac 11's, Technine's, sawed-off shotguns, .44 Bulldogs, .357 magnums, and some Rambo looking shit with laser beams on them. They came in on *bidness!*

A bitch with a blue bandana tied over her nose walked up to the DJ booth and put a single hollow point bullet into the man, who was just spinning records only seconds before. Now his brains were all over his laptop.

"Alright muthafuckers," the bandana chick began. "Y'all know what it is. We got this bitch surrounded and locked down! So ain't no one getting out of here less we ***let*** you out. Anybody get on some funny shit or even ***sneeze*** in this bitch, we blowin' yo gotdamn nose off!" she said into the microphone. "All y'all gotta do is give us what we came foe and y'all will live to see another day. Up dat dough, them jewels, them car keys, and all that good shit." ***Pop! Pop! Pop!*** She busted the .45 in the air and chunks of ceiling collapsed on the floor.

The women moved like professionals; smoothly and quickly. Some had garbage bags, and some had duffle bags. They went from person to person, removing them of their money and valuables. There was about six women on "S" standing on the table tops, the bar, and two of the stages. Their guns were at the ready, monitoring everyone in the club and making sure no one "reached" or tried to be a hero.

Rarr! Rarr! A man tried to sneak his cellphone out of his pocket to call 911 but was spotted. His life ended before he could even grab the phone. He layed in a pool of blood as patrons around him screamed in horror.

"Shut the fuck up! Or get cho shit pushed back too," one of the women said, swinging her gun back and forth at the terrified people on the floor.

Strippers were in the back trying to hide their cash and hide valuables when 2 assailants walked into the locker room.

"Everybody let me see your hands," an Amazon chick with a camouflage ski-mask said. She had a Tech-nine with a blue laser beam on it. That royal blue dot stopped bitches in their tracks. Eyes wide, frozen like a deer in headlights.

"Please don't– " ***Rarr! Rarr!***

One of the strippers were silenced immediately. The top of her head flew off like a convertible and painted the dancer behind her with bone, brains, and blood... the three B's. These women didn't come to play no games. They was about dat action!

"Don't *NOBODY...* say a muthafuckin' word. Or you'll end up like that bitch."

Strippers swallowed their screams and a few of them pissed on themselves. The smell of urine filled the air and tears flowed like the Mississippi river, but none of the strippers dared to even snivel.

The assailants opened all the lockers and confiscated all the cash and valuables. As they were backing out, one of the robbers asked, "One of you Cinnamon?" They all shook their heads no. One of the dancers raised her hand to speak.

"What?"

"Sh-sh-she was on stage when y-y-y'all came in," she said, shaking uncontrollably.

"Aight," camo ski-mask said and walked out.

All around the club, patrons were being relieved of their wallets, rings, watches, keys, necklaces, and shitloads of cash. The surveillance videos were already being erased and taken by two girls, who had the club manager at gun point as he opened the main safe in his basement office.

"Now thaaaat's what I'm talkin' bout'!" A dark-skinned woman with a pink ski-mask on said as the huge safe door swung open. The club kept hundreds of thousands of dollars in singles to cash in for their customers. And the safe was

LOADED for the weekend rush. Fridays and Saturdays were their busiest days.

The girls filled two Glad bags with money before knocking the manager out cold with the butt of a .357 and went back upstairs.

At the same time, the "house mother"— a trusted employee who bagged the dancers' money and logged their amounts on a legal pad– was being defiant.

"The Lord's gonna get you heathen women for taking what doesn't belong to you," she told the robbers.

"Bitch! I know you ain't trying to act all high and mighty. Ho, you work in a stripclub," a redbone with a yellow bandana tied around her face said.

"These girls trust me with their money. I—" **WHACK!** The old woman got smacked across her face by a pistol. An immediate gash opened up in her forehead as blood gushed forward like the Red Sea.

"Oh my God!" she said, holding the fresh wound. "Lord Jesus, whyyyy?"

"Bitch open up the goddamn safe and quit playin'. We ain't gonna ask you no more. If you wanna live to see another day, open that muthafucka up now!" **WHACK!** She was socked in the nose with the barrel of the gun. The crunch of bone confirmed it was indeed broken on contact.

The old Madea-looking lady dropped to her knees and fumbled with the combination. They pushed her out of the way once it was open. Big Ziploc freezer bags full of cash was inside. Each with a different name on it: Starr, Gushy, Cinnamon, Boom-Boom, Thick um, Kreamsicle, and many more. The women pulled the bags out and threw them in their own duffle bags.

"Lord forgive them for they know not what they do," the woman groaned.

"Old bitch, we know EXACTLY what we doing," yellow

bandana said, pointing her 9mm at the house mother. "I'll see you at the crossroads sooner or later. Have a baked pie waiting for me." **POW!** She squeezed the trigger and put one bullet between the old woman's eyes. Her and her girls walked out of the room singing the classic Bone song:

"And I'm gonna miss everybody. And I'm gonna miss everybody, hey, and I'm gonna miss everybody..."

The Stripclub was *literally* being stripped. Every single dollar on the floor and the stages were gathered. The cash registers at the bars and the door were all emptied. Even the top shelf bottles of alcohol were being taken. Ace of Spades, Dom P, Ciroc, etc.

A few people who tried to make a run for it or be a hero were added to the fatalities list, including a bi-sexual bride to be who was having her bachelorette party there that night.

She was in the bathroom stall getting her pussy ate by a stripper with a 6-inch tongue when the melee broke out. She heard the ruckus and commotion and peaked out to see what was going on. After witnessing the events, she told Layla what was popping off and the dancer stormed out of the bathroom to go and grab her money bag before it was taken. The bi chick let her go as she tried using her phone to call for help. She couldn't get any reception in the bathroom, so she climbed out of the tiny window, phone in hand, and as soon as she landed on the concrete outside of the building, her fingers began dialing. But she only got a couple numbers in before the phone was snatched from her and smashed against the building. A wide-body 5'5" woman with a black beanie and gray ski-mask was standing there.

"Going somewhere?" she asked before blowing the would've been bride's heart out the back of her purple dress. Ms. Bi-sexual was no more.

"Who da fuck is Cinnamon?" was asked several times by several women. When no one offered up any info, everyone was

told more bodies would get shot up until Cinnamon was pointed out or came forward. She was ratted out instantly.

Hiding underneath a table in a neon green thong, Cinnamon was grabbed by her long brown weave and dragged on stage. The woman who snatched her up snapped her fingers at blue bandana in the DJ booth, who then spoke into the microphone.

"The ho you see up on stage is a dirty snake bitch! Her name is Cinnamon, and she likes to steal her fellow co-workers' tips when they're not looking. She also likes to steal bitches men too. Throwing salt on hoes' tricks and all kinds of other foul ass shit. Ain't that right Cinnamon?"

The brown-skinned cutie with the gold body glitter was shaking like a dice game. She was a nervous wreck. The woman who held Cinnamon by her hair bitch-slapped her and the terrified exotic dancer whimpered like a wounded puppy.

Blue bandana pushed a few buttons on the laptop and Ludacris and Shawana's "Gettin' some head" came on the speakers.

"Dance bitch," she was told.

Scared to death, she got up and did what they asked of her as tears rolled down her face. The chick who dragged her on stage had a sawed-off Pump in her hand and watched as Cinnamon tried her hardest to be "exotic" and still hold it together. Frightened hostages and horny men snuck glances at the stage, not wanting to miss the show, even though they were face down on a dirty floor being held at gun point.

A chubby woman who was barely five feet and wore a Chucky Halloween mask walked on stage and shoved a Desert Eagle in Cinnamon's mouth. Cinnamon froze and showed butterball her palms.

"I ain't say stop dancing bitch! Now suck this D.E. to the beat and keep that body moving," the chubby funny voice bitch told Cinnamon as she fellated the big gun.

There was some gangsta niggaz and D-boys in the crowd who was mad as hell that some bitches was sticking them up for their shit, but as they laid on the grimy stripclub floor, it was a lot of hard dicks throbbing that were extremely turned on by these ride or die bitches who came in on straight G-shit! The kind of bitches them niggaz wished was on ***their*** team.

"Lay on your back, rest on your elbows, and show us that pussy bitch," the chubby, Chucky mask-wearing woman said.

Cinnamon got on the floor and slowly took her thong off. She cried and gyrated to the music, quietly praying to God that she'd live to see another day and make it home to her 6-year-old son Aaron.

I was gettin' some head, gettin' gettin' some head...

The Too $hort sampled DTP chorus blared out of the speakers. Bass rattled the whole club as Cinnamon spread her legs, lifted her butt off the stage, and showed nothing but her hot pink insides.

The woman holding the sawed-off looked to her left. The stripper named Gushy was laying face down on the other side of the stage. They locked eyes and GG nodded. The shotty got reloaded and the woman dropped to her knees and said, "Your pussy's caused a lot of problems, you know that? Well bitch, call me the muthafuckin' problem solver," she rammed the pump all the way in Cinnamon's vagina, making her scream in agony at the top of her lungs.

Cinnamon tried to back up to get the shotgun out of her womb, but the chubby bitch standing behind her held her in place by her shoulders. Cinnamon cried, wiggled, and flopped around like a fish out of water.

BOOM! BOOM! Cinnamon's ovaries and fallopian tubes got pushed up to her lungs as her pussy burst open like an

exploded *Hot Pocket* in the microwave! Blood and flesh splattered all on the

woman who pulled the trigger. Cinnamon's clit ricocheted and landed on the trigger woman's shoulder; she flicked it off like it was a piece of lint and stood up. She exited the stage and told her goons, "let's bounce." She looked over at Gushy one more time, she was still laying on her belly, arms spread out to her sides like an airplane, but had a big ol' smile on her face.

Some of the robbers had already hit the parking lot and used the keys they lifted off the customers to steal the cars of their choosing. A Mercedes SLS AMG 600, a Camaro Z4 drop-top, a Cadillac CTS Luxury, a big body Yukon Acadia Denali on 30-inch Forgiato's, and a bowling ball grey and white Ranger Rover on 28-inch Lexani floaters. Everyone else hopped into the rides they came in, bags of cash and valuables in hand, and hit the highway.

The shakedown at Encore began at 12:03 a.m. At that exact time, every stripclub in Wisconsin from the big ones like Silk Exotic, Sugar Shack, Oval Office, and Heartbreakers to the small hole in the wall ones Grand Daddy's, Show Time, Border Lounge, Club Bristol, and Fox Tail were being robbed and experiencing the same dilemma. Sixty-six adult establishments in all.

Most of the assailants were women, but there was a sprinkle of men in the groups here and there too. But for the most part, it was predominantly female. A simultaneous caper that was pulled off efficiently with ruthless precision. It was the most organized robbery in Wisconsin's history.

132 people were killed. 209 were injured. 28 million dollars was taken. And over 80 million in jewelry, cars, and other merch was stolen. 22 million dollars' worth of damage was done, and millions of questions were left on people's minds as to who was behind what the media called, "The Stripclub Capers."

"GIRL, you a fool! I wish I coulda recorded dat shit on my iPhone, so I could watch dat shit over and over again," GG said, taking a pull on the grape Swisher blunt.

"Girl please. You do NOT wanna see a va-jay-jay get blown off up close," Quintasia told GG. "Bitch clit and pussy lips was all on me and shit. I swear her muthafuckin' pubes got in my eyes. I thought you stripper hoes shaved y'all shit. Damn," the trigger woman said, rubbing her eyeball unconsciously.

"Shit, we *DO*. But that nasty bitch don't. She trifling for real," GG said and choked on the OG Kush.

"Naw, ***WE*** triflin'! Tryfe Lyyyfe!" Quintasia said. She was TLB and also the sawed-off pump toting woman who squeezed the trigger in GG's foe's woman parts.

They were in an apartment building on Villard that was owned by the BBC. It housed various members of TLB and THOT Gang; the crews who took part in the Stripclub capers, that were masterminded by none other than the BBC.

Rose was up north on some takeover shit with Becky, so GG and Summer divided up the takes for all 3 crews. Quintasia and her girl Catalina (aka "Cat"), a half black, half Russian cold blooded killer who spoke seven languages were there to collect on behalf of TLB. A native chick named Nymphy and a South African woman who went by the name "Calendar" were there for THOT Gang.

GG was smoking on that good-good while she gave them their share of the robberies, (which had been delivered to her at the apartment building the very next day for processing). This was a 100 million dollar job that they pulled off. Each click would get 9.3 million in cash. The cars were all shipped to a chop shop in Chicago where the VIN's would be replaced and then put on the black market along with some of the jewelry

they took. That would bring in another 20 million for one nights job. Not bad.

Each crew would pay the participants of the capers a "production fee", and those who showed the best efficiency and took care of bidness would receive a "loyalty bonus."

The guns taken off people's persons and from club offices would be distributed equally amongst TLB and THOT Gang since BBC weren't a 'field team' in constant need of new weapons like the other two clicks.

"You right, you right. Y'all is the trifest. My bad girl," GG said, blowing smoke at the ceiling fan. "Y'all bout dat life FOR REAL!"

"Damn right. Muhfuckaz ain't seeing TLB," Quintasia said, taking the blunt from GG.

Calendar cleared her throat. "Um, ***or*** THOT Gang. We ain't no punks neither," she added.

"Alright, alright. All y'all bout dat life. Damn, y'all worse than niggaz," Summer said, putting the last of the money in a duffle bag. Everyone laughed as the blunt got passed around.

"Alright, before y'all bounce, let me break this shit down," GG said as she stood up. "Y'all know da business, tell everybody to lay low for a sec. If they **MUST** spend some of this dough, tell 'em to do it out of town. No extravagant lavish purchases all of sudden, nah mean? The pigs finna come down hard and try to crack some bitches. So, make sure y'all people keep they cool. They street bitches so they know the routine. You don't know shit. You ain't ***seen*** shit! The best bet is for muthafuckas to go on vacation or a cruise or some shit," GG said as she paced back and forth in her black yoga pants and sports bra.

"You know what? A couple of us was just talking about Fiji a few weeks ago. Maybe we should go there or some exotic island," Nymphy said.

"Barbados or Anguilla would be nice," Catalina added.

"I need a vacaaaaaaaaaation. I'm going to Decatur where it's greater to see if I can double up this paper," a chick named Frosty sang.

"Yeah, that's a good idea. Shit. Just be smooth, chill, and keep everyone in check. No dumb shit. Let the heat die down for now." GG said. All the women in the room nodded as everyone got to their feet. Hugs were given, duffle bags were grabbed, and everyone began to leave.

"Oh yeah, tell Lyza to hit me up," GG said.

"Ok. You got another mark for her?" Quintasia asked.

"Mmhm. Show do," GG said, laughing.

"Aight. I heard how y'all got down on Young Racks. Summer, wit cho freaky ass!" Quintasia said and laughed.

"Girl, fuck what you heard. You know it's whatever for the dollar," Summer said.

"Everything must go!" Cat said.

"Hit it all, get it all!" Calendar and Nymphy said in unison, shouting out THOT Gangs' motto.

These three clicks of women were a group of killers, hustlers, robbers, and all out stomp- down bitches! The things they plotted and executed were not your average every day petty hustle. These women were about their money and doing BIG THINGS. That small-minded, miscellaneous shit wasn't even worth their thoughts. They had the ambition, drive, and heart of a hungry lion! And on that fateful night of the Strip-club Capers, they not only marked their territory by pulling off an unthinkable heist, but they conquered the motherfucking jungle. G style!!!

The mass amount of honey Beez on or around the dead bodies in all of the strip clubs was puzzling to the authorities. And why was there honey? They knew a calling card when they saw one, but they'd keep that part from the media.

For GG, Summer, and Rose, it symbolized Bad Beez in this Bitch! *This is what the fuck we do B. Run up in shit. Think it's sweet like this honey? R.I.P honey*. But for TLB, it was Tryfe Lyfe Beez. Sting your ass and Bounce! *We die? We die. Fuck it, it's the Lyfe we lead.* THOT Gang and their Breezy were geeked from the lick too. They sprinkled more dead bees than the other two crews because they didn't actually have a B in their name. But they were some Busser ass, Boss top-giving Bitches Bout whatever!

So, they sipped Tequila Honey Bee drinks and agreed that everyone could now get the honorary Bee tattoo somewhere on them. Motherfuckers were official now. All three clicks could represent the Bee on them. The Brazen, Bravery of these Beautiful, Body Bagging women earned the right to represent the Bee after this move. And in weeks to come, hundreds of women from all three organizations would be inked with *the* HoneyBee.

They all laughed and chatted a bit more while sipping. It was something about the Tequila Honey Bee that made ya feel smoothly sweet. Once the drink was gone, everyone parted ways in a cloud of weed smoke. Just like bitchez, quick to leave when the drank all gone... But at least they were all millions more richer now.

#The Takeover

7

ROSE/APPLETON

"Cuuuuz, what's good mami?" Nacho said to Rose as she let him inside of her hotel suite.

"Shit. Bout to sow up this town," she said, closing the door after giving him a hug.

Nacho was a big dude. 6'2" 327 pounds. He got his nickname from the food he consumed the most. Nachos were his favorite. He was full-blooded Puerto Rican and high-up in the Latin King organization. His mom and Rose's mom were first cousins.

After the big indictment on hundreds of Kings on Milwaukee's Southside happened in '97, Nacho fled to Brazil where Rose's uncle, second in command in the Colombian Cartel, resided. He helped Nacho secure a new identity, including a 12 hour procedure that altered his facial features, got his most distinguishable tattoos removed, and schooled him on real "mob life" before returning him back to Milwaukee where he'd flood the streets with more South American drugs than the states had ever seen!

"So, what chu find out?" Rose asked him as they sat on leather chaise lounge chairs.

"T-dub got a nice lil crew. Call themselves Mud Money. His

babymamma is a Mexican bitch named Selena. That's how he got plugged. Her Grandpa ***IS*** the Mexican Cartel. Of course, ain't no love between us and them, but they ain't never tried to move on our shit cuz they don't want no smoke," Nacho said.

"So, he da one with that gray shit then?" Rose asked, referring to "Gray Death," the grayish/purple color dope that was just as good if not *BETTER* than the shit they were slangin'.

"Yep. That's him. They got some bodies under they belt too. Took out Skinny Tone and da Northside Riderz, Goony and his crew, and recently Brown Bag and his Bag Boyz," Nacho told her.

"*They* merked Brown Bag?"

"Yeah. You know he *stayed* with security. They got him pretty good on some Mission Impossible shit," Nacho said, referring to the demise of kingpin Brown Bag.

"A crew of trained professionals hacked into Brown Bag's security system, disarming the motion detector sensors to his mansion in Oconomowoc. They gassed his crew to sleep by putting an anesthetic vapor in the ventilation system. That Nitrous Oxide shit.

From the roof top, they came in through the windows like Black Ops or a special forces SWAT team or something. They tied Brown Bag and thirteen members of his crew up. When they woke, they were tortured until they were told were their stash spots were at. After the robbers got the information they came for, they slit Brown Bag and the Bag Boyz' throats and took their bricks and a million in cash that Brown Bag and them were in the midst of counting and bagging up before they got gassed to sleep."

"Wow. Them niggaz is gooooood," Rose said, quite impressed.

"Not ***that*** good if this fool let down his guard enough to show GG where he keep his shit at," Nacho said, shaking his head.

"Yeah, well. You know how it goes... the power of the P. Ain't it a beautiful thing?" Rose said, smiling and rubbing it in knowingly.

"Yeah, yeah, yeah, whatever," Nacho said, waving her off. *Always on her Pussy rules the world shit.* "Anyway, the Mexicans ship that shit up here in stuffed animals. They got people in the Post Office, Fed Ex, and UPS on the payroll. So T-dub is able to get those big shipments without any red flags going up. He then sends bears stuffed with money back to the Cartel in Mexico. Since it's in American dollars, the Cartel makes a shitload of profit once they transfer that into Mexican currency."

"Hm. Pretty good operation they got going on. But why didn't I know about this before?" Rose asked her cousin.

"Cuz you been focusing on yo legit businesses and shit lately. Which is cool, clean up that dope money. And you said, as long as y'all ain't losing no money in the streets, ain't no use in going to war. And although they got that A-I, T-dub nem operate primarily in the other Midwest states," Nacho told her.

"So, if we hit them without them knowing who did it, we should be good then right?" Rose asked.

"Well, it is risky. They got eyes and ears EVERYWHERE, just like your uncle. So, heads are gonna roll regardless. Most likely on T-dub's side, cuz Selena's Grandpops is gonna want answers to why they shit is missing."

"We gonna have to be ready for war if any leaks drip on our name though ya know? Shiiiid, you know them fuckers love to cut off heads and hang 'em up like fucking Christmas decorations and shit! It's gonna be a Draco and MP5 everywhere we go kinda time. But if you can get one of TLB to go undercover on a wifey mission, we might be able to find out when the big shipments come in and *where* and make a nice move on they ass. Cuz that ain't all the shit they got that GG saw. Whatever's at his crib is probably only like a QUARTER of what they really got," Nacho said.

"Damn, he holding like ***THAT?***"

"Mami, come on now. He plugged wit da Mexicans. They the only other ones other than us that's really moving shit. Plus, like I told you, he do a lot of business in South Dakota, Iowa, and Minnesota. Getting that *WHITE MONEY*."

"Speaking of *WHITE* money, you got my shit?" Rose asked him.

Nacho nodded, "Yeah cuz. But man, are you sure it's safe up here?"

"Look. It's a fucking goldmine in this bitch! We gonna flood the town, take out the competition, and quadruple our money. Before Appleton even know it, they gonna have a full on epidemic on their hands. They won't even know what hit 'em," Rose said.

"Ok mami. I hope you can trust that white bitch. You know how they is," Nacho warned her.

"I know, I know. But I been watching her. She good people," Rose told him.

"Chula said something about her getting knocked and she didn't rat?" Nacho said.

"Yeah. Held her own like a soldier. I'm telling you, she got BBC in her blood bro. Straight down ass bitch for real. And her sister? Man, a muthafuckin' solider! Straight up. Oh yeah, which reminds me. She had a lil problem the other day and I need you to exhort some revenge for her."

Nacho leaned forward with a wicked smile on his face and rubbed his palms together, "Oh yeah? Hmmm, what chu you need me to do cuz?"

~

THE TWO GIRLS walked into Amber's house giggling.

"I'm telling you Ambs, there's no way *possible* someone can even do that." Delilah said.

"Like, yes, it is. It's TOTALLY possible. I bet you I can. I'll videotape it and everything," Amber told her friend. They were debating whether or not it was possible to have sex while a girl was in the "splits" position.

Amber did the splits at school and a cute boy said he wanted to fuck her just like that, and the debate began from there.

"Whatevs. Come on, let me do your hair so I can hurry up and meet with Cody," Delilah said, grabbing the CVS shopping bag with the pink and purple hair dye kit Amber bought.

"God, I don't know WHAT you see in him. He is like sooo lame. And what the fuck, you even said he has a little cock," Amber said, opening her bedroom door. She was looking at Delilah while she spoke. Delilah's face froze and her mouth dropped as she stood in the doorway and dropped the bag of hair care products on the floor. Amber couldn't understand what was wrong with her friend's sudden mood change until she followed her gaze. She turned around to see what had stopped her friend in her tracks. They both screamed like bitches in a horror flick.

All over Amber's beige bedroom walls was *R.I.P. Nugget*—written in blood. Hanging from her ceiling fan was the body of her pet German Sheppard, "Nugget", and its decapitated head sat atop Amber's pillows. Its eyeballs and tongue were removed and placed on her nightstand.

Amber burst into tears and then fainted...

"TURN DOWN FOR WHAT!" Bucky shouted along to the Lil Jon song that blared out the speakers. He was on top of the bar with a half empty bottle of Hennessy in his hands, waving it back and forth in the air.

Rose, GG, Becky, and her friend LuAnn walked into Bucky's

"Skittles Party" at Cold Shots Nightclub looking like a million bucks. 4 dimes that came to shine!

The club was filled with mostly college aged white kids who were very drunk and/or high. So, when the four of them walked in, each in a different color Versace dress and heels, all eyes were on them! And to top it off, Rose and GG had their BBC diamond chains on; they were blinging hard.

It was 11:47 p.m. and the party was in full swing. Their plan was to break off in two's and work the room, letting their presence marinate. So, GG and LuAnn went one way, and Becky and Rose went the other.

Bucky's fake ass crew all wore custom T-shirts that had **PM** emblazoned with rhinestones on them, and each member's names were airbrushed on the back. They also wore backwards baseball caps and big baggy jeans falling off their asses.

"Hey LuAnn, over here!" Bucky shouted, waving her over to where he was at. She and GG walked over to the bar and looked up at the red headed hillbilly gangster wanna-be. He smiled and his big Bugs Bunny overbite teeth stared back at them. GG did all she could to keep from laughing at him. *So that's why they call his buck tooth ass "Bucky" huh?* She thought to herself. He jumped down off the bar and was inches away from where GG stood. He looked her up and down and licked his dry thin lips.

"Want some Henn dog, sexy?" Bucky asked, holding up the big liquor bottle.

"Nah daddy. I like my liquor like I like my men...WHITE...and *STRONG*," she whispered in his ear.

Bucky's dick went from 0 to100 ***real*** quick as his mouth dropped open. He blushed beet red and GG smiled at him, patted him on the cheek, and turned on her heels. She sashayed away, making her big booty wobble like waves in the ocean. Her skin-tight red Versace dress clung to her curves, leaving nothing to the imagination. Bucky stared at that fat ass in awe.

"Who's your new friend Lu?" he asked LuAnn.

"Oh her? That's Gushy," she replied.

"Gushy? What kind of name is that?"

"I don't know. Ask her yourself. I gotta go," LuAnn told him as she walked off to catch up with GG.

"Oh, I will. I motherfucking will," Bucky said, taking a few thirsty gulps from the Hennessey bottle.

Meanwhile, Rose was on the dance floor, sandwiched between Lincoln and Steve (both of Pill Mobb), as she wound her Latin hips to Krizz Kaliko's "Follow The Drip." Her BBC piece glistened under the fluorescent lights, blinding people. Lincoln had his hands on her hips and his semi-hard crotch pressed into the crack of her ass.

"Where've you been all my life J-Lo?" he said into her ear.

She threw her head back on his shoulder. "Making movies I guess," she said, and they both laughed.

Steve was in front of Rose, staring at her tan "Butter Rican" cleavage as he humped her pelvis. Both Steve and Lincoln were off key trying to keep up with her, but she just kept doing her thing in time to the beat anyway. *These white boys show ain't got no damn rhythm,* she thought to herself.

Becky sat at a table and observed it all. Her new girls had already made quite an impression as the ethnic beauties infiltrated the party and had all them white boys' tongues wagging like dogs in heat! What GG and Rose was doing to them is exactly what BBC wanted Becky to do in *their* environment as well. She was taking notes and soaking up mad game, live and in color.

"Becky! What up girl? Glad you could make it to my shindig. It's off the chain ain't it?" Bucky said, staggering as he walked up to her table.

"Yeah. Pretty dope bash you got going on here. The music's lit too," Becky said.

"I know it! I hired a DJ from Milwaukee. He's got that heat," he said, all in her face.

"Jeez Bucky. Back up with your hot ass liquor breath," she said, leaning back in her chair.

"Awww Becky. I don't know why you always gotta diss me. We could make a good team ya know? Bucky and Becky. Becky and Bucky. Yeah, it has a nice ring to it, don't cha think? We could be Mr. and Mrs. Pill pusher," he said and laughed.

"Um, like... no. I'm good. You know– "

"Yeah, yeah," Bucky said, cutting her off. "I know. You only date niggers right? What the fuck ever *REBECCA*. Well, you know what? I only fuck with them too. I don't fuck with you white bitches no more. I be tapping BLACK ass!"

"Oh, really now? What black girls have you fucked before Bucky? Huh?" Becky asked, raising one of her eyebrows.

"Lots! You don't know 'em cuz they ain't from round here," he said defensively.

"Mmhm, whatever. If you say so Bucky."

"Bitch, I *DO* say so! And I bet your punk ass, five cock-sucking grand that I'll get with your black friend Gushy too!" Bucky told her.

"Um, I highly doubt that. She don't fuck with broke dudes. She's an exotic dancer, so if you don't have that moola, she won't even give you the time of day," Becky said.

"Bitch, I ain't no broke nigga! Me and my niggas is ballin'!" he said, getting all red in the face. "You see this shit, I got bowls of pills all around this motherfucker! Pill Mobb do it big," Bucky said, sweeping his arms across the room, bouncing around animatedly and sweating like a mad man.

Becky looked around and nodded her head. There were dozens of candy dishes full of pills on the tables, bar, on a pool table, and a pinball machine. Each candy dish/bowl had a different kind of pill in it; Adderall, Oxycontin, Percocets, Ecstasy, Vicodin, Fetanyl, Seroquel, Xanax, and many others piled up as "party favors" for the guests to help themselves to.

"You're right. My bad Bucky. You *are* the shit. You're doing your thing up in here," Becky said.

"Damn right I am! You better recognize. Hmpf," he said and walked off trying to strut all tough. But since he was super wasted, he ended up tripping and falling flat on his face, breaking his almost empty Hennessey bottle in the process. Becky stifled a laugh as he got up and tried to play it off like he was so cool. *What a lame*, she thought to herself.

He got up and fell multiple times. It was a stoner's comedic dream how ridiculous he looked.

Rose may have been on the center of the dance floor grinding on the two uncoordinated no-rhythm having white dudes, but she was still able to observe her surroundings from where she was. She saw all the custys help themselves to the party favors in the candy dishes, giving new meaning to the term "skittles."

She saw when Bucky was animatedly talking to Becky, probably getting rejected like he always did by her. She saw how cool, calm, and collected Becky remained even to his obvious hostility. Rose liked that in her. That told her she was good under pressure. Self-disciplined and cool as a cucumber. The more she observed Becky in action, the more she knew this white chica was perfect for the BBC.

Rose also scoped out how Pill Mobb flashed bankrolls of cash while taking pics on their smart phones. They posed throwing up different hand signs; an **A** for Appleton, a **P**, and an **M**. Lit blunts in their mouths, handfuls of pills. Their arms around women. They were flicking up good. Obviously for their Instagram, Snapchat, and Facebook Pages.

Rose peeped how the eyes of men *and* women lusted after her and GG. While they weren't the only 2 minorities there, the other ones were born and raised in Appleton, so they were practically white anyways. She and GG were fresh faces in a new city. Glamour queens that looked like something on the cover of Black Men or Straight Stuntin' magazine. Their swag, aura, and sex appeal automatically pulled people into their zone.

Rose nodded her head as she canvassed the scene and took mental notes. White people turnt up too... in they own way, but shit, they could still party like a muthafucka! And she had to admit it, she was on business, but she was really enjoying herself. *This new environment was fun and easy*, she thought to herself.

She smiled, knowing that taking over Appleton and getting rid of Pill Mobb would be like taking candy from a baby. It was about to go *diz-own*!

THE NEXT DAY while the city slept in, Rose was up at the crack of dawn banging Rick Ross' "Hustlin" in her Audi A7 Premium.

Everyday I'm hustlin' Everyday I'm hustlin'

GG was in the passenger seat as Rose drove around Appleton, Wisconsin and broke it all down to her.

"We got 20 different pills on deck. You already know the popular ones; Perks, Oxys, Vikes, and shit. But we also got Depakote, Cyclobenzaprine, Dilaudid, Trazadone, Zanny bars, and all kinds of shit. No matter what it is, we doing two for 50. Nacho got me 10,000 of each pill for starters. The way me and Becky crunched numbers, we should be able to move 200,000 in a week. That's 5 mil right there. And that ain't including the Ex. Then we gon' do $150 for a gram of boy and $100 for a gram of coke. That's wackin' the comp by 25 percent, plus our shit is ten times mo potent than anything these fools ever had. On the weed tip, we only selling kush. No Reggie, no mid or weak ass loud, none of that shit. Just Blue Dream, Peyton Manning, Banana Blaze, and Cherry Popper. Nothing under a zip, and we dumping it for $200 an ounce and letting Britney run that."

"Becky's little sister?" GG asked.

"Yeah. She's in high school and you know them teenagers smoke hella weed. Plus, she rolls with that party crowd up here, so once they know she got that good good on deck, she'll have all the schools on lock, ***plus*** the college kids," Rose said.

"She ain't ready for BBC yet though," GG said.

"Oh, she not only getting BBC, but she got some BBC in her." Rose laughed to herself. "But nah, not yet anyways. But I figure we can give her $400 off each pound she sells. That's a two G profit for us. Then Becky told her girls who bartend that she'll give them two Geez a week to dump them pills in the club for her. So, we got them on deck too. Some of them pop, so that two Geez gon' end up coming back to us anyways," Rose said.

"So, who gon' move the boy and coke?"

"I wanna get a couple THOT Gang bitches up here and put them in an apartment. Becky can introduce them to the main users and let them be runners. We only gonna deal to a select few cuz it's a lot of C.I.'s around this bitch. But the muthafuckaz who get high consistently and don't fuck with them people, we gonna supply 'em. According to Becky, we should be able to move a couple bricks of each a week. ***EASILY***," Rose told her.

"Damn girl, for reals? Shit, I can fuck with that," GG said, nodding. "That's what's up. So, what chu want me to do then?"

"The Stripclub up here is weak as a bitch. It's called Beansnappers. I want you to headline out there to bring out all the rich white dudes with a Chocolate fetish. You know Bucky's ugly ass gonna show up. Work his stupid ass over until he gives you the info we need to they stash spots and plug. I'm gonna work Lincoln over, then when we hit 'em..." Rose trailed off.

GG nodded. She knew how it would end up for Pill Mobb. Rose picked up her gallon of water off the floor and took more gulps like she was dehydrated.

"Damn girl, you been drinking like a muthafuckin' fish. What's up with that? I know yo ass gotta piss drinking that much damn water," GG said, looking at her homegirl funny.

"Mmhm, that's the point," Rose said, pulling into an apartment complex called Crest Tree. She parked the purple Audi and opened the driver's side door. "Wait here ma, I'll be back," Rose said, hopping out of the car and running into the building...

"YEEEEAH BABY. That's it... ooh yeah," the white man moaned as he rubbed the hot urine into his skin. Rose was squatting over him, standing on a bed covered in plastic as she urinated all over his stomach, chest, and... face.

"Come on sexy. Pee in my mouth," he said, going *ahhh*. Rose moved up a little bit and aimed at his lips. He caught a mouth full of piss, gargled, then spit the yellow liquid onto his hairy, tan chest.

The pee would not stop spraying. Rose had drank three gallons of water for this specific "arrangement" and her bladder was full to the max.

The white man's penis was a violent red and stood straight up as he stroked it up and down, giving himself a hand-job. Urine ran all down his body and slid onto the plastic sheets. He looked up at Rose's pretty beige pussy as the lemonade-like fluid gushed from her like a faucet. His secret kinky fetish was being delivered by the most beautiful woman he'd ever seen.

For the finale, she sat on his face and pissed straight down his throat while he licked her clit. The sensation of relieving her full bladder *and* having her pussy ate at the same time was such a nasty, naughty, erotic feeling, that he made her cum hard and long.

"Ohh...my...Gaaawd!" She screamed, as her orgasm made her shake and shiver. She squeezed her pussy muscles and let the last of her pee trickle down his throat while her thick, creamy cum followed behind and filled his mouth.

Rose grabbed his hair and banged his head into the bed. She grinded her pussy on his face, giving him a real moustache ride. She threw her head back and moaned at the ceiling. "Yes! Yes! Oh, fuuuuck yessss." He slurped up her fluids greedily and nibbled on her clit. Unbeknownst to him, Rose actually LIKED her oral sex rough and aggressive. A little bit of pain heightened her freaky exxxperience. "Oh Tom! Chew that pussy motherfucker! That's it. Yes! Harder goddamnit! Oh shiiiit," she screamed as she wound her hips and came again. Her second orgasm overlapped the first one in waves of pure bliss and X-rated satisfaction.

After they were done, she got off the bed and went to the bathroom to clean herself up. Tom handed her a US Bank white envelope with one hundred $100 bills in it.

"We're having steak for supper tonight," he said as he toweled off. "It would be nice if you could make it."

"Mm, alright. I'll see what Becky wants to do," Rose said as she opened the envelope and counted her fee.

"Gail loves you ya know? Not as much as me. But..."

"Tom, Tom, Tom. You kinky little boy," she said as she slipped her Manolo Blahniks on her pretty feet. "You wouldn't know love if a Mack truck full of it ran over you," she teased.

He laughed nervously. "God you're gorgeous. You are the most beautiful specimen I've ***EVER*** laid eyes on," he said, kneeling down and kissing on her pedicured toes.

She looked down at him and shook her head. "Well, I gotta

run. We'll try to swing by later ok?" she told him as she headed for the door.

"Try to come, please," he begged.

"Oh, but Tom, I did... several times," she said, smiling and left.

PART II

PLOTTIN'

8

MA BABY

A bunch of women in the FCI Dublin Federal Penitentiary in Dublin, California were huddled around the flat screen Television in the dayroom.

"Every Stripclub in Wisconsin, sixty-six in all, was robbed at gunpoint by groups of renegade women. Hundreds of people were injured and murdered. Some believe it was an inside job, but authorities still have no suspects in custody nor any leads. These ruthless women got away with tens of millions of dollars in cash and possessions. If you have any information, you are urged to contact your local law enforcement or the FBI–"

The news woman was drowned out by enthusiastic chatter amongst the inmates.

"DANG THEM BITCHEZ IS GANGSTA!"

"Hell yeah, I wonder who pulled that shit off?"

"Them hoes had they shit together!"

"Yo, I hope they left the country."

"Ma baby, you know some down ass bitches in your hometown like them?"

"Yeah, I know a few ride or dies. But they ain't capable of pulling no shit like that though. But shit, I been gone for a seven piece, and shit changes like a muhfucka. Obviously hoes out there on some trill shit in the cheese state," Ma Baby answered. She was the only inmate in the institution from Wisconsin. And ever since the Stripclub Capers became nationwide news, everybody got geeked about her often slept-on hometown.

But she was proud that they were on the map and getting some shine, even if it was a negative publicity of sorts. Bad publicity is better than *NO* publicity. And they ain't been headlining news since Jeffrey Dahmer's crazy ass ate them people back in the day. Not even Dontre Hamilton getting killed by the police in 2014 wasn't enough to make the news like Michael Brown in Ferguson or Eric Garner in New York. It's as if Wisconsin was a non-existent state that no one gave a fuck about. Maybe that's why they were so wild. Crying out for attention like kids when they're being ignored and neglected.

Ma Baby was from the cold, hard streets of Milwaukee, Wisconsin. She represented her city in the joint always and to the fullest. She had the Brewers glove with the famous **M** in the middle of it tattooed on her right hand. Always twisting her middle finger around her ring one and throwing an **M** up, letting other women know she wasn't no punk bitch from the Midwest. She was from the motherfucking **Mil**!

Ma Baby had been locked up for seven and a half years on a thirty-year sentence for drugs and gun trafficking. So far, she spent four years in Aliceville, down in Pickens County Alabama. And she did two years in FCI Tallahassee before coming to Dublin.

Marisol "Ma Baby" Rivera was a 36-year-old half Puerto Rican, half Filipino woman that stood 5'10" and was built like a stallion! A lot of people often told her she looked like Selma

Hayek but with chinky eyes. She took it as a compliment seeing that the *Desperado* actress was one of her favorite Latina leading ladies.

On them Milwaukee streets, Ma Baby was that **BITCH!** Not only was she a true Latin Queen, but her baby daddy Nacho was plugged with the Colombian Cartel. Even though they weren't together too long, they still did plenty of business with one another. They helped each other get richer, but he was smarter with the people he chose to keep around him than she was. Her inner-circle had leaks, and everyone knew leaks couldn't hold no water when the pressure's on. So when her workers got knocked, they set Ma Baby up to save their own ass. When it was all said and done, Ma Baby got slammed! 30 years for her first-time offense. She was only 28 at the time. They had given her more years than she'd even been alive!

Ma Baby was out on bail for a year from ‘08 to ‘09 and was about to flee the country before her sentencing, but her own sister tipped the Feds off before she could board that private plane heading for Tokyo. For that act of betrayal, Ma Baby's only sibling was strung up to a fence ass naked on the 35th street bridge on National. Her breasts were cut off and **SNITCH** was carved into her body over and over. Her tongue was also cut out and stapled to a dead rat that hung around her neck on a shoestring. It was a gruesome murder, a crucifixion of such that sent a clear message to those that even contemplated telling... snitches ended up in ditches. So, ***DON'T*** do it. Or else!

When she was out there, Ma Baby was a leader. She groomed young teens who had the potential to be something great. It was a handful of them that she grew very close to and considered as her daughters. They were young, beautiful, intelligent, and had heart. But most importantly, they were about their muthafuckin' paper!

Those three chicas were the only ones who held her down

for the last seven and a half. Every month, she got a $1,000 money order put on her books. She was also sent lots of novels and magazines. It always came under various fake names because it was decided while she was on bail that if she ever had to do time, there would be no letters, visits, or phone calls because the FEDS monitored EVERYTHING. And Ma Baby did not want her young protégés to pop up on the alphabet boys' radar.

So while they kept their distance and stayed invisible, they were still very much there for her. They did not miss one month in the last 91 of them that she'd been incarcerated for. And that made her feel proud to know that she had trained them well.

They also put her on dozens of social media and pen-pal websites. And through those, she acquired a few sugar daddies AND mamas as well as some consistent pen-pals that helped her pass the time.

"Rivera, come to the Sergeant's station," was announced on the PA system. Ma Baby got up and left the women rambling on about the Stripclub Capers to see what the hell the C.O. wanted with her.

"Go put on your state issues. The Warden wants to see you," she was told by a guard.

Ma Baby changed into her khaki prison uniform and walked to the administration building. It was a nice summer day, so she took her time as she pondered why the hell she was being summoned. She hoped it wasn't a family death or anything serious. That's usually the only time they called you up...for bad news.

Her mom was 58 years-old and just got over breast cancer a year ago. But the treatments had left her drained and weak to the point where doctors didn't think she'd fully recover.

Her mom also had primary custody of Ma Baby's daughter Anita. A bright beautiful young girl with long brown hair and a smile that could light up the city. They were her only two family members she had left. The only people in the world that she loved unconditionally.

Ma Baby chewed on her lips and tapped her feet nervously as she sat in the waiting area. Finally, a half an hour later, she was ushered into the warden's office.

Warden Whiteside was a short, jovial man whose comb-over rivaled Donald Trump's. His triple chins wobbled when he spoke. The girls in Dublin called him "turkey neck."

He was a crooked, sweaty, sausage finger of a man who got his dick wet by knocking off some of the inmates' time. *30 years is 30 years. If this muthafucka think I'm spreading my legs for his fat ass, he got another thang comin'. I ain't goin',* Ma Baby thought to herself as she entered his massive office.

There was military memorabilia all over. Medals, plaques, statues, flags; even a real grenade in a glass box.

The floor to ceiling window behind his U-shaped cherry oak desk gave him a marvelous view of the lush green acres that spanned out for miles and miles beyond the prison.

Family photos of his also fat wife and children sat on his desk in gold picture frames. Ma baby quickly committed their images to her photographic memory.

"Ms. Rivera, how do you do? Come, come in. Have a seat," the warden said with outstretched arms as he pulled out the empty chair in front of his desk. There were two other chairs next to hers already occupied by a man and a woman. Both of them wore black suits. But instead of pants, the woman wore a knee length black skirt. They had "FEDS" written all over them.

"Ms. Rivera, this is Agent Holis and Special Agent Bradshaw. They scheduled this meeting because they'd like to ask you some questions," Warden Whiteside said.

Ma Baby looked over at the stiffs.

"What for? I don't know shit, and I ain't ***seen*** shit," she said sternly.

"Ms. Rivera, you don't even know what we came to speak to you about," Agent Holis said. Her honey blonde hair was slicked back and pulled into a tight bun. Her make-up was minimal but perfect. Sharply arched eyebrows framed her piercing green eyes. She looked like one of those upper-class "uppity" white bitches, and Ma Baby disliked her immediately.

"It don't matter *what* you came to ask me. Whatever it is, I don't know shit. And I ain't **SEEN** shit!" Ma Baby told her.

"Now, now, Ms. Rivera. There's no need to be rude. These nice people flew all the way here from Wisconsin just to see you," the warden said.

"Wisconsin?"

"Yes. Your hometown. We're from there too," Agent Bradshaw. "I'm originally from West Allis, and she's from Kenosha."

"Ok. That's nice. Fine and dandy and all that honky-dorey shit. But what does that have to do with me?" Ma Baby asked.

"Well, you still have what, 18 and a half years left do to on your sentence before you go home right?" The blonde bitch asked, smiling all smug and shit. Ma Baby sat there and stared at the condescending bitch. "Anita will be almost 30 by then. And your mom, well with all of her health issues, who's to say she'll even make it that long."

"You bitch!" Ma Baby shouted, getting out of her seat. "Don't chu ***dare*** speak about my family."

Everyone else rose to their feet defensively, awaiting some kind of confrontation. Agent Bradshaw stood between Ma Baby and Agent Holis.

"Hey, hey, hey now. Everybody just settle down. Ms. Rivera, no need to get nasty now. Agent Holis was just stating the facts," Warden Whiteside said, trying to diffuse the situation.

"Look. Just have a seat Ms. Rivera. Or shall I say, ***Ma Baby?***"

Agent Bradshaw said. "Just hear us out. Then we'll be on our way ok?"

Ma Baby stubbornly sat back down in her chair and everyone else did the same. She balled her fists up and her hazel eyes shot daggers at the female federal.

"We're trying to solve the Stripclub Capers. This was a hundred million dollar plus job. It was pulled off by an organization of women. Who? We don't know. But we think you do. Or if you DON'T know, we think that you can find out," Bradshaw said.

"We know your record. Stand up gal. Never rolled over on your people or gave up your supplier. Well respected in the streets. ***STILL*** respected in the streets. You're a 'hood legend'. You were a smart woman Rivera. You surely weren't on our radar. Your mistake was trusting those in your circle. You thought they were valid, but they got knocked and threw you under the bus to save their own asses. But it's like that when you play the game," the blonde FBI agent said as she smiled at Ma Baby.

*Punk ass ho. I'll wipe that smile off yo face **REAL** quick!* Ma Baby thought to herself.

"We've spoken with the warden. Your institution conduct has been good. We see you move and groove with the shakers. Diaz, Evans, Guerra, and Ms. Brown. Women with clout and money. You don't network with peons. You have your own little Posse in here, not to mention your little tenderoni plaything Ms. Coleman. But all of that is irrelevant, Ms. Rivera. We want you. We can let you go. Open those doors so you can go home and be a mother to your daughter and take care of your mom... all you have to do is go undercover and work for us," Agent Bradshaw told her.

Ma Baby laughed. "You want ***ME*** to be a C.I. for ***YOU?!?*** That's funny. You fuckers are fucking hilarious you know that?

You must ain't read my files if you think I'd ever work for Y'ALL!"

"Ms. Rivera. You would rather do 2 more decades in the penitentiary then be out there free to raise your daughter? To be there for her Sweet 16? And her high school graduation? You're willing to miss all of that cuz of some stupid moral street code? Your daughter is at that critical age in life where she needs her MOTHER. You don't want her to go the route you did do ya? Nah, I know you don't. You don't want her to get knocked up by some deadbeat loser before she even finishes high school do you? You know more and more kids are 'active' these days. Sex has gone totally mainstream," the warden said.

Ma Baby stared at the floor teary-eyed. Whiteside's words were hitting close to home and had her feeling some type of way. Ma baby was only there for the first three years of Anita's life before she got locked up. She already had missed a lot in her child's life.

"Look. We'll make it look like your case was over-turned and in 3 months, we'll set you free. You'll go undercover and hit the streets. We'll even supply you with the dope to sell so people won't think twice about you being home so soon. While you're doing what you do, find out who pulled that job. That's our main focus. But we would like to get a few dealers off the streets too. So, along the way, you can assist in helping us clean up the streets," Agent Bradshaw said.

"BY SETTING up muthafuckaz with the drugs that ***y'all*** putting out there?" Ma Baby asked dumbfounded.

"Well... not necessarily. A lot of drugs have been flooding the state of Wisconsin lately, and we have a feeling there are some powerful organizations around our parts that are deeply connected to the Cartels. Washington is in an uproar. Heroin is up 20% over this time last year. Everyone is fucking panicking, and the **DEA** and us are under a lot of fucking pressure to start cracking down," Bradshaw said.

"Hmpf! Funny that there's a governmental 'panic' going on now that heroin has flooded the **WHITE** community. Awww, little Kyle, Courtney, and Peter are hooked on **H**. Now there's pandemonium. Ha! Y'all let the shit destroy ***our*** neighborhoods, now that it's in ***your*** backyard, and affecting your world, now all of a sudden y'all care and wanna play supercop and shit," Ma baby said.

"Listen here you little ghetto tramp! We're doing **YOU** a fucking favor. We could let your dyke ass rot in this mother-fucker for an eternity! So don't go talking your bullshit about ***OUR*** community. We don't have broken homes and shitty slums—"

"*Christine*. Please," Agent Bradshaw interrupted his partner, putting a hand on Agent Holis' shoulder to calm her. Unbeknownst to Ma Baby, Agent Christine Holis was actually dealing with a pandemic situation in her life as they spoke. Her twin sister Courtney was hooked on heroin, and she could not get that vicious monkey off her back for nothing in the world. Indeed, the issue hit very close to home for her.

"Man, I hear what chy'all sayin'. But I ain't no rat. I woulda *BEEN* out if I would have told on my plug. But fuck dat shit. I did the crime, I'm uh do da time," Ma Baby said, holding her chin up high.

"Hmpf. That's too bad. It really is. Looks like you'll have to do another 25 to life for the murder of Rhonda Sims," Agent Bradshaw said.

"*What?* I ain't kill Ratchet Rhonda," Ma Baby said.

"Oh yeah? Well, maybe you didn't. But we do have written statements from several inmates saying you two were sworn enemies in here. And not even a month ago, she was murdered in her cell. All the clues point to you. Well... at least, *NOW* they do," Agent Holis said.

"What the... Y'all trying to frame me? Mr. Whiteside, you know I ain't kill Ratchet Rhonda. I- "

"Ms. Rivera, I know nothing. If they put together a case against you for the murder of that woman...well, you know they have the highest conviction rate in the country," Warden Whiteside said.

Ma Baby began to sweat. *These motherfuckers are black-mailing me*, she thought to herself. *They tryin' to put me* ***UNDER*** *the jail. What the fuck?!?*

"Save yourself, Rivera. Go home to your family. Work for them. You wouldn't be ratting on your people. You have no one left remember? They either turned on you or left you high and dry. Why protect some people you don't even know? And if you ***do*** know them, so what? Are they more important than your mother and daughter? Think of your family Rivera. They need you," the Warden told her.

"Yeah, Ma Baby. Sofia and Anita need you. Come work for us. Get paid a nice salary and enjoy life. Or spend the rest of yours behind ***THIS*** motherfucker and never see your goddamn family again!" Agent Holis threatened.

Ma Baby looked from the warden to the agents and back to the warden again. A million things were going through her mind at that moment. She was fuming mad as she shook her head not believing how they were coming at her.

The agents stood up and smoothed out their suit jackets. "You have two weeks to decide Rivera. Let Mr. Whiteside know when you make your decision. For you and your family's sake... let's hope you make the ***right*** one. We'll be in touch," Agent Bradshaw said, extending his hand.

Ma Baby looked at his hand and stood up herself. "Can I go now?" she said to the warden. He nodded and she left his office without bidding the agents farewell.

Later that night, she took her anger and frustration out on her celly's face.

"Yeah bitch... eat my pussy ho! Eat this muthafucka like you mean it," she growled as she rode her young tenderoni Carol's face. Ma Baby pressed her palms down on Carol's sweaty forehead and grinded her hips in figure 8 motions against the young woman's mouth. Ma Baby had already orgasmed four times in an hour, and now she was going for lucky number five.

"Mmmm, lick dat pussy... lick dat pussy... licky licky liiiick. Ohhh shit," Ma Baby moaned.

Carol could hardly breathe. She was trying to move her head side to side to catch a little air, but Ma Baby would just grab her hair harder and press her pussy into Carol's face. She got more aggressive every time she dared stray from Ma Baby's hot button.

"Fuck yeah! That's it bitch. Put your tongue up in there. Got damnit yes! **Yes! Yes!** Yeaaaah!" Ma Baby shouted as fireworks exploded in her gut, causing her to cum again. Liquid fire oozed out of her pussy and down her PYT's throat. Carol slurped up Ma Baby's juices like she was devouring a watermelon rind! She dug her fingers into Ma Baby's soft boriqua booty cheeks and moaned loudly as secretions went in her nostrils.

Carol sucked, licked, slurped, nibbled, and moaned enthusiastically to let Ma Baby know how much she enjoyed servicing her.

Even after her body stopped convulsing, she still sat on Carol's face, slumped over, gasping for breath and not wanting to move. Her long hair was matted to her face, neck, and titties.

Carol thought she might suffocate if this bitch didn't get up soon, but she didn't dare signal for her to move or even mumble in protest. After all, Ma Baby was the Dom and Carol was her sub, so she played her position accordingly.

"Damn, bitch. You show know how to make a girl feel better," Ma Baby said as she finally got off her young play thang's face.

Carol was mixed; half black and half white. But her complexion was very fair, which made her look more white than black. So seeing her whole face flush **red** from being rode for over an hour— made her look like a human strawberry.

Her nose, lips, and cheeks shone with milky secretions. Ma Baby had that thick "glistening" cum that looked sexy as hell to be a bodily fluid. Plus, it was yummy too.

Ma Baby cupped Carol's cute face in her palms and licked her own sweet juices off the girl's face with long, slow, light strokes of her tongue.

"Mmmm... do I taste gooood?" Ma Baby moaned. She licked Carol's face like it was an ice cream cone, and Carol pinched and twisted her own nipples while Ma Baby licked her face clean. Her little bi-racial pussy was ***soaking*** wet. It always was after servicing her Dom. She hoped Ma Baby would let her get her rocks off tonight too.

"Mami, may I have permission to speak?" Carol asked in her soft, shy, baby voice.

"Yes, you may," Ma Baby replied.

"You've never been so wound up like this before. What the matter ma?"

"It's a lot of shit babygirl... a lot of shit," Ma Baby said as she stood up and cleaned herself with baby wipes. "I don't really wanna get into it right now though. Just thinking about the shit is gonna piss me off all over again!"

"Ok mami, my bad. If you ever wanna talk, I'm always here for you," Carol said.

Ma Baby looked at the obedient young girl. She was so cute and adorable; like Selena Gomez or Hayden Panettiere. She was only 20 years-old, but she looked no older than fifteen! She was doing 12 years for some guns that her brother convinced her to take the rap for since she had no priors. But since the artillery she had claimed were some illegal black market guns from Russia and Afghanistan, they banked her ass with a dozen piece.

Young, dumb, and naive, Ma Baby took her under her wing and turned Carol into her lil boo thang. She showed her the ropes and became her protector. They had been cellmates for the past 8 months and things were A-OK. But now with the new shit the FEDS and nem brought to her, she didn't know ***what*** to do!

Ma Baby wasn't no snitch. She absolutely HATED rats. She wasn't no informant. That was "police shit." But damn, if they put the Ratchet Rhonda murder on her, she knew she would NEVER see the light of day again. And on top of *that*, with a fresh murder charge, nine times out of ten, she'd be shipped to a new joint. Most likely U.S. Coleman in Wildwood, FL, where all the more severe high-risk inmates go. That meant no more sweet Carol and her terrific tongue skills. For the first time in her life, Ma Baby was actually contemplating working for "them people." Just the thought of it made her want to throw up. Who would've ever thought that it would come to this? She got a 30 piece for keeping her mouth shut. Now she had to open her trap or die in prison. And the fucked up part about it is, they were right. Her daughter was at that crucial age where she needed her *mother* to steer her in the right direction before it was too late. It was 2019 and those streets were not kind to the youth. Especially in Milwaukee. They were growing up faster and faster these days. It was way more different now than how it was back in the day when Ma Baby was a shorty. With all the new technology and social media they have now, it was a new ballgame.

Tears slid down Ma Baby's face as her thoughts plagued her and ate away at her soul. She sat on her bunk and bawled her eyes out. Carol was in shock cuz she NEVER saw Ma Baby cry before. She knew something had to be deeply troubling her.

Carol sat next to Ma Baby and wrapped her up in her arms. She stroked Ma Baby's hair as she cried on her chest.

"Whatever it is Mami, it's gonna be alright," Carol said, consoling her.

A week later, Ma Baby was getting her hair braided when a C.O. told her she needed to go to the administration building. *Not again. It ain't even been two weeks yet,* she thought to herself.

She went through the same routine as before. Changing into her prison issues, taking the long walk across the compound, then sitting in the waiting area for a while. This time when she entered the warden's office, he was alone. It was dark because he had the blinds closed.

"Ms. Rivera, how are you this afternoon?" he said as he ushered her to a chair.

"I'm cool Warden," Ma baby said and crossed her legs.

"Good, good. Have you given any thought to the proposition that was extended to you?" he said as he began circling her chair.

"Yeah. A little bit. But I thought I had 2 weeks?"

"Well, you do. But I was just checking to see if you made a decision yet," he said, stopping in front of her. She looked up at Turkey Neck's chins swaying back and forth. ***Yuck***.

"Nah, not really. I mean, it's a very hard decision Turk— uh, I mean, Warden."

"I do not understand Rivera. I'd choose family over anything else. There would be nothing to think about. My loyalty would be to my family," he said.

"Yeah, well you don't know about where I come from. Liars and rats are the lowest pieces of shit on the totem pole in my world. And I sir, pride myself as a woman of integrity."

"*Pride?* Ha! Many many people have died foolishly over that thing called *pride*, Rivera," he scoffed as he began to pace back and forth behind her. "Pride is excessive self-esteem ya know? And many people tend to swallow that 'self-esteem' when their back is against the wall. A lot of women come into my office and swallow... *pride* if you will, just to get home to their families as soon as possible."

Ma Baby said nothing. She sat there and tapped her foot. She didn't know she was giving the warden a nice shot of her thick ass thigh. With her legs crossed, it just made the prison khaki pants hug her thighs even more. That got Whiteside's blood pumping.

"Your hair looks pretty today Ms. Rivera. Those zig-zaggy cornrows are very erotic," he commented.

"Uhhh, thanks?" she said in surprise, not knowing how to respond to what he said. She could feel him hovering over her and it gave her the creeps. She turned slightly and caught him whiffing her hair.

"Ahhh, you smell lovely too," he said, smelling her neck.

Ma Baby's face scrunched up as she leaned forward out of her chair to get out of his reach.

"Umm, Warden White—"

"Shhh. I can get you anything you want. ***ANYTHING***. Pot, cocaine, liquor. Whatever you fancy. You scratch my back. I'll scratch yours," he said, stroking her long, braided hair. Ma Baby stood up and began to protest as she backed into the front of his desk.

"Look Warden. I'm good. I- "

"Listen you ungrateful bitch," he said, grabbing her by the shirt collar and getting up in her face. "I'll have you transferred out of here **ASAP** on a murder rap. Pronto. You understand? Comprendo amigo? How long do you think your little cellmate Ms. Coleman will last without you here to protect her? These fucking bulldagger cunts will eat that pretty naive little mutt slut alive! Maybe I'll even take her for a test-run," the warden said and laughed shrewdly.

He let go of her collar and ran his big clammy hands up and

down Ma Baby's body. He groped her heavy breasts and round buttocks as his fat belly trapped her against his desk.

The warden flushed red and perspiration beaded all over his doughy face. Ma Baby could feel his erection growing through his slacks as he molested her. She refused to breathe in his hot Doritos breath as he spoke.

"You're a RIPE little thing Rivera. Yes. I can tell that you workout and keep in shape. None of your womanly parts are all saggy or cottage cheesy like some of the women here who let themselves go. Uh uh, not you baby. Mmmm, you're soft and firm. Me likes that," he said as he unbuttoned her shirt.

Ma Baby was trapped and scared. Normally, she'd knee a man in the balls if he tried to take advantage of her. But this piece of shit was practically GOD in here. He had her life in his hands. If she fought him or refused him, the rest of her time would most definitely be Hell.

"Ooh, look at those pretty puppies. Take your bra off so I can see them," he said as he looked at her buttermilk cleavage.

She did as he asked and held her breath as his hairy sausage fingers admiringly stroked her nipples. She was too angry to cry. She just closed her eyes and chewed on her lips as he bent down to suck on one of her peanut butter-colored nipples.

"Mm, you like that Rivera? Hmm?" He asked as he sucked her breasts and pawed her. She didn't answer him. She opened her eyes and looked over at his family photos. Ma Baby made a promise to herself that his fat ugly wife and his bratty ass kids would pay for ***his*** sins one day.

"Tough little cunt aren't cha?" He said as he grabbed her face and squeezed his fingers into her jaws. Nose to nose, he snarled, "Let's see how big and bad you are with my cock in your mouth you little spick bitch!" he said and slapped her across the face with an open palm. He threw his head back and laughed, causing his turkey neck to twerk like a big booty bitch in a music video. He unbuckled his belt and put his hands on Ma Baby's shoulders, pushing her to her knees.

Warden Whiteside stepped out of his pants and tighty-whitey's and palmed the back of Ma Baby's head as he plowed his fat pink dick into her mouth.

"Oh yeeeeah, I knew that pretty mouth would feel good around my cock," he said as he thrusted back and forth. "Mmhm. I couldn't stop staring at those big juicy lips of yours when you came in here last week. I knew I had to have you. Ohhh God that feels fucking good."

Ma Baby closed her eyes as the warden fucked her face. He palmed the sides of her head like it was a volleyball and dug his fingers into her freshly braided hair. She was raving mad and wanted to bite his dick off! But instead, she kept her cool and plotted her revenge while he continued to violate her.

After about five minutes, he pulled himself out of her mouth and slapped her across the face a few times with his penis and wiped it off on her cheeks and chin.

"Stand up," he barked. She did so slowly, and he grabbed her by her shoulders and spun her around. He put his hand in the middle of her back and pushed her forward, bending Ma Baby over his desk. With her face and chest smashed into the top of his desk, she could barely move. She tried to wiggle free of him to stop him from pulling down her pants. But even though he was a fat bastard, he was much stronger than her. And his massive frame that held her in place outweighed her by at least 150 pounds!

"Be still and take this white cock you Latin whore," he said as he finally got her pants down. He ripped her cotton panties off and threw them in the swivel chair behind his desk. He aimed his drippy penis at her fat pussy and put his elbow into her back to hold her still as he rammed her.

"Ow!" she screamed. Ma Baby hadn't had a dick inside of her for 8 years, so her womb was tightly closed. And the warden had a thick girthy tool that stretched her wide and hurt like hell.

"Aww yeah. You're a tight little cookie aren't cha? Mmhm. Spick pussy is always good pussy," he said, pumping in and out of her. "Fuck, this is some *GOOD* snatch honey. Ooh, yes it is," he said as he grabbed the back of her neck and squeezed it hard.

"You like this fat white cock don't cha whore? Admit it. It's better than nigger cock and spick cock combined isn't it?" he said and pulled her hair, making her neck snap back.

"Say something back ***bitch!*** Talk to me goddamnit," he said and slapped her on the ass repeatedly as he pounded into her. **Whop! Whop! Whop! Whop!** The sound of skin slapping against skin echoed like thunder in that office.

Ma Baby knew from previous experience that if you talked dirty to a man or gave him any kind of enthusiastic sexual encouragement, that usually helped speed up the process. She felt nauseous and disgusted. And as much as she hated having to do it, she swallowed her *pride* and played along anyway.

"Oh yeah big daddy. White cock *is* the best papi. Mmhmmm. Warden...fuck...this... Puerto-Rican...pussy...motherfucker! Oh yeah baby. Ooh yeah. Mmmm that feels SOOOO fucking good! God, you have the biggest cock I've *EVER* had inside of me. I wish I would have *been* fucking you. Fuck! I love the way you fuck me papi. Fuck me, fuck me, fuck meeee," she moaned as she began throwing her ass back at him and winding her hips.

The warden laughed triumphantly.

"Yes, whore. Work that pussy like you spick bitches do so well. Ohhh FUCK!"

"Yeah daddy. Ain't nothing like this tight... hot...juicy...spick pussy. You feel how wet you got me baby? I'm dripping all over your ginormous cock," Ma Baby said seductively. She flexed her pussy and did kegels on his dick. She looked back over her shoulder at him and flickered her tongue at him and he lost it.

"Holy motherfucking fuuuuuck!" He shouted as he deposited a half pint of sperm inside of her pussy. "Oh my God! Ohmygodohmygodohmygod!" he uttered and collapsed on her back. Thank God he still had his shirt on or his hairy, sweaty man-boobs and jelly belly would slime up her back! She could feel his thick cum oozing out of her and running down her leg. Ma Baby felt sick to her stomach and wanted to throw up.

"Damn Rivera. That's gotta be one of the best fucks I done ever had," he mumbled into her shoulder blades. "Was it good for you too?"

"Mmhm. That was just what I needed baby. Some good dick will always get a girl's mind right," Ma Baby said dryly.

After his breathing returned to normal, the warden slid out of her with a loud slushy "plop" sound. He wiped his dick off on her red butt cheeks and slapped her on the ass one more time for good measure. **SMACK!** He walked around to the back of his desk, opened a drawer, and pulled a small box out of it. Plan-B was written on it. Then he opened his little mini-fridge that sat next to his desk and took a bottle of water out. He popped the little pill out of its cellophane wrapping and handed that and the water to Ma Baby.

"Take it, can't have you walking around preggers. I *did* shoot a helluva load in ya," he said as she grabbed the bottle and pill from him. He grabbed some Kleenex and wiped his still moist penis off while she popped the pill and washed it down with the water. She wasn't trying to get pregnant by no fat, white, rapist piece of shit either. She was glad he was prepared, but that also told her he did this sort of thing on the regular. Don't no normal dude keep boxes of Plan-B on deck.

He watched as she took the pill and told her to show him her tongue to make sure she didn't "cheek it." She said *ahh* and stuck her tongue out to show him that she did swallow it.

Then he told her to go into his office bathroom to clean herself up before she left, and she did that too. She stayed in there for a while, staring in the mirror even after she washed her pussy out. *I'm slicing your dick off* ***personally*** *myself one day motherfucker*, she said in the mirror.

"You alright in there? You didn't fall in did ya?" the warden said after he knocked on the door and chuckled.

"No, I'm fine," she said as she gathered her composure, opened the door, and smiled at him. He returned that smile and palmed her curvaceous backside.

"You're glowing Rivera. I take it that was good for you?"

"Oh yes. It was the best sex I ***EVER*** had Tur– uh, Warden. How can I ever repay you?"

"Well well now. Maybe you can ***CUM*** back in a couple of days," he laughed at his innuendo. "Mmm, you can let me eat that pretty Puerto-Rican pie of yours. Yeah, that'll be real niiiice. *Real* nice. I'm sure you've been letting those carpet munching skanks lick your twat, but you've never had cunnilingus until you've had a SEASONED expert white guy go down on ya. And let me tell you honey, I can eat a peach for hours," he flickered his tongue at her and made it wave. She almost threw up in her mouth.

"Mmm, I can't wait," she said and kissed him on the cheek. "Oh. And Warden? Can you call them agents and tell them I'll take their offer? You're right, I need to think of my familia. Nothing is more important than ***family***," she said, stressing that last word.

"Smart girl. Very smart of you. I'll do that right away. I'll call you back down in a few days so we can get more acquainted with one another also," he said, rubbing his palms together. "And uh, shave your snatch bald for me will ya? It's damn good, but I like my gals with hardwood floors. Smooth as marble ya know what I mean?" he said, smiling.

She patted him on his big beer belly. "Ok daddy. I'll do that *just* for you. In the meantime, I'll keep this pussy tight and juicy for you. Don't chu be giving all my big white dick away now either. I don't want you spent the next time we hook-up," Ma Baby said.

"Wow, you're a HOT feisty mamasita," he said, getting all hot and bothered again.

"Oh... you ain't seen nothing yet!" she said and walked out of his office plottin' her revenge.

9

SUMMER

The click was due to go to Zurich in 2 weeks for their bi-annual "drop off," and Summer was busy racking up her frequent flier miles, plotting hard and collecting from her "sponsors."

On deck, she had athletes from the NBA, NFL, MLB, UFC, and NHL. She also had several actors, directors, and studio executives. Summer had six rappers, two R&B singers, a hit music producer, and a whole Rock band that "shared" her. Also, a couple of pop star chicks, even a well-known "Vet" one. Rounding out her "sponsor rolodex" were several businessmen and powerful moguls in different industries. They all wanted to fuck with her, so she "invoiced" them for her services.

She knew she was beautiful, smart, and a **SUPER** freak! And unlike a lot of pretty women who stupidly gave up their goods for "free" like the dumb bitches they were, Summer was bold about her game. Her time is money, and if motherfuckers wanted to be with her, they were going to pay up!

Some may call her a whore, a prostitute, a call-girl, or whatever. She didn't give a damn *what* a person called her. Just as long as they didn't call her broke! Cuz that is one thing she said she'll ***NEVER*** be. Broke hoes is a no-no fa sho! And she didn't respect broke bitches. How could a woman be struggling to pay her bills, live check to check, and barely scraping by when so many trick ass men were out there cashing out on bitches just to spend time with them? She just didn't understand those dumb chicks. Pussy is a goldmine! Even the raggediest, most beat up piece of pussy can earn its way in the world, so what does that tell ya?

Not that *hers* was like that though. She kept her pussy tight and intact. She did kegels all day every day to keep her walls strong and firm. And a few times a week, she soaked in a vinegar bath. Vinegar was an acetic acid that preserved whatever contents soaked in it. So, she used it as her special secret tightening weapon. It kept her nookie A-1.

But many of Summer's sponsors wasn't even fucking her though. They bought her shit and cashed her out just for her to be their arm candy at some event or award show. To be the beautiful "trophy date" to make *them* look better.

She was very well-versed and worldly, so she could mingle with any crowd and immerse herself in any conversation, no matter the subject. She was bright, witty, funny, and quick on her toes. She was the most "well-known" member in the BBC because of her music video and modeling appearances. Summer had her own level of celebrity status. But what those stars and athletes that she networked with *didn't* know was, Summer Thompson was a thorough ass hood bitch. Raised in the gutterest of Ghetto's. She let the pretty face and bangin' body fool people into believing the fantasy-like dream she was selling them. Summer was as ruthless and cut-throat as they came. A down ass trill bitch from the Mil. And the only thing she gave a fuck about was BBC and her muthafuckin' money!

Summer was a skilled chameleon that could adapt and survive in any situation. She wasn't judgmental about how others chose to live their life. She encouraged people to do them. Just don't be fake about it. That's why her "sponsors" loved her ass so much; cuz they could let loose and be themselves with her behind closed doors.

Many of them had off the wall kinks and fetishes that they were into that their wives or girlfriends (and in some cases, husbands or boyfriends) would NOT fulfill for them. Stuff like taking a piss or shit on them. Or fucking them in the ass with a strap-on. Yes, it was some kinky ass dudes and females out there that wanted that shit. They got down with the EXTREME EXTREME. And like the old saying goes, what his bitch *WON'T* do, he'll get another chick ***TO*** do. And that's where Summer came in at.

"Oh yeah baby. Give it to me, give it to me, give it to meeeee! Fuck! Give me that big... **BLACK** ... cock!" The four-time Academy Award winning actor growled as he chewed on the pillow. Summer was behind the fifty-something year-old man wearing a nine-inch black strap-on around her waist... *fucking* him.

"You like that? Huh motherfucker? You like how I fuck your little pink ass?" she asked, swatting his old hairy white butt cheeks.

"Oh yes! Yes! Of course I do. Aaargh," he grunted as he reached between his legs to caress his saggy balls. In the blink of an eye, the lights in the huge Presidential Suite flipped on. Summer grabbed the man by his hair at that exact moment and yanked his head back. They both

looked in the direction of their intruders; frozen.

Blinding lights flashed at them as a group of paparazzi women snapped away with cameras. The lighting quick sounds of the photogs' shutter pics filled the room while Summer and the actor paused in complete shock.

"Front page news."

"His wife'll ***LOVE*** this."

"A-list actor with homo-erotic kinks. I can see the headlines now!" The women rattled off quips before smiling and closing the door once they got their pics. In and out. 60 seconds flat.

Summer pulled out of him and was the first to speak. "What the fuck? How did they get in here? Oh my God... this is gonna ruin my career. You're a married man," she sobbed.

He sat up in alarm, running his hand through his disheveled salt and pepper hair. "Calm down honey. I-I-I'll find out who those fucking pap smears were! I won't let this get out. **I CAN'T** let this get out. Oh God, if my wife finds out... she'll fucking get *every* fucking thing! Oh man. Goddamnit!" he said and punched the wall.

"I knew this was a bad idea. I shoulda never got involved with you. You said no one would ever find out. They had cameras. I-I... I was still ***inside*** of you. They got our faces," Summer cried.

He tried his best to console her, assuring her it would be alright. At the same time, he wondered how the women got into the suite in the first place. He could've swore one of them looked like the maid that was lurking around on their floor when they first came up.

That mystery plagued him up until he got the call that unless he came up with five million dollars in CASH--all hundreds, unmarked bills, in two days--all the pics and video of him and Summer would get sold to TMZ and other media outlets.

The famous actor complied and also bought Summer a blue 2020 Bentley Continental GT as a sort of apology for getting her wrapped up in all this mess. He then assured her that they gave him the master copies of the pics and video and he immediately destroyed them.

When he told her that their privacy wouldn't be invaded again and suggested a trip to St. Tropez, she declined his offer, saying she couldn't afford to take that kind of risk again.

She broke it off with him, driving the brand new Bentley

away from the Beverly Hills Restaurant they had lunch at. As she pulled off, she saw his sad puppy dog face in her rearview mirror. Summer smiled and turned on Jay-Z's "On To The Next One" and rapped along to it.

"DAMN! THIS SHO' is some good stuff," the Pastor said as he leaned back on the plush couch, wiping at his nose. On the table was a mountainous pile of cocaine in the shape of a white volcano. He'd been dipping his face in it Scarface style for the last twenty minutes, getting high as the moon!

Summer sat beside him in a purple lace thong. One arm draped over his shoulder while her soft caramelly titties with their hard, brown nipples brushed up against his arms and back.

"It's really good stuff ain't it daddy?" She cooed in his ear seductively.

"Mmhm. You really found me some Grade A this time baby," the Pastor said, going in for another face-full. They were lounging in an elegant hotel suite in downtown Dallas, Texas. The same acclaimed city where the famous preacher at hand led a 100,000 member Christian congregation. He had a nationally televised show that aired every week all over the world. He was one of the most popular ministers in history and was looked up to by millions of people. And because of that, he was also one of the highest paid, earning a seven-figure salary AFTER taxes.

When the group of paparazzi women busted through the door, he was in the middle of taking a snort of coke off Summer's breasts.

"What the?..." he looked up at the bright lights as cameras flashed rapidly. His whole face was ringed with white. As he put two and two together, panic sobered him up instantly.

"Coked up Pastor."

"The only thing whiter than the Pastor's Jesus is his nose."

"The father, the son, the holy coke. I can see the headlines now!" The women sniped at him.

Then they bounced just as quickly as they came, slamming the door behind them. The distraught Pastor went into a frenzy, pacing the floor and griping about his marriage, church, and reputation. Summer ran her same spill about her name being publicized as a homewrecking devil woman and being dragged through the mud by the media. He then assured her he'd do everything in his power to protect her from any harm or career damage.

The blackmailers called with the five-million-dollar ransom for the master copies and the Pastor quickly cleared out his personal savings account that held 3.7 million in it. He also dipped into the churches renovation account/fund that was going toward expanding their already massive amphitheater and got 1.5 million out of there. $200,000 of that went to Summer as an apology, telling her to do some traveling around the world with some of it until the heat died down. Just in case the blackmailers did indeed still have main copies and released them anyway, at least, she'd be out of the country and away from scrutiny.

She thanked him for his generosity and kissed him good-bye. She told him she didn't know when or *if* she'd see him again, but she was gonna take his advice and go abroad for a while.

"I'll keep you in my prayers," she said as she walked out of the Pastor's life for the last time... a couple million dollars richer.

~

Free Larry Byrd, let a nigga out. The Mil ain't the same 'till them birds fly south!

They were in the Mayfair mall shooting the music video to "Free Larry Byrd," a song put together by his niggaz. It featured a killa verse from the incarcerated rapper that was recorded over the phone, letting the streets know that even though he had to do a 'lil time, he was still going hard for the Mil.

Summer was the featured video model. And because she had love for all her fellow Milwaukee artists, she took a severe pay cut and told his homies to give her five geez and she'd make the video hot! Shit, she earned five figures being eye candy for the likes of 50 Cent, Lil Wayne, Young Thug, Lil Baby, Jeezy, and others. But it was deeper than money when it came to her hometown.

Everybody wore FREE LARRY BYRD T-shirts in an array of colors for the music video. Summer had a picture of the rapper's face air-brushed on the front of her extra small white wife beater. It was tied in a knot underneath her breasts to show off her six pack abs and diamond studded **BBC** belly button ring. She also wore a pair of black coochie-cutter spandex shorts with *Larry Byrd* written on the ass. Half of her booty cheeks popped out of the bottom of them. An air-brushed pic of a white dove spreading its wings was on the crotch. And since her pussy was so fat, the dove looked like it just swallowed a big ass owl as it jutted out in 3D.

They were about 100 deep in that bitch. The director and cameraman glided the expensive video camera on pulleys in the air as they shot from different angles. People were packed on the escalator as they bobbed their heads, flashed gang signs, and mouthed the words to the song. Summer was front row and center as the camera zoomed in on her. She twisted her hips rhythmically, throwing up M's, flipping her hair from side to side, and looking all glammed up like the Bad Bitch that she is. Her whole aura commanded attention as she put on a spectacular performance like a true professional.

"Alright. Annnnnnd CUT!" The director yelled through a bullhorn. "Take five. We'll pick back up in the food court," he said as the music cut off and all of the video participants headed for their next destination.

"That ho think her shit don't stank, wit her yellow ass," a nappy-headed female a few feet behind Summer said.

"Mmhm girl. Just cuz she been in a few videos and shit, she think she all that. Funky pussy ass bitch. She ain't on shit," another chick with a raspberry weave responded to her friend's remark.

"Show ain't, wit her bussdown ass. I heard Hustle Gang flipped her in the studio. Bitch prolly got something since she sucks and fucks so much dick!"

Summer stopped in her tracks. She knew they were hating on her, spitting venom and spewing lies because of their own insecurities. She received a lot of hate from women because they were jealous of her and envied her. It didn't take a genius to see that Summer was much prettier, classier, and had way more "G" than 99% of the bitches out there!

She turned around and knew immediately who the culprits were. Two brown-skinned, chicken head bitches wearing knockoff Gucci outfits and cheap ass Payless looking heels. Summer laughed at them bum hoes and turned her back to them. *They **DEFINITELY** ain't worth my time*, she said to herself and began walking again.

"Girrrl, you see dat? She turned around like she was gon' say somethin'."

"Hmpf. Yellow ass bitch don't want no smoke!"

"Damn right she don't! Fuck around and get jumped in dis muhfucka." They high-fived each other and laughed.

As people congregated in the food court waiting for the

next scene to be shot, Summer walked into an interesting conversation.

"I'm telling you, that nigga P-Yella got the city on choke. Byrd dat nigga, but if P-Yella get *ON* on? He gon' blow," a jet black Akon looking dude with a Pelle coat said.

"Man, Byrd hot. But shiiid, Party Harrrd is da truth yo! That nigga got **STUPID** bars," someone else said.

Then a female made a comment about Cheese Marshall being her favorite rapper. On and on it went about who the best to ever do it from Milwaukee was: Coo Coo Cal, Baby Drew, P-Yella, Larry Byrd, Party Harrrd, and countless others. Summer had her own opinions but kept them to herself. She had love for anybody who put on for the Mil. Rico Love was probably the most famous, but he didn't rep the Mil like that.

Her city wasn't really on the map yet. Not like they ***should*** be anyway. Atlanta, New York, Florida, Cali, even Texas, were the main staples in "KNOWN" hip-hop regions. And Summer wanted so desperately for someone, *anyone* to drop that flurry of hits that bust the doors wide open and show muthafuckaz how the Mil *really* got down! But cats was basically just local legends. Many of them had the potential to go MUCH bigger if they could just stay their ass out of jail and focus on dropping hits. That's why Summer did everything she could to promote her slept-on city. From radio interviews to her modeling spreads in SHOW, Phat Puffs, XXL, and Straight Stuntin', she shouted out her city.

She threw up "M's" in music videos, photo shoots, and on all of her social media pages. She held it down for hers, that's why she got more love than she did hate, especially from all the street niggaz.

Dudes walked up to her and asked for pics as she strolled around the food court. They hugged up with her while their homies snapped flicks with their camera phones. Smiling and posing from different angles, she turnt up to set the visuals off.

Always making sure to pose from a side view and poke her round ass out so a "shot" of that donk could be seen.

No doubt, many of those flicks would soon make their way up North to all the Wisconsin penitentiaries to show niggaz locked down what's out there waiting for them when they come home, knowing that seeing pics of muthafuckaz having fun and living life geeked inmates up. Motivating those who were on the "inside" to get their shit together and blueprint a master plan so they could get out and ***stay*** out!

A couple of the Milwaukee Bucks players came out in support and made a cameo in the video. Summer got cozy with them and exchanged numbers with one of them. *Now that's how you ball. While these D-boyz think they stuntin' with they lil pieces, this nigga rockin' a Vanheron Constantin Tour de I'lle watch. That muthafucka STARTS at 2.5 million.* Summer said to herself, impressed with the pro ball players taste in wrist wear. She knew she had to fuck with him in the near future in some kind of way. He had a famous wife, so she was going to have to be real discreet. And from the way he fucked with his eyes, and licked his sexy lips, Summer knew he wanted to get with her too.

From a distance, Summer could still see those two chicken heads who was talking shit. They stood in the crowd looking ratchet as they mean-mugged her. As they shot the food court scene, she made sure to put some extra swag in her moves as she turnt up and did her thang. She still kept an eye on her haters because they made her want to shine even harder!

But Summer was a creature of habit and knew drama was in the air, and it was only a matter of time before shit popped off. It was inevitable. And as the practices of a soldier went, she was always aware of her surroundings.

"Annnnd Cut! Perfect y'all. We got it. Now for those of you who were told will be in the block scene, we'll see you on 24th and Brown in one hour. Make sure your whips are clean and your rims are extra shiny," the director said into the bullhorn and then handed it to his assistant. The director walked over to Summer and told her they'd meet at the pet store to shoot her solo scene later that evening. She said "cool" and headed to Victoria's Secret to do some shopping with sponsor money.

The two spiteful women trailed her as they griped about how light skin bitches always getting all the shine and thinking they was better than everyone else. Hate and envy was spewed forth in every ignorant insult they spat.

Meanwhile, Summer knew they were following her. She could see them in the glass of all the stores she walked by out of her peripheral. Summer's stride was sleek as a panther and as poised and confident as a supermodel. Her tight buns hung halfway out of her booty shorts as Larry Byrd bounced up and down like a seesaw while her hips switched in figure 8 swivels. Her right arm swung back and forth like a kid on a swing set. Everyone eyed her with either awe or envy or *both*.

She knew she wasn't gonna get any shopping done on this and thinking about how she hadn't put the floo-flops on a bitch or two in a minute, she re-routed her destination and headed for the parking structure, leading the hood "rats" to her mouse trap.

She exited the mall, her red bottom Louboutins click-clacked loudly on the pavement as she strode toward her black Cadillac SRX premium with the 24" deep dish Asanti's on it. Bad Bitchez rode slick too.

A few seconds after she entered the parking garage, she heard the mall doors open and close as more heels click-clacked on the ground. *Dumb bitches don't even know that* ***silence*** *is the key to an attack*, Summer said to herself as she pulled her keys out of her purse. She chirped the alarm off her Lac and heard the heels trotting at a hurried pace behind her.

"Hey bitch! You thi—"

WHACK! Summer turned around and punched the woman

in her mouth before she could even finish her sentence. Two teeth flew out of the chick's mouth and skidded across the concrete. She fell flat on her ass in surprise as she held a hand up to her bloody mouth.

Her friend didn't even have time to react before Summer grabbed her by her bogus ass, curly fries-looking weave and rammed her face into a Chevy Equinox parked nearby. A streak of blood ran through the white paint as her nose burst open on contact. Summer kneed the bitch in her stomach, and she crumpled on the pavement next to her friend.

The two hating bitches sat their stunned, holding their bloody injuries while Summer hopped in her 'Lac and put the car in reverse. Not caring if they were in the way or not, she backed up over what felt like a speed bump but was actually one of the hating hoes' legs. A terrifying scream echoed off the concrete pillars as her foot was broken in three pieces ***instantly.***

Summer saw the teeth prints on her knuckles as she looked at her hand on the steering wheel. *Damn.* She shook her head and put the car in drive, dipping off on they ass. Handling her business quickly and efficiently, she didn't even have to say a word to get the job done. *I bet they don't try to run up on another bitch*, she said to herself. Summer glanced in her rearview mirror real quick, then put on Larry Byrd's *4-1* snow record.

~

"WHAT'S GOOD MA?"

"Hey daddy! What's poppin' witchu? I ain't heard form you in a minute. What, you forget about a bitch or something?" Summer said.

"Forget *YOU?* Never. I just been touring like crazy and promoting the album. You know it just went Diamond, right?"

"Yeah, I heard. Congratulations," Summer said to the hard core gangsta rapper who just sold 10 million units of his latest album. He was currently THEE hottest thing in the music industry.

"Good lookin'. Thanks, I appreciate it. Shit, I still think I have you to thank for the success of the first single though. Shit, you made that video what it was," he said.

"Aww, thanks boo. Ya know... you can thank me with a lil trinket next time we get together," she told him.

"Say no mo. Speaking of which, when can a nigga see yo fine ass mami? I can put you on a private flight right now! Fly you straight to New York."

"Well, I'm shooting a video for my shmoo Larry Byrd right now. Buuuut... I can probably ***CUMMMM*** tomorrow," she said and giggled.

"Oh yeah? Mm! Witcho freaky ass," he said and laughed. "That's what's up. Cool then. Ummm... I was thinking, you don't know no white hoes that get down so can we have a ménage?" he inquired.

"Ahh, so you wanna ménage it up huh? Well, I might be able to make that happen. I do know a ***BAD*** ass white bitch. Strapped like CoCo and everythang," Summer said.

"Word???"

"Yup. But you gonna have to break bread if you want us *BOTH*... at the same damn time."

He laughed. "Ma, you know that dough ain't no issue for your boy. Just call her up and I'll have a jet waiting for y'all to leave at noon tomorrow. And uh, bring them toys that I like."

"Ok daddy. I gotchu. We'll see yo sexy ass tomorrow." She said and disconnected. Summer walked back to the front of the pet store after she put her phone up. They were about to shoot her solo. A scene of her in a barely-there bikini with exotic birds sitting on her shoulders, arms, and hands.

She walked down the reptile aisle looking at iguanas, lizards, and... SNAKES! A venomous idea popped into her head as she stared at the slithery creatures through the 3-inch glass that they were caged in. Ball Pythons, Garter snakes, Blood Pythons, Dumeril Boas, Taiwanese Beauties, Albino Boa Constrictors, Redtails, King Snakes, Brazilian Rainbows, and many others. A malicious smile spread across her face; *somebody's in for a rude awakening*, she mused to herself.

FRESH OFF THE MARQUIS JET, Summer and Becky breathed in the muggy New York City air as they gathered their Louis Vuitton luggage and was escorted to the stretch Maybach limousine that awaited them. The plane ride to NY was the first time the two of them got to bond on a one-on-one basis. Before Summer called requesting her assistance, Becky had only kicked it with Rose and GG. Summer had been on her own little mission at the time of Becky coming into the picture and didn't have time to chop it up with her until now.

"I'm telling you girl. This nigga is ***NOT*** who he portrays in them videos and songs. He's a whole type of *other* muthafucka. And because I'm in move bussin' mode, it's time for his fake ass to pony up and run that dust. He gon' do it cuz he don't want his gangsta rep to be tarnished," Summer said.

"Wow, I still can't believe he gets down like that. I mean, I listen to all of his albums. He talks about shooting people and how he'll bury his rivals. Heck, he's been shot six times and wears bulletproof vests to his press conferences and award shows. I woulda NEVER thought that he uh..." Becky trailed off.

"Yeah, I know what you mean. I thought the same thing. But one thing I learned from being in the entertainment industry is you can't judge a book by its cover. Trust me. I have plenty of celebrity sponsors that are like ***WAY*** out there. Shiiid, just last week, this NFL star wanted me to take a shit on him. A real...live...doo-doo," Summer exclaimed.

"Noooo. Get out!"

"Dead serious girl. It's nasty, but if you gon' break bread, I'm gonna give you what chu want. So, I ate plenty of Taco Bell for like three days straight, and when it was time to meet up with Mr. Football...I got the job done. It was messy as hell and nasty as a muthafucka! But hey, that's what he wanted. Our girls busted in as he was rubbing it all over his neck and chest. I had another turd hanging halfway out my ass, in mid-drop, when they snapped away with their cameras. He was ***EXTRA*** generous to not let that shit,– pun intended– get out to the media," Summer laughed.

"Like eeew. He's won fricking Super Bowls and plays with feces? Geesh. That's crazy. So, the girls will be prepared once we get ol' boy how we want him?" Becky asked.

"Yeah, they know the drill. Since you most likely will be the thickest, BADDEST white bitch dis mog ever laid eyes on, you'll be able to get his nose wide open. We'll get him to pop this exclusive Molly GG got for me and lace his drink, so he won't be on guard. He's a street nigga so he's always on high alert. And you know he beefin' wit a couple niggas, so he always got his homies and security around. We've gotta get him alone, *very* wasted, and so full of lust that he won't be suspicious about anything. Cuz I'm telling you, dude is paranoid as hell and always sharp when it comes to details. So, we gotta get his ass open like a 7-11. And that's where *YOU* come in."

"Ya want me to put my Snow Bunny game down huh?" Becky said and giggled.

"You know it! Make him fiend for that white thang while we do our trife thang. Oh, try not to let your eyes pop out of your head when you see his dick," Summer said as they pulled up to the Waldorf Astoria in downtown Manhattan.

"Why?" Becky asked.

"Cuz he's *EXTREMELY* hung," Summer said.

Becky's eyes got big and her heart sped up quickly. Becky

was cuckoo for Cocoa Puffs for big dicks! She licked her lips in anticipation, wondering just how big this dude really was.

"Let the shoooow begin," Summer said, stepping out of the Limo.

I'd rather be ya N-I-G-G-A
So we can get drunk and smoke weed all day
It don't matter if you lonely baby, You need a Thug in your life
Cuz them bustas ain't lovin' you right

TUPAC WAS SUBBING from the speakers in the immaculately plush 3-bedroom penthouse as the famous rapper swigged from his Ciroc bottle in one hand, then took big puffs from the purple OG-filled Backwoods in his other hand. He choked loudly and blew big clouds of smoke to the ceiling.

"Damn, I can't believe how bad you is," he said to Becky. He was standing behind her and rubbed his crotch against her backside as they both swayed to the music.

Becky was wearing skin-tight Miss Me jeans that looked like they were painted on and a turquoise half-blouse that hung off one shoulder and showed off her flat tan stomach. Her four-inch Manolo Blahnik heels made her calves look even more defined and enhanced her 50-inch ass to the max, making it protrude outward even further than it in already did.

Becky smiled and danced, basking in the rapper's praise and attention as she puffed on a blunt that her and Summer shared. He was the first real-life celebrity she ever encountered, and despite her usual cool demeanor, she was a jumble of nerves in his presence. But the weed was helping calm her down a little bit as she focused on her seduction tactics. *Don't fuck up. Give him that snow he's craving for*, she coached herself.

Summer looked on with her honey colored eyes while Becky gyrated her huge assets against the multi-platinum rapper. He had on about nine or ten heavy chains, iced out like a muthafucka as he two-stepped and got bent.

A few of his homeboys lounged around sipping Crown Royal and smoking B's. Some of them played Xbox One for a stack of cash in the middle of the floor.

Summer walked around barefoot with her tight leather mini-skirt showing off her scrumptious legs and bubble butt. She tossed her silk blouse on the couch and sashayed around the living room in a black lace bra. Her fat titties squeezed together and sitting up higher than a lifeguard chair, making all the men salivate over her sexiness.

Becky bent at the waist and touched her toes. The rapper's eyes got big as saucers, looking down at that big stupid ass sway side to side on his semi-erect dick. Becky could feel that monstrosity through his jeans and her pussy got wet.

"Daddy, we trying to turn up. Tell your boys to bounce so we can have some privacy," Summer whispered in his ear as she pressed her soft breasts into his muscular back. He grabbed a handful of Becky's ass, and she bounced it up and down against him.

"Yo. Babygirl, you know I keep my dudes close. We can go in the other room and make shit happen ya know what I'm sayin'?" he told Summer.

She smacked her lips. "Shit, how we supposed to get buck wild like how you want when yo niggaz in the next room?" Summer said.

"It ain't stopped us before did it?" he said.

"Maybe not. But you never had two fly ass bitches ready to go X-rated ham on you like we came to do," Summer informed him. Just then, Becky turned around and wrapped her arms around his neck, pressing her big titties into his tatted up chest.

"Grab my ass baby. Palm that motherfucker," Becky said in his ear. "Feel how soft that is? I'm gonna make it clap on your cock while you fuck my brains out," she said and licked his ear.

Summer pressed harder into his back and licked his ***other*** ear while Becky spit dat G!

"My cunt is so fat and so wet, just ***thinking*** about what I want you to do to me and what I want to do to you. But I'm not with the whole audience thing. I want to fuck you and suck you all around this penthouse. Every room, every surface, and every piece of furniture in this motherfucker. But I'm a screamer. And honey, I get *LOUD!* And what we're gonna do to you? *YOU'RE* gonna get loud. You don't want them to hear that do ya baby? Me and my girl want you all to ourselves. Whaddaya say?" Becky looked at him and batted her big sky blue eyes.

He looked down at the pointy nipples straining against her blouse. *Damn her nipples are hard.* He looked around at his boys smoking, drinking, and playing the game. He was sandwiched between two bad bitches. Probably the baddest bitches he EVER had! What could go wrong? He'd been jammin' wit Summer for a minute, so he knew she was straight. He could relax and do the damn thang like never before. It was true; he couldn't really let loose like he always wanted to with his guys nearby.

Becky could see the wheels turning in his head as he contemplated who knows what. On impulse, she dropped to the floor and did the splits. Everyone stopped what they were doing as she twerked her butt cheeks one at a time in tune to the music. She looked over her shoulder and opened her mouth. She wiggled her turquoise tongue ring at him.

"Let's do this daddy," Summer cooed in his ear.

"Yo! Y'all gots to ride out," he said, snapping his fingers at his boys. "Come on, bounce. I gots business to take care of. Come on muthafucka... let's go!" he said, rounding them up.

"Man, you sure?" one of them asked, grabbing his pistol off the table and putting it in his waistband.

"Yeah nigga, I'm sho'. Now let's go man. Y'all ain't gots to go home but chy'all gots to get the *HELL* out of here," he said, rushing them to the door.

Some of them put their half smoked blunts in the ashtrays while others took a few more swigs from the liquor bottles before setting them back on the table. They gave him some dap as he told them he'd holla at them later.

As soon as his boys left, the whole tough guy gangsta persona melted away. In front of *them*, he wouldn't kiss no females cuz that was frowned upon by niggaz in that world. They thought, "who knew *whose* dick a ho was sucking out there these days." But as soon as that door closed and he threw on the safety latch and security chain, he sauntered up to Becky and grabbed her by the waist. He pulled her close until half of his chains slid down the top of her blouse as he shoved his tongue down the white girl's throat. His kisses were sloppy and urgent. Hard and aggressive as he slobbered all over her mouth, smearing her red lipstick all over both of their faces in the process. *Gosh, he's the worst kisser ever*, Becky sighed to herself. She tried kissing him back but was overpowered by his massive tongue. He grabbed her 34Ds and moaned into her mouth. Summer crept up behind him and nibbled on his earlobe. He was sandwiched between two beautiful women and loved it!

"Let's turn up with these Pac-Man's," Summer said, holding a yellow pill (with the famous video game character on it), in front of the rapper's face.

"You know I don't pop pills ma," he said, breaking his kiss with Becky.

"What? I thought you partied like it was nobody's business," Becky said, quoting one of his biggest club hits.

"I do. I just don't fuck around like *that*," he said, palming Becky's phat ass. She wriggled out of his embrace and slowly walked over to the windows overlooking the city. She twirled her blonde hair around her finger and pouted.

"This shit is lame. I came to party with the hottest rapper

the industry has ever *seen* and you're telling me you don't turn up like 'that.' Like, what the fuck is that supposed to mean?" Becky said, putting a hand on her hip.

"Yo, what's up with your girl ma? Don't she know not everybody gets down like that?" he said to Summer.

"It ain't like that daddy. She listens to so much of your music, she thinks you do all the shit that you rap about. She don't know that a lot of it is just entertainment," Summer said.

"Yeah, well..." he grabbed his Ciroc bottle and took a couple of swigs.

"Look daddy, my girl is cool. She just likes to party ***HARD***. And she feels like a muthafucka ain't feelin' her if she gotta turn up alone," Summer told him.

"But it ain't even like that yo. You know I does the damn thing." he stated.

"Daddy, I know. It's just... well this is her first threesome and she really likes you and..."

"You're my dream man! You're tall. Dark. And handsome as hell. ***AND*** you're straight up gangster. I fucking love thugged out Bad Boys," Becky said in her best Valley girl voice. She removed her top and tossed it on the floor. She didn't have a bra on. "You see how hard my nipples are?" She said, pinching the bubblegum pink eraser tips that stood out like firm earplugs. "*You've* got 'em like this. I've never been so turned on in my life," she paused to lift one of her heavy breasts up to her mouth, so she could flicker her hot pink nipples with her tongue. The rapper stood there amazed. On ten!

Becky fixed him with a sky-blue stare as she slowly unzipped her Miss Me jeans. As she walked towards him, her hourglass hips swayed seductively with each step. "No one... is hotter than you. You're the best to ever touch a microphone. You're the fucking bomb, daddy," she said in a husky voice. Her pants were so tight, she struggled to peel them off her hips. Dude just stared at the front of her jeans. They were unfastened enough for him to see the top of her turquoise panties. It looked like she was concealing a pot pie in her crotch. Her pussy looked *THAT* fat! He licked his lips in anticipation as Summer kissed and licked on his ears, neck, and shoulder blades.

"It's cool though. Since you won't pop with us, you can at least put a pill or two in ***THIS***," Becky grabbed his hand and shoved it down her pants. Fat wasn't the word to describe her smooth, clean shaven pussy. What he felt was something *BEYOND* describable. He thought he was touching a boxing glove, it was so big and poofy...*AND* it was wet!

"Goddamn!" he shouted.

"Mmhm, her pussy fat as a ***bitch***, ain't it daddy?" Summer whispered in his ear. He turned halfway and looked back at Summer as she smiled at him.

Becky removed his hand from her panties and sucked on his fingers like it was a dick. She moaned and looked directly into his eyes.

"I came to fuck and to be fucked," Becky said and walked towards the master bedroom. He was in such a trance, he forgot to grab his pistol that he ALWAYS kept near him off the table before following Becky back to the room. He didn't seem to notice Summer hanging back.

Once they were out of sight, Summer grabbed the blunt roaches out the ashtrays, the half-drunk liquor bottles she sealed in zip lock bags, and placed them in her huge Burberry purse. She unlocked the front door and joined the festivities.

When she entered the bedroom, Becky was already naked, and the rapper was about to dive between her tan legs and eat that pretty pink pie. Summer pulled his LRG jeans and boxer briefs off before he went all the way downtown. His chains clink-clanked around as everyone got into position.

While he ate Becky out, Summer tossed his salad and blew

kush in his bootyhole. He giggled like a schoolgirl and wriggled back and forth while Summer tongued his "Hershey Highway."

To Becky, his oral sex game was just like his kissing: wet and sloppy. He tongue fucked her, but had no clue what he was doing. She tried to position her clit on his mouth, but he just kept dipping his head lower and tonguing her insides. She faked an orgasm then said, "God that was hot! Let me suck your cock now baby."

He sat up with his back against the headboard, revealing to Becky what he was actually working with.

"Holy guacamole! You've got a fucking horse cock," Becky said in surprise. He did have a battering ram of a penis. 14 inches long and the circumference of a can of whip cream! Its head was the size of a small plum. Becky looked at that black anaconda and almost came on herself. *For real* this time.

Summer passed him the lit blunt and an Ex pill. "Shove this in my pussy daddy," she said, spreading her legs wide and bussin' it open for him. He inserted the Ex into her vagina just as Becky clutched his pole.

"I've never seen anything like it," Becky muttered in disbelief. Thick veins pulsed beneath the jet black beast, making it look like garden snakes were slithering under his skin. A shiny teardrop of pre-cum coated his helmet crown as Becky held him with both hands like a baseball player does a bat. She licked his tip slowly, tasting his salty delight and savoring its spiciness. "Mmmmm," she moaned enthusiastically.

Her tongue went to work, circling laps around his swollen head. When her tongue ring played in his pee hole, it sent chills through his body. She looked up at him with those big blue eyes and took half of him into her hot, eager mouth.

"Ohhh shit," he moaned, took a hit of the blunt, and blew smoke into her pretty white face.

"Suck that dick white bitch! Hell yeah. Dammmmn girl," he

moaned, grabbing the back of her head and pushing down on it.

Becky showed him why white girls held the oral sexxx crown down! She moaned on the dick while she glided it in and out of her mouth in meticulous strokes. She relaxed her throat and let the head of his dick pummel her tonsils like it was a punching bag! She had no gag reflex, and all those days in high school her and her friends spent competing to see who could get the most of a soda can in their mouth was paying off now.

Becky's mouth was nice and spitty. Her saliva coated his Mandingo pipe and made it shine like black patent leather. "God, your cock is so hard... mmmm, so ginormous. And so...***BLACK!***" she said, filled with lust. She rubbed his dick across her face in lustful admiration. His oral skills and kissing game may have been whack, but the sheer sight and taste of his black beast had Becky so wet that pussy juice ran down her legs.

Summer looked on from the side lines in awe. *Damn, this bitch is **COLD** on a dick*, she thought to herself, feeling a bit intimidated.

Becky put the whole 14 in her mouth until her nose was buried in his pubic hair and her bottom lip rested on top of his balls. His toe knuckles popped and cracked as they balled up in his socks.

"Damn bitch! Ain't nobody *ever* been able to take all my meat before," he said in shock. She looked up at him and batted her long eyelashes like a peacock's feathers. She slurped up and down from the tip of his dick on down to his big hairy balls. Her mouth made loud vulgar suction-like noises as her head bobbed up and down, up and down.

Becky swallowed his entire penis in one swift dive, then came back up to lap circles around his pee hole with the tip of her tongue. "Mmmm, you like that honey? Hm?" she said as she took his piece out of her mouth and slapped herself across the face with it several times.

"Mmhm. I've been a bad...bad...girl. Daddy, slap...me... with...your...big...black...cock!" she said, holding his heavy penis and hitting herself with it. The bitch was off da radar, talking filthy nasty and showing just why niggaz nicknamed oral sex "Becky."

He threw his head back and closed his eyes. Becky opened her mouth and Summer put the special Ex pill on her tongue. Becky cheeked it and resumed sucking his dick. When she got to his head again, he could feel her tongue ring opening up his pee hole as the hard-turquoise ball invaded the tiny sensitive area tenderly. Well, he *THOUGHT* it was her tongue ring. She was really putting a Molly inside of him and coating it with spit until it dissolved, and he didn't even know it.

"Sllllll," he moaned between clinched teeth as he raised his ass off the bed. Summer dove down and sucked his balls while Becky went ham on his dick. Dude was flying high off the weed and being double served by two fly ass freak bitches. Both of their fat asses were tooted up in the air side by side. It looked like a big white heart and a big caramel heart glued together.

The pill kicked in quickly, heightening his senses and making him even hornier. He thought it was just the two dime pieces blowing his mind that had him feeling like he did. When in fact, it was pure MDMA running though his system.

"Fuck this. I'm ready to ***fuck!***" he growled, pushing both the women off him. He grabbed a super large condom off the night-stand and put it on as Summer grabbed her bag of goodies. Becky laid down on the bed and grabbed the back of her knees, pulling them up to her ears for him. Her pink pussy opened up like a blossoming flower.

"Damn that muthafucka pretty," he said, kneeling between her legs. "Lips so fat, they look like two pink hot dog buns!" He rubbed his dick up and down her wet entrance.

Becky looked down at his Billy club and couldn't believe her luck. She was a "Size Queen" that loved her cocks big, fat, and black! The bigger the better since she liked a little pain during sex. And she could tell that his dick was about to hurt…soooo good. It took a minute to get up in her because she was so tight. But when he finally did work his way up in that thang, he went *ham* on her pussy. He pounded Becky out and filled up her insides with more dick than she ever had in her life! She was loving getting stretched out and stuffed from wall to wall. He went so deep, she could've sworn he was poking her lungs. She could hardly breathe, but she still got her white girl porn/dirty talk on: "Oh yeah! That's it. Mmm fucking fuck yeah! Oooh so good. So good. God, your cock is huge. Fuck my tight white pussy...with your big black cooooock," she growled.

"Yes! Yes! Mmm fuck. Give it to me daddy. Tight...white...pussy...big...black...cock," she chanted and panted between thrusts. "Awww yeah. Awww yeah. You're in my stomach," she whine-moaned. Her dirty talk turned him on even more. Summer was having a hard time doing what she was doing behind him because he was in beast mode.

When he flipped Becky on all fours, he became deranged! That was the biggest, fattest ass he'd ever seen. And it was real. Not even a sista was that muthafuckin' strapped. He thunderclapped Becky's backside as he pounded into her. He began sweating like a mad man as his New York Yankees fitted hat fell off his head. The rapper's balls slapped the back of her thighs with each pump, making it sound like effects in a drum machine.

Becky flipped her hair over her shoulder and looked back at him. "Oh fuuuuck, you feel so good inside me. Mmmm, fuck my pussy daddy. Fuck me like you've never fucked another bitch before! Ohhhhh yeah. That's it."

He dug his fingers into her waist as she began throwing it back at him. He couldn't believe she was taking ALL this dick like a champ. Her pussy walls squeezed his penis in a tight vice grip. She kept going on him.

"Slap my ass! Pull my fucking hair! Mmmm yeah. Oh God, yes daddy yes. Fuck yeah! Punish...me...with...your...big...black...**COCK**! Arrgh!" she howled. Sex and obscenities filled the air, passionate exchanges and lustful body collisions bounced off the walls.

The gangsta rapper was gritting his teeth, foaming at the mouth, and making unintelligible sounds. Sweat coated his chains and made them bling even harder. The lubed up fingers Summer had in his ass went unnoticed as he slapped Becky's butt, yanked her hair back, and fucked her with every ounce of his being.

He held nothing back. The drugs made him feel like Superman!

Even though she didn't want the banging of her life to end, she had to fake an orgasm when Summer gave her the signal. Which wasn't hard since her pussy was dripping like a Jheri curl in the 1980's.

"Ok daddy. I can't take anymore. I tap out," Becky said, pushing him out of her. He sat there winded and grateful that she stopped him cuz he needed to catch his breath. And he was feeling dehydrated as fuck!

As if reading his mind, Summer passed him a drink. He didn't stop to think when she could've grabbed a glass or what was even in it. He just saw cubes of ice and frosty condensation misting the glass and gulped it down greedily. For the first time since they entered the room, he actually looked at her and saw that she had his favorite toy on.

"You got one for her too?" he asked, raising his eyebrow.

"Mmhm, sure do. Mami, grab that ya dig out the bag and put it on," Summer told Becky.

"Oh. And here daddy," Summer said, handing him two Ex

pills. "Put these in her. One in her pussy, and one in that big ol' ass!"

After Becky pulled a 7-inch white penis strap-on out of the bag next to the bed, she bent over and let him put an ecstasy pill in her asshole. Then she turned around and spread her legs. There was a big gaping hole in her vagina where his dick was just minutes ago. He dropped the Ex into her cave like you do cubes of ice in a cup.

Becky giggled and fastened the strap-on around her waist. The one Summer wore was a 9-inch black one. Summer handed her a bottle of lube. Becky still couldn't believe one of THEE hardest, most gangster rappers that ever lived was really down with this shit.

It was his turn to get on all fours now. Summer knelt in front of him and lit a new blunt. She inhaled deeply, then blew smoke in his face. Becky got behind him, slathering the fake white penis with lube. He wiggled his black hairy ass impatiently. His chains clinked like wind chimes on a cool spring night.

He looked over his shoulder and said, "I've been a naughty, naughty boy. Punish me mommy," in a soft, baby voice. Becky shrugged and whacked him on his butt. Now the roles were reversed and he wanted to be dominated. *We do whatever for the dollar*, Becky reminded herself, quoting the BBC motto as she still couldn't come to grips with what she was about to do. Surprisingly, she slid the strap-on into his anus fairly easily. She damn near fell in on the first stroke. *Hmpf, someone does this an awful lot.* She started whacking him on his ass like he did her a few minutes ago.

"Now suck my dick nigga! Suck this big black dick you muthafuckin' bitch nigga," Summer said in an aggressive deep voice. She grabbed his head and shoved the fake dick in his mouth. Summer thrusted forward and backward, fucking his face.

Becky looked at Summer and scrunched her nose up. The look said ***eew***. Not only was this some way out stuff, but a hint of shit filled the air as Becky went deeper and deeper into his anal cavity.

"Oh yeah. White dick feels so good up my black ass," he said in a strange, weird, unrecognizable voice. He looked back at Becky pumping in and out of him and said, "Gimme that white dick. Fuck me!" Summer and Becky got into a perfect in sync rhythm as they fucked him from both ends. Although he didn't have long hair, he did wear a Doo-rag as a prop. He told Becky to pull it like it was his hair while she hit it from the back. A few seconds later, the paparazzi women barged in, taking pics with their blinding cameras and hurled comments at him:

"Gangsta nigga loves dick."

"Hard on the outside, Likes it hard and ***INSIDE!***"

"From rocking mikes to sucking swipes."

"Hardcore and on all fours. The New York Times is gonna ***LOVE*** this!"

The drugs slowed his reaction as he froze like a deer in head lights, trying to comprehend what the hell was going on. When reality sunk in, he looked around for his pistol. It was ALWAYS close by. But not this time. He would've blasted on the intruders had his strap been in reach, but it wasn't.

The paparazzi chicks got what they came for and ran out of the penthouse before he could react. Summer and Becky were screaming and putting their clothes on. He knew something wasn't quite right, but he pushed it to the back of his mind while panic overcame his thoughts in a tidal wave of fear and paranoia.

He was already on the phone calling his boys as he pushed his ménage à trois participants out of the penthouse in a frenzy. Gun cocked and in his right hand, he fumed and waddled around the crib like a penguin.But murder was on his mind.

When he got the call a couple hours later about the hush money, he had no choice but to oblige. Being that he was newly certified ten times platinum, his price was a bit higher than the other celebs Summer had set up. 20 million in cash in 48 hours or else! He did what they asked, all while trying to get to the bottom of who had set him up. It was either a member of his crew or them bitches. He had a gut feeling it was the latter.

All in all, Summer had went on a nice little sting. Recruiting THOT Gang bitches to pose as blackmailing paparazzi, she took advantage of high-profile celebrities during their most vulnerable moments, knowing that they had EVERYTHING to lose by not complying. She set up her biggest sponsors for one last payout, knowing she could never see them again. But she was playing with fire, taking Grim Reaper chances with the wrong guy when it came to the rapper dude.

Several men and women fell for the "okey-doke" and forked over that unmarked cash though. Summer hit they packets ***HARD.*** 70 million dollars total. 20 million of that went to THOT Gang. The other 50 was going with BBC to be deposited in their off shore bank accounts. Yup, Summer was ready to go to Switzerland.

10

BECKY

The fish in the pond is not the catch of the day. Violation hits close to home but ultimately, the ball's in your court. If you have mercy, you too will be forgiven.

Becky shuddered when she read her horoscope. This was not one of those "good luck" ones. This particular one made her feel eerie. But despite the red flags telling her to stay in the crib and have a chill day, she knew she had to hit the streets and handle her business.

Ever since Rose had come into her life, things had progressed quickly. She now had an endless supply of "skittles" and with their 2 for $50 deal they gave, she was quietly sowing up Appleton and the surrounding cities. She even had people coming from as far as Marinette to shop with her.

BBC had taken her to some clubs and events where Big Ballerz and high-profile cats were, and she was an instant success with brothaz who yearned for fine thick *whiteness.*

It seemed like every other day, she was on a flight or the highway to a new city. Miami, Houston, L.A., St. Paul, Indianapolis, Atlanta, and of course Milwaukee. Rose and GG were teaching her the art of "finessing."

"Finessing is a skillful art of handling a situation. It's the smooth performance of getting what ***YOU*** want while making another person think it was ***THEIR*** idea to give it to you in the first place. And as a bad bitch, we put the ***FINE*** in finesse," GG told her.

Becky was soaking up mad game from her new friends and loving every minute of it. She was having the time of her life and getting some real good "fucks" thanks to the new crowds she was brought around. She was still wilding out over the episode that went down with her, Summer, and the rapper. *All that good cock and he's fucking gay,* Becky said to herself and shook her head.

She was now the Queen of rolling Blunts. After Rose's enlightenment on pipes, she and Britney threw all of theirs away and asked Rose to teach them how to masterfully roll a B. Which is what she was doing while sitting in her white SLK Class Benz at the gas station as she waited on Poobie.

BBC was slowly infiltrating Mud Money, T-dub's click of Ballerz, one member at a time. They knew all of their hangouts, so the girls were to mingle in said places and just-so-happen to get with one of them.

Poobie was a big gambler who loved to play craps at Potawatomi Casino. It didn't take him long to get at the hot blonde who swooped in and won a quick seven thousand dollars and got up to leave while she was still ahead. He asked her to stay, blow on his dice, and be his "good luck charm." She did, and she must have been a rabbit's foot because he won 42 geez that night. He gave her 12 of that and she gave Poobie her number.

On what was supposed to be their first date, he was running really late. Becky told him before-hand that she didn't know her way around Milwaukee like that, so Poobie told her to meet him at the gas station on Sherman and Capital and they'd go from there. After almost an hour of waiting, he texted her saying some important business came up and he'd be occupied for a few more hours. He told her to go to the mall or a movie in the meantime, and he'd meet up with her later. "I'll make it up to you times 100," he texted with a wink emoji.

"Fucker!" she fumed, blowing Peyton Manning Kush smoke against the woodgrain dash. She was all dolled up in clear platform stilettos with a six-inch heel, a tight body-hugging white Dolce & Gabbana dress that had a plunging neckline that went damn near to her belly button. There was so much cleavage exposed, she had to "adjust" herself every few seconds because the girlz were one move away from a wardrobe malfunction!

She checked her Facebook wall and POF messages while Big Sean rapped "I Don't Fuck With You" from her Pioneer speakers.

Becky bobbed along to the irresistible lyrics and sang along: *I don't give a fuck, I don't give a fuck, I don't give a fuck* in her white girl valley voice.

Since she was in the Mil, she figured she might as well try to meet up with one of the other Ballerz she'd been chatting with online. A dude on POF who went by the username "Deep Pockets" had left her a couple of messages. His profile pics were stuntastic! Him with thousands of dollars fanned out in his hands. Him with diamond necklaces clenched between his teeth to show off his gold grille. One pic was of him leaning up against a Porsche truck on 28" Davins. He definitely looked the part, so she hit him up and told him she was in Milwaukee and would like to meet up.

He gave her directions to his chill spot on 15th and Locust and she punched it into her GPS. When she got there, she was skeptical about parking her car on the decrepit block. She knew she was in the hood, and while there were a few donks and SUVs on big boy rims out there, none of them shits compared to Becky's clean ass Benz on 24" white Santorinos.

It was the middle of the afternoon so there were people

posted up and down the block. There were two dudes sitting on the porch when she walked up to the house Deep Pockets gave her the address to.

"Dammmmn, shorty! You fine as a muthfucka," a nappy fro dude with a Bobby Brown gap in his front teeth said as her heels click-clacked up the sidewalk.

"Um, is... Deep Pockets here?" Becky asked. She tried not to scrunch up her nose at the peons sitting on the porch. They smelled like they hadn't bathed in *months!* Their B.O. over powered the weed smoke they were blowing in the air.

They both looked to be in their early 20's. Gap tooth wore a huge over-sized Black T that looked like a dress on him. Dirty, baggy jeans, and a pair of crusty black and gray Air Force Ones that were balled up like fists and crinkled at the toes. He also wore two big ass fake gold chains that looked copper, and a big earring in his ear that was so artificial it made Cubic Zirconium look like flawless ice!

His friend who was slobbering all over a blunt looked a little better in the face, but not by much. He was a brown skinned cat with big lips and natty, fuzzy dreads. He was tattooed from the neck down with a few on his face as well. He was very skinny and wore a white wife beater that had black and gray ash stains all over the front. His big fake Gucci belt held up some four sizes too big for him Levi's, and his knock off Jordan's had definitely seen better days. These dudes surely weren't up to her standards.

"Yeah mami. He in da crib. Go on in," the one with the dreads said.

She smiled politely and walked up the steps. They peaked under her dress as she passed them, and they whistled at the thick white flesh that made their mouths water.

When she opened the front door, more weed smoke followed by some loud Meek Mill blasting greeted her. A dude was sitting on a beat-up couch bagging up some dime bags of weed on the living room table.

"Hey shorty. I see you made it. Come in. I'm just finishin' up dis bidness," he said.

"Uhhh...are you...Deep Pockets?"

"Yeah babygirl. Who else is I gonna be?"

Becky raised a quizzical eyebrow and thought, ***clearly*** *not the motherfucker in the POF profile.* He was at least 80 pounds heavier, two shades darker, and tons of swagger *LESS* than who she thought was a nice candidate on the internet. *Damnit, I've been catfished!* Becky said to herself as she thought of an excuse to get out of there.

"Ummm, I see you're busy, so maybe I'll stop back another time," she said, backpedaling to the front door.

He stood up. "Hold up ma, I'm good. Come chill, we can smoke something and kick it. It's all good yo," he said as he walked over to her. Just then, the front door opened, and his two bum ass friends walked in.

"Yo, D.P., shorty strapped like a terrorist! Look at her big stupid booty," Gap tooth said, walking up on her and brushing his fingertips up and down her back. She shuddered and her skin crawled.

"Um, look guys. I uh, I only came to say hi. But I really need to be going," Becky told them.

"Nah, nah shorty. You said you wanted to kick it wit a nigga when we was on da phone, and dat's what we fittin' to do. Kick it!" Deep Pockets said as he walked up to her.

"Yeah ma. We don't bite. We some trill niggaz. Let's blaze some loud and do da damn thang," dreads said, twirling her long blonde hair around his finger.

"Mmmm, you smell good too," Gap tooth said, sniffing her neck. The three of them surrounded her and she tensed up, holding her breath. They stunk so bad, she thought she was gonna faint.

Weed smoke was blown in her face as three sets of hands began molesting her body, squeezing her butt, grabbing her breasts, stroking her arms. She could feel their semi-hard ons through their dirty jeans as they rubbed up against her.

"Guys look. I'm not—"

"You're not ***what***?" Deep Pockets interrupted, grabbing her face and squeezing her jaws together like some kind of fish. "You finna kick it wit us babygirl. You fine as a muthafucka. You know you white bitchez want that Mandingo dick," he laughed crudely.

"Yeah babygirl, y'all *love it!* And you about to get what you came foe... times three!" Gap-tooth said.

"No, I— "

WHACK! Someone slapped her booty. Hard! She tried to make a run for it, but they grabbed her and pushed her toward the couch. D.P. snatched her purse off her shoulder and threw it on the floor. They tore into her like some animals. Ripping off her panties, sticking fingers in her pussy, pulling her titties out and roughly twisting them.

"Ow!" she screeched at the harsh intrusion of fingers probing her dry vagina. She was getting her neck and titties bitten at the same time and it hurt like hell.

"Damn her pussy fat. Look at that pink muthafucka."

"Yo, I'm finna get me some of this white monkey."

They spun her around and smashed her face into the arm rest. D.P. was holding her wrists and had his knee in her back. Becky could hear a belt unbuckling and zippers being pulled down. *Oh no,* she cried to herself. They had her dress hiked up above her waist, her fat white ass was sticking out like a full moon.

You know I'm bad. I'm bad, you know it...

Everyone stopped and looked in the direction of Becky's big white D&G purse on the floor.

"What the fuck is that?" Deep Pockets said, and absentmindedly released her wrists. With his knee still in her back, he bent down and grabbed her purse.

"That's just my babysitter calling," Becky lied. She knew it was Rose. "Please, just let me answer it and tell her I'll be home late. We can party and I'll suck and fuck all of your black cocks reeeal good," she said, turning on the seduction. "I do love Mandingo cock. I can't wait to have all three of you inside of me. But let me just tell her, I'll be home late."

The dudes looked at each other while the Michael Jackson ringtone continued to play. The way she said "cock" like how the white hoes in porn do turned them on! But they were still a bit hesitant.

"Nah. You don't need to answer it. Just turn da muthafucka off," D.P. said, taking his knee out of her back.

"*BAD?* Who da fuck has MJ for a ring tone? Bitch, this ain't 1988," Gap tooth said, and they all laughed.

"Ok. Just let me turn it off then, please? I am like soooo ready for your Mandingo cocks," she said, turning them on with her Snow Bunny dialect. "Gosh, I swear she's just gonna keep calling and calling. I definitely have to turn it off, so we won't be rudely interrupted again," she said, holding out her hand.

The naive youngster handed Becky her purse and the tables turned *really* quick. Becky pulled her Glock 17 out of her purse. She cocked it and pointed it at the young men as she stood up. Tits still hanging out of the plunging neckline, she pulled her skirt down over her hips.

"You cocksuckers were gonna ***RAPE*** me?"

"Yo! Chill out ma, put that— "

"Shut up, you ugly gap tooth motherfucker you!" Becky yelled, pointing the gun in his face. He held his hands up nervously.

The dude with the bogus dreads dived for the loveseat where they kept a .40 Cal under the cushions. **Blockup!**

Blockup! Blockup! Becky popped him 3 times, shattering his ribcage and exploding his kidney. He screamed in pain and twitched on the floor.

She pointed the Glock at the other two while she tucked her breasts into her dress. Her pointy pink nipples were hard as they visibly pushed through the thin fabric. Becky's face and neck were flushed hot pink as she looked at the wide-eyed peasants huddled next to each other with their hands up.

"You low-life pieces of shit! You were about to rape me," she shouted, feeling volatile.

"Yo ma, look— "

Blockup! Becky shot gap tooth in his arm, sending him flying into the couch as blood sprayed on D.P.

"Aaargh! What chu shoot me for? Damn!" he yelled as he clutched the bullet wound.

"What motherfucker? You were about to violate me you sonuvabitch!" ***Blockup!*** She shot him in his other arm.

Violation hits close to home...

Becky shuddered and pulled the trigger again. ***Blockup!*** Half of his calf detached from his body. "Ahhhh!" he screamed in horrific agony.

She heard rustling behind her and saw the wounded dude with the dreads trying to claw underneath the couch cushions. She walked up on him swiftly and put the hot barrel of the Glock to his head. ***Blockup! Blockup!*** His skull cracked in half like an eggshell. The couch and floor were painted with blood, brains, and dreadlocks.

You know I'm Bad. I'm Bad, you know it...

Everyone turned to look at Becky's purse. Her phone was going off again and that seemed to trigger her, making ***her*** go off. Something inside of her snapped!

"You cocksucking sonuvabitch douchebag! *Bad* Bitches have Mike as a ringtone," she said, walking up on gap-tooth. ***Blockup! Blockup! Blockup! Blockup!*** "***I'm*** BAD motherfucker. Laugh now, you worthless piece of dog shit!" ***Blockup!*** She filled the now dead man's body up with hot lead, Swiss cheesing him up *real* good. His body slumped forward in slow motion like a tree being chopped down and crashed into the glass coffee table in front of the couch. Glass sprayed in the air like confetti, then rained down on gap tooth's back.

Deep Pockets had pissed on himself, witnessing the angry white girl kill his partners. She was the true definition of not judging a book by its cover. She was obviously "cray-cray," but something he couldn't quite put his finger on puzzled him about her. She was flushed red and breathing heavy. Beads of sweat dotted her forehead and lips. And her nipples... they were on swole something serious!

Deep Pockets silently prayed to Jesus, Allah, Budda, and whatever other God was known to man that she wouldn't take his life too.

"P-p-pleeeease babygirl. Don't– " ***Blockup!*** Becky shot at the wall behind him, missing his head by inches... on purpose.

"I ain't none of your 'babygirl' you dirty rapist cocksucker you," she snarled, penetrating his cowardly eyes with her tumultuous sky blues.

The fish in the pond is not the catch of the day.

"Who the fuck were you posing as on POF? Cuz that sure as hell wasn't your fat ugly ass," Becky said, waving the pistol in his face.

"Uhhh, da-dat was my cousin yo. H-h-he a pretty boy baller n-n-nigga," Deep Pockets stuttered. "He d-don't do da internet thang tho. So, I..."

"Pretended like ***YOU*** were him? You fronting ass degenerate turd. I oughta fucking kill you just for being a fucking poser."

If you have mercy, you will be forgiven.

"But you know what?... I'm gonna let you live."

Oh Thank you God. Allah. Jesus. Budda. Jehovah. Whoever up there answered my prayers, he silently praised to himself.

"Get naked!" Becky ordered.

"What?"

"Fucker, did I stutter? I ***said***, get ***NAKED!***" Becky bared her teeth like an angry tiger and put the Glock to his forehead. He did as he was told. ***REAL*** quick!

She could smell the stench of urine that had soaked his lower body. She was surprised he hadn't shit himself yet. His dead homies' bowels had been released as soon as their hearts stopped beating.

"Awww, look at the little wee-wee you got there," Becky taunted as she smiled at his shriveled-up dick that looked like a black turtle hiding in its shell. "Mandingo my ass! I've had French fries bigger than that thing," she laughed. "God, you're fat. You should work out more. All that gut hanging out everywhere. That's gross. Uh-uh, so *not* attractive. Ok, so here's what I'm gonna do fuckboy. I'm gonna teach you not to EVER, *EVER* even think about violating a woman ever again. You wanna be big and tough with your petty hustling ass? Huh? I'm gonna make sure you remember ***THIS*** white bitch. Now get in the kitchen douchebag," she barked.

Deep Pockets got up on a wobbly legs and tripped over his dead homie, falling into glass, cutting up his arms and hands. She kicked him in his ass, and he hurried to his feet, trotting to the kitchen and hoping she didn't change her mind about sparing his life.

"Sit," she said, pointing at an old stool sitting next to the kitchen table.

"Deep Pockets?! Ha! You're a joke. You're a bum! Your friends are bums. You're a phony," Becky spat as she looked around the kitchen. "Fake ass jewelry you clowns are wearing. Where'd you get that bullshit from, the Milwaukee Mall?" she said, rifling through kitchen drawers. "Bingo!" she pulled out a big steak knife.

Becky walked over to Deep Pockets slowly and seductively,

looking like his worst nightmare. It looked like she was working in a butcher shop. Her white dress was splattered with blood and pieces of internal organs. She held a big knife in her hands that had a sharp 8-inch blade gleaming from the black handle. She sat her Glock on the stove and held the knife up to eye level.

The ball's in your court...

She looked down at his feet. “I thought I said get naked motherfucker. That means **EVERYTHING!** Take your goddamn socks off before I go ISIS in this bitch.”

He did so obediently, and she snatched them out of his hands and draped them over her shoulder. Becky put the tip of the knife under his chin as she bent down and put her nose against his. Her titties dangled like two big exotic pieces of forbidden fruit. Even with death at his front door, he still eyed her amazing cleavage.

“Nice, aren't they?” Becky said as she lightly ran the tip of the knife along his jawline. He swallowed the lump in his throat and nodded. Tears welled up in his eyes.

“Go ahead... touch ‘em,” she whispered. He didn’t move. She added pressure to the knife until it broke skin and a drop of blood dripped from his cheek. “Touch them!” she ordered. His hands flew up and caressed her magnificent breasts.

“Oooh yeah,” Becky moaned. “Ya see. I get off on rough shit. Pain is my thing. I damn near orgasmed after I shot your peon friends. Look at how wet I am,” she hiked the hem of her dress up around her hips. Sure, as shit stinks, the bitch’s bald pink pussy was glistening with thick strands of pussy juice. Deep Pockets couldn't believe it!

“Yeah, I like a little violence,” she laughed. “Maybe I’m sick in the head, who knows,” she shrugged and smiled. “But it has to be on *my* terms. You tried to take advantage of me because you thought I was some weak little white bitch, right? Yeah, that's what your dumb ass thought. But you slipped up when you gave me my purse. Didn't think little miss snow bunny was packing did ya? Now look. Your homeboys are dead. And you're..." Becky grabbed his nut sack and quick as a flash of lightning, she cut off his testicles in one fluid swoop of the knife. "Castrated!" She said as his screams sounded like 1,000 horror movies playing at once. He crumpled to the floor, holding the bloody area where his nuts *USED* to be.

Becky grabbed one of his socks off her shoulder and put his hairy, severed testicles in it. Then she tied the top of the sock in a knot and just like that went from smooth to psycho.

"You lousy scumbag motherfucker you," she yelled, pummeling him with the sock that had his balls in it. He kept one hand on his crotch while using the other arm to try and shield himself from Becky's wrath. "I can't believe you cock-suckers were gonna take advantage of me" she screamed.

"You worthless...piece...of shit!" With each word she spat, she swung the sock of balls. It made a disturbing sound as it connected with his face, neck, chest, and back. Becky beat him over and over with it like she was playing Whack-a-Mole. She went from spewing obscenities to spitting the Big Sean lyrics that were still in her head.

"You little stupid ass bitch, you little dumb ass bitch. I got a million trillion things I'd rather fuckin' do, than to be fuckin' with you!" He rolled around the floor and she stood over him, raising the sock of balls high and bringing it down hard. She was full of rage, anger, and felt betrayed, even though she didn't know them clowns.

"I'm gonna fix your little red wagon, you fake ass mother-fucker you!" Becky screamed in his face loudly.

"You will never...ever...try to rape...another...woman...again! Do...you...understand me?"

"YEEES! Yes! Please," He screamed and cried.

"I guess you need a **BAD BITCH** to come around and make it up. I guess drama makes for the best content, everything got a bad side even a conscience," she rapped/yelled and swung the sock like a baseball bat. ***PLAK!*** It caught him across the mouth in the middle of him screaming and knocked a tooth down his throat. Blood filled his mouth like a glass of red wine.

Becky seemed possessed. She was in a violent zone that she'd never encountered before. And there was no denying it, she was turned on like a motherfucker! Her nipples were burning hot and hard as diamonds. Her vagina secretions ran down her legs as if her pussy was crying streams of joy. She beat Deep Pockets vehemently with his own testicles and in a damn sock!

The ball's in your court.

She smiled an evil grin at the horoscope entendre. *It sure is*, she thought to herself.

Finally, when her arms got sore and the sock was bloodied all the way through, she dropped it on his flailing body as he rocked back and forth on the dirty linoleum floor. Breathing heavily, she flung her sweaty blonde hair out of her eyes and looked down at him. "Look at me motherfucker," she sneered and kicked him in his back with her high heel.

"You gonna tell the police who did this to you?... and them?" she pointed towards the living room. He shook his head sobbing. Becky raised the bloody knife. "What, you piece of shit?"

"No, no... I won't say a word. I swear to God," he pleaded.

"Good boy. Because if you breathe a word of this, I'll come back for you and finish the job. You're lucky I didn't cut your fucking dick off you incompetent pile of slime. But you could have just gotten another one of those. Anything woulda been an upgrade from that lousy thing you got between your legs," she laughed. "So no, I didn't want that. They don't make prosthetic balls though, so you're out of luck on the functioning testes tip. Plus, I did the world a favor. I don't know if you already have kids or not, but you sure as ***fuck*** won't be able to impregnate any chick dumb enough to let you touch her with your evil ass rapist sperm, you prick! So be very grateful. Punk ass motherfucker, you could've ended up like your pee-on friends in there," Becky said and grabbed the Glock off the stove.

"Get on your stomach," she ordered him. He painfully rolled over and squeezed his eyes shut. Tears fell like rain on the kitchen floor while he anticipated a bullet to the back of the head. **WHACK!** Becky slapped his butt cheek.

"You've got a FAT ass too Deep Pockets. A fat ***lard*** one. Not fat and pretty like mine though," she said and spread one of his cheeks to the side. "Fat disgusting motherfucker!" Becky rammed the Glock in his asshole. He screamed a loud piercing shrill that could've woke the dead.

"How does that feel you dirty sonuvabitch? Huh? Doesn't feel good to be violated does it?" Becky said, fucking his asshole with the Glock. She shoved it in and out as fast and hard as she could. He passed out from the pain and shitted on himself. Well, he shitted on the gun actually.

Becky pulled the shitty gun out of his rectum and wiped it off on his skin, writing RAPIST with his feces on his back.

BLOCKUP! She put a bullet in his right buttock. "Since you wanna be a rapist asshole, I just gave you a new hole in your *ASS.* You fucking asshole!"

Becky grabbed a dish towel off the sink and dampened it. Then she grabbed an empty garbage bag out of one of the cabinets. She began wiping down everything that she touched, and she threw the gun and knife into the garbage bag.

She left the kitchen and gathered up the bums' blunt roaches and other paraphernalia with the tip of her fingers, putting them in the garbage bag as well. She grabbed her purse and looked down at her dress. A $2500 Dolce & Gabbana piece ruined! She decided to empty the dead men's pockets and take their bags of weed to compensate her for ruining her dress.

They only had $1700 total between the three of them and about a pound and a half all in dime bags, but she threw it all into the garbage bag too.

She did one more quick walk through, making sure she wiped off all of her prints. Even though they weren't in the system, she didn't wanna take any chances. Who knows who else she'd have to "body" in the future, so she was being cautious.

She left the trap house quickly. No one on the block didn't really seem to pay her any attention as she hurriedly hopped into her Benz with the big black trash bag. Used to hearing gunshots ring out in the hood was as common as seeing the sunshine to them. Luckily for Becky, they didn't see shit nor hear shit. At least, that's what they'd tell the police when they showed up in an hour. She knew Deep Pockets wouldn't say a word of who did it. Too afraid and embarrassed, he'd keep his fat mouth shut and save face. Plus, he didn't know who she really was anyway. She took her POF profile down instantly, just to be on the safe side.

Before Becky got on the highway to make the two-hour trip back to Appleton, she had to pull over in a McDonald's parking lot and masturbate furiously. The violent images of the murder kept playing before her eyes over and over while she drove, making her extremely horny. So, she parked the Benz and rubbed one out behind the tinted windows. She moaned and thrashed about in the driver's seat as she humped her hand.

When she got home, she burned the dress and told Britney all about what went down. Her little sister stared in wide-eyed amazement as she listened to Becky give her the detailed play by play of her first ever murder. Just telling the story got Becky riled up again and she had to excuse herself to her master bedroom where her trusty vibrator "Batman" went to work on her pussy until the batteries died.

11

BRITNEY

Britney was driving in her purple Ford Fusion SE, a gift from Rose because she was doing so well in her kick-boxing and Martial Arts classes.

Ever since they propositioned her with the offer to sell exclusive strains of Kush, she got down immediately. The money was POURING in. Everybody and they mama was hitting Britney up for them $200 ounces of flame. They were selling like hotcakes! All the other muthafuckas who previously sold weed, now couldn't even get a quarter zip off. Something one of her best custy's Eric was telling her as he sat in the passenger's seat.

"Brit, you know we go way back. That's why I'm telling you this. The pot pushers are really starting to talk. There's been some ramblings bout snitching you out to the po-po," Eric said as he admired the fat fluffy bag with 4 ounces of Banana Blaze in it.

"I even got wind that some of them were planning on robbing you."

"Oh yeah? Who is that?" Britney asked while she counted the $800 cash Eric gave her.

"Fucking Greg Wombek and Todd Borland," he said, putting his nose in the bag and smelling the delightful marijuana aroma.

"Those crappy weed selling douchebags? Hmpf! Ok. Well, thanks for letting me know Eric. You're an awesome friend."

"No prob Brit. I wouldn't want anything to happen to you. This weed, at these prices, is the best thing that's ever happened to me!" he said enthusiastically.

Britney nodded and bid him farewell. As she drove off, she began to think. She was moving hella Kush, so it was only natural that there'd be ***some*** kind of jealously. But she didn't think other dealers would drop dime on her or try to rob her. Rose and Becky had schooled her on the rules to the game and gave her Drug Dealing 101. But she didn't think any of that would apply in Suburban Appleton.

Plus, after it was widely speculated that she was behind the decapitation of Amber's dog, all the high school and college kids were scared of her and looked at Britney in a new light. That was some mob shit, and it garnered a new level of respect from her peers. But it seemed as if that wasn't good enough. A new BOLDER demonstration would have to be done to make those scheming bastards think twice about plotting on her.

She thought back to Becky's confession from a few days ago. *Murder.* Two Men. Wow, she knew her sister wasn't one to fuck with, but she didn't know she had it in her like ***that.*** But what other choice did she have? They tried to rape her, and when she got out of the situation, one of them reached for a gun. "Kill or be killed," Rose told them once. "If you hesitate for even a half a second... you could die."

Ever since she looked Becky in her eyes, listening to her disclose how it's "really no big thing to kill a person." Britney wondered if she could ever do it herself. God knew she'd been crying herself to sleep over the whole Deemontay betrayal since it happened. And she sure as hell wanted to kill his dog ass!

Swiping through pics in her phone of him and her hugged up made her bawl her pretty little eyes out. “How could you?” she’d cry as tears and snot ran down her face.

Now with the new information Eric gave her, feeling betrayed and violated by people wanting to do her harm, murderous rage bubbled up inside her. She gripped the steering wheel until she thought her knuckles would break. “Motherfuckers won't ***ever*** play me again,” she sneered as she plotted her own retaliation.

12

GG

GG had been putting A LOT of highway miles on her peach Lexus LS the past couple of weeks. Making the two-hour drive from Milwaukee to Appleton gave her plenty of time to think and strengthen her plot on bringing down Bucky and Pill Mobb.

Ever since the Stripclub Capers went down, the ones that got hit in the bigger cities like Milwaukee, Madison, and Green Bay were choosing to go on a hiatus. The clubs in the smaller cities couldn't afford a break, so they quickly made the necessary repairs and were back open for business in no time. With all the disgruntled customers who were "regulars" at the big establishments not having anywhere to go to get their jolly's off, the lesser known clubs who re-opened saw a tremendous increase in business.

GG spoke to the owner of Beansnappers and told him if he REALLY wanted to see an influx in customers, his best bet would be to add a "chocolate" main attraction to spice up the usually vanilla atmosphere. Many white men had a secret fetish for sistaz and with her skill set and moves, he could easily re-coup the money he lost from having to close shop and fix the damages done to his club.

She auditioned for him and showed him why they called her "Gushy."

As soon as the waterfall trick was done, he had the club manager put her name on the marquee in big bold letters. "You are now our featured headlining dancer," he told her.

The promotion they put behind her was a massive campaign to drum up business. It included several paid radio slots with her saying, "It's been a drought on adult entertainment. But things are about to get wet. *Gussssh.*" They also put a half page ad in the local newspapers in all of the surrounding cities with a picture of GG in a barely-there bikini doing the splits in front of a waterfall. And it was all a great investment.

Her first night was on a Friday, and with the debut of some new moves she'd been practicing, her performance was an instant success. She made $18,000 that night. As word of mouth spread, the blitz of social media posts, messages, and tweets practically blew up the internet overnight about the hottest stripper in the country.

So when Saturday came around, Beansnappers had been filled to capacity with a mile-long line in the parking lot full of eager men and a few women waiting to get a glimpse of Gushy's set. Doctors, lawyers, politicians, judges, and athletes alike...all white, the high society wealthy poured in. Saturday was also when Bucky and his crew made their first appearance to check her out in action. They showed up loud and boisterous. "Pill Mobb in the motherfucking building!" Bucky yelled, looking twenty years late in the fashion department with his 90's hip-hop attire. Baggy jeans, a football Jersey that hung to his knees, and Jordan Flight 23 sneakers. His flunky white boy click surrounded him with similar attire. GG was giving a lap dance when she locked eyes with Bucky from across the room. She gave him the "I'll be done in one minute" finger while he stood as still as a statue with a bottle of Hennessey in his hands.

After the dance, she collected her tips and made her way over to Bucky. The twist in her hips was so erotic, it made his whole crew ogle with their mouths dropped. The only thing she wore was a white G-string. Her breasts were exposed and bounced freely like two big brown water balloons as she walked.

"Hey daddy..." she said, sauntering up to him. "Remember me?" she put a hand on her poked out hip.

"Fuck yeah I do! I was just telling my niggaz about you," Bucky said.

GG raised an eyebrow. "Your niggaz huh?" she questioned, thinking, *does this white dude know he is NOT black?* "Soooo, what was you saying daddy?" she said, rubbing up and down his arm.

"Uh, ummm. Just how fly you were," he stuttered and blushed.

GG looked at all nine of the white boys. They all looked like hillbilly rednecks. But they were flossing the best jewels. Diamond bracelets and rings. Platinum chains, gold links, all with iced out pieces on them. Diamond studded earrings. A few of them smiled and showed their snatch-out diamond grilles.

GG was shining like moonlight on the ocean. Her shimmery coconut body glitter glazed her skin from neck to toe. And because of her chocolaty hue, the fluorescent lights in Beansnappers made her look like an exotic work of art that radiated from every angle.

"So, I guess y'all came to see the show huh?" GG asked. They all nodded. She rolled her nipples between her thumb and forefinger until they hardened. "Well, I'm about to go on in a few minutes so get ready for the event of your life," she said and turned to go. "Oh yeah, one more thing," she turned to Bucky and grabbed the back of his head, bringing it down to her left breast. "Bite it! Suck it, baby. Mmmm, be my good luck charm tonight," she ordered as she smothered his face in her mammary glands, trying to cram that big muthafucka down his throat.

He chewed on that black nipple like it was bubblegum as she moaned and egged him on. "Yeah, that's it my nigga. Do it to a bad bitch like she likes," GG said while staring into his homies' eyes. After she had enough, she grabbed his hand and shoved it in her G-string and waterfalled him. Then she pulled his hand out and shoved his fingers into one of his boys' mouth, who eagerly sucked GG's cream off Bucky's fingers.

GG pulled Bucky off her tit, kissed him sensually on the lips, and sashayed away. Booty cheeks wobble-dee wobbling with each step she took. Pill Mobb stood in awe at the hot black Goddess that was unlike anything they'd ever seen.

For her show, there was a beautiful cascading waterfall projected on the wall behind her. And because of the multiple projectors mounted on the ceiling and walls, they were able to make it look like a stream of water was running down the front and sides of the stage as well.

The lights dimmed and the DJ introduced Gushy. She strolled out to Kelly Rowland's hit song "Motivation."

Go, go, go oh lover, don't you dare slow down

Go longer, you can last more rounds.

GG wore a white see-thru lace kimono with her white G-string bikini underneath. On her feet were white thigh-high suede "fuck me boots."

Push harder, you're almost there now. So go lover, make mama proud

She sensually worked the intricate pole that was not your average stripper prop. This was a specially made black light pole that ran from the ceiling to the floor. It had neon globules floating up and down inside of it; making it look like a giant Lava lamp.

GG's athletic moves were admired as piece by piece she peeled off articles of clothing. She was upside down and snaking down the pole. She was suspended in mid-air and swinging around dozens of times, holding on to the pole by only her legs. She did a front flip while in the upside-down splits position and caught the pole with one hand at the top and slid down it in a ringlet motion as if her body were a curly fry. The stage was showered with money and roses. And it actually looked like they were floating in water. Bucky bogarted his way to the front of the stage. A five-inch stack of hundreds was in his hands. GG got on her knees and twerked for him. Bouncing her big buttocks up and down while looking back over her shoulder at him. He admired the huge camel toe that looked more like a moose mouth in her tiny white G-string. He slapped her ass with hundred-dollar bills lustfully. His boys made it rain a few hundreds themselves. Pill Mobb didn't believe in tipping with one's. Franklins were more ***their*** style!

And when we're done, I don't wanna feel my legs

And when we're done I just wanna feel your hands all over me baby

GG crawled on all fours like a Panther back to the pole. She stopped, did a handstand, and humped the air facing the crowd. Her hair dragged across the stage as she spread her legs in a wide Y. She flexed her pussy and sucked the G-string fabric INTO her vagina. It disappeared like a magic trick. You could still see the string around her waist, but the rest? Gone! Her fat black pussy sparkled under the luminating lights. Every white man in Beansnappers had a hard on. But they hadn't seen *NOTHING* yet.

GG wrapped her legs around the pole and flipped herself

up as she crawled toward the ceiling. No one could see her unfastening the latch that held the pole in place at the top. She slid down like a fireman and pulled her G-string off completely. She was now fully nude.

Baby I'm a be your motivation go, go, go, go

Motivation. Go, go, go, go.

She mouthed the words to the song and turned her back to the crowd. By now, men were standing on the bar and tables, even hoisted up on other patrons shoulders gazing at the Gushy show. The waterfall projecting on the wall behind her parted like the Red Sea so that she could be the center of attention. It was as if the descending stream had separated itself to make room for the Gushy Goddess.

Uh, girl I turn that thing into a rainforest

Rain on my head, call that brainstorming.

GG put her hands on top of her head and made her booty cheeks clap. The loud smacking of her buttocks could be heard over the music and it sounded like a thunderstorm. That was because her pussy was so wet and gushy, her secretions ran down the crack of her ass so when those cheeks clapped together, the moistness just made the claps resonate and echo louder. The people in the club joined in and clapped along with her butt cheeks.

GG stood up straight, sandwiching the pole between her ass cheeks as she began spasming her buttocks in wide fluid movements. They flexed and clapped, making it look like her ass was an Eagle flapping its large wings. They clapped against the lava lamp pole and men drooled on themselves like babies.

I won't let ya get up out the game

No, so go lover, gon' and make me rain.

When Kelly Rowland hit that last note, GG's ass cheeks clamped down on the pole like the jaws of life. She dropped to her hands and knees, detaching the pole from the ceiling.

"Holy shit!"

"What the fuck?!"

"Whoa!"

To the crowd, it looked like her ass had ripped the stripper pole out of the floor and ceiling.

GG laid on her stomach with the pole still in her ass crack and did the splits. She looked over her shoulder as she began tossing the pole in the air with her ass like marching bands do a baton. She flexed her glutes and made it hurdle the pole 3 feet in the air then catch it between her cheeks before it'd hit her back. She did this 24 times to show them just how talented she was. Just in case anyone thought her trick was a fluke that could only be thrown in the air once or twice, she proved them wrong. Like nah, she went hard 24/7. Hence the number "24."

After the 24th catch, she put her legs together while still on her stomach and made her cheeks clap; the pole still resting in her crack. She wiggled around the floor, cumming like crazy and lubing up the pole. Because it was technically a black light, her thick streams of cum could visibly be seen as it made the pole look like white splatters of paint was all over it.

When the song ended, GG hurdled the pole out with a forceful thrust of her ass, making it roll to the side of the stage. Then she sat up and cocked her legs wide for the audience to see.

When she threw her head back, the waterfall projection returned in full, flanking her now as she contracted her pussy muscles and did the waterfall trick, but making the cum gush out in an arcing stream. It looked like how when a man pees. But everyone knew it wasn't piss. It was Gushy... gushing on stage. Squirting like crazy!

So much money rained on the stage, it looked like confetti on New Year's Eve in Times Square! The place went fucking bananas. They roared with applause, praise, and cheers. It was so loud; people couldn't even hear the fire marshals on their bullhorns trying to clear the place out. With the mile-long line outside, someone dropped dime, saying it was most likely way over capacity inside. And it was. So they were there to eliminate the safety hazard.

GG kept a duffle bag near the stage just to put her tips and other gifts in after her set. After she swept the stage clean, she changed and knew Bucky would be waiting for her. Before he could even speak, she put a finger to his lips.

"Let's go daddy. *Now!*" she dragged him by the arm toward the back exit. "Text your boys and tell them to drive your whip. ***You*** will be taking me to your place," she instructed, tossing him the keys to her Lexus.

She sat in the passenger seat with the duffle bag, listening to Rick Ross' "Rich Forever." She took inventory of the gifts people threw on stage: roses, earrings, cruise tickets, stuffed animals, and exotic chocolates. Then she counted up her cash to another successful night, almost 60 geez.

Been winning so many years

And the future is bright now it's very clear.

When they got to his condo, she sucked him off as soon as they got inside. Giving him the blow job of his life in the foyer because she knew he'd cum quick if they fucked first. But with his first nut out of the way, she could pussy whip him like she needed to.

"Damn boy, yo nut taste goooood," she said, licking his dick head clean until he couldn't take it.

"Fuck! Alright alright already! Gosh," he yelled, snatching his dick out of her hand and leaning against the wall. "Fucking ay! You're an animal baby. That was the best BJ I've *ever* had."

GG smiled and got off her knees. She smacked her lips and walked to the living room. "Nice place ya got here daddy. I hope you got some vodka for me, cuz you know I only *DO* white," she said seductively.

He smiled, his big Bugs Bunny teeth on display. “Yeah, some of my niggas drink that shit so I keep some around. But you know me, I only do ***brown***,” he said, walking up on her and squeezing her fat ass.

“Mmmm, don't I know it daddy. And after you do ***THIS*** brown, you'll never want anything else in yo life,” GG said.

“Is that right?”

“Mmhm. Once you go black... you don't go back,” she smiled and caressed his dick through his pants. He broke away from her because he wasn't ready for round two yet, so he walked over to the liquor cabinet.

“I’ve got Grey Goose, Ciroc, Belvedere, Abso—”

“Give me that Grey Goose baby. Da goose gets me loose,” GG said and giggled naughtily.

“You want ice with that?” he asked, sounding like a bartender.

“Nah, I'm from the hood, we drink straight from the bottles yo.”

“Hell yeah! That's what’s up,” he said happily, as he brought a full bottle for her and a bottle of Hen for himself back to the living room.

“My nigga,” she said, accepting the Grey Goose bottle from him. They sat on his expensive suede furniture and chopped it up. She unzipped her boots and got comfortable. Bucky popped a few pills and offered her some, but she declined. She lit up a blunt she had in her purse instead. They vibed out to some Stunna 4 Vegas for a half an hour before she suggested they take a shower together.

Bucky wasn’t buff, but he had a naturally athletic build. He was skinny with a slight six pack. His skin was white as notebook paper with freckles ALL OVER. He had an average six-inch penis that curved slightly to the right. It wasn't too small, and it wasn't too big. For most women, it was actually “just right.”

They soaped each other up with Armani Code body wash in his marble and glass steam shower. Bucky began feeling the euphoric effects of the pills he popped, making him extremely sensitive to touch and tingle all over. GG played into this by lightly brushing up against his skin with the loofa like it was a feather.

"Damn my nigga, you got a sexy ass cock," she said, stroking his ego and making him feel like something he was not.

"You like that don't cha baby?" he asked, playing with her nipples.

"Mmhm. Ain't nothing better than white cock... my nigga," she whispered in his ear, then licked his earlobe with the tip of her tongue.

"Yeah. And nothing is better than black cunt," he said, dropping to his knees. GG propped one foot on the edge of the tub to allow him access to her sweet waterfall. "God, you're pinker than bubblegum," he said, as he spread her vulva with his fingers and began licking her insides.

GG looked down at him. Water sprayed on his back as his redhead bobbed up and down, sucking her pussy like it was a juicy orange peel. She had to admit, *the man sure could eat some pussy. For real for real.*

He flicked his tongue across her engorged clitoris and used it like a jackhammer. She grabbed his big ears and humped his mouth ferociously until she came. He reached under her and thrust a wet finger inside her butthole and she orgasmed again! Shaking so wildly, she slipped and brought him down with her as she fell under the streaming shower head. They both laughed as she rolled him onto his back and mounted him.

"Oooh Bucky," she moaned as she slid his curvy red banana dick inside of her box. Bucky had never felt a hotter, tighter pussy in his life. He didn't know she kept her walls contracted on purpose. She wasn't naturally that tight. But she wasn't no "hallway" either.

"Holy motherfucking *FUCK*, Gushy," he screeched.

"What daddy?" she cooed.

"Fuck, you feel good," he said, grabbing her wide fleshy hips. When he was in her to the hilt, she hovered over him and began riding him like a stallion. He leaned forward and took her chocolate nipples into his mouth and sucked hungrily on them.

"Oh yessssss," she moaned as her hips did figure 8's on his dick. Her feet were flat in the tub, so she was able to push herself up using her legs until only his head was inside of her. They both looked down at his exposed dick until she made it disappear into her molten hot womb. Up, down, up, down, up, down, she worked his dick just like she worked a stripper pole; skillfully and pulling out all the stops.

GG threw her legs on top of his shoulders and leaned back on the palms of her hands as water sprayed down on her chest and stomach. She humped up and down, side to side, while he gritted his teeth and palmed the sides of her ass. The sound of wet skin echoed in the glass shower stall, mingling with the running water. Steam rose up and intensified the smell of their sex in the air.

Bucky had no rhythm and was throwing her groove off, so she told him to be still because she couldn't handle all of his dick.

"Let me steer this ride daddy. You're... oh, you're too big for me," she lied. He stopped moving and let her grind against his pelvis until she orgasmed. He thought more liquid was coming out of her vagina than there was shooting out of the shower! After her convulsions subsided, she stood up against the marble wall panting for breath.

"Fuck me good and hard daddy. Show me how Pill Mobb gets down," she said, holding one leg up and putting it behind her ear. Bucky held the base of his violently red dick and rubbed the head of it up and down her clit piercing. The blue veins in his cock throbbed and pulsated, looking like tiny worms beneath his skin. He thrusted into her creamy black pie as he palmed her calf and held it behind her head. Her pretty toes brushed against the misty marble wall as she did Kegels on his penis, squeezing it tightly with each thrust.

"Oooh...nigga... my...nigga...damn...dis, white dick...is...so...good," she moaned. GG knew calling him a "nigga" would pump up his ego and make his delusional mind really think he was a "brotha."

Bucky sucked on her neck and pounded into her passionately. His balls slapped her like a speed bag. **Pap! Pap! Pap! Pap!** "Fuck yeah. Take this white cock bitch. Take it!"

"Oh yes! Give it to me. Fuck me just like that Bucky. Gimme that huge King Kong cock daddy," she screamed. GG didn't even use the word "cock;" white bitches did that shit. But she knew hearing it form a sista would turn him up. So, she over-exaggerated her dirty talk and made it sound authentic.

Her pussy piercing rubbed against his dick with each stroke and made his bones shiver.

The curve in his dick was the perfect angle to hit her G-spot and she gushed all over his dick. Bucky looked down at himself going in and out of her. He couldn't believe his eyes. It looked like he stuck his dick in a bucket of ice cream! His joint was slathered in thick white custard. That shit blew his *mind.*

GG did what he did to her earlier; she wrapped a hand around his backside and stuck a finger in his bootyhole. He tensed up and stopped pumping. But she knew white people were freaky muthafuckaz who loved "assplay." Bucky clenched his cheeks together tightly and made an O with his mouth. His eyes rolled to the back of his head and GG smiled. She stuck her tongue in his open mouth and humped his dick while driving her finger in and out of his ass.

He followed her cue and began thrusting again. He almost

slipped and lost his balance, so GG brought her leg down and wrapped them both around his waist. He may have been slim, but he was strong. He held her up and showed her that he could handle her thickness. And despite having absolutely no rhythm at all, she thought he was a half-way decent fuck.

"Damn, nigga. You's...a...*beast,*" GG panted as he palmed her ass cheeks and fucked her relentlessly.

"You goddamn right! I told your ass I was gonna give you good cock in your hot black pussy. Didn't I? Didn't I?"

"Yes! Hell yes you did!" GG shouted.

He slid out of her and bent her over. GG held the tub's faucet and tooted her fat ass in the air. Bucky dropped to his knees and tongue fucked her bootyhole.

"Oh Bucky! Shit, nigga shit!" she screamed. *He's really into ass-play I see*, GG thought to herself as he made her squirm in delight.

"Mmmm that feels good. Eat that black ass. Yeah nigga, slurp that big muthafucka," she coaxed him. He tossed her salad like a pro. Sucking her ass and pussy at the same time until she squirted all over the place.

"Ahhhhh shiiiiit!" she yelled.

He got behind her and rammed his dick into her sopping wet pussy, fucking her doggystyle. Water rained down over her back as he slapped her ass cheeks and fucked her like a power drill.

GG made her booty clap like it did on the lava lamp pole at Beansnappers and he couldn't believe his eyes. It flapped like waves in the ocean, moving in directions he'd never seen before!

Used to pulling white girls' hair during sex, he grabbed GG's and yanked her head back hard! That forced water to shoot in her face and down her throat. She choked and gagged on a mouthful as it also ran up her nose.

"Oops, my bad," he said, realizing he got a bit carried away. She recovered quickly after catching her breath and began backing that ass up, meeting him halfway. **WHACK! WHACK!** He spanked her ass as his orgasm bubbled inside.

GG knew he was close, so she reached down and grabbed his balls. He slid in to the hilt and stopped. His pubes rested on her ass while she caressed his balls and grinded against him. He didn't have to move. Her pussy muscles became like a fist, opening and closing tightly around his shaft. Milking him and jerking him off with warm wet walls that felt like paradise.

He threw his head back and hit Mariah Carey high notes as he busted his nut. Her pussy pumped him dry and covered him in her own gush of slimy cum in the process. Bucky drooled on her back and turned red as a stoplight as he busted the nut of his life! He shook and bucked and thrashed deep inside of her while she continued to squeeze every drop of cum out of his tender balls.

By the time she was done with him, they had fucked in every room in his condo. GG stroked his ego and puffed him up until he felt like he was ***THAT*** nigga. Her game was so smooth, she had the mogs nose wide open on the first night. He was wasted off his ass and pillow talking like a muthafucka. After a couple of more "fuck-a-thons," she knew she'd have all the information she would need. *This shit is a cake walk,* she boasted to herself when she snuggled up on his chest by the fireplace. She looked in his eyes and could tell he was in love already. Some women could make a man sprung in no time, and GG was one of those bitches. The baddest of the baddest. A Boss bitch with a cold heart that thrived on money and moving up in the world. Yeah, GG was a Bad Bee who just drizzled honey all over her future mark. Soon, he'd get stung like a motherfucker.

. . .

Bzzzzzzz.

There are reasons behind every action. One's past might be a current reflection or a mandatory distraction...

13

LYZA

The day before the Big Thangs Poppin' Party was to be held at the Sybaris pool suites, GG texted T-dub and told him a female friend of hers was throwing the BTP party and she said he could invite three people. GG told him if he wanted to see her "new moves," he and two of his guys could come through. Since he hadn't seen her in a minute, he said he would.

When T-dub showed up to the Chalet swimming pool suite with two of his niggaz Green Mans and Deucey, Lyza--now going by the name Tamika--answered the door. The first thing T-dub noticed was her beautiful eyes. They were the color of pecans and sparkled like diamonds. The second thing he noticed was the huge "T" tattooed on the side of her neck. She'd later say it was the initial for her name, but really it stood for Tryfe.

"What's good? Who are you?" She asked, looking him over from head to toe. He was rocking a double-breasted maroon Croc-skin coat with Luxe silk pajamas underneath. Black Maison Martin Margiela leather slippers were on his feet, and he had on more ice than a freezer.

He checked her out too. She wore skintight gray leather pants that showed her thick thighs and dangerous curves. A black Donna Karen silk blouse that showed off her toned midriff barely covered her swollen breasts. Her black open toe Stella McCartneys made her usual 5'3" frame stand 5 feet 7 inches tall. Diamond hoop earrings hung from her ears and she had a pink diamond ring in her nose.

Lyza had a flawless blemish-free graham cracker complexion that was smooth as butter. Her lips were full and glossy pink. T-dub could smell her enticing perfume, which was Michael Kors' *Rose Radiant Gold*. The sista was drop dead gorgeous to him.

"I'm T-dub," he said, licking his lips. "Gushy said I could come thru wit two of my peeps."

Lyza nodded her head. "Yeah, ok. That'll be $500...each," she said, holding out her hand.

"What? She ain't say nothin' bout no cover charge. I thought this was a free ya dig?" T-dub said.

"Baby, ain't *NOTHIN'* in life free. This is the Big Thangs Poppin' party. Which means, shit finna be jumpin' in this bitch. Only exclusive V.I.P. muthafuckas is welcome in here. Obviously if Gushy invited ya, you ain't no bum ass nigga. And from the looks of you, I can tell you're doing quite well for yourself, with your fly ass," she smiled. "But if you don't wanna pay the $500 door charge, then you can hit it my dude. Bye Felicia!" she said all business.

T-dub ***liked*** her. She was pretty but street. Direct and real. The bitch had mad swag and was one of the finest redbones he'd ever seen.

"Ok, ok. I can dig it ma," he said, peeling off five Franklins from his knot. His boys did the same and Lyza stepped aside and let them in.

"Yo, what's your name babygirl?" T-dub asked.

"Tamika," she said and showed him a set of pretty white teeth.

The BTP was really a faux party that GG threw together to get T-dub and Lyza in the same room. Him and his boys were the only males there. The rest of the attendees were all women. Fifteen in all. And every last one of them were cold blooded killers. Tryfe Lyfe Bitchez were in the building, posing as average chicks.

The Sybaris was a luxury hotel suite that was as close to paradise as one can get. The Chalet suite was a huge multi-level room with a tropical waterfall and a 22 foot heated swimming pool that had a waterslide running from the upstairs bedroom loft to the huge pool on the first floor.

Everyone was in "lounge wear," so there were silk teddies, sexy lingerie with garters and heels, and many wore the complementary terry cloth spa robes, which were big and fluffy like cotton candy.

There was an array of exotic foods on a table filled with lobster, shrimp, caviar, chocolate covered strawberries, grapes, bananas, hot wings, and buttery croissants. There was a champagne pyramid with dozens of champagne flutes full of Moet stacked four feet high in the shape of a pyramid. There was also a silver platter full of pre-rolled blunts of Gorilla Glue#4 for the guests to help themselves to, which they did.

The suite was a smoke-filled factory. Clouds were blown in the air while a female DJ played the hottest new Hip hop and R&B tunes from her laptop in a makeshift booth in the corner. Nadia, the 6'3" Russian, walked around in a pink bathing suit and 6-inch Giueseppe Zanotti

Heels, passing out daiquiris and Patron shots. Her legs went on for miles! And her ass cheeks were round and firm. They didn't move much when she walked because her rigorous workouts kept them compact. But they still looked good as a muthafucka!

GG and Starburst, a half-Chinese half-Cuban stripper from THOT Gang, were the main entertainment. They had a pole setup in front of the fireplace, and they worked it simultaneously for the group of women and T-dub and his boys.

Lyza purposely lounged on a cream sofa by the sliding patio doors all by herself. She was puffing on a blunt and eating grapes when T-dub walked over to her during the stripper's intermission.

"What's good Tamika? I see you getting chopped by yo dammy," T-dub said.

"Yeah. I'm kind of a loner. But you can hit it a couple of times if you want."

"Hit what?" T-dub said with a mischievous smile.

"Boy, sit down," she said, extending the blunt to him. "I see you got jokes."

He laughed and sat next to her. They talked and smoked and fed each other grapes. She was good at making a person feel like they'd known her for a lifetime. Her story was so genuine and deep, people couldn't help but to be into her from the jump.

She fed him the same back story she'd told so many times before. She told him how she's a part-time caregiver to the elderly and grew up on 39th and Vilet as the only child to a crackhead single mother. When in fact, Lyza Williams really grew up in Detroit and had eight brothers and sisters. Her mom was a mean drunk that had six baby daddy's. One of whom Lyza shot dead when she was eight-years-old. She zoned out as she reflected back to that day.

The man had been molesting lil Lyza for five months when one day he came over and beat her mother Gwen to a bloody pulp. They were both drunk, belligerent, and ransacked the house as they fought from room to room.

He punched Gwen like she was a man, leaving trails of blood all over the floor. Shaking with fear and tears in her eyes, little Lyza went to the hallway closet and grabbed the revolver her mother kept in a shoe box. She stood over Marcus while he pummeled her mother on the bathroom floor.

"Stop! Stop it now!" she screamed, holding the gun with both hands and shaking like a bobble head doll.

He stopped and looked over his shoulder at the little girl. "Bitch get your little snotty nose ass back in the living room before I kick your ass too," he said and resumed punching Gwen.

Pop! Pop! Pop! Pop! Pop! *Lyza squeezed the trigger five times. One bullet for each month he'd been molesting her eight-year-old body. He died on top of her mother. who screamed louder than she had when the mog was beating her.*

All of her brothers and sisters gathered in the bathroom doorway and looked at the bloody mess with saucer eyes. Lyza dropped the gun, left the bathroom, and went back to the living room, and curled up on the couch with her favorite doll. When the police came, they took one look at Gwen's face and knew it was a justifiable homicide. But the murder of the man Gwen "loved" sent her into a tailspin.

She went nuts, and two years later, she was put into a psych ward where she was strapped down with a straight jacket. Lyza and her siblings were broken up and put into various foster homes where more physical, mental. and sexual abuse took place, forcing her to kill her abusers one after another. By the time she was thirteen, she had killed six men and one woman and still had no problem sleeping at night. It didn't take long for her to realize that Lyza Williams was a numb soul with no conscience at all.

When she began running the streets with Detroit's finest, the drug dealers tried grooming her for the dope game, but her passion was in killing. Once word got out that a pretty young bitch who looked like Lisa Raye (in her Player's Club days) would body a nigga for a little bit of nothing, Lyza's career as a street assassin took off.

The more her work took her to different states, the more she began meeting like-minded women, who she was sometimes referred to work with in order to carry out the job on a mark. This led to loyal friendships that grew from a bond built on murder. And on Lyza's 20th *birthday, Tryfe Lyfe Bitchez was born with nine other bloodthirsty cutthroat killers from Cincinnati, Minneapolis, Chicago, Gary, Des Moines, St. Louis, and Milwaukee. Over its six-year existence, they grew to be 127 strong with more "Fresh Fish" in the making waiting to be* ***TLB*** *certified.*

When GG heard rumors about the lethal bitchez in her early stripping days, she put word in the wind that she'd like some "work done." Nadine, a short babyfaced sista, approached GG after the club one day saying TLB got her message. They chopped it up at an after-hours spot and not long after that, BBC was bringin' plenty of business to TLB as they eliminated their foes and put a chokehold on the game.

The two crews had mutual respect for one another because they were both good at what they did. BBC got money in dozens of ways. They were ultimate finessers with a million and one hustles. TLB were contract killers who could kill a man or woman a million and one ways and got away with it.

During the early stages of their relationship, Rose flew the main TLB members to Brazil so they could learn some effective torture methods and unique murder procedures straight from the cartel to add to TLB's repertoire.

During that two month stay of "training" in South America, it was agreed upon that the two clicks would link up and form an alliance as two powerful all-female organizations that looked to persevere in the world. BBC wanted power and wealth and TLB wanted respect and notoriety. Rose promised them that and so much more. And that's how Tryfe Lyfe Bitchez became the first branch on the BBC family tree.

On the outside, Lyza was a beautiful enchanting woman. Short, bow-legged, and redbone. Her soft black hair with the brown streaks in it fell to her shoulders. She had tasteful tattoos on various parts of her body, and she kept her nails and toes done.

She had nice C cup titties and a fat ghetto booty that made men bite their knuckles whenever she walked past them. Her pussy was super tight because the only time she had sex was when she was "undercover," playing the girlfriend role to her next victim. She had no interest in sex, and she didn't even masturbate. She really was a loner who didn't believe in pleasure.

On the inside, Lyza had ice water in her veins. She had no heart. It had long ago blackened and died during the years of mental, physical, and sexual abuse she endured as a child. She had love for no one. Not even herself. She killed so easily and without abandon because she had no qualms about human life. She was like a zombie inside, a shell of woman; and she knew it too, but Lyza didn't give a fuck!

Everyone she killed, she felt honored to relieve the world of them. Obviously, they had wronged someone if they were on her hit list, so they deserved to die was how she felt about it. If they crossed somebody or pissed a person off enough to want them dead, in Lyza's eyes, their death was justifiable. She did not care. At all.

Lyza and her girlz made people widows, parentless, childless, and siblingless. That was life, and that's the way the cookie crumbled. If a muthafucka chose to live the street life and got robbed or killed because of their chosen profession, oh well. Life's a bitch and then you die.

When she was 22 years-old, she got her tubes tied and burned off so she could never have children. Though she didn't enjoy sex anyways, she still did not want to get pregnant on the job. She knew she'd die by the same gun that she lived by one day. And Lyza did not want her kids to go through the pain of not having a mother there for them. So, she made the conscious decision to forego children.

She'd never been in love and knew that she would never experience that feeling either. She was too emotionally paralyzed to feel... ANYTHING. But the reality of knowing that was what made her "acting" seem more authentic than even the best performances ever portrayed.

Lyza could cry and tremble at the drop of a hat, and you'd swear she was really a heartbroken woman when she confronted a two-

faced lover or cheating boyfriend. Lyza was the best at what she did. Her facades were the most believable masks those looking from the outside had ever seen. Only TLB and BBC knew the real Lyza. And even then, they didn't know how far she'd ***really*** *go.*

"So, you think you and me can kick it sometime babygirl? Since you like seafood, we can go to Red Lobster then hit up the IMAX or something. Check out one of them 3D flicks, sip some drank, blow some smoke, and just chill," T-dub said, tendrils of kush smoke wafted from his nostrils as he looked at her, breaking her from her reverie.

To him, she was a hood bitch with sensual swagger and a gangstress flair. The type of bitch he wanted on his team. That's why street niggaz found her so appealing. Lyza was irresistible to them. She looked good, smelled good, and was cool as fuck. She was a chameleon that could blend into any environment. She also had a way of making total strangers feel comfortable around her. Like they'd known her all of their life.

"Yeah. I think we can do that daddy," she said, swinging her leg over his knee. "You seem real cool and shit. So why not?" Lyza pulled her phone out so they could exchange numbers. T-dub had no idea he was about to let the devil, in female form, into his life as soon as he hit the SAVE button in his contacts.

From across the suite, GG peeped them on the low. She smiled as that old school song "Another One Bites the Dust" came to her mind.

14

ZURICH

The three of them kicked back on a 12 passenger private plane, sipping $3,500 bottles of Chateau Margaux. They had more suitcases and trunks than an airport baggage claim. But their luggage wasn't full of clothe; it was packed with MONEY and two bags had gold bars in them.

It was that time for them to make their first "drop" of the year into their Swiss Bank Accounts. A bi-annual tradition they'd been doing for the last 3 years now. This was their biggest haul yet with $210 million dollars on deck.

Ever since they found out money wasn't taxable and can't be fucked with in offshore accounts, the BBC began transporting their dough by plane to Switzerland.

Harold was their pussy-whipped banker who laundered their money and didn't ask questions, cuz he got to hook-up with each of them every time they came for their week-long trip.

Whenever the girls came to Zurich, they rented a massive $10,000 a week villa that boasted 6 bedrooms, 8 bathrooms, a movie theatre, and a four lane bowling alley inside. Not to mention, an Olympic size indoor/outdoor pool separated by an Egyptian grotto.

Fresh off the plane, they *each* took a limo loaded with the luggage straight to the bank. This ride was always their favorite time because they were each alone with their thoughts, cruising through the Global center of the world for banking and finance, to appreciate how far they came from hard times brought tears to their eyes. Looking at the beautiful landscape behind tint with millions to transport brought more tears to their eyes. That ten-minute limo ride was the only time they were truly vulnerable.

Harold greeted them with big hugs as he helped each lady bring their bags into his Swiss place of business, always eager and rolling out the red carpet for them as he should.

It was a long process of money-counting machines and stacks of paperwork. BBC weren't just making deposits. They were cleaning their dirty money, investing in various stocks, bonds, and portfolios as well as shifting funds from one business to the next one. The head of their empire was called Lipstick Enterprises, a privately held chartered corporation owned by Rose, GG, and Summer. Lipstick Enterprises had various subsidiaries such as BBC Corp. and Passionate Venture Capital Inc., which were smaller branch businesses that dealt in a specific category. Each served its purpose as being an offshoot under the Lipstick umbrella without being directly tied to it for tax and finance purposes.

BBC had their hands in everything from agriculture and tech to import/exporting. And of course, all things entertainment. New subsidiaries were formed every time they came to Zurich. Harold was a banker, CPA, and business lawyer all in one, so he efficiently helped them complete their tasks twice a year, and in return, they gave him mind-blowing sex and a very generous payday. This time, they gave him $5 million once all of the documents were taken care of and the money was cleared.

They told him they'd see him at their villa in the morning and he smiled like a kid in a candy store. His baby dick got hard at the thought of having those three exotic beauties at his disposal for the next few days. Harold was cuckoo over them bitches. But then again, who wasn't?

THE FOLLOWING EVENING, BBC dined in a five-star restaurant that had a breathtaking view of the lit-up city at night. Before going in, they smoked three blunts in their rented Aston Martin, so they were super hungry when they ordered, and they ate like QUEENS.

Their table was adorned with entrees: sautéed soft-shell crabs with wild rice, lobster bisque, jumbo shrimp with Bermuda onions, fried veal, and buttered shallots sprinkled in marsala, Alaskan King crab legs, and stuffed Japanese mushrooms.

They sipped cocktails, ate like they never heard of food before, and laughed until they cried, just enjoying time with each other.

"Girl, that honky crazy as a muthafucka with his lil ass jolly rancher dick," GG said.

"Jolly rancher? Shiiid, I've ate jolly ranchers bigger than his dick!" Summer said and slapped the table. They all laughed.

"He swear he be doing something too, chica. All like 'take this big cock. You love how it feels you up don't cha?' And I'm all screaming at the top of my lungs like "oh yes, Harold. Oh God!" Rose said.

"He can eat some pussy tho'. That's about all he's good at," GG said.

"Well, he's damn good with our money," Summer said.

"Hell yeah he is. Shit, our investments have tripled in damn near no time! And with these new endeavors we just formed, we 'bout to see them *BILLIONS*. Now that's a **B** I wanna say I can claim," Rose said and tore into some crab legs.

They just formed an Entertainment corporation that would house a Record Label, Film production company, Modeling Agency, Event planning business, and chain of Nightclubs, Bar & Grilles and Stripclubs.

Under the BBC publishing umbrella would be magazines and books of various genres for all kinds of readers.

Their clothing line was launching in the fall, and they had a BBC fragrance in the works that should be ready to debut by Christmas. But besides the lucrative businesses in motion, Rose had been plotting a whole other takeover.

"Check this out y'all," she began after taking a sip from her giant margarita. "The key to success is longevity. And the only way for us to sustain such a run until we're old and gray is to have people in high places. So, if need be, we can call on them for help when the time comes."

"Mami, what chu talkin' bout?" Summer said.

"We can't take over the world without help. We bust the most important moves to further our empire with who? TLB and THOT Gang. Now just think if our two most trusted allies were politicians, police officers, lawyers, doctors, P.O. s, and other significant positions of power and importance. What we need to do *NOW* is start breeding our familia for the future. We're gonna need people we can TRUST on the inside of those fields that we'll never fully get to infiltrate. Sure, we got muthafuckaz on the payroll at the bank or running our stores and shit, but what if we ever get knocked? Look at Ma Baby, we ain't got no Correctional Officers on our team who could make sure she straight. What if that was one of us? We ain't got no P.O. s on deck who could look out for us. No judges to rule in our favor. Ya nam sayin'?" Rose said.

"You right. But that's why we got all this cocksucking cash to bribe and pay them muthafuckaz in those occupations," GG said.

Summer and Rose looked at each other like *cocksucking cash?* GG smiled. "I been fucking with that whiteboy Bucky a lot," she said, laughing.

"Giiiirl, you stupid. Anyway ma, we gotta think bigger than that. What if you were on trial facing life and you had Lyza as your judge and Nymphy as your lawyer? You'd be able to sleep at night cuz you know shit is gonna go in your favor, you feel me?" Rose said. GG and Summer nodded and sipped their drinks.

"Between TLB and THOT Gang, we got 306 ***official*** members and hundreds more in training. What we do is sit down with them and see who has an interest in what. See what they wanted to be when they were a little girl. I bet a lot of them wanted to be nurses, doctors, and all kinds of shit. Then we send those bitches to school. Just like we train them in this hood shit and finesse game, we pay for their education. Then when they get Bachelor's, Master's, and P.H.D.'s and shit, they'll be in the position to further our organizations by being on the *INSIDE*," Rose said, looking at her homegirls.

"Kinda like how we did with Myesha?" Summer asked. Myesha is a non-active THOT Gang member who was gutted in a street fight real bad when she was 20 years-old. She almost lost her life, but she pulled through by the grace of God. Because she had two shorties, BBC told her they'd get her out of the street life and into a better environment. Myesha wasn't no hood bitch to begin with. She grew up in a middle-class family with BOTH parents and plenty of money.

But the streets intrigued her, so she began running with hood bitches and almost paid the price with her life. Now she had a 10-inch scar across her stomach to remind her of the life that she left behind and was never for her.

BBC bought a car dealership in Madison, Wisconsin and made Myesha the head honcho of it. She was now a conservative CEO who sold cars and plugged the BBC, TLB, and THOT Gang with a slew of new cars on the regular. All the women had to do was come in with a shoe box full of cash and the paperwork would be doctored up so the authorities wouldn't question the purchases and they'd drive off the lot inhaling that new car smell.

"Yeah, just like Myesha," Rose said.

"That's what's up. Hell yeah, I can dig that shit girl," GG said.

'"Yeah, that's a brilliant idea," Summer added.

"Ma, if we have a bitch in ***every*** occupation, in ***every*** field imaginable, looking out for ***OUR*** best interest... Shiiid, we'd REALLY rule the muthafuckin' world," Summer said.

"Exactly," Rose nodded.

They all looked at each other and raised their glasses, "Let's do it!"

During dessert, an Italian gentleman from across the room sent them a $5,000 bottle of wine. They nodded from their seats, thanking him. When it was time to leave, he had already instructed the maître that he'd foot the bill. So, after they were told their five-figure meal was already taken care of by the gentleman in the blue Versace suit, they walked over to his table to thank him.

"Three beautiful women in a foreign country should have to pay for nada," he said in a heavy Italian accent. He kissed each of their hands as they introduced themselves. "Hello Queens, I am Angelo, and this is my cousin Ricky," he said, gesturing to the man sitting across from him.

"Well Angelo, that was a very gracious thing you did. We appreciate it greatly. I'm Rose, and those two are Summer and GG," Rose said, introducing the trio the men.

"You are quite welcome," he answered her, but looked in Summer's eyes.

"How long will you ladies be here in Zurich?" he asked.

"Mmm, a few more days. Why?" GG asked, looking at the handsome man with his jet black hair slicked back. He had that tough guy, Mark Wahlberg look that she found incredibly sexy. But he only had eyes for one woman.

"Because, I wanted to know if Ms... Summer is it?" She nodded. "Would accompany me to lunch and a shopping spree," he said.

"Shopping spree?" Summer said, raising an eyebrow and loving the sound of those two words.

"Yes. But of course, you'll pick up some things for your friends too. At my expense... naturally," he smiled and his brilliant white teeth blinged like a toothpaste commercial.

"Well, I don't see why not. Sure, I'd love to," Summer said and told him where he could pick her up at the following day.

She brought back Hermes Birkin bags and Christian Louboutins for Rose and GG. She had shopping bags from all the upscale boutiques for herself. Prada, Gucci, Valentino, Balmain, Fendi, and Louis Vuitton. Dude had spent over $100,000 on Summer and she didn't even have to give him the pussy... although she *wanted* to.

He was smooth, suave, and manly. His accent was sexy, and his intellect was a bridge between street and book smarts, which *REALLY* turned her on. When he dropped her off in his Rolls Royce Phantom, he kissed her on her cheek and told her he'd see her again soon. She was so wet and horny, she had to go get herself off.

She took a hot bubble bath in her private Carrara marble sunken tub. The people who rented the villa last must've had a kid because they left behind a rubber ducky in the bathroom. When Summer cleaned her pussy, her hand lingered over it while her mind wandered to Angelo. Sexy. Ass. Angelo. She closed her eyes and had the orgasm of her life! Was it him or the pent-up sexual frustration? She wasn't for sure, but when her orgasm settled, she opened her eyes and looked down at the rubber ducky she had in her hand. *What the fuck is up with me?* She thought to herself as she threw the floating toy on the floor. She was in such a zone, she had used the closest object to her to get off with. *Damn, I'm wilding,* she said to herself and laughed.

As she rinsed off, her thoughts returned to the mysteriously demure Angelo. Summer sensed he was more than the import/export businessman he portrayed to her, but she wasn't gonna push the issue. *Yet*. She'd find out more about him all in due time. As well as what his sex game was like, cuz she was really fiending for his Italian dick. She closed her eyes and pictured him whispering dirty things in her ear in Italian; words she wouldn't understand but would sound sexy as hell coming from his heavily accented voice. Summer shuddered and got goosebumps. "Angelo," she whispered as she tugged on her nipples. She grabbed the rubber ducky off the floor and went for round two until she hit another plateau in the warm bubble bath.

Afterwards, she leaned her sweaty head against the marbled tub as she thought about what had been an enjoyable, successful trip to Zurich. The extra perks and amenities were a plus as she reveled in the joy of wealth and new opportunities.

She, Rose, and GG had decided earlier that day to make Becky an honorary member of the Bad Bitchez Click as soon as they got back to the states. Things were looking up, and life was good. Then Summer looked down between her legs at the rubber ducky that was still halfway inside her pussy, and she had an idea. *I'm about to fuck up da game with this one,* she said and smiled.

15

PIG SHIT

For the most part, different divisions of law enforcement didn't like each other. FBI, DEA, ATF, etc. and then inside of the police department, you had the Homicide, Robberies, SVU, and Narcotics and so on. The reason they were so leery of one another was because it's one huge rat race on the inside.

Everyone was constantly trying to climb the "corporate ladder" and get promoted to a higher position of power. In a sense, it's no different from how the gangs operate in the streets. Overprotective of their territories, many officials were quick to lash out if they felt like someone was stepping outside of their jurisdiction or trying to make a name for him or herself off someone else's case. This led to stepping on toes, sabotaging foes, and lots of cutthroat activities taking place as people looked out for self and tried to prosper as best as they could.

No one wanted to be at the bottom of the totem pole. With all the grunt work that comes along with being a foot soldier, the back-breaking tasks, putting in long hours, and shit loads of over time only to remain in a stagnant position for many years sucked the soul right out of those who once had a passion for fighting crime.

That was not an option for the Power Squad (a.k.a. **P.S.**); they weren't hearing none of that flunky bullshit. P.S. were a bunch of rouge officials who played by their ***own*** rules. They were hungry, passionate individuals who decided to band together to pave their own way, cementing their ***own*** future by taking their destiny into their ***own*** hands. The Power Squad was a hierarchy force that would not be denied their goals.

P.S. worked together scratching each other's backs by using the exclusive resources afforded to them by their respective departments to crack a case. Power Squad were absolute BEASTS in the field! Not only for their keen "police intuition," but they also used street smarts and a by any means necessary approach when it came to getting the job done, which meant none of them had a problem getting their hands dirty. That's why muthafuckaz in the streets called them **P**ig **S**hit.

THEY RAIDED drug spots only to confiscate drugs and guns to plant on *other* criminals they wanted to lock up. Or they'd keep the dope and give it to their informants to sell. Whatever "illegal" money was found would always go into P.S.'s pockets.

They coerced confessions, many of them false, by threatening peoples' families and loved ones. They beaten people, framed people, and in a few instances, *killed* people. They were renegades that didn't see themselves in "that" way. In their own twisted minds, they felt their actions and tactics were justifiable. That they were ridding society of the scumbags and filth that populated the world. Even if they had to "bend the rules" a little bit.

And as of late, Pig Shit had been bending *plenty* of rules. Trying to get to the bottom of the Stripclub Capers meant ruffling lots of people's feathers. Since the job was done by mostly females, the child protective services were called on single mothers, women were pulled over and cavity searched, many were roughed up in front of their kids and boyfriends. And any woman with a criminal past or ties to the streets were harassed wherever they went.

The consensus was that it was an inside job. So, P.S. interrogated the main employees of all Wisconsin stripclubs and more strippers than one can count! They also kept many of them under surveillance to see if they'd lead them to any clues. But everything was pretty much a dead end because nobody knew anything.

There was no useable evidence from any of the crime scenes and all of their suspects of interest turned out to be innocent scapegoats. They desperately needed a lead of some kind. That's why the Power Squad (all 42 of them) were having a conference meeting at their secretly leased "headquarters" in downtown Milwaukee.

"We've gotta get Rivera on these streets now before this case gets any colder!" Homicide Detective Wilson Moncrief said. "The longer we go without any info, the harder it'll be to solve."

"Yeah, with all these women involved, you know she can get to the bottom of this quicker than we can. The streets will talk to her. She's a LEGEND out there! But it's like they aren't scared of us anymore. We've literally been on people's ***ass***, and they still aren't saying shit," said Lucy Peterson from ATF.

"I know exactly what you're saying guys. I agree 100%. It's like they're calling our bluffs when we try to crack down on them. That's how I ***know*** it's bigger than some street gang shit. They are protecting some organization that is way more powerful than your run-of-the-mill thugs or click of drug dealers," agent Bradshaw said.

"We're seriously thinking the cartel. It's gotta be," Agent

Holis said. "But how a bunch of African-American women on a street level ties into the cartel is what's leaving us baffled. I mean, are they just working with *anyone* now?" she said, sending a subliminal diss. The black members in P.S. didn't seem to notice the cheap shot from the "undercover" racist federally.

Christine Holis single-handedly blamed black folks for all the illegal drugs in the United States. As if blacks had the means to grow and import drugs from foreign countries, bypass U.S. customs, and distribute them to every city in America. In her fucked up ignorant thinking, it was "black people" who were to blame for her twin sister Courtney's heroin addiction. Even though it was Courtney's babydaddy, a white man, who introduced her to boy. And her two drug dealers that she alternates copping from are also both white.

"We always thought Rivera had ties to one of those Latino Cartels because of her daughter's father. But after the Latin King indictment, we believe he was one of the many who was murdered and never found. I mean, it's been 22 years and he hasn't resurfaced. But by returning her to society... um sorry, the *streets*, we think she'll lead us to her old connection as well as expose the one tied to all of these drugs and capers that's avalanched our state," Agent Bradshaw said.

"Ok, so what's the hold up?" Officer Dumall from the robbery division asked.

"Well, she's agreed to cooperate. But only if we let her cellmate and lover Carol Coleman work with her," Agent Holis informed him.

"And?"

"We're having a hard time getting clearance for Ms. Coleman's release because she's deemed an extreme liability. She's young, weak, and gullible. She can be easily manipulated, which is a risky flaw in the field," agent Bradshaw said.

"Hell, that's great! Rivera can play puppet master and pull Coleman's strings. She's in her 20's right? Well Rivera is knocking on 40, so Coleman should have no problem weaseling her way in with the younger crowd to find out whatever we need to know. And if she's really naïve as you say she is, she won't be hard to control on our end," Detective Moncrief commented.

"Yeah, that's how we feel too. But you know the higher-ups are skeptical. Bitching and moaning about having to put another paid informant in the budget and yada yada yada. We already have to roll the carpet out for Rivera so the streets won't be cautious around her. So, to include her lover in the plan... well, you know how those tightwads are," Agent Bradshaw said.

"Hmpf. I already know who it is. It's Pasternicks' fat ass isn't it?" Frank Quaid from the DEA said.

Bradshaw, Holis, and two other feds nodded.

"I knew it! That fat, sloppy, penny pinching sonuvabitch. Look Bradshaw, kiss a little ass you know? Butter the cocksucker up. You know brownie points go a long way with him. We need Rivera out here. Fuck, we'll fund her our damn selves if we have to! Hell, besides these damn Stripclub Capers, there's so many other going-ons, we've been having a field day trying to tap into. But money is power, and these fuckers are out here getting A LOT of money, which is making our mission much harder."

"I don't like being out of the loop. I want to know who's doing what and with whom out there. We keep hearing about this all female gang of assassins, but what I thought was a myth is starting to sound more and more like a reality. And I want names. I want faces," Lieutenant Sterling said.

"Yeah. The way they murdered 130 people and shot up 200 more...these women are ruthless! This could very well be the infamous female killers we have been hearing about for all of these years. I thought it was some made up bullshit too. But now..." Mrs. Fitzgerald from Homicide said and shrugged.

"We see what a gang of women are capable of doing," someone from ATF said. The room grew silent. Men and women sipped coffee and wrestled with their own thoughts.

"Look guys. The day after tomorrow, I'm going golfing with Pasternicks. I'm gonna sell this to his ass like my life depends on it. Before we're on the 8th hole, he'll give me the greenlight. We'll have Ma Baby home and on the streets working for us before this month is over with," Agent Bradshaw said.

"And you're sure we can trust her?" Officer Dumall questioned.

"Yeah man, she's a..." one of the snooty agents stopped mid-sentence and looked around.

"She's loyal. But she loves her family more than anything. If she crosses us, we'll make her family pay for it. And fuck, we're holding her life in our hands. She's the one that's a snitch now, and we'll make sure she knows *we* hold her cards in ***OUR*** hands. At any time, if she gets on some funny shit, we'll expose her to the streets and let them have their savage way with her," Agent Holis said.

"Throw her to the wolves you mean?" Frank Quaid said with a mischievous smile.

"Yup. They find out she's working with the law, and they'll slice that bitch's throat like a ripe tomato. And Ma Baby, will be...no mas," Agent Holis said and laughed. The rest of the room filled with light laughter as everyone nodded.

"When we solve this case, there will be medals of honor and lots of promotions to go around. But in the meantime, let's continue ruffling some feathers. Keep your ears to the street and do what you've got to do to uncover information. It's time to ***really*** get our hands dirty now," Agent Bradshaw said with a smirk on his face.

Everyone in Pig Shit had their own plans with what would come from solving the Stripclub Capers. This was a huge opportunity. The kind that not only *made* careers, but took one to the next level. For many though, they just wanted to recruit these ruthless women to do side jobs for them. Everyone within the Power Squad had their own hidden agenda.

16

GIRL TALK

The women were in the spacious backyard of the "Greenhouse," their lavish mansion in Fox Point. They built a mini-campfire using cherrywood and lounged around it on a warm summer night. They all sat in the grass surrounding the bonfire a few feet away from the outdoor Olympic sized swimming pool. The bright orange blaze from the fire reflected off the water, casting a hypnotic color off its surface. They had bottles of alcohol and a basket of snacks and fruit nearby. Rose unzipped a pink Reebok gym bag and cleared her throat.

"Chicas, I proudly present to you...BBC bomb!" she said, pulling out a Ziploc freezer bag full of weed. GG, Summer, and Becky sat up and huddled around Rose as she held the bag up high. With the fire burning bright, everyone could see the uniqueness of what was in the bag. This wasn't your everyday weed.

"Whoa!"

"Is that shit *REAL*???"

"Holy Guacamole!" Becky said. They all looked at her sideways. "Whaaaaat?" she said, blushing hot pink. Rose smiled and opened up the plastic bag as she took a big chunk of marijuana out and placed it in her palm. All four of them huddled up like a football team, almost bumping heads as they stared at the magnificent bud.

"This is ***OUR*** new strain of cannabis. Ryan, our genius scientist guy, has been in the lab growing, mixing, blending, and breeding different strains like crazy to come up with the perfect kind just for us. And I'll be damned if this ain't us to the T!" Rose exclaimed.

The chunk of weed in Rose's hand was lime green. It had royal blue stripes going through it and glittery gold polka dots. It was very silky, with fine layers all over that made it look like mini-cabbage.

"The color of it as y'all can see is the same mint green as money. The blue stripes you see is the same ones you see on what?" Rose asked.

"Them Franklins baby!" Summer said, referring to hundred dollar bills.

"Riiiiiight," Rose said. "The gold, well, that there is self-explanatory. We all *SHINE* something fierce! Can y'all smell it?" Everyone put their noses in her palm and this time they *did* bump heads. They "ow'd" and giggled, then they all took a whiff.

"Gosh that smells good," Becky said.

"Hell yeah! Giiiiirl, I wanna ***EAT*** dat shit," Summer commented.

"As you should...what you're smelling is an exotic combination of ***us***. Pineapple cuz that's your favorite fruit GG," Rose said, nodding towards the curvaceous stripper. "Somali ROSE is representing me. And that sweet chocolate is cuz of you two," she directed at Summer and Becky. "Summer, that's your guilty pleasure and comfort food with your sweet-tooth having ass.

And Becky...well you just loooooove you some chocolate ***MEN*** don't cha girl?" Rose said and smiled. The white girl blushed a deep red.

"All these yummy scents mixed together and made into one AMAZING smell for us to enjoy while we blow our mutha-fuckin' brains out! And it's marinated in honey cuz we Bad Beez of course," Rose said full of excitement.

"Dammmmn girl. This shit so pretty, it don't even *look* real," GG said, taking the bud out of Rose's hand and holding it up in the air to inspect it with awe from all angles.

"Oh, it's real alright. And exclusive as fuck. I got ten pounds of it for us right now. That should last us a minute. Since this is all we gon' smoke on from now on, all our previous per-per Kush is retired y'all. If it ain't BBC Bomb, mami, don't put it in your lungs. We ain't even selling this shit. This is exclusive BBC certified *ONLY*," Rose said as she pulled a box of blunts out of the gym bag.

"Bullshit ain't nothin'. Girl, let's see what this shit bout!" Summer said as she snatched the blunts out of Rose's hand and ripped open the package...

Twenty minutes later, they were all higher than giraffe's pussy! Laughing, choking, giggling, and rolling around on the Burberry blanket they laid on the grass.

"Damn girl, this shit got a bitch seeing stars," GG said, looking up at the sky.

"Bitch, those ***ARE*** stars," Summer said and laughed.

"Naw ho. I'm seeing some ***OTHER*** kind of stars."

"Yeah, yeah, whatever. You just high," Summer said, rolling her eyes.

"We're *ALL* high," Becky said, giggling. "But you know what? I like this. Just us girls bonding. We've got our BBC Bomb. Got our snacks. A fire going. Our drinky poos..."

"Wait, wait, wait. Drinky poos? Girl, you are *sooo* white," GG said, and they all laughed.

"Yeah, so? I don't pretend to be otherwise. Isn't that why you accepted me?"

"You're right chica. We fucks wit you the long way cuz you're just...Becky. You don't try to talk or act black like the white bitches that be around a lot of niggas. And that's what's up ma. Shit, I ain't never even heard you say *nigga* before," Rose added.

"Umm, that's not a word I'm comfortable with. I mean, I know it's a terminology for some people, but I just don't think a white person should say that shit. Period! Even if it's with an *a* and not *er*. It's still racist and derogatory. Like fucking Bucky and his douchebags throw the N-word around like they really are black or something. I fucking hate that shit," Becky said.

"Girl, who you telling? That mog be like, my nigga this, my nigga that. One time I heard him say 'on my mama my nigga!'... I looked at that fool like *really?*" GG said.

"Well Becky, I think that's 100 of you," Summer said and hit the blunt. Once she exhaled the smoke she continued. "I don't like when white people say that shit either. Straight up, I be ready to slap a cracker! Sorry."

"No, no... it's cool. I totally understand where you're coming from. I be wanting to slap a cracker too when I hear them say that shit," Becky said. Everybody laughed.

GG hit the blunt and said, "You cool peeps, Becky. For real for real, we been looking for a DAB like you for a minute now."

"DAB?"

"Down Ass Bitch," GG told her.

"Oh. Sorry I– "

"Don't know the slang like that. I know. *We* know. But that's fine. We're all different. I mean, even though we've been around each other for most of our lives and have some of the same tendencies, we still have our own unique personalities and traits. That's what makes BBC so special. We're the same, but we're not the same. You get me?"

"Yeah, I get you GG. You guys mesh. You gel. That comes with time. How long have you known each other anyways?" Becky asked.

"Well, me and Summer went to grade school together. We've been friends since we were both eight-years-old. We didn't meet Rose til high school. But we've been inseparable ever since. We have our moments, our disagreements, and whatnot. But we don't feud. We fight *FOR* each other. Never against one another. That's why we're so tight."

"I can see the chemistry you guys have. How you finish each other's sentences and talk shit to each other. That's a special closeness. I don't really have that kind of bond with anyone. I mean, I used to with my BFF, but after she passed...I don't know. Me and Brit-Brit are tight. But there's a lot she doesn't understand because she's still a kid and has a lot of growing up to do. She looks up to me so much that it's hard for her to form her own identity," Becky said.

"I feel you. My sister was the same way. Everybody called her a mini-Summer, following in my footsteps. She was..." Summer sighed heavily and trailed off.

"Oh, I didn't know you have a sister," Becky said.

"Well, I don't...not anymore. She got killed four years ago. She was only twelve."

"Oh my God! I'm so sorry," Becky said, clamping her hands over her mouth. Summer told her how her little sister April was a bright, pretty girl who wanted to be a supermodel when she grew up. Their crackhead mother had been a hype for a decade when one of her smoking buddies introduced her to meth. That wasn't an inner-city drug, so Summer was shocked to see the psychotic effects it had on the woman who birthed her.

One day, April called Summer crying and told her how she locked herself in her room because their mom was going bananas on her, trying to get her to have sex with some junkie dude for drugs. Summer was in Chicago doing a video for Lil

Durk at the time, so she sent Rose to go get her sister for her. By the time Rose got there, April was sprawled on the living room floor, naked and dead. Her skull was bashed in by a clothes iron that was a few feet away from the body. Summer's mom was nowhere to be found. It took Summer two months to track down her dopefiend ass mother. And when she did, she stabbed the woman 88 times, killing her and spitting on her body before setting it on fire in an alley. She never found out who the meth-head was that raped and killed April, but that didn't stop Summer from going on a psychotic killing spree, murdering every meth user she could find in Milwaukee county.

Rose and GG compassionately rubbed Summer's back while she told the traumatic story. Becky listened in horror as everyone held tears in their eyes.

"I just japped out! Stabbed her over and over again like when I first killed a man when I was sixteen. Bitch ass mutha-fucka raped me on my way home from the store. After he finished, I grabbed a beer bottle nearby, broke it, and sliced his ass to shreds! I ain't been the same since."

"Wow...I can like, totally relate. I fucking spazzed out when those fuckers tried to rape me a few weeks ago," Becky told Summer.

"Yeah. Rose told us about that. Was that the first time you killed somebody?"

"Yes. It was like an out of body experience too. I mean, I knew I was capable of violence...maybe even killing. But I didn't think it would be so..."

"Easy?" Rose asked.

"No."

"Therapeutic?" GG said.

"Hot! I mean, I was fucking turned on like a motherfucker! My nipples were hard as steel, and my pussy was sopping wet! I had to frickin' masturbate in the car not even ten minutes later," Becky told them.

"But you know why that is though? For some people, murder is an aphrodisiac for them. A lot of TLB kill for thrills. That's why they chose murder as a profession. But it's not for everyone though. Some people have nightmares and can't sleep after they take a life. Some people become so haunted that they go crazy and commit suicide," Rose said.

"What about you? Can you sleep?" Becky asked her.

"Like a newborn baby after sucking its mama's titty! But I've killed...mmmm, let's just say, my fair share of muhfuckaz. So, I'm numb to it. I'll keep it real though, it was hard at first. I was seeing the people I bodied everywhere I looked. It began with my high school sweetheart. I walked in on him fucking a bitch I had beef with. And he knew I was beefing with her ass. I shot his dog ass in the chest three times with his own gun. Then I blew her mutha-fuckin' head off in pure rage. But I was young then. Blinded by love. Naïve to men and their bullshit. I'd never kill for something so dumb again though," Rose said as she looked up at the sky.

Becky looked at GG. "GG, have you... ?"

"Mmhm. My first body was ten years ago. Some niggaz tried to rob me. Ran up in the spot, took my dope and money. They caught me slippin'. But they ain't know or ***think*** I was strapped tho. Before they hopped in the car, I aired they ass out. ***BOW! BOW! BOW!*** I took my shit back, plus they pistols, and left them slumped over and stankin'. I didn't really flip out afterwards, cuz they tried taking something that didn't belong to them so I ain't feel bad. Fuck 'em! I'll see 'em in hell. Since then, I've had no problem pulling a trigger. I'd rather not, but if I got to, I will."

Everyone nodded their heads in silence as the flames crackled in the still night. Becky sighed loudly. "Yeah, well, I left that fat fucking piece of shit alive to think about his transgressions. Now every time he goes to pee, he'll remember me." All the girls chuckled lightly.

"Damn ma. You really beat da nigga wit his own nuts?" Summer asked.

"Yup. Sure did. Cut those crusty fuckers right off, put 'em in a sock and pummeled his motherfucking ass with them."

"Girl, you's a beast! I don't wanna piss ***you*** off," GG said.

"I bet he won't be trying to get at no more Becky's wit the good hair," Summer said.

"No more babies for him," Rose added.

"That was the point. To prevent any future rapist spawn he'd even ***consider*** creating. But screw that phony cocksucker. What about you guys? Y'all ever want to have kids?" Becky asked them. Everyone grew silent for a moment.

"Mmm, I do...one day," GG said. "Maybe when I'm in my mid-thirties I'll be ready to settle down and do the mother thing. Let Trey Songz's fine ass impregnate me or something."

Summer smacked her lips. "Beeyotch please. In yo dreams. ***Anyway***, I'm not so sure about the whole kids thing myself. I mean, I do, but I don't. We live in a cold world ya know? And I wanna protect my unborn seed from harm. Any pain he or she would endure on earth. Hell, I couldn't protect my little sister ya know? And knowing how karma is, my shorties would probably end up going through HELL for all the dirt that I've done," Summer said.

"Umm, what about you Rose?" Becky asked. GG and Summer tensed up, eyes got big as tires as they looked back and forth from Becky to Rose.

"It's cool chicas, relax. She didn't know," Rose said, referring to the touchy subject. GG and Summer exhaled at the same time.

"What?" Becky said, looking confused.

"I can't have children mami. I ...I almost died at birth, so my insides have been fucked up since the day I came into this world," Rose told her.

"Oh my Gosh! I didn't know. I'm so sorry."

"Nothing to be sorry about mami. It's not your fault. Shit, it ain't ***MY*** fault either. My reproductive organs never formed like they were supposed to. Just one of those cruel things life throws our way ya know? Shiiiiid, I didn't find out I couldn't have kids until I was trying to make a baby. I was 19 and had a horny boyfriend at the time. Dude used to buss so many nuts in me, I was like, 'why ain't I knocked up yet?' So, we both went to the doctor and had some tests done. They told me I'd never have a child. I guess that's one of the reasons my heart grew so cold too. I mean, we all have our demons and situations that made us into the women that we are today, but I think my turning point was when that doctor said I'd never be a mother. Cuz that's something I always looked forward to being ever since I was a little girl. So, when he said that shit, something inside me just snapped! I walked out of that place a different person. Seeing the world through new eyes and no longer giving two fucks!"

Everyone was quiet for a while, their hearts aching for Rose's inability to conceive a child. "Spark another B somebody. We need to switch up the mood," Rose said. Summer grabbed a blunt and lit it over the bonfire.

"Chica, you gonna burn that pretty face of yours off doing that shit," Rose commented. Summer took three long puffs and passed it to Rose. "Girl, I'm the expert smoker here. I know what I'm doing," Summer said and began choking and coughing. Everyone laughed as GG patted her best friend on the back until she regained her composure.

"Ok expert," GG teased.

"What...ever...girl," Summer said, still coughing a bit.

"So, what about you Becky? You never said if you want to have shorty's or not."

"Yes, I do. But kinda like you GG, I want them in my mid-thirties or so. I wanna find the right guy. I don't just want any ol' body for a baby's father because I'm definitely not the marrying type of girl. I like my independence too much. So, once I zero in on a potential candidate, I'll keep him around until it's harvesting time," Becky said, and everyone laughed.

"Mami, you so crazy," Rose said, passing the grape Swisher full of BBC Bomb to Becky. She inhaled it deeply.

"Yeeeeeeah, this *is* that bomb tho."

"So, no potential sperm donors yet?" Summer inquired.

Becky thought about it for a minute. "Nah, not good enough to procreate with."

"You ain't got no main bootycall?" GG asked.

"Mmm, I have a couple," Becky said.

"Who's your freebie then?" GG asked.

"Freebie?" Now Becky was puzzled.

"Girl, you ain't tell her 'bout the freebie rule?" GG asked Rose.

"Naw, we haven't gotten around to that yet."

"What freebie rule?" Becky asked.

"Look ma," Summer began. "If you gonna fuck wit us, those days of giving up the poonanny to any everybody for free is **OVER**! I know you like big dicks and get off on wild shit, but as a Bad Bitch, our pussy is just as *exclusive* as this weed we smoking on," she paused to inhale the sweet marijuana. Tendrils of smoke wafted from her nostrils like a sneaky dragon as she continued. "Niggaz pay for dis pussy. Directly or indirectly, a muthafucka is gon' break bread to get between our legs. We are Bad Bitchez, and we hold ourselves in high regard."

"Which means, we made a pact some years ago to keep one or two studs on deck that we really vibe with and who are good in bed. We hook up with them freely. Whenever. However. Wherever. With no ulterior motives. We don't ask them for nothing or expect anything but good sex. Hell, we even treat them every blue moon to a lil shopping spree or gift or something," Rose said.

"Wow... a freebie huh? Well, that makes sense. So, it's pretty much a rare breed of man that is way different from other guys, has his stuff together, and his sex is unforgettable right?" Becky said.

"Right!" Summer, GG, and Rose said in unison.

"So, I have to narrow it down to one or two guys?"

"Becky, you're a grown ass woman. We're not gonna tell you who you can and can't sleep with chica. That's up to ***you***. But we value ourselves and feel we deserve to be compensated for our time in the sack. You remember us talking about when we hook-up with guys that we don't even orgasm most of the time? Fuck that shit! So, when we do get a muthafucka whose sex game is on point and he can actually make us cum, we keep his ass around to fulfill our sexual needs and desires. But we keep that number low. Like, I have two, and GG and Summer both have one. That's by choice though. You might have eight dudes who are beasts in bed, and you may want to keep four of them on deck as freebies. That's up to you, nam sayin'? Just try to narrow it down is all we suggest. The other four keep 'em around, just tax they ass! But there are *some* good men out there that deserve to get treated like Kings by us. Rub their feet, give them long, slow head for hours, spend money on them, hold them down, etc." Rose said.

Becky nodded. "Yeah, I get whatcha mean. I'll have to think on who I want to put into that freebie category. I do wanna hear about you guys' freebies tho. Come on now, I want details. Spill the goods everyone."

GG took the blunt out of Rose's hand and took a couple of puffs. "I'll kick it off," she said, blowing out smoke rings. "I met a fly ass nigga named Frank at a concert a few years ago. Tall, chocolate, and sexy as a muthafucka! He ain't no D-boy or nothing, and that's cool. He owns a construction company in

Minnesota. We exchanged numbers and got together like a month later when I headlined a club in St. Paul. Girrrrl, the dick was so good, da nigga made me forget ***my*** name!" GG said and laughed. "He's a slimmer dude. Built kinda like Mayweather. But damn is he strong! Probably from slangin' cinder blocks and concrete around. He can pick my thick ass up and carry me from room to room fucking me. His stamina is amazing! He's thirty-eight now, but I'm telling you, the nigga dick-whipped me so good the first night, I thought he took a Viagra or something. But I slept over at his crib a few times and watched his ass like a hawk! Cuz I was like, ain't no way his dick is ***this*** hard and always ready like it is without him poppin' some Molly or Viagra or some shit. But nope, he's just a naturally good lover. He don't do no drugs. Don't even smoke weed. He sips a lil Remy every now and then, but that's it. Shit, dude just off da radar wit da dick! I already be coming like a muthafucka anyway, but Frank makes me squirt **OCEANS!** Damn, I'm getting wet just thinking about him. Shoot, somebody go next. Damn," GG said, fanning herself and rubbing her titties.

"Well, my freebie is Party HaRRRd. That's my nigga yo! We been jamming since high school. Way before he became a rapper and he was just hustling ass Dee. That nigga knows how to PUNISH the pussy! He be beating this muthafucka up like Mike Tyson in the 80's. He has this beautiful curve in his dick that strokes my G-spot so perfectly, I just lose my mind when he up in me. I don't know how he does it, but he be hitting so many untouched places inside me. He be swiveling them chocolaty hips and be all up in my guts like no other man ***EVER*** has. Plus, Party da one that turned me out on that eating ass freaky shit. He put his tongue in my yellow booty one day and I damn near fell in love with him! Then he let me do it to him and it's been on ever since. Keeping it real witchu, he da one that turned me out on all *kinds* of freak shit. Cuz of him, I learned the Alvin, Simon, Theodore trick, and all kinds of other demos. S & M, Voyeurism, all that. Yeah, Party HaRRRd is my boo thang y'all," Summer sighed and fanned herself as she blushed and smiled from ear to ear. "Hell, we even made a sex tape...a couple of them in fact."

"What?!" Rose said, eyes wide as she sat up.

"Girl, stop lying," GG said shocked.

"Naw, I'm for real. I know we talk about not putting ourselves in a position where we can be extorted or blackmailed for some personal shit, but...I don't know. I trust Party. And well, I was the one who actually suggested it and had to talk him into doing it cuz he was hesitant at first.

We watched the Ray J and Kim Kardashian's tape one day and I wanted to put they weak ass flick to shame. So we did!" Summer said, smiling big.

"Girrrrl, you gotta show us that shit!" GG said.

"Mmmm...maybe," Summer said coyly.

"Whatever chica. It's my turn," Rose said, sitting Indian style. "My dude's name is Running Horse. He lives on the Rez in Oneida. Thug ass native cat with a dick to his knees! *Mmm.* We both like that rough shit. Pushing, biting, slapping, pulling, strangling, scratching, yelling, screaming, clawing at each other like wild animals and shit. He's the *only* one to ever make me squirt! He's got this move where he folds me up like a human pretzel so I can't move. Then he chokes the shit out of me while he's deep in my guts. Mami, I cum more than GG's crazy pussy ass," she said with a chuckle. GG gave Rose the finger. "Then we have this slapboxing demo where when I ride him like a bull, we go ham slapping the shit out of each other. My face be stinging and burning like a muthafucka, but damn that shit turns me on and makes me cum like crazy!"

"So, who's the other guy? Didn't you say you had two freebies?" Becky asked, looking pink and flushed after listening to Rose recount her sexual trysts with Running Horse.

"Yeah Rose. Go head and tell her about the *other* one," GG

teased her. Summer giggled like a schoolgirl. Becky looked at all the girls' facial expressions and knew there had to be some kind of inside joke going on.

"Whaaaaat?"

"Yeah mami, tell her about lard ass," Summer said, laughing.

"Whatever ho," Rose said, waving her middle finger at them. "You just mad cuz ain't none of yo niggaz got a tongue game like him," she sniped at Summer. "Anyways," Rose continued, returning her attention back to Becky. "I fuck wit this big ass dude named Weezy."

"Big, fat, Rick Ross, Biggie Smalls looking muthafucka," GG said.

"He's a big dude. Got a big beard, a big belly, and a BIG..." Rose trailed off and smiled. "I'm telling you chica, this nigga could win the pussy eating championship if he wanted to. And I don't usually go for the bearded type cuz that shit is itchy, especially against my thighs when they be eating my pecan pie. But his beard is soft and fluffy like cotton candy, and it smells like lemons. He's got this big hurricane-like tongue that twists and twirls so fast it'll make your head spin! When he eats my pussy, I cum in thirty seconds flat. And he won't stop until I bust eight or nine nuts. I be shaking and screaming and begging him to stop. Punching him in his head when he get to chewing on my clit like I like it done, and I be tapping out, trying to push his ass away, like *please. I give, I give. Uncle!*" Rose said and laughed. "He's cool though. He get a lil money, and I plug him with a brick or two here and there. Shit, when you find a carpet muncher like him, you gotta keep dat on deck!"

"We feel you ma, but shit...that nigga fat as hell. Don't he crush you when y'all fuck?" GG asked.

"He ain't never on top. Either I'm riding that dick or he hitting it from the bizaaack. Gotta help him burn some calories somehow, nam sayin'?"

"Mhm. Whatever Rose. You need to tell his fat ass to get a whip he can fit in. Da mog always hopping out of coupes like he a little dude or something. Nigga, you four-hundred pounds, why you squeezing yo greasy ass into two doors?" Summer said.

"Don't knock him, that's just his style. He's a coup nigga. It's what he likes. I am gonna get him a Denali for his birthday though."

"Yeah, yeah, yeah, enough about Fat Albert. Your turn Becky. Which nigga do you fuck with the most that be putting it down on you?" GG asked.

"Hmmm, I'll probably have to saaaay...this one guy named KK. He's originally from Milwaukee, but he's been in Appleton for some years now. He's a big buff dude with gold teeth and lots of tattoos. He's a hustler too. One of the only ones who actually knows how to get money and do something with it. I had to beat up one of his babymamas in the club one night though. Bitch came at me sideways and I had to open up a can of whoop ass on the hoe!" Becky said and everyone laughed. "Anyhoo, his sex is like ***thee*** bomb. His cock isn't as big as I'd prefer it to be– "

"With your size queen having ass!" Summer interrupted.

"Hell yeah, I'm a size queen! But hey, KK still got a nice one. It definitely gets the job done. When he fucks me doggystyle, he chokes me *and* pulls my hair at the same time. That shit feels sooooooo fucking good. I'm getting wet just thinking about it. He's very passionate and animalistic when we fuck. But I know he has a little assistance. He loves his Molly and weed combo, so he's always high when we hook-up. But I don't care. The sex is still the bomb diggy."

"You be sucking the shit out of his dick too?" Summer asked.

"Why of course. Every chance I get. That's mandatory. I ***LOOOOVE*** sucking cock!"

"Bitch, you ain't gotta tell me. I ***saw*** you in action," Summer said.

"Mami, whatchu talking 'bout?" Rose asked.

"Girl look. This bitch is a ***MONSTER*** on the dick! You hear me? Pure beast I tell ya. I ain't gonna front, this bitch had me intimidated as hell. She puts them porn bitches to shame! Now I know why so many niggaz be running to white hoes and shit. You gotta see one in action to fully understand. This bitch here took *ALL* fourteen inches of dude's dick down her throat with ***NO*** problem! Then she got to slappin' herself across the face with it. Talking about, '*I been a bad, bad girl. Punish me.*' Seriously y'all, this girl is an animal. I thought them porn hoes was faking and shit. But after seeing Becky's intense enthusiasm... she was getting *OFF* on that shit! She ain't lying when she says she loves sucking dick. She was in cock heaven wit ol' boy!" Summer told the Bad Bitchez Click.

"Damn skippy I was! Nothing is better than sucking a big ol' black cock."

"So that's why niggaz nicknamed oral sex 'Becky.' Cuz you white bitches some *freaks*," GG said.

"Nah, they named it after *ME*. Because I'm the world's greatest cocksucker! White girls gimme *Becky*," she said, quoting the Wiz Khalifa lyrics to his song "We Dem Boyz."

"Well, that's good. Get ready to put them *Becky* skills to use for BBC then," Rose told her and stood up. "Follow me chicas." Everyone stood up and stretched. Rose padded barefoot through the grass and slid open the back patio doors. They walked into the mansion, went through the kitchen, and out of the door that led to a four-car garage. The automated lights came on when they entered, and a lone car sat in the middle of the garage shining like a brand new whip on a showroom floor.

"Check it out ma," Rose told Becky, handing her the keyfob to the brand new 2020 AMG Mercedes Benz with the gullwing doors. Becky chirped the alarm off and walked up to the car cautiously as if it was a deer that would run off or something. When she opened the door, it lifted up like the Batmobile and made a "chhh" sound.

"Mami, you're an awesome woman. Beautiful, smart, funny as hell, and you ain't no punk ho! You make absolutely ***NO*** apologies for who you are and that's real shit right there. Ain't nothing fake about you Becky, and we admire that," Rose said. GG and Summer nodded.

"You are the Bad Bitch we been looking for. A white girl with swag, flava, be dripping sauce, and you about your cash. And we've decided from this day forward, you are *officially* a part of the Bad Bitchez click... that is, if you *want* to be."

"Are you serious?" Becky asked in disbelief with tears in her eyes.

"Yup. This car is our gift to you. You're one of us now baby. But this *is* til death do us part mami. Ride or die," GG said.

Tears slid down Becky's pretty face as she began to shake. "I-I-I...I don't know what to say," she stuttered.

"Say you're BBC and put that muthafuckin' chain on girl," Summer said, pointing to the platinum necklace with the iced-out BBC Medallion dangling from the rearview mirror in the car. Becky slid into the palladium silver Benz and sat in the custom gray leather bucket seat. She gripped the steering wheel and looked in the rearview mirror. Her mascara was running, and her eyes were bloodshot red. She looked like a hot mess, but this was the best day of her 27-year-old life. More tears ran down her face and fell in her lap. Becky grabbed the necklace off the mirror and put it on. The flawless diamonds sparkled against her sexy tan skin.

"I'm a Bad Bitch now. Forever and always until the motherfucking wheels fall off! BBC for life. Woot, woot!" She said, smiling. All the girls laughed and group hugged.

"Welcome to the family chica."

"Glad to have you on board."

"You's a Bad ass white bitch now!" GG yelled.

"Thank you guys. This really means a lot to me. I won't let you all down. I promise!" Becky told them all teary eyed.

"Just know that you are pledging your life to this organization. It's only one way out this mami," Rose said.

Becky stroked the yellow diamond Honey Bee on the BBC chain. A lot of people claim that ride or die shit but lack what it takes to be authentic...*heart*. Becky had the heart of a Lion. The *I don't give a fuck* attitude of a person who's tired of the world and its bullshit. It didn't matter her color. She was a real bitch. And they knew it, that's why they invited her into something so exclusive. To be a part of something only three other women were in was like winning the lottery for Becky. It wasn't about the money for her, she *been* had that. It was the sisterhood of some loyal people, who would *kill for you* or *kill you* if you crossed them. Yeah, this was the fam she wanted to represent. She knew the consequences. Death was a high possibility. Fuck it, we gotta live it up til our time is called anyway.

Becky shrugged, "Ride or Die. I know what it is. I'm in this bitch." They all high-fived and laughed. They were now FOUR strong.

17

FRESH OUT

Marisol "Ma Baby" Rivera and Carol Coleman walked out of the Dublin Federal penitentiary on an early morning, holding hands and cheesing from ear to ear. Finally, they were both FREE. After years of incarceration, they found their way out of the belly of the beast. It may have been under some fucked up circumstances, but freedom was freedom once an inmate set foot out of "those doors."

A limo took them to the airport where they flew first class to Milwaukee, WI. Ma Baby told Carol it was best that she left her past behind her in Phoenix, Arizona in order to start over fresh with her new life in Wisconsin. And since Carol's brother and friends pretty much left her for dead after she got locked up (out of sight, out of mind), it didn't take much convincing for her to forget about them, the same way they did her. So, there would be no notifying anyone that she was out of prison. Not even her own mother. As far as Carol was concerned, her future involved Ma Baby and Ma Baby only.

Back in Dublin when Ma Baby revealed to her celly what the FEDS wanted her to do for them, Carol urged her to do whatever she had to do to get out of that hellhole. Ma Baby taking their offer and saying Carol would be her partner made the young girl light up like a Christmas tree. In that moment, she felt truly loved and wanted. Something she never felt before. Now it was just the two of them. Dom and sub. Ride or die. With a new lease on life. But they both knew wasn't no turning back now.

The FBI set up a private bank account for Ma Baby with $100,000 in it. A four bedroom four bathroom 3,700 square feet fully furnished house in Menomonee Falls, where they would now call home was waiting for them. In the three car garage was a brand new Infinity QX80 luxury SUV that Ma Baby requested and a Chevy Impala 2LT for Carol. Unbeknownst to either of them, both cars were rigged up with high-tech recording devices so the alphabet boys could listen in on them and track their every move. The house was also bugged and had hidden cameras in various rooms and outside the property as well.

After landing in Milwaukee, they took a cab to their new home. Ma Baby was already used to living large (in her life BEFORE prison), so she'd seen better. But Carol on the other hand was extremely ecstatic about their new place.

"Oh mami, it's beautiful!" Carol gushed.

"Well, I'm glad you like it. I told those pigs to make sure our living conditions is A-1 for me and my sugar thang," Ma Baby bragged and hugged Carol. The young mulatto girl snuggled into her Dom's warm bosom and one thing led to another. Before long, they were scissoring each other in their new Queen size bed; having their first orgasms in the free world at the same time.

After showering the sex off herself, Ma Baby told Carol she'd be home later cuz she had some business to take care of. There was a Gucci purse with $25,000 in it left for Ma Baby on the dresser. She gave Carol 3 geez and told her to go grocery shopping and pick up some knick-knacks for the house. Carol complained about not knowing her way around the new city. Ma Baby pointed to the iPhone X on the nightstand.

"You've heard of Google ain't cha? Well, that's your phone, so use it. Plus, your car has GPS, so I think you'll be fine. I'll see you in a few hours baby," she said and kissed Carol's forehead. Ma Baby grabbed her own iPhone and got in her whip. It was time to see what the streets been up to while she was away.

Shit definitely changed. Businesses and stores she fondly remembered were now replaced by new businesses or tore down completely. Some of her old trap spots were boarded up and abandoned, becoming real "Bandos" now.

New faces and cars populated the blocks she knew all too well. Eight years ago, hustlers were still riding old schools; Chevy's Monte Carlos, Donks etc. Now it seemed like everyone was on their "foreign" kick. Benzes, Lexus', Audi's, Beamers, and Maserati's stormed through the streets bangin' Future, Young Thug, Team East Side, and Trippie Redd tracks from the woofers rumbling in their trunks. Her city had changed. Shorties as young as twelve were out there racked up with sticks on their hip. And now that there was more money to be made, the murder rate increased as plenty of blood was being shed for that almighty dollar.

Ma Baby's job was to get to the bottom of the Stripclub Capers and knock a few mid-level drug dealers in the process. But Ma Baby had other intentions. She'd give the FEDS the info they needed to solve the Stripclub Capers cuz she doubted anybody she fucked with was behind it. She only rolled with hustlers who sold; not *stole*.

But in the meantime, she would be putting money up to "retire" on and move her mother and daughter out of the country where the FEDS wouldn't be able to find them. Take the money and run was how she looked at it. She figured five million dollars would be enough to buy some nice property in a foreign land and lived the rest of her days soaking up the sun, tanning, swimming, chillin' and raising her shorty. Ma Baby didn't tell Carol about these future plans and wouldn't do so until the time was right. Most likely when they were on that plane headed to their final destination was when she'd inform her. The girl was so young and naïve, she would most likely tell on herself without even knowing it. So, Ma Baby would have to keep her sugar thang on a very short leash. Ma Baby knew the FEDS would try to get info from Carol on the sly whenever she wasn't around, so the less she knew, the better.

Ma Baby spent an hour riding through the Mil. From the northside to the southside, she surveyed her beloved city. When she crossed the 35th street bridge, she got the chills. Maybe the ghost of her rat ass sister was still on that fence, waiting for her to cross it so she could haunt her for the rest of her days. Ma Baby shrugged off her superstitions and turned V100 up. She missed her favorite radio station and was pleased to hear they still played the hottest in Hip-Hop and R&B, even though they played a million commercials per hour!

She knew her daughter would be home from school by now and couldn't wait to see the look on her face when she surprised her. Anita adored butterflies, so Ma Baby stopped and bought some figurines and rub-off tattoos of butterflies for her daughter. The house her mother and daughter lived at on 70th and Orchard was one she never saw. The crib she had bought for her mom in New Berlin was confiscated by the FEDS once she got knocked, along with Ma Baby's six-bedroom, five bathroom mini-mansion in Brookfield. So, while her mom and daughter's new home wasn't a shitty crib in the hood, it was a far cry from the lavish digs they *used* to have. Her mother was also no longer a homeowner; she now had to pay her rent like the majority of the other common folk in Milwaukee. Well, Nacho technically paid the rent since he took care of all the bills for them. They knew the FEDS would be monitoring her mother's finances and spending habits after Ma Baby went to prison, so they played it safe and made sure Sofia lived a moderate, low-key lifestyle.

Before she got out of her Infinity truck, she left the iPhone the FEDS gave her on the passenger seat. After she got her daughter's gifts, she stopped at a cellphone shop in the hood and bought herself an S10 Android from Boost mobile. She wasn't stupid. She knew those phones provided to them were tapped. So she'd be moving and grooving with her own untraceable phone.

Not only were there butterflies in the bag she was holding, her stomach was also full of them as she stood on the front porch ringing the doorbell. Her mom answered the door and damn near had a heart attack she was so shocked!

"Mamasita! Wh-what?..."

"I'm home mami!" Ma Baby said and wrapped her itty-bitty mother up in her arms. Both of them cried tears of joy and spoke enthusiastically in Spanish. Anita heard the commotion and came into the living room to see what was going on. When she saw her mother, she almost peed on herself.

"Mama?" Anita said in disbelief. Ma Baby dropped to her knees and opened her arms wide. Anita ran full speed ahead and leaped into her mother's embrace, tackling her as they rolled around on the floor hugging, kissing, and laughing.

After all the tickling, giggling, and fun died down, Ma Baby kicked back in the recliner while her daughter curled up in her lap like a kitten. She didn't tell them how she *really* got out the joint; she just said she won her last appeal and they released her immediately. Ma Baby promised Anita and Sofia that she'd never leave their sides ever again. Her mother told her to get comfortable while she cooked them a home cooked meal. Sofia commented on how much Ma Baby had "filled out" quite a bit since going to prison; she was still about to get one of the best meals she *ever* had.

Ma Baby's new figure was an attractive thickness tho. Eight years and 23 pounds later, her daily hook-ups she ate in the joint had contributed to her already curvaceous body. It turned her into the brickhouse stallion that she was today. Ass, hips. and thighs were ***STUPID*** fat! She had a little bit of a tummy, but nothing she couldn't work off at a *real* gym and tighten up with a personal trainer. Ma Baby was an Amazon built like Khloe Kardashian.

Ma Baby told Anita to call her father and tell him to come over right away because there was an emergency. When Nacho asked what was wrong, Anita just said, "Please Papa, just come right away. Hurry!"

Not even twenty minutes later, Nacho was barreling through the front door with his chrome Smith-n-Wesson in his hand. "Anita?! Sofia?!" he called out, surveying the living room. He could smell the delicious food coming from the kitchen and heard pots and pans clinking around. He peeked around the corner and saw his daughter's grandmother humming a tune to herself as she stood over the stove cooking one of her mouth-watering dishes.

"Sofia, is everything ok? Anita called and– "

"*I* told her to call you," the voice behind him said. Nacho turned around and saw the mother of his only child. He hadn't seen her in almost eight years. She hadn't aged a bit. To him, she was still the most beautiful woman he'd ever met. It was true that prison "preserved" a person, but Nacho could tell something was different about her. The look in her slanted eyes and her whole demeanor was something he couldn't quite recognize nor put his finger on. He knew prison changed a person; he just didn't know how much it had changed Ma Baby. Especially with all the shit she had to go through during her last few weeks before she got out. One thing was for sure to him though; she was thicker than he'd ever seen! His eyes practically popped out of their sockets when he looked at her coke bottle figure. She had on skintight jeans and a tight pink tank top. The whole outfit was small and curve hugging. Nacho could see her ass from the *front*. Her hips flared out like the bottom of a pear, and her pussy looked like an upside down mountain between her legs. He licked his lips lustfully. "Ma, what the?..." he stopped short of saying 'fuck' as Ma Baby smiled and walked up to him. They hugged for a very long time and all the old memories came flooding back for the both of them.

"Papi, you done got fat," Ma Baby said, patting his big stomach.

"Yeah, and you got fat girl. But in all the right places," he said and squeezed her bodacious butt. She swatted him away playfully and wiggled out of his embrace.

"You scared the hell out of me with that call," he turned to his daughter and said. "Don't be doing that Nita."

"Oh, chill out! I told her to do it to get your ass over here ASAP. Now I need to holler at chu. Come on," Ma Baby said, leaving the kitchen. He had to refrain from howling like a wolf at a full moon when he watched her gigantic ass switch out of that kitchen. It looked like she had two pumpkins stuffed in the back of her jeans! He had to hit that. She'd been gone for an eight piece too? He knew that pussy was the bomb dot com. His dick was getting hard just looking at his sexy ass BM.

They walked outside and got into his green Camaro LT. The whole inside was mint green suede. The floors were custom dark green chinchilla carpet, and there were TV's *everywhere*!

"Damn boy! I see you still pimpin' out cho rides."

"You know it ma. Kick yo shoes off and feel that soft chinchilla under your feet," Nacho told her. Ma Baby kicked her platform wedges off and rubbed her toes through the soft, thick fluffy carpeting. It was so soft and silky, she just closed her eyes and moaned.

. . .

"LIKE THAT DON'T CHA?" he said, smiling.

"Mmmmmhmmm."

"Yeah, that's dat shit right there. But yo, you wanna tell me how the hell you got out the joint ma?"

Her eyes flew open as she came back to reality. She cleared her throat and said, "I won my appeal." There was an uncomfortable silence in the car as he looked at her for a minute.

"Last I heard, you used up all of your appeals."

"That's what I thought too. But the courts fucked up on one of my demos and had to grant me another one because they didn't follow proper protocol on some shit," she told him.

"Oh yeah?" Nacho said, suspiciously looking into her chinky eyes.

"Yeah. How else would I get out?"

"That's what I was thinking. They gave you 30 years and all you did was 8? You ain't wired is you?" he said, half serious, half joking.

"Nigga don't play with me. You know I don't roll like that," Ma Baby said defensively, her heartbeat racing a mile a minute.

"Shiiiid, I don't know *how* you roll ma. I'm just saying. I ain't seen yo ass in eight muthafuckin' years and you just pop up out the blue like Houdini. What the fuck would *you* think if you was me?"

Ma Baby wiped her sweaty palms and said, "Look, I feel you papi. But you know me. I'm a stand-up bitch through and through. Dem crackers fucked up in they court system and I caught them slippin' so they had to let a bitch go. So here I am..."

"Aight, aight. If you say so. Muthafuckaz gon' shit bricks when they find out you home. I'm telling you yo, shit done changed Ma Baby. Your name still ringing out here, but you inspired a lot of bitches to form they own clicks and shit. It's plenty hoes out here doing their thing now."

"I know. I heard. All I been hearing about on the news the

last couple of months is how high our homicide rate is and about them Stripclub stick-ups. Them was some gangsta ass bitches who did that shit! Do you know who pulled that shit off?"

"Nah, it could be any of these female clicks out here. It's real in the field ma. It's mo bitches popping they guns than niggaz is nowadays. Shit is crazy yo. That's why I stay to my dammy," Nacho said, looking out the window.

"Mhm. Like you don't know what's movin' and groovin' out here. Boy, don't play with me."

"Shit, I ain't playing. My boy got a lil car detailing shop and I be working on cars and shit now. I'm just trying to stay out the way ma. These young niggaz and hood bitches crazy as a muthafucka, I'm telling you. Everything is GangGang this, and GangGang that," he said.

"Nigga, you got on like a half mill worth of jewelry fool. And I used to get fashion mags in the joint, so I know that ain't no cheap ass knock-off bullshit *Nacho.* What is that, Ferragamo?" she said, hitting it on the head. His icy watch, necklace, and earrings were blinging something fiercely! "And to top it off, you bust up in Ma's spot with the pistol like you ready to shoot up da– "

"Bitch, our daughter called me sounding like some shit was going down. So, hell yeah I came in on bidness!"

"Well, it's nice to know you still got *somebody's* back."

"Yo, don't go there with me. You knew the agreement before you went in. *NO* contact cuz of... well, you know. But we still made sure you was straight didn't we? Sofia ain't had to pay one bill since you been gone. And I put up a nice lil nest egg for you," Nacho said.

"I know, I know. It's just...I don't know. I wish I coulda talked to y'all or got some pictures or something. I was a long way from home and I– "

"Was homesick. I feel you mami. But shit, you home now,"

he said and wrapped his arm around her shoulder, pulling her into him. She inhaled his expensive cologne. Whatever it was, it smelled ***good***. Her nipples began tingling as she thought back on all of their wild ass sexcapades back in the day. ***Hmmmmm***.

"I wanna go see my chicas that's been holding me down. Where they at now?"

"Ma Baby, you won't believe what they on now. They ain't the same teenagers you put on game years back. These bitches a whole nother breed of women now," Nacho said.

"Well, I've seen Summer in plenty of magazines and music videos doing her thang. I even saw her on TMZ once, coming out the club with Young Dolph." Ma Baby said.

"Yeah, they all got their own thang jumping off. They even got a newbie on deck, a white bitch from Appleton,"

"White bitch? Appleton?"

"Mhm. She cool as fuck too wit her thick ass."

"Hmpf. Whatever nigga. Take me to go see my chicas. I wanna see what my bitches been up to. They rolling with white hoes now?"

As Nacho put the Camaro in drive, Ma Baby used her Boost Mobile phone to call her mom and tell her she'd be back later for dinner. When she hung up, Nacho pointed to the Infinity truck. "That you?"

"Just a rental," she responded and turned the radio up. Nacho looked at her sideways as Jeezy and Jay-Z rapped about how they done "Seen It All." Nacho too had seen it all. And he knew rentals had their own special license plates on them. The Infinity, however, had state-issued *regular* plates on them with fresh vehicle registration stickers.

Nacho called Rose to see where she was at. She told him they were chillin' at Summer's condo by the lakefront. He told her he was gonna swoop through for a minute because he had to holler at her.

"Alright, we'll be here. We just smoking our BBC Bomb," Rose said, inhaling a fat ass blunt.

"Oh yeah? I still ain't had none of dat shit. Save me some."

"Fool, you ain't no **BAD BITCH**. That's why you ain't had none," Rose said, laughing.

"Whatever puta. I'll be there in a minute," he said and hung up.

"Had some of what?" Ma Baby inquired.

"Oh, they got they own weed now. It's supposed to be dat flame!"

"Damn, they doing it like that huh?" Ma Baby said. Nacho just nodded and cranked the music up. Ma Baby was his baby-mama and all, and she was a down ass thorough bitch back in her day. But he wasn't getting positive vibes from her. Something just wasn't sitting right with him. He was sketchy about her sudden release from prison. And all the prying questions was weird cuz she was *never* the "nosey type" before. But now the bitch had more questions than Family Feud! That was suspicious. His street senses told him to be alert and watch her ass closely until he knew what the fuck was ***really*** going on.

NACHO WAS the size of *two* human beings. He was built like an offensive lineman and as wide as an SUV. So, when Summer opened the door, she couldn't see Ma Baby standing behind him.

"What up my nig?" Summer said, greeting him with a high smile.

"Shit. Came to kick it wit you heifers for a little bit and introduce y'all to a new friend of mine," Nacho said.

Summer looked confused. "Friend?"

"Yeah bitch!" Ma Baby said, stepping out from behind Nacho. Summer screamed at the top of her lungs like Freddy

Kreuger was coming after her. Rose and Becky ran to the door to aid and assist their homegirl. Becky had a 9mm with the lemon squeeze clutched tightly in her hand. Rose saw what Summer was screaming for and began screaming loud as hell too! Summer and Rose rushed Ma Baby and three-way hugged her. Becky just stood there looking confused. Nacho leaned against the wall and smiled.

"Girl, what the fuck is you doing here? Did you break out?" Summer asked.

"Naw mami, I'm free. I won my appeal!"

"Chica, I thought you used up all your appeals," Rose said.

"Got my shit overturned cuz of an error by the courts. So here I am," Ma Baby said, opening her arms wide. Rose hugged her again, picking her up and spinning her around this time.

"Ma, we've got *sooo* much catching up to do. Come on," Rose said, grabbing Ma Baby's hand and pulling her into the living room.

"Where's GG at?" Ma Baby asked.

"She's putting in work up in Appleton headlining this lil stripclub up there and handling some business," Summer said. Ma Baby's ears perked up upon hearing the word stripclub. She took a seat on the butter soft white leather couch. *Nah, it couldn't have been them*, she thought to herself.

"Say whaaaa? *Stripclub*? Lil GG stripping now?"

"Umm, lil GG ain't so little no more. Mami thicker than you, Ma Baby. She all grown up now," Rose said.

"Speaking of *thick*. Ma, you done bulked up like a muthafucka! Look atchu girl. What, you been in da joint pumping iron and shit?" Summer teased and laughed.

"Girl, forget chu. I was in dat bitch eating like a muthafucka. That's all you can do. Especially when you're depressed cuz you got a 30-year sentence. But I was in the gym too tho," Ma Baby said. She kept looking over at Becky who was also eyeing Ma Baby skeptically and still holding her heat.

"Aw shit, my bad," Rose said, peeping out the body language between the two. "Put that shit away girl, she cool. She family. The one we told you about," Rose told Becky. "Ma Baby, this is Becky. Becky, this is Ma Baby."

Becky put the gun back in her purse and stood up to shake Ma Baby's hand. *So, THIS is the one who taught them everything they know huh?* Becky thought to herself. For some reason though, she got a bad vibe from Ma Baby when she looked into her slanted hazel eyes.

Deception will enter your world when you least expect it. Stay on guard to protect those you love, or the cost will be detrimental.

Becky's eyes got big and her heartbeat sped up as she thought about her horoscope she read that morning. "Something wrong?" Ma Baby asked Becky, sensing her sudden change in demeanor.

"Uh, no. You just...uh, you look so much like Selma Hayek— "

"Yeah, I get that a lot," Ma Baby said and smiled.

"Um, well, it's nice to meet you Ma Baby. I've heard a lot about you."

"So, who is she?" Ma Baby asked Rose.

"This our girl. Shiiid, she's one of us now. BBC for life, right Becky?" Rose said.

"Yup. BBC for life!" she responded but looked at Ma Baby while she said it.

"BB *what?*" Ma Baby asked, looking confused. Summer and Rose looked at each other. They didn't think they'd be seeing Ma Baby for another seventeen years. When she got locked up, they were her "soldierettes" in training. Back then, Ma Baby's click was called "Milwaukee Mami's," and that's what Summer, GG, and Rose used to scream, throwing up the double M's wherever they went. But after Ma Baby got knocked and Rose and them found out it was the Milwaukee Mami's who dropped dime on their own leader, they chose to *NOT* rep the double

M's no more. They would not be affiliated with anything as disloyal and snake-ish as those backstabbing rat hoes.

So, once they dismantled the Milwaukee Mami's, bodying the ones they could get to because six of them were put into witness protection and were ***still*** out there somewhere living under new identities, most likely far far away, they decided to form their *OWN* exclusive organization. A real one built on loyalty, honesty, trust, and a sheer passion to get money and succeed at all costs! So, in the fall of 2010, the **B**ad **B**itchez **C**lick was born.

Rose and Summer took turns explaining to Ma Baby about **BBC** and why they decided as a group to move in a "new direction."

"So y'all ain't reppin' double M's at all?" Ma Baby asked with obvious hurt in her voice, looking like she was about to cry.

"Nah chica. We just couldn't. Even though *YOU* wasn't no rat, we still didn't wanna be associated with anything that was," Rose told her, on some real shit.

"All them punk ass hoes rolled over on you, Ma Baby. They had Milwaukee Mami's tatted on them. We got our shit removed. What we look like representing that shit? You know how the streets talk. Muthafuckas woulda been at our heads too. Knowing how them bitches was disloyal snitches and sent you up the river opened our eyes to how people's integrity goes out the window when the heat is on," Summer said. Everyone nodded in agreement.

Ma Baby felt guilty hearing Summer talk about the same kind of "rat" she signed up to be. But she didn't let it show. "I feel you. It's just... well, I built Double M. Y'all know– "

"Ma, you know da biz. *NO* associating or being affiliated with snitches. Rats get they shit pushed back. **PERIOD!** You da one that taught them dat shit. They did what was right," Nacho said, speaking his two cents.

Ma Baby nodded her head sadly and looked at Summer's Tuyserkan Persian rug, thinking how beautiful it was but also wrestling with her thoughts. She knew they were right. Even worse, she was now the "rat" in that same category that they despised so much. How the tables have turned! She still wasn't sure how they converted her. *If they only knew. They'd probably push my shit back too.* She felt sick to her stomach and wanted to throw up.

"Don't trip tho Ma Baby. When you see the structure we got and how we killing the game, you'll agree that it was for the better. You'll be proud of us," Rose said, trying to cheer up her mentor.

"I feel you. It's just... well, I thought y'all was still holding it down. I saw Summer in all those magazines and music videos throwing up M's and I figured she was sending me a message. Letting me know y'all was still out here reppin' for me. Shit, I got the love y'all sent me every month. The money orders, books, magazines, and cards. Y'all held me down like a motherfucker, and I really appreciate that," Ma Baby said.

"Shit, you know how we do. We look out for ours! You brought us up and showed us the ropes. How to get money and win. We wouldn't be where we are today if it wasn't for you. But them M's I was throwing up? That's just me representing the city Ma Baby. You know I'm a true Milwaukeean til I die. I wasn't throwing up ***two*** M's either. Just one. I didn't want people to get it misconstrued wit Milwaukee Mami's. Cuz as far as I'm concerned, and no disrespect Ma, but ***FUCK*** Milwaukee Mami's! I'm from da Mil. But I'm a **REAL** bitch. A ***BAD*** Bitch!" Summer said. Ma Baby grimaced when Summer said "fuck Milwaukee Mami's," but she bit her tongue because she knew the hatred Summer felt toward the click she started was for the chicks who told on Ma Baby, so she let the comment slide.

Becky blazed up another blunt and asked Ma Baby if she'd like to try *their* weed. Rose told her about the exclusive strain they had concocted for them and Ma Baby was impressed. Even tho there was plenty of drugs in prison, she chose not to indulge. She had to stay sharp and be on her toes at all times in the clink. Because if you got caught slipping just *once*, that may be your last. Now that she was free, her curiosity and old love for weed got the best of her. Ma Baby didn't have to take no piss tests. She was fresh out and hadn't smoked in 8 years. She accepted the blunt from Becky and took a long pull of the sweet, potent BBC Bomb. She began hacking right away, coughing for like three minutes straight. Drool ran from her mouth and she turned "STOP" sign red.

"Take it easy chica. You know your system ain't used to this shit. And the weed these days ain't *NOTHING* like it was ten plus years ago," Rose said, chuckling and patting Ma Baby on the back. Ma Baby's already Chinese looking eyes got blood-shot red and even lower. She was instantly high from the one toke. Nacho snatched the blunt out of his babymama's hand.

"Man, let me try dis shit and see what it do," he said, taking a few long drags. He held it in for a minute while smoke wafted from his nostrils. "Mm, it's ok," he said and passed the B to Summer. He began gagging on a cough he was trying to hold in and all the women started laughing at him as they watched his eyes water and face turn red. Sweat beaded his face and he was unable to hold it any longer; he coughed and choked relent-lessly as he released the rest of the smoke.

They all chopped it up, smoked BBC Bomb, and caught Ma Baby up with what's been going on since she'd been gone. They didn't reveal how they had the drug game on lock though. They just said they had some legit businesses that were very prof-itable, which was true. Rose knew Ma Baby used up all of her appeals because she was the one who paid for and kept in contact with her lawyer. So, until she found out the *real* reason why Ma Baby miraculously got out, she'd be tight lipped about her underworld organization. Rose didn't want to assume Ma

Baby was working for *them* people, and she had a hard time even ***thinking*** her mentor was like that. But this wasn't Rose's first rodeo. She'd seen *plenty* of people get out early in exchange for testimonies or becoming informants. She'd seen a lot of shit during her time in the streets, so it wouldn't surprise her *too* much, but it would break her heart if that were the case. Rose knew Ma Baby for many years. She practically raised Rose since she was 13. So she highly doubted that the woman she looked up to and brought up in them cold hard streets could be an opposition now, but Rose put nothing past no woman or man. You just never knew. But just to be on the safe side, she'd keep her close and find out what was what first.

Summer, being the smart woman that she was, peeped how Rose steered clear of mentioning their criminal activities. She followed Rose's lead, talking only of their legitimate endeavors and speaking on her modeling gigs and the new sex toy she was in the process of making.

"Really? What's it called?" Ma Baby asked, blowed out of her mind!

"Duck Me! It's a vibrating rubber ducky that...penetrates you," Summer said with a wicked grin.

"Damn, that sounds hot!"

"It is. Wait til it's finished. Y'all gonna love it!" Summer said enthusiastically.

"Ok, ok. That's what's up. But shiiid, now that y'all know a bitch is home, is y'all gonna throw a bitch a welcome back party or what? Shit, I wanna get turned up and shake my fat ass. Don't get it twisted yo, a bitch still got it," Ma Baby said, snapping her fingers and swiveling her hips. "Plus, I wanna meet me some fine ass nikkuhs and do da damn thang!"

"Fa sho, fa sho. You know we got you girl. We gonna hook it up for you," Summer said.

"Chica, I'm finna call Dre right now and tell him we wanna rent The Rave out for a night. All the big ballers and anybody who's anybody gonna show up. The streets ain't never forgot about you Ma. You's a muthafuckin' legend out here, so everybody gonna be there to pay homage," Rose said.

"Hell yeah, now that's what I'm talking about!" Ma Baby said and gave Rose a high five.

"Yeah, we gonna make this Mil-town's most memorable event the city has ever seen. Ma Baby is home bitchesssss! Get ready," Summer shouted.

18

TEAR DA CLUB UP!!!

Word spread like wildfire from the streets to social media that a welcome home bash was being thrown for a legendary figure from Milwaukee. Anybody who was anybody showed up to The Rave, a multi-hall concert venue, that night. Muhfuckaz pulled up in Porsche trucks on 30's, 745's and 750's, Benzes, Rolls Royce's on Davins and all kinds of other fly ass cars were banging the latest rap tunes. Niggas had they ice game on drip. Their wardrobes were baller chic: Louis Vuitton, Prada, Armani, Maison Margiela, and plenty of Gucci.

But it was the WOMEN who showed up and showed out in clicks, shining like new money. Go Getter Girlz(3G'z), Ca$h Money Bitchez, Cherry Street Chick$, Women With Attitudes (WWA), Redbone Divaz, and Dirty Dames. The heels were high, and the skirts were short. Everyone's hair and nails were on fleek. Titties and ass were out in epic proportion as their diamonds and beautiful skin blinged magnificently under the fluorescent lights.

The woman of the hour wore an elegant spaghetti-strap purple dress that came to mid-thigh. On her feet were black leather Altuzarra boots that had a six-inch stiletto heel on them. Carol, whom told everyone she met Ma Baby online, was by her side wearing an Elie Saab gown that had a slit up to the waist and Stella McCartney heels.

Bouncers at the door took the $1,000 admission and pat searched everyone they let into the club. The BBC stood in V.I.P on the balcony checking out the attendees as they came in and commented on everyone's choice of attire. DJ Butta had the music banging, and later, Party HaRRRd would perform on the main stage. THOT Gang, the rap group, would also be doing tracks off their new mixtape.

The Rave was filled with marijuana smoke and everyone had bottles, not *glasses*, in their hands. T-dub and Mud Money was in the building dripping sauce. Cats from Murder Mob, 2-1, TPC, Drip $quad, and Dreadheadz were all there reppin' their crews. But the deepest of them all was THOT Gang. They were over fifty deep in that bitch! And because their rap chicks were gonna rock the stage for the first time, they were *extremely* turnt up!

BBC came down to the main level to greet all the guests as Ma Baby networked and met new acquaintances. T-dub, who had "Tamika" on his arm, strolled up to Ma Baby.

"Yo, I've heard a lot about you Ma Baby. You a legend out here. It's nice to finally meet you," T-dub said and introduced himself.

"It's nice to meet you too T-dub," Ma Baby said, shaking his hand. She stared at the blinding MM piece dripping in diamonds on his necklace. Milwaukee Mami's flashed in her mind and she had to shake off the memories.

"This is my girl Tamika," he said, the two women nodded at each other. Ma Baby thought the redbone beauty looked familiar but couldn't remember where she knew her from. Lyza, on the other hand, knew *exactly* who Ma Baby was. At one point, Ma Baby was on Lyza's radar to get robbed until she found out one of her cousins was a Milwaukee Mami member. Then she fell back from her 2-11 plans. Up until then, she had trailed the infamous Latin Queen and posted up at some of the same spots and events she was at to learn all of her moves. What was so ironic was, after Ma Baby got knocked, Lyza was hired to murder Ma Baby's cousin for testifying against her. Lyza did the job by suffocating her to death with a pillow. Now here stood the two women all these years later. Lyza knew she didn't look the same anymore. She'd lost a lot of weight and grew her hair out. Ma Baby, on the other hand, looked *exactly* the same, just thicker now.

"I got a homeboy who would loooooove you," T-dub said, looking Ma Baby up and down.

"Oh yeah? Well tell him to buy me a bottle and we can talk," she said, telling him she'd be around. Then she went to do more congregating.

Big Mama Drawz, a 6'8" Amazon sista from THOT Gang, was turned up and really drunk as she bumped into people and staggered through the club. "Damn bitch. Move! Get da fuck out my way yo," she slurred to the people she towered over, men and women alike. Her height and weight were already intimidating enough to anyone who looked at Big Mama Drawz, but she was also a thug ass bitch that took no shit. She was a bully all her life and was a *stomp down knockout* artist who thrived on drama. "What da fuck you looking at hoe? Huh?" she asked a big nosed chick from WWA.

"What? Ain't nobody looking at yo big ass. You better fall back." The courageous woman told Big Mama Drawz. Nadia stepped between them and pulled Big Mama Drawz away before shit popped off.

"Girl, you know we chillin' tonight. Just be cool. You know these hoes don't want no smoke," Nadia told her.

Meanwhile, Becky was puffing on a blunt while Poobie

rubbed on her booty. "Babygirl, you know you strapped," he whispered in her ear. "I'm tearing this muthafucka *UP* later on!"

"Mmmmm, you promise?" Becky cooed, grinding against him. "Cuz not only do I want you to tear this pussy up, but I want you to fuck my little...pink...asshole too." Poobie's eyes popped out of his head like a cartoon character and he got a raging hard-on!

"Damn, you freaky as a muthafucka," he said. She smiled and continued to seduce him.

Neef, a tall chocolate brother with 360 waves and white gold diamond teeth, walked up to Ma Baby with a bottle of champagne in each hand. "So, I hear you're the woman all of this is for," he said. Ma Baby took a step back and inspected the nicely built hustler whose mouth looked like a disco ball.

"Yeah, something like that," she said and smiled.

"I'm Neef. My boy T-dub said me and you would hit it off. And umm, I'd have to agree with him," he said, checking Ma Baby out and handing her a bottle of Ace of Spades. In her boots, she stood 6'4" which was an inch shorter than Neef's 6'5" basketball frame. They popped their bottles and toasted as the cool bubbly frothed over.

"To new beginnings and solid friendships," Neef said, raising the gold bottle in the air. Ma Baby followed suit and clinked her bottle against his before they both drank from them. *I'm giving this nigga the best pussy he's ever had in his life tonight*, Ma Baby vowed to herself.

GG and Summer hit the dancefloor as they showcased their choreographed hip-hop dance moves. A circle of people surrounded them as they wound their hips and shook their jiggly parts in sync to the music. They were both professional dancers, so they made it look easy. Rose, always the observant one, stood off to the side smoking a blunt while watching her chicas in action. They truly were a click of Bad Bitchez and couldn't nobody tell her otherwise. In the meantime, she was gonna pull up on that Carol bitch and screen her. That girl was green as a pool table and most definitely wasn't from Wisconsin. Rose wanted to find out who she really was.

By the time Party HaRRRd hit the stage, the Rave was jam packed! Diamonds blinged under the dense fog of weed smoke while all the different clicks threw up their sets. Everybody was on ten when Party performed his street classic, "It's Real In Da Mil."

It's real in da Mil, my city's a battlefield,
Poppin' bottles poppin' pills we do it for drug deals.
Bitch it's real in da Mil, a hunid clicks dat kill,
So you mogs better watch what you say out cho grill!

GG and Summer got on stage with him while he did his set. They twerked, popped, and gyrated on the rapper while he rocked the mike for the excited crowd who sang along to every word. After doing eight songs, he passed the microphone to Summer.

"Give it up for my nigga Party HaRRRd y'all. Milwaukee's finest in this bitch!" she yelled. Party smacked Summer on her butt, threw an M up, and exited the stage to loud applause. "As y'all know," Summer continued. "This is a welcome home party for my homegirl Ma Baby. Some of y'all know her, and some of y'all know *of* her. She's been gone for a minute. But now, one of the realest bitches in the Mil is back and better than ever! So, show some love for my girl, the woman of the hour...Ma muthafuckin' Babyyyyyy! Get up here mami."

Ma Baby smiled and walked toward the stage. The crowd parted and gave her a big round of applause. People whistled and cheered as Ma Baby stood next to Summer. She was feeling like a Boss Bitch again. Then Rose took the stage, followed by

Becky, and she was quickly reminded who the *NEW* Boss Bitches of the Mil was. BBC stood behind Ma Baby as she grabbed the microphone.

"First of all, I want to thank my chicas for putting together this dope ass bash for me. They brought the city out for real for real. And to all y'all who showed up to this muthafucka, I appreciate it. Everybody's thousand-dollar admission is a donation to the Ma Baby fund. *Meaning*, y'all funding a bitches pockets. So good looking on that." Everybody in the crowd laughed and she continued. "A lot of shit done changed since I been gone. I see muthafuckas is coming up in the world, doing it stupid big, and that's what's up! New clicks out here holding it down. Get your money. Rep your crews. Shine on the haters. Shake twelve and continue to prosper. But remember this, the most important thing to have in these streets is **LOYALTY**. Without it? You're *NOTHING!* Death before dishonor. Bullshit ain't nuttin' ya feel me?"

There were some hell *yeah's*, *amen's*, and *preach!* shouted out by people in the crowd. Ma Baby passed the mike to GG and everyone gave her another thunderous round of applause.

"Give it up one more time for Ma Baby y'all. A real-life Milwaukee legend. Bitches better recognize! Now for all my hustlers. All my ballers. Get ready to stunt and turn the fuck up for none other than THOT Gaaaaaaaang!" GG screamed into the mike. Five members of THOT Gangs' rap group came on stage as a bouncy, deep bass track vibrated from the speakers.

We get moneyyyyy, twenty foe sev,
For that root of all evil we'll give you bitchez hell.
We get moneyyyyy, three sixty five,
You play wit my paper somebody gots to die. (Hey!)

The all-girl rap group performed their hit single "We Get $." Gia, Black&Blue, Traycilla, Ms. Prada, and Candy Yamz were the five MC's in THOT Gang. They were some sexy ass street bitches with mad bars. The crowd rapped along to the bangin' ass song that was burning up the streets. The rest of the THOT Gang click got on stage, backing up their girls. They went through their bangers, "Bitchez Rule The World," "Pussy Iz Power," "Hoes Up, Niggaz (Ain't) Down," "I Wipe My Ass Wit Hundred$," "Killwaukee," and a few more songs. THOT Gang threw money into the crowd, proving niggas wasn't the only ones who made it rain. Even though they were a fairly new group, they still rocked the stage like vets. Two days prior, they recorded a new joint called "THOT (Anthem)" and this was the last song they performed. It really set the club off.

Them Hoes Over There them hoes ain't square,
Them Hoes get down, they down hell yeah!
Them Hoes Over There they don't play fair,
They'll take yo shit then bloody up yo hair!

IT WAS a crunk ass anthem like Luda's "Move Bitch" and it had everybody geeked! Muthafuckas began throwing elbows, pushing and shoving, and a mosh pit formed. Big Mama Drawz had a big bottle of Grey Goose and started flinging the white liquor into the crowd, wetting people up. One of those who got doused was Vicky, the big nose chick she got into it with earlier.

Vicky mugged Big Mama Drawz and threw two W's up followed by a stiff middle finger. That was the green light. Big Mama Drawz smiled and threw the bottle at Vicky, but she ducked just in time. It cracked a Go Getter girl that was standing behind her in the forehead. Big Mama Drawz dived into the crowd and began swinging at Vicky, but the big nosed girl had a good bob and weave game, which caused Big Mama Drawz to fire on innocent bystanders. Men and women were getting clocked left and right. This led to their friends retaliating. And before you knew it, ***everyone*** was fighting.

THOT Gang jumped off the stage like wrestlers off the top rope! Niggas was whoopin' men and females. Bitches was going in on females and men. Everybody was high and drunk so the intoxication from the drugs and alcohol fueled people's adrenaline and numbed their pain. BBC looked at each other and shrugged like, *fuck it, let's tear da club up!*

Becky was the first to bust a muthafuckin' move. She elbowed a bitch and blood sprayed from the woman's nose like a water hose. Somebody grabbed Becky's long blond hair and yanked her head back. Knowing all kinds of fighting techniques, Becky threw her dome backward and head-butted whoever was behind her. Even in the loud ruckus, she could hear the crunch of bone when she connected with their face. She threw another elbow to the stomach of whoever was behind her, and they finally let her hair go.

Rose came up out her heels and was drilling bitches left and right, knocking hoes out with one punch. Niggaz was admiring her "hands" while she went ham on muthafuckas.

GG and Summer stood back to back, taking on three or four people at a time. Dudes and chicks. "This...is...B...B...C... mutha...fucka!" GG yelled, using some woman's face as a punching bag. Blood, teeth, weaves, high-heels, and jewelry were flying everywhere, laying all over the floor and getting trampled on by hundreds of feet. Tables, barstools, and bottles were being smashed against people's heads and bodies, causing people to be sprawled out on the floor unconscious.

THOT Gang was going nuts! Pita, Nymphy, Chula, Sandra, Jordan, Redd, and many others were showing bitches why they were one of the hardest females clicks around. Candy Yamz swung the mike chord like a whip as she clocked people upside their heads with the microphone. The DJ was still playing THOT Gangs music, so the hardcore tracks doubled as a soundtrack to the club brawl that resembled something from an action flick. It amped people up even more as fists flew and kicks were delivered.

Ma Baby had a Latino chick laid flat out on top of the bar while she pummeled her face with expert knuckles. "Y'all wanna come to *MY* party and fuck up some shit? This my night hoe!" she said, ramming the woman's face into the chestnut wood bar top.

Carol, on the other hand, had not been doing so well. Not a fighter in the least bit, she was knocked out cold at the beginning of the brawl by a nigga she rejected earlier in the evening. Still salty at getting shot down, he saw Carol trying to run for cover when shit broke out and he grabbed her from behind, spun her around, and punched her on the chin. She fell like a ton of bricks!

Luckily there were no guns in the club or else, there would've been some dead peeps in that bitch. But that was a good thing though because it took it back to the old days when people had to use their hands instead of pistols to settle disputes. So with a full-on bar brawl, it showed who actually had fighting skills and who didn't. And Becky, the lone white girl in a sea of black and brown bodies, was one of the best and thriving on it all. "Bring it on you cocksuckerrrrrrrs! I'm a Bad ass white bitch," she yelled, punching everyone in her path.

Big Mama Drawz finally got ahold of the bitch who kicked the whole thing off. After closing both of Vicky's eyes shut, she threw the girl's limp body over her shoulders and spun in circles, using Vicky as helicopter propellers. Big Mama Drawz hit everyone in her vicinity like a tornado, including members of her own click while screaming, "On the G... I'm the truth!" over and over.

Ma Baby jumped off the bar like she was a Kung-Fu fighter. Feet first, her six-inch stiletto heel drove through some chick's eyeball. Then she stomped on the bitches head and yelled, "I miss this gangsta shit!"

The brawl lasted twenty-three minutes--an eternity when you're fighting–before the lights came on and the police swarmed the venue on their bullhorns. "Alright goddamnit! Everyone... break it up. You all will be arrested for disorderly conduct and battery," a whiny voice said. There were hundreds of niggas in the club compared to the dozen or so officers. Everyone stopped fighting and looked around at each other. It was a non-verbal communication of the streets that they knew all too well. *FUCK TWELVE!* DJ Butta knew it too, so he put on Kendrick Lamar's "Alright." When it got to the part where he said:

And we hate Po-po, wanna kill us dead in the street fa sho...

That set it off! They looked at the boys in blue like, *fuck you muthafuckaz. Y'all must be crazy if you think you getting all of us*! Then someone yelled, "Let's get 'emmmm!"

Everybody in The Rave, men and women, bumrushed the police. Those pigs didn't stand a chance! They were tackled, trampled, beaten, and pistol whipped with their own guns. They were handcuffed and maced with their own pepper spray. They were tased by their own taser guns. They were stripped of their uniforms and got pissed and spit on. They were shown the *ultimate* disrespect like they'd been doing to minorities for years. With all the police brutality and killings of innocent black men the last few years by the hands of the police, it was a breath of fresh air to retaliate. This was a physical reparations of sorts for minorities. Even though there were a lot of African-American cops there, no one gave a fuck! If they were twelve, they got fucked up.

It was a liberating scene for many, and the shit went viral as cellphones captured the streets' justice via Snapchat stories and Facebook live. Squad cars were stolen and taken for joyrides while others were vandalized, shot up, and set on fire. All the acts of police brutality against blacks finally came to a boiling point at Ma Baby's welcome home party. It became the night niggaz and bitchez united and chose to rise up and ride on their oppressors.

They whooped the police, tore the club up, and even though there were some pretty bad injuries, nobody died. There was a lot of damages to the club that BBC would later pay for, but it was a historical night. NOBODY backed down. Everybody stood up for their peeps and held their own; some better than others, but it was all in good fun. And it showed the community that they *could* unite if they really wanted to.

BBC was unscathed and Ma Baby went home with Neef, having her first "consensual" sexual encounter with a man in 8 years. The sex was off the radar for both of them. They fucked until the sun came up, and she even cooked breakfast for him butt-ass naked. She was enjoying her newfound freedom, but when she saw him pull out a digital scale and box of sandwich bags, she was brought back to reality. She had a job to do, so she better start "fishing" now.

PART III

CONSEQUENCES

19

DOUBLE TROUBLE

Ever since Becky officially became BBC, her clout and status in Northern Wisconsin shot *way* up. Her business was booming like a car stereo on a hot summer day. And this was *not* good for her competitors. Specifically, the J-Twins.

Jessie and Julie Ainsworth, two petite brunette snow bunnies who recently turned 33, were registered nurses who'd been slangin' pills for the past six years. The last three of those, they became users of their own product. Getting high on their own supply was what turned those gray eyed beauties into pure pill heads.

They sold to support their habits and keep up with their lavish lifestyle of designer handbags and expensive shoes. But now that Becky's two for $50 deal was out there, everybody and they mama went to shop with her. She had the streets on lock. The J-Twins were always "civil" when they saw Becky. They knew she was a psychotic bitch that loved guns and practiced Martial arts. They didn't want no smoke with her. So, they co-existed on the pill hustling circuit. Plus, they sold their pills for less than she did, so they didn't really see her as a threat to their income faucet. But when that faucet began to dry up, the twins began calling their custy's and asking about the slow up.

They got various answers. "I'm quitting." "Money is funny." "Haven't felt like popping." And yada yada. The J-Twins knew their customers, so they knew all those excuses were bullshit. No one wanted to keep it real with them and really tell them they were taking their business elsewhere. The twins shrugged it off and just indulged more for themselves. This didn't go over well with their plug and boss Patricia Clooney, the head Hospital Administrator.

Because of her position, Mrs. Clooney was able to order double and sometimes triple the amount of medication needed for the hospital. And since the state was the one paying for it, she manipulated the books to make the inventory logs look legitimate. When in fact, the shipments that came in were well over the expected amount. Those extras went to Jessie and Julie to sell, and they gave Patricia a nice cut to keep herself in fur coats and glittery diamonds. When she confronted them about the lack of money coming in lately, they told her that business was just slow.

"Yeah, but the pills are obviously still going up *your* noses, but *I'm* not seeing any money. What the fuck?" Patricia scolded them one afternoon.

"Chill out Patty. We'll get your money," Julie said.

"I fucking better goddamnit! I'm trying to go to Bora Bora for the holidays, and I wanna buy all new shit for my trip," she told them.

Wanting to satisfy Patty and not get on her bad side, they decided to bribe the streets with free goods to get the information they were seeking in regards to their declining business. It didn't take long for the pill heads to spill the beans about

Becky's two for $50 deal. Not only were the twins shocked about the unbeatable bargain Becky was offering, but also the fact that no matter what the pill was, she had it on deck.

"Where the fuck is that cunt getting all of those pills from?" Jessie asked Julie. The twin shrugged and suggested they do their own investigation to get to the bottom of what Ms. Big Booty Slinkowski was up to.

They knew where her parents stayed. They surveilled the place for a few days and didn't see Becky, but they did manage to tail her sister Britney around the city. Her frequent stops of running in and out of various houses were obvious signs that the young girl was dealing. The twins thought she was slinging pills for her big sister, so one day, they approached her when she stopped at a gas station.

"Hey, it's Britney right?" Julie asked as she strolled up to the teenage brunette as she pumped gas at Kwik Trip.

Britney furrowed her brows. "Um, who wants to know?" she asked, looking back and forth at the skinny twins with the long stringy hair.

"Oh, we're some old friends of Becky. She said if we couldn't get ahold of her, you could probably help us out," Jessie said.

"Oh, alright. How much are you guys looking for?"

"Um, we've got one hundred bucks. Can we get four perc thirties?" Julie said.

"Percs? Um, you know I only got Kush right?"

"Kush? You mean weed?"

"Yeah. I don't fuck with nothing else. Becks musta told you that..." Britney paused and looked confused. Then she became skeptical. "What did y'all say your names were again?"

"Um, I'm Jessie, and this is my sister Julie."

"Oh, ok. Well, look, I can call Becks and have her give you guys a ring, or you can just talk to Sally at Dr. Jekyll's," Britney said.

"Wait, bartender Sally?" Jessie inquired.

Britney looked at the twins and was growing increasingly leery about their intentions. If they fucked with Becky, then they had to know her number one pusher was Sally. Unless...

"Hey, you bitches ain't the police are you?"

"Whoa, whoa, whoa, now. Come on," Jessie protested.

"How are you gonna insult us like that? Do we look like the damn police?" Julie said.

"I don't know *what* the fuck y'all look like, but your shit isn't adding up. So, answer my motherfucking question. Are y'all the motherfucking police?" Britney demanded sternly.

"No honey, we are *NOT* the police. And look, we'll buy some of your kush. We love weed too. So, can you hook us up?"

"For $200, I can get you an ounce."

"That's cool. Go get one hundred out the ATM Jess. And pay for her gas too while you're at it," Julie instructed her sister. "We didn't mean to ruffle your feathers or anything. I apologize about that. It's just been a long day. We're just trying to mellow out ya know?"

"It's cool. No biggie. Thanks for picking up my gas tab. I'll have to go get the bud tho. Can y'all wait here?"

"Sure. How long will you be?"

"Not long. Twenty minutes tops," Britney told her as she hopped in her Ford Fusion. As she drove off, she immediately dialed Becky and relayed her interaction with the twins.

"Brit-Brit, stay away from those hoes. Do not sell them *ANYTHING!* You hear me?"

"I hear you sis."

What the fuck are those cunts snooping around in my business for? She said to herself after she hung up with Britney.

Rivals are after your crown, but in the game of Chess, the Queen is the most important piece on the board.

Becky was out of town when Britney had a run in with the twins, but she made sure she got back to Appleton ASAP. She knew she'd have to confront the J-Twins sooner or later once they found out she was supplying all of their custys. Becky had put word on the street to all the pill poppers not to reveal how much she was selling hers for because that's when competitors feel threatened and shit usually ends up popping off! But obviously, someone had opened their big ass mouth and blabbed about her shit.

Two heads are always better than one,
But there's only one head on a coin...
And it is the heads on Roosevelt who will always win.

BECKY WAITED for the twins outside the hospital they worked at. She leaned against the gray Kia Optima smoking a blunt of BBC Bomb until they got off. Caught up in their own grumbling about Patricia on their backs, they didn't see Becky posted against their car until they were a few feet from the parking space.

"Hello ladies. I heard you been looking for me. Well...BOO! Here I go," Becky said as she threw the half smoked blunt on the pavement and stepped to them. The twins stopped in their tracks, completely caught off guard and scared shitless.

"Uh, Becky. How've you been?" Julie asked.

"Bitch, don't 'how've you been' me! What the fuck are you running up on my sister for? Asking her questions and shit. Y'all don't shop with me. What the fuck are you on?"

"Well, first of all, it was extremely rude of your sister to say she'd sell us bud and then never even coming back to do so. We waited in that parking lot for two hours for her and she never showed."

"*Your* bad. I told her don't serve y'all shit! When the fuck y'all pill snorting asses started smoking weed?"

"Rebecca, we've always smoked weed. Just because we dabble– "

"Bitch, cut the bullshit. What's really good?"

"What's good? Gosh Becky, when did you become so...ghetto?" Julie said.

"Look, what's good is we don't appreciate you stealing our custys. How are we supposed to make any money with you selling two for fifty everything?" Jessie said.

"Ho, that ain't my problem. Sell your shit two for 40 and I'm sure you'll take all my business."

"Hmpf. Be serious now. We wouldn't make any kind of profit that way. We're still trying to figure out how *you're* even profiting. I mean, come on, twenty-five a pill?"

"Bitch, don't worry about my profits. Mind your own damn business. It don't cost you a dime to stay the *FUCK* up outta mine!"

"Listen here skank," Jessie said, losing her cool. "I'm tired of you calling us bitches and hoes– "

"Oh yeah bitch? And what the fuck are you gonna do about it? *Ho!*" Becky said, walking up on them. Becky grabbed Julie's hair and pushed her head forward, making her head-butt her sister. "I'll whoop *both* you sluts right here in this parking lot," Becky yelled as the twins held their foreheads in pain and disbelief. "It's over for you two. I'm running shit now. Get it through your pilled-out heads. This is ***MY*** city. Accept it or move around. But if I find out you whores is asking about me, talking to my sister, or trying to fuck around in my business... I'll come for you cunts. And mark my words, you will *not* like the outcome." Becky flinched like she would punch them, and they both stumbled backwards with their hands up in surrender.

Becky kicked their car as she turned around. "See ya...in a Kia," she taunted. "Who the fuck drives Kia? You bitches ain't about y'all money. This bitch ass car. Ha! Get your shit together Ainsworth junkies," she said and walked off.

The twins immediately ran back into their place of work

and relayed the events that just took place to Patricia Clooney. Now that the head administrator knew the reason behind her sudden cash drought, she could do something about it. And the only thing she knew was to drop dime.

"Hello, Appleton Police Department. How may I direct your call?" A woman on the other end of the telephone asked Patricia.

"Yes, I'd like to report some drug activity."

20

CAROL

Carol Coleman had settled into her domestic role as the "submissive housewife." Her job was to cook the meals, keep the house clean, do the grocery shopping and laundry, and have an eager tongue ready for whenever Ma Baby wanted to be serviced. And that began to become less and less with each passing week.

It seemed like the only time she got to taste her Dom's sweet peach nowadays was when Ma Baby brought home some dude she wanted to have a threesome with. Carol never understood why Ma Baby wanted to share her with another man, but she refused to complain. Her job was to do whatever was asked of her. If that meant sucking dick or letting a dude fuck her, so be it. Ma Baby was her master, and she was the willing slave that did whatever was required to please her and make her happy.

Carol began learning the ins and outs of Milwaukee as she googled new places to go and ventured out in her cream Chevy Impala to explore her new city. One day, she ran into Ma Baby's friend GG at the Walmart on South Oklahoma. Unbeknownst to Carol, GG had been following her for a couple of days.

Seeing nothing out of the ordinary, GG chose the Walmart encounter to make her "coincidental appearance."

"Hey, ummm Karen right?" GG said, snapping her fingers like she was trying to recall Carol's name as she walked up to the young mulatto girl.

"Carol," she said, correcting her and extending her hand to GG.

"Oh yeah, Carol. That's right. My bad. Nice to see you again," GG said, shaking Carol's hand. "You here with Ma Baby?"

"Huh? Oh, no. Just me. I'm doing a little shopping for the house that's all," Carol said, looking into her shopping cart.

"That's cool. I just came to get a few knick-knacks myself," GG told Carol as they cruised the store and chatted. GG could tell just from a few minutes of conversation that the young girl was *really* naïve. Her demeanor was one that gave off a lonely, isolated vibe, and GG exploited that. When Carol told her she and Ma Baby were friends with benefits who just became roommates, GG found this to be interesting. And from the sound of the conversation, the "benefits" part of their relationship was not being exercised at the moment.

GG knew Ma Baby was rolling with Neef pretty tough. And word on the street was she and him were bussin' moves on the hustling tip. BBC had yet to be invited to Ma Baby's crib, so GG was gonna try to get the inside scoop herself.

"So how come I've never saw you around the Mil before?" GG asked Carol as they pushed their shopping carts into the parking lot.

"Oh, um… I moved here from St. Louis not too long ago, so I'm a newbie," Carol lied.

"St. Louie huh? What side?"

"Um, the east side," Carol said.

"Oh, ok. Cool. You know all about Freddie's then."

"Ooh yeah. That was my spot."

"Hmpf." Freddie's was an afterhours spot on the south side of St. Louis, and it had been shut down for years. This was the first lie she caught Carol in. "Well, since you probably don't know too many people here, wanna hang out with me for a while?" GG asked.

"Wellllllll, I don't know. I really should be getting back. I need to make dinner and..."

"For what? Ma Baby is out with Neef, and you know she won't be home til late. *If* she even comes home at all tonight."

That seemed to piss Carol off that GG knew more about what Ma Baby was doing and with *whom* than even *she* knew.

"You know what? Fuck it. Let me drop this stuff off at home and then I'll ride with you, if that's ok?"

"Sure girl. Now ya talking! I'll follow you then we'll go from there," GG said.

Back at her crib, GG helped Carol put away her stuff and snooped around on the sly. The way the crib was furnished and set-up seemed stale to GG. She knew Ma Baby liked bright colors that were loud and extravagant, and her house was the complete opposite of that. It didn't feel like a real home. They had no pictures or mementos or anything that made the place feel personal. Something just wasn't right about it to GG and it gnawed at her conscience.

Once Carol changed, they hopped in GG's Pontiac G6 GT convertible and hit the streets. GG had already texted some of her homegirl's in THOT Gang and TLB, telling them she was bringing some fresh meat through so to play it cool.

THEY DROVE ALL OVER MILWAUKEE; the eastside, northside, southside, even Brewers Hill. They puffed on BBC Bomb all afternoon and Carol was lightheaded and giddy. "I don't think I've ever been this high before," she told GG and giggled as they walked up to Chula's spot on 77th and Carmen.

"Yeah guuuuuurl, you ain't never smoked nothing this good before," GG said as she held Carol's arm to steady the wobbly girl. Chula opened the door as they walked onto the porch.

"What's good bitch? Glad you could make time to see a ho," Chula said, greeting GG with a hug.

"Bitch, whatever. You know I be on the road and shit."

"More like the *pole*. Yo ass ain't that busy."

"Shut up ho," GG laughed. "This is Ma Baby's um, friend, Carol. Carol, Chula. Chula, Carol." The two women shook hands as Chula's blue nose pitbull sauntered up and sniffed Carol's crotch. She tensed up in fear.

"Smurf, get yo ass out that girl's coochie," Chula said and kicked at the dog. It whimpered and scurried away. "Ol' freaky ass. I'm sorry 'bout that ma. He loves sniffing new pussy."

GG and Carol kicked off their heels and walked on the plush carpeting to Chula's den. Carol noticed tall green blocks piled on the table as they walked past the kitchen. It had to be at least 50 pounds of weed in that muthafucka. GG grabbed a Ginzu from the kitchen and began slicing up the whole pineapple she brought with her.

"Girl, you and them damn pineapples all the damn time. Don't be getting juice and shit all on my furniture. This shit is Egyptian leather." The den was a small immaculate room with a floor to ceiling glass door. It had iron gates on it. The drapes were open so they could look out at the backyard at Chula's garden. Chula sat in her chair, a specially made recliner that vibrated and gave intense massages. It held secret compartments for drugs and weapons, was temperature controlled, and had her name stitched into the arm rests in cursive.

GG placed the pineapple on a plate and sat it on the crystal glass table. She ate chunks of the fresh pineapple right off the knife.

"So, you Ma Baby's friend huh?"

"Yeah."

"What's up with her? I ain't seen her around in a while," Chula said.

"I don't really know. I ain't seen her much myself lately either," Carol told her, folding her arms over her chest. Chula and GG exchanged glances. Carol's body language gave her away. Chula already knew the demo. They were gonna get the girl zooted and find out who the bitch *REALLY* was. And since they knew she was gay, they'd play on that and seduce her on the low.

"Hmpf. Well, it is what it is. Girl, whatchu been up to?" GG asked.

"Shit girl. Same ol' thang. Getting money and sucka duckin'."

"Mmhm. I heard that," GG agreed.

They chopped it up for a little bit before Chula had to excuse herself to handle some business. While she was gone, GG put her hand on Carol's leg.

"You aight mami? You're offly quiet. Everything cool? We can leave if you want."

"Naw, I'm good. Shit, I'm just high. Plus, I don't wanna interrupt y'all thang."

"Interrupt? Girl please! You better jump on in the convo. Don't be acting like you all shy and shit," GG said as she reached over and began tickling her. Carol, a ticklish chick by nature, erupted in a fit of giggles.

"GG... STOP! I'm ticklish girl." GG straddled her and continued tickling her. Carol tried to get from under her, but GG was cockstrong. A thick stallion that had the mulatto girl trapped by muscular thighs. When Chula walked back in, GG told her to get in on the festivities. GG grabbed Carol's wrists and held them over her head.

"Get her girl," GG instructed. Chula was kneeling on the couch, tickling Carol's armpits, ribcage, and belly. Carol laughed hysterically. Tears ran down her beet red face. This went on for at least ten minutes until Chula's right titty popped out of her tank top and brushed against GG's face. Everyone froze in their tracks. The perfect Puerto-Rican C cup with the big brown nipple held everyone's attention. It rose and fell as Chula breathed deeply. GG looked at Chula, then at Carol, then shrugged her shoulders as she faced Chula's exposed breast and took the nipple gently into her mouth.

"Ohhhhhhh," Chula moaned and shuddered. She cupped the back Of GG's head and drew her closer. GG sucked that beautiful tit and lavished the small areola with her tongue. Carol sat there, underneath them, just looking on in awe. Her own nipples were hardening watching them.

When Chula pulled her left breast out, Carol licked her lips looking at the cone shaped titty. GG stopped what she was doing and told Carol to "take care of the other one." Carol was hesitant. She loved Ma Baby and wasn't a cheater. However, all that talk of her with Neef and other people knowing what Ma Baby was doing in the streets when ***she*** didn't even know was a major pang in her heart. So, when Chula grabbed the back of Carol's head and brought it to her chest, she submitted and took the left tit into her mouth. Together, Carol and GG sucked and tongued Chula's titties for a full fifteen minutes. Moaning, slurping, and gasps of breath floated in the air until Chula could no longer take it.

"Yo, any longer and I'm gonna squirt all over my damn self!" she said, getting up. She stood in front of them with hickies and saliva all over her Hispanic hooters. "I'm gonna fix myself a drink. Y'all want one too?" They both said yes. A few minutes later, Chula returned with a tray of Bahama Mamas. She gave Carol her drink first, then GG picked up her glass last. "To friendship and good times," Chula said, raising her glass.

"To friendship and good times," GG and Carol said as they clinked their glasses and took a drink. Chula sat back in her recliner and rolled a blunt. She turned on her 80-inch flat screen and played the movie *"Menace to Society."* They watched the hood classic and got drunk and high. The mickey that Chula slipped in Carol's drink was working because the normally shy girl was now all loopy and talkative. She seemed to comment on every scene that took place in the movie.

"We used to have parties like this all the time in Phoenix. Motherfuckers drinking, playing cards and dominoes, dancing, making out, sitting around talking shit," Carol commented.

GG listened on but didn't say nothing. *Phoenix huh? That's where she's from. I knew she wasn't from the Lou!*

When Cane went to see Jada Pinkett's baby daddy in the joint, Carol slurred, "See, muhfuckas always pull that *'I don't wanna see you in a cage like this'* shit when you locked down. They don't fucking know how important visits are to us. Specially in Dublin."

Bingo! Gotcha bitch. GG now knew where Ma Baby met this silly young girl at.

"I feel you boo. I was locked up in T.Y. and ain't NOBODY come see me," GG lied. Carol hung her head somberly, thinking of all the times she wished her family would come visit her. GG felt the mood shift and scooched closer to Carol and wrapped her arm around her. GG stroked Carol's hair and shoulders tenderly while they sat and watched the rest of the movie. Everyone was in tears at the end when Cane got shot up.

"My brother used to talk about how this was his favorite movie. Though I never watched it before now, I can see why he loved it so much. It's a hood classic!"

"DAMN RIGHT IT IS," Chula said, taking Carol's empty glass off the table to go refill it. Carol didn't notice her grabbing the glass with a napkin, and she sure as hell didn't know Chula put the glass in a Ziploc bag in her kitchen, so they could give it to their inside connect at the police department to lift the fingerprints off it.

Chula returned with a *new* glass of Bahama Mama laced with a strong sedative that would knock her out cold! And ten minutes later, that's exactly what happened. While she was unconscious, GG and Chula stripped Carol naked and recorded themselves doing things to her that would be used as "ammo" in their plans later down the road.

Cuban Doll rapped in the background: *Now it don't take much to get a bitch gone, five bandz on yo head send you home...* GG and Chula smiled at what they were able to uncover. Poor Carol had no clue that she was just a sacrificial pawn in an elaborate scheme that was going to get a lot of muthafuckaz checkmated.

21

SHIT HITS DA FAN!

"Oh yeah big Bill. Fuck my pink puckered asshole! Oh my God... your cock feels so good," Gail Slinkowski screamed.

"Ooh fuck, oh fuck, oh fuck, I'm coming baby," Bill Shultz announced as he pounded Gail's backdoor. "Here it comes honey!" Gail pushed him out of her asshole, turned around, took his slimy penis into her mouth, and guzzled his liquid seed down as he erupted in her throat. She sucked, slurped, and licked until his glands were raw nerves. He had to push the cock hungry slut away before he shattered into a billion pieces!

"You're one hell of a woman Gail. Gosh," he panted. The phone rang and she picked it up and handed it to him.

"Hello? Yeah Dale, what's up buddy?" Bill looked over at Gail with a look of horror on his face. "What?!? You gotta be shittin' me! There's nothing there. Why the fuck am I just finding out about this? I'm telling you Dale, I've known the Slinkowski's forever. They don't mess around like that. Yeah, yeah, ok. I'll be there in a minute. FUCK!" Bill disconnected the phone and ran his hands through his silver hair.

Gail, who sat up straight when she heard him mention the

Slinkowskis, was becoming frantic. "Bill, what's wrong honey? Did something happen to my girls? What the– "

"Gail, calm down. Please. The department is en route to your house. They have a search warrant...for drugs."

"Drugs?"

"Yup. An anonymous caller said that drugs were being sold out of the Slinkowski household."

"What? Why that's absurd. Simply ludicrous! We don't– "

"Gail, I know hun. But...they said Rebecca and Britney Slinkowski were witnessed selling narcotics and marijuana from your home, so a search warrant was issued. I'm sorry."

"That's insane! Give me my phone, I'm calling Tom."

"Uh, you better call Becky first and let her know what's going on," Bill said. She looked at him puzzled but did as she was told. She relayed the information to her first born. Becky was at her own place in Menasha at the moment. She tried to assure her mother that there was obviously some kind of mistake. But she said she'd meet her at the house shortly. When Becky hung up, she got rid of the pills and weed she had on her person in case they had a warrant for her place too. She had a stash house where the bulk of her merch was kept at and she was 90% certain NO ONE knew about it. But she called her little sis and gave her the message too. Britney said there was nothing at the house, but she'd leave her friend's place right now and meet Becky at the ranch.

Becky seethed and cursed as she drove her Ford Escape Titanium to her family's home. She knew who dropped dime and what this shit was about. And for that, they would pay!

~

"FAM, you wanna tell us why we finna merk this bitch?"

"Cuz the ho ain't right man. Bitch need to be dealt with," the angry rapper growled.

"Man, it sure is a shame to have to kill such a fine ass bitch."

"Hell yeah dog, all that sweet yellow ass going to waste. Can we at least fuck her before we body da bitch?"

"Look here you ignant ass niggaz, that's what's wrong witchu dumb ass muhfuckaz in the first place. Always thinking witcho dick! That's how niggaz always end up in some bullshit, all over some punk ass pussy," the rapper said, referring to himself more than anything. He had fell for a big booty and a pretty smile. Then was blackmailed. Him? *Blackmailed*? He was from the cold hard streets of Queens, NY. He'd been shot, stabbed, jailed, and all kinds of ruthless shit. But never had he been conned by some video bitch who threatened to reveal his down-low activities that could ruin his Hip-Hop career forever! The bitch tried to play like she ain't have shit to do with it, but he knew better than that. He knew what was up. Now it was time for the ho to meet her maker.

The rapper and his thugs loaded up all kinds of artillery as they cleaned handles and bullets with different color bandanas. Nines, Mac's, Desert Eagles, even an AR-15 were ready to blow up some shit. He took it back to the turf war days when him and his boys suited up in all black, ski-masked up in stolen cars, and fanned shit down! Two trap cars waited for them downstairs as they all put on gloves and masks.

Meanwhile, Summer was snapchatting live from Hot 97 as she and Kay Slay gave an interview for the debut of her Straight Stuntin' Magazine cover. "Y'all make sure y'all come down to the club tonight to celebrate the hottest cover to ever grace Straight Stuntin' cuz this shit straight *fire!*" she said into the microphone while also capturing the footage on her phone.

It was announced that New York's top five MC's would be performing that night. No names were given, but everyone speculated about NY's finest. Would it be Hov? Kiss? Nas? Who? One thing was for sure, the bash was going to be off the radar!

Summer hugged Kay Slay and Funk Flex, telling them she'd see them at the party later. Her and her east coast mami's Kari, Princess, and Bombay headed for the elevator as they laughed, took selfies, and high-fived each other.

What most celebrities and people in general failed to realize was that their constant presence on social-media, specifically the LIVE feeds, was like a GPS for their whereabouts. Twitter, Instagram, Snapchat, and Facebook Live made it possible for anybody and they mama to show up announced to wherever the person they were "following" was at. Which is why the gangsta rapper knew *exactly* when and where to roll up on Summer.

Her and her girls exited the ten-story building absorbed in conversation. Bombay got a text saying their Uber was pulling up any minute. As she looked up from her iPhone 11, she heard tires screeching to a halt. Two ratchet cars pulled up bumper to bumper, a handful of masked men dressed in black hopped out with guns a blazing! By the time Summer and them realized what was happening, it was too late.

"You set the wrong nigga up hoe!" Gunfire erupted in a barrage of bullets and smoke. Everyone hit the pavement as Kari reached for her baby nine in her purse. She stood up and blasted on the assailants, hitting two of them. "Bitch ass ni– " was all she got out of her mouth before the AR knocked her head off her neck like some kind of video game.

Summer, feeling woozy, reached for Kari's gun, which fell right next to her. She grabbed it and squeezed off rounds while she lay on her side, slowly losing consciousness. She heard a man yelp and knew she had shot one of them too. Then everything turned to black...

~

WHILE SUMMER WAS GETTING POPPED up and the Slinkowski's

crib was getting raided, Patricia Clooney had her feet kicked up on her desk, hands clasped behind her head, with a big ol' smile on her face. Her two flunkies sat in front of her looking nervous.

"Relax, bitches. I took care of those Slinkowski cunts."

"What? How?" Jessie asked.

"Ohhh, I just tipped off the police about their extra-curricular activities. Those little whores should be in handcuffs as we speak," Patricia said, laughing.

"Oh my God! You didn't?!" Julie Ainsworth said.

"Yes...I did. Now you two should have no problem selling our merchandise anymore. Those bitches won't be dealing anything anytime soon."

"Patty, I don't think that was a good idea," Julie said, her teeth chattering suddenly.

"Yeah, she's gonna find out we had something to do with it," Jessie said.

"She won't find out shit! And let's just say that she *does*? What's she gonna do?"

"Are you fucking kidding me? The bitch ***SHOOTS*** at people. Look at this," Jessie said, pulling up a video on her phone. It was of her shooting at Amber's feet the day they came to fight Britney.

"She's freakin' nuts! And she fucking hangs with black people and ghetto bitches," Julie said.

"Pipe down. She's not gonna do shit. The police are gonna be on her like flies on shit! She'll be a good little girl from now on. And besides, I highly doubt she knows who ratted on her," Patty told them. The twins looked at each other, knowing better. Becky was no dummy. And once she put two and two together, they knew there would be trouble. And they were scared to death.

22

UNTRACEABLE

Britney had been mistaken about there not being anything in the house. She had two unsmoked blunts that she'd forgotten about in her drawer. The police acted like it was two *KILOS* though as they ushered her off to jail. Becky was wilding out and cursing them all to hell as they led her baby sister out in handcuffs to the squad car. Becky was ranting that it was *her* weed, but they found it in Britney's room and wasn't trying to hear that shit.

"Don't say a word Brit. I'll be down there in a sec to get you out. You cocksuckers have nothing better to do than arrest people for some petty ass weed?" Britney yelled at the cops.

Back at the station, the police tried to rattle the teenager, thinking she was a naïve little girl, but they didn't frighten her one bit. She was schooled by the best! They wanted her to rat and tell who was selling all the drugs in town. But all they got from her was an "Oh puh-lease" eye roll.

By the time Britney's parents, sister, and lawyer showed up, the detectives hadn't gotten more than two words out of her. But they let her know before she left that they'd be watching.

In the days that followed, Becky laid low as she witnessed unmarked cars follow her and try to track her every move. She sent messages to her workers to stop pushing until further notice. She instructed Britney not to slang either while she plotted her next move. Once she felt everyone knew their duties, she flew to New York to be by Summer's bedside while she recovered from her gunshot wounds.

The information she got from BBC was that Summer was the sole target. Her girl Princess was the only unharmed survivor in the ambush and she relayed the events to BBC. After some discussion about who it could be, it was Becky who told them she was 99% sure that it was the rapper they had the fling with. Who else would say, "you set the wrong nigga up hoe?" They knew all of Summer's sponsors were high powered officials and celebrities, but the only hardcore street muthafucka she staged a walk-in on was ol' boy.

"So that niggaz got a death wish huh?" GG said, stroking Summer's hand as her girl laid up in the bed with lots of tubes hooked up to her.

"That fag ass nigga ain't street. We gonna show his dick in the booty ass how *REAL* street muthafuckaz get down!" Rose said.

BECKY HAD ice water in her veins. It seemed like as soon as everything was going good and on the rise, someone was always lying in wait to bring her down. First her and her family, her hustling, and now trying to assassinate Summer. She had revenge on her brain, and as the heat died down, she went to work.

She now traveled wearing a short black wig that looked like a bob. Kind of like Uma Thurman's hair in *Pulp Fiction*. She also wore bigger clothes that didn't hug her coke bottle curves. That way, she could move and groove inconspicuously. Rose got her a Town & Country mini-van to get around in under the radar.

Becky trailed the J-twins, following them around the clock 24/7, learning their every move. Their "business" definitely picked back up since Becky put a halt to her hustling operation. Dumb bitches never knew they had a tail. They thought shit was sweet. Becky was able to put a tracker on their car, hidden cameras in their house, and a hidden app on their cellphones that allowed her to hear all of their calls and see their texts.

Jessie had a junkie boyfriend whom she'd go and see every couple of days. He'd shoot heroin while she snorted crushed up pills off his penis. Then, it was a drugged-out fuck fest.

It was a dark, moonless night when Becky made her move. She had a backpack of goodies: night vision goggles, lock breaking tools, and other spyware. She was able to peer into the first floor bedroom of Jessie's boyfriend's house and watch them do their routine thing. She scrunched up her face watching the two *very* pale, bony bodies ram into each other while they bumped uglies. They both came loudly, and thanks to the drugs, nodded off into la la land soon after.

Becky went through the back door wearing latex gloves. She crept into the bedroom where the two junkie lovers lay passed out. The room reeked of sex, ass, and stank. She gagged at the stench as she stood over the bed. *Funky cunt bitch needs to wash her pussy*, Becky thought to herself. She dug into her backpack and pulled out two needles loaded with uncut Colombian heroin. First, she injected the man and made it look like he had shot himself up, leaving the needle in his arm. He never even budged.

Jessie stirred as Becky grabbed her arm and injected her veins with the pure dope. Her eyes shot open and she looked into the big ocean blue eyes staring at her through the dark hoodie. Jessie tried to reach out with her free hand, but that boy was an instant paralyzer.

Becky smiled, the grim reaper in female form came to collect another soul. “Your sister’s next bitch,” she whispered as Jessie’s body twitched and shook for a few seconds before it went completely still. That familiar arousal began to wash over her body; wet pussy, hard nipples, heavy breathing. Killing really was an aphrodisiac for her.

Becky put the needle in Andrew’s hands, making sure his prints were on it before tossing it on the bed. It would look like he shot his girlfriend up then himself. Becky left the same way she came in and disappeared into the dead of night.

BECKY WAS TAUGHT by a mechanic in Minnesota on how to dismantle brakes to make it look like they’d been wearing thin. While she was laying low and plotting her untraceable acts, she practiced on a couple of junk cars until she got the satisfactory results she wanted.

It took her an hour and a half to “tamper with” Julie’s car. The plan was for the brakes to fail as she sped toward the hospital once she got the news that her sister had OD’d. Knowing the distraught woman would be crying, speeding, and frazzled, her carelessness would most likely send her through the windshield and end her existence on impact. There might be another bystander injured in the process, but at this point, Becky didn’t give a fuck *who* died! She wouldn’t be pleased until everyone who crossed her and her loved ones were in the motherfucking dirt!

Becky parked down the block from the twins’ apartment with the wire-tap app open on her phone...waiting. The call came in three hours and seventeen minutes after Becky left Jessie and her boyfriend D.O.A.

"Hello?"

"Yes, may I speak to Julie Ainsworth please?"

"This is her. Who is this?"

"Um, ma'am, my name is Steven Gorgdborg with the Appleton Police Department. I'm calling in regards to your sister Jessie."

"Jessie? What's wrong? What's happened to her?"

"Ma'am, there's been a...uh, incident. We got a call about a domestic dispute at Mr. Andrew Shultz' apartment– "

"That junkie bastard. I'll kill him!"

"Um...that won't be possible. He's dead. And your sister was also pronounced D.O.A. by the medics." "Wait. Wh-what?"

"Yes, it appears to be fatal heroin overdoses. They are on the way to St. Elizabeth's Hospital... now if you'd like to– "

Julie hung up on the cop as she tearfully threw on some clothes and bolted from her apartment. Her whole body was shaking as she attempted to get into her car. She dropped her keys on the pavement multiple times before she finally managed to get the door open. Once she started the car up, she rested her head on the steering wheel as she sobbed uncontrollably.

"Why Jess? Whyyyy? Fucking H? You know better than that. Andrew, you no good rotten son of a bitch! You killed my sister," Julie screamed as she punched the dashboard over and over.

With rage coursing through her, she put the car in reverse and sped out of the parking lot. AC/DC was blasting at full volume as she whipped her Kia to and fro. Had the music been down a bit, she might have heard the break-pads screeching. Becky smiled as she watched her distraught foe zoom out of her complex at max speed. *Only a matter of minutes and those bad boys would be non-existent*, she gloated to herself.

And sure as shit, by the time Julie hopped on the freeway, there was not a smidgen of brakes left on her whip. When she tried to brake while zipping around cars, her foot went straight to the floor. Stomping hard on the left pedal only to find it touching the mat made her panic. She began honking her horn like a wild woman as she shouted at passersby's. "Get the fuck outta my way!" She side-swiped cars and trucks. She couldn't even get on the shoulder of the road because an eighteen-wheeler was clogging up the lane going fifty miles per hour. She swerved through traffic like a car chase in an action flick. She felt like she was in the *Matrix* as she gripped the wheel tightly. Her sorrow turned to panic as her heart rattled her chest cavity and sweat poured down her back. "Please God, don't let me die. Not like this Lord," she prayed and wept.

As soon as she said that, the highway patrol jumped behind her, flashing its lights. Julie zigged and zagged, passing cars at an alarming rate. Now she was in a real-life car chase, just not by choice. Her exit for the hospital had at least four cars making the exit as well. "Fuck it," she said to herself, crossing her fingers on the steering wheel.

She made a sharp right and side swiped a Hyundai Elantra, dragging it into the F-150 that was in front of them, sending it straight into the cab's rear. Metal and glass made a sickening sound as a two-car crash turned into a six car pile-up. The domino effect of the collision was extremely fatal. Cars rammed into each other back to back.

Julie tried to ride the rail and made a sharp left that caused her car to flip up into the air at least fifty feet. The Kia did gymnastic summersaults for what seemed like *forever* until it finally pounced on the concrete and did half a dozen more flips. Eventually, it landed on its roof, wheels in the air, and spinning wildly.

A Wal-Mart semi tried to brake and swerve around the upside down Kia, but couldn't do so in time. It rammed the compact car into the opposite lane into oncoming traffic, where more cars throttled the Kia like a game of bumper cars. The vehicle pile-up was a tragic barrage. Cars burst into flames, bodies were thrown from windshields, including Julie. Glass and limbs covered the street as smoke and fire filled the air. Shit was hectic!

23

BRITNEY

The last few weeks in App town had been crazy. People were OD-ing, robberies and burglaries were on the rise, and there had been some random shootings that had baffled the community. Britney knew the real reason behind the chaos though. Her homegirls, the Bad Beez, had set up shop, bringing THOT Gang and TLB to the A and was supplying the city with enough drugs to keep every man, woman, child, and their pets high for months! The dope was pure, the pills were grade A, and the weed was fiya!

Becky let Britney in on who dropped dime on them and had their house raided. The J-twins and their boss Patricia had sent incriminating texts to each other, openly discussing their snake moves. Becky recorded it all on her spyware. When she saw what they said and how they planned to take the Slinkowskis down, Becky's blood boiled to the max! She hated snitches, and the deeper she got into the game, the more she transitioned from a semi-square snow bunny to a hood bitch in training.

GG and them had introduced Britney to all the classic hood movies like *Belly, New Jack City, Menace To Society, Bout It, Paid*

In Full, and Scarface. Movies she had never even *heard* of before. But once she watched them, they became a constant staple in her viewing repertoire. A life she had never even lived before had sucked her in, and she became addicted to the adrenaline rush that came with the drama and danger of the drug game. She changed all of her social media handles to "Brix-Brit" cuz she had bricks of kush on deck and felt like the female Scarface.

After the incident with Amber's dog, and the gossip of the police raiding her spot, Britney became a local celebrity and was viewed as a mob ass gangsta bitch that was *NOT* to be fucked with. And one Saturday evening, she demonstrated that...

One of the richest, spoiled kids in Appleton, Laura Rosenburg, decided to throw a huge party at her massive home since her parents were on a cruise for their 20th Anniversary. But this was no ordinary party. On the flyers and invitations that she gave to every high schooler in Outagamie County, the headline read V.S.P. To anyone in their thirties or forties, they wouldn't know *what* the hell V.S.P. meant. But for the younger generation who had their own lingo and slang and could hold an entire conversation using just emojis, they knew exactly what it meant...Vodka Soaked Party.

When Brix-Brit and her friend Tanya pulled up to Laura's crib in Becky's SLC-Class Benz, the party was in full swing. There were cars and kids on the front lawn, music blared from the house, barely clothed girls grinded on horny teenage boys, and everybody was turnt up!

Four of Laura's friends stood guard at the front door. In order to be admitted inside, you had to agree to two varieties of "soaking" that would be administered. This was a Vodka Soaked Party, which meant there would be no alcohol drinking on the premises. If you were gonna get tipsy, it would come through an unusual form.

For the females, there were vodka-soaked tampons that they'd insert inside of their coochies, walking around while the strong liquor seeped into their walls and flowed through their bloodstream. For the males, there were vodka-soaked condoms. One of the girls at the door gave a guy entering the party a quick BJ or hand job to get the guy erect and then roll a vodka drenched condom onto their penis and secure it to the base with a rubberband, so even when they went flaccid, it would not fall off. The little bit of vodka inside the tip of the condom would eventually find its way inside the dudes' pee hole and into his bloodstream. It would also soak into the shaft through his open pores.

The other choices were to eat vodka-soaked fruit (wop): watermelon, grapes, cherries, apples, kiwi, strawberries, etc. Or they could choose to be injected with a syringe full of the white liquor, heroin style– in their veins.

After choosing the tampon and fruit selection on one of the girls' tablets, Britney and Tanya were brought into the foyer where a little privacy curtain hung in the corner. Another girl stepped behind the curtain and pulled out the tampons while Britney and Tanya pulled their booty shorts and panties down to their knees. The girl handed them the Grey Goose drenched tampax for them to insert, which they did before pulling their undies and shorts back up.

"Oh yeaaaah, whatcha got in the bag Brit?" the door girl asked. Britney grabbed her book bag off the floor and opened it. "A pound of kush for the party. Some new shit that will knock your fucking socks off," Britney said, smiling.

"Cool. Make sure you get a spray bottle and drench it after y'all find someone to break that shit down. There's plenty of new bottles laying around so help yourself. Have fun."

"Ok, thanks," Britney said, zipping her bag up and heading into the living room. "Broccoli" was blasting in the elaborate surround sound system. White kids danced off beat and rapped along, "*In the middle of the party hoes get off me...*"

Everyone greeted Britney with hugs, fist pounds, and "what up" head nods. A couple of girls made room for her as she sat on the tan leather sofa. "Hey you guys, I need some help with this," Britney said, sitting her book bag on the glass table and pulling out its contents. Everyone's eyes got big watching Brix-Brit pull out the lime green saran wrapped brick of weed.

"This is a new strain of Kush. It's called TUK. Turn Up Kush. It's an upper like coke which gets you turnt up, but it also mellows you out too. It's the perfect balance. Oh, and it makes you ***super*** horny too," she said. Her and Tanya giggled hysterically.

"Wow. That's awesome. Are you gonna be selling this stuff?" a hazel eyed cutie asked while stroking the brick.

"Yeah, eventually. But for now, this is a party favor, so let's enjoy. Somebody grab a spray bottle and something to break this shit up with," Britney instructed. Tanya unwrapped the brick of TUK and a loud aroma filled the room unlike anything those kids ever smelled before.

"Holy shit!" "Mmmmm." "That smells amazing!" "Damn, I want some of that now!" Kids commented left and right. A couple of dudes came back with the requested items: a spray bottle filled with Apple Ciroc, a cookie sheet pan, some scissors, and pliers. They dove in stabbing and pulling at the brick of weed, breaking off chunks while the girls used their pretty hands to break down the large pretty buds. They sprayed the Turn Up Kush with the vodka, letting it soak and marinate. The tampons in Britney and Tanya's pussy had them tipsy ASAP.

"Ain't...no...telling...what...I...might...finna...be onnnnn!" They stood up and shouted as they made an appearance in the rest of the rooms. The place was packed. People were either naked or in swimsuits out by the huge swimming pool. People were popping fruit in their mouths like skittles. Others were shooting up their veins with vodka right out in the open. There were blowjobs being given against walls, sex being had on counters and furniture, make-out sessions everywhere you turned, laughter, moans and chants of encouragement filled the air.

The girls went into the kitchen. While Tanya loaded up a bowl of wop, Britney was busy unraveling rolls of paper towels. She looked on the back patio and saw her arch nemesis Amber giving her ex Deemontay a lap dance in a lawn chair. Her blood pressure rose, and she gritted her teeth with vengeance. Tanya walked up to her with the bowl.

"Here Brit..." she looked out the window too and saw why her friend was so tense. "Brix don't let those two douchebags get under your skin girl. Fuck them. They aren't shit," Tanya said, her words temporarily calming the storm.

"You know what ma? You're right. Screw them," Britney said, taking a few pieces of cantaloupe out of the bowl and popping them in her mouth. She grabbed the two cardboard paper towel rolls and stormed out of the kitchen.

Back in the living room, people were loading up their weed pipes with the vodka soaked TUK. "No, no, no! Damn junkie motherfuckers!" Britney shouted. "Put those fucking pipes down. We're steamrolling this shit." Britney pulled four boxes of blunts from her bookbag and threw them on the table. "Any of you fuckers know how to roll a B?" A few people raised their hands. "Get to rolling then. And make sure they are tight," Brix-Brit instructed like a Boss. She and Tanya made perfect size holes in the paper towel rolls, three on each side. Once all the blunts were rolled, they stuffed a quarter of a blunt in each hole and lit the exposed tips. The bottom of the paper towel was blocked with a wet washcloth. The user was to put their mouth at the top, engulfing the big round opening like a dick, and inhale deeply. Doing so would light up all six cherries. The steamroller full of smoke wound its way to their mouth and they'd be high as a kite! This was 20 times better than a bong. A petite chick named Amy was the first to try a go at it, but she choked and gagged so hard, she nearly threw up.

"Fucking rookie. Let me show you how it's done. Gimme dat shit," Britney said, snatching the steamroller out of the girl's hands and taking a monster hit on it like a pro. Britney held the massive amount of smoke in her lungs for thirty seconds before tendrils wafted from her nostrils like a dragon. Desiigner's eerie song "Timmy Turner" bumped in the background. It was the perfect soundtrack to Brix-Brit's kush smoking demonstration. Over fifty people stared in awe as she didn't let out a single cough. She blew enough smoke to make a locomotive jealous! "Now *that's* how you steamroll," Britney said, passing it to Tanya.

Word got around the party about the steamrollers and people from upstairs, downstairs, and the pool area staggered into the living room where Brix-Brit was holding court. When Amber and Deemontay walked in, the room grew silent. Britney lit the second steamroller and blew smoke in their direction. "Hey Tay...Amber," she said sarcastically. Everyone looked to and fro, waiting for shit to pop off, but Brix-Brit was on some chill player shit. She wasn't worried about them.

"Turn up Kush...that new flame. Want some?" She said, extending the steamroller to Deemontay and Amber. They looked at each other in surprise and shrugged. Being the pothead that he was, Deemontay wasted no time reaching for the steamroller from his ex.

"Thanks Britney," he said, putting his mouth around the opening.

"It's Brix," she corrected him and got up. She and Tanya squeezed their way through the mob and went out back to the huge pool to get some air.

"Those fuckers were shaking in their boots Brix. Everyone

for sure thought you were gonna open up a can of whoop ass," Tanya exclaimed.

"Nah, as long as that cunt stays in her lane... I'm gonna let shit slide...for now," Britney said. What Tanya didn't know was how eager Britney was to get her second go at Amber. She knew the outcome would be different this time. In the months since their epic fight, Rose honored her word and got Britney enrolled in numerous self-defense classes. She knew Jiu jitsu, Taekwondo, Krav Maga, and Kickboxing. She took to it like a beast, becoming one of the top student's in each of her classes. Brix was itching for Amber to jump slick or even look at her wrong, and she was gonna show that bitch a thing or two.

Britney and Tanya lounged by the pool, bobbing their head to rap and pop tunes and chopped it up with a few people.

"Brix. Major cutie at 12 o'clock is checking you out," Tanya said.

"Huh? Who?" she said, looking around. Then she spotted him. A tall black dude standing on the opposite end of the pool. He was eating a bowl of strawberries and burning a hole through Brix with his penetrating stare. Brix smiled at him nervously and he smiled back, revealing a mouthful of diamonds. Her nipples hardened and her knees got wobbly.

"Ooh crap Brix, look, he's coming over here," Tanya whispered. His walk was sleek and confident. Like a lion or a panther. All the girls ogled him as he moved. He wore skinny jeans with a royal blue Gucci Polo shirt tucked in. He wore designer royal blue leather sneakers with cream soles. His chain blinged with an iced out cross swinging from it. Diamond studs in each ear, and a presidential Rollie adorned his wrist.

"What's up shorty? I couldn't help but notice how fine you are. You killin' all these bitches in this party ma. What's your name?"

Britney swallowed hard but quickly regained her composure. Even though her heart was beating like crazy! “Hmpf. What’s *your* name?” she said, turning the tables on him.

“Ohhhh, ok. Flipping da script on a nigga huh? Aight then. I’m Gutter,” he said, extending his chocolaty hand. She shook it and held it for a tad longer than usual.

“Nice to meet you Gutter. I’m Brix.”

“Brix? Wait, you da chick I been hearing about wit dat good green on deck?” he asked.

“Yup, one and the same. Why you look so shocked, Gutter?”

“Shiiiiid. I-I- ain’t expect...” he trailed off.

“What? You didn’t expect me to be white?”

He didn’t say it, but yeah, he didn’t expect the bitch to be white. And so young. She had a babyface that was flawless but had the body of a grown ass woman!

“Nah, every race gets money. You just, I don’t know, you wasn’t what I expected that’s all.”

“Well daddy, don’t judge a book by its cover. It’s more than meets the eye,” Brix said.

“I feel you ma, I feel you,” he said, lustfully licking his lips and drinking in her banging curves. Britney introduced him to Tanya, swapped numbers, laughed, fed each other fruit, and got to know one another. Gutter was from Memphis, Tennessee and had that thick country accent to prove it. He was 20 years old and came up to visit his moms, who met some rich white dude and moved to Stevens Point. He had heard about the V.S.P on Facebook and decided to check it out and see what it was about.

“Yeah, this how we get down in the A, Gutter,” Brix said, laughing.

“Shit, y’all crazy. Bitch at the door pulled my piece out and got to sucking on it like a vacuum before she strapped the jimmy on. That muhfucka busted tho. I had to give her a magnum to soak,” he said, laughing. “But just the idea of this shit, it’s bananas!”

"So, did you get the magnum put on?"

"Hell yeah, they put a rubberband around my shit. This shit tight as a bitch!"

"They?" Brix said with a raised eyebrow.

"Yeah. I guess ol' girl who got me up told her girls how I was slanging, and two other chicks came behind the curtain. I had three snow bunnies on they knees, stroking my dick and looking at it like it was some kind of unicorn or something. One held my piece while another put the rubberband on. The other bitch stroked my balls. Shit was wild!" Gutter said, shaking his head in awe. Now it was Britney's turn to lick her lips. She had only had sex with Deemontay, but her teenage hormones were raging. She'd become a regular *Pornhub* visitor and used the vibrator Becky got her for her 17th Birthday.

They walked around the backyard talking, laughing, and puffing on vodka soaked blunts full of weed he brought with. "This that Blue Dream ain't it?" Brix commented, blowing gusts of smoke. He looked at her in surprise.

"Yeah fool, I know my shit, I'm a weed connoisseur," she said, smiling. "So, tell me something Gutter. You got at least 50k in your mouth, and another 50 or better on your neck and wrist. You the birdman or something?" Brix asked, passing him the blunt. They stopped under a plum tree and smoked.

"Well... I do a little of this... a little of that...but my passion is rapping tho."

"Rapping huh? Kick me something then," Britney requested. Gutter looked her up and down for a minute, then took three more drags from the blunt before handing it back to her.

"From the dirty to da Midwest, where da shorties real thick/ Gimme a nurse for this verse, cuz it's real sick/ Think I finally met a real bitch, the baddest of 'em all Ms. Brix/ I'm tryna preheat that oven so I can taste her cake mix/ Vodka soaked party? Man this some new shit what a trip/ Liquored up condom on my dick and fruit got me blitzed/ Only came to visit but I might stay for a bit/ and I ain't Gene Simmons but I gotta get me a kiss/" Gutter leaned down, palmed the back of Britney's head and brought her mouth to his full lips. He moaned as soon as he tasted her sweet cherry lip-gloss. He devoured her lips and tasted traces of strawberry still on her tongue as they passionately kissed under a full moon and sky full of stars. Her short, curvaceous frame melted into his muscular 6'2" stature and she felt like *that's* where she belonged.

Gutter's strong hands found their way to her big bubble butt that was so fat yet so firm. He didn't know white bitches were really built like that. He could've sworn those Kardashian chicks had surgically enhanced bodies, but since he'd been up in Wisconsin, he hit plenty of spots where the white girls had bodies like sistahs! They were naturally thick from all the hormones in the cows. All that good milk and dairy they were accustomed to in the dairy state had these snow bunnies with hips, tits, and ass for days! Gutter had never had sex with a white chick before, but he was quickly catching *jungle fever*. And 17 or not, he vowed to fuck the sexy honey dip in his arms.

After a five minute make-out session, they walked hand and hand back to the pool area. Brix had the biggest smile on her face until she saw Deemontay and Amber in the Jacuzzi. She was sitting on his lap with her back to him. It was like Amber had Britney radar cuz she immediately locked eyes with her and gave her one hell of a mean mug. Amber leaned her head back on Deemontay's shoulder and whispered something to him. He looked at Britney, said something to Amber, and they both laughed...at her? Oblivious to the tension in the air, Gutter put his arm around Brix's shoulder and asked her to shoot pool with him. She said cool and they went inside.

It was after midnight and the party was jumping! Brix-Brit, Tanya, and Gutter were downstairs in the game room. A huge room with two zebra clothed pool tables, arcade games, and pinball machines lined the walls. A drunk group of people were playing beer pong in the corner, and a PS4 was hooked up to a 50-inch TV.

THEY WERE HAVING FUN, laughing and kicking it while Gutter showed the girls how to hit trick shots. Amber and Deemontay came down dripping wet with bath towels wrapped around their waists. "We've got next," Amber announced, looking at Britney. The people playing on the other pool table said they could have the one they were on because they were almost done. Amber, feeling froggy, said, "Nah. I wanna play on *this* one," she said, pushing a couple of Gutter's pool balls into the table pockets. Gutter scrunched his face up and was about to check the colorful hair bitch when Brix put a hand on his chest. Tanya stepped up first.

"Listen Amber, I don't know what the fuck your problem is, but that shit wasn't cool."

"Shut up, bitch. Get the fuck out my face!"

"Fuck you bitch, you don't wanna– " Amber put her palm on Tanya's face and muffed her. *Hard*. When Tanya tried to react, Amber shoved her into a bookshelf full of board games. Tanya stumbled backwards and fell flat on her ass. Chess pieces, Monopoly boards, and Battleship pieces rained down on her body. A few people chuckled while others gasped.

"What, bitch? You want your ass whooped again? I know you did that shit to my dog you fat cunt," Amber said as she stepped to Britney. Quick as lightning, Brix karate chopped Amber in her throat. She bent at the waist, holding her neck as she choked. Brix uppercut Amber in the eye, grabbed the back of her hair, and pulled her head down to her knee. Amber's chin connected with Brix's knee and two teeth flew out of her mouth. Brix did a spin kick, her four-inch wedges clocked Amber on the side of the head. She went down like the Twin

Towers. That's when Brix pounced on her and unleashed a fury of rapid fists, elbows, and slaps like she was Bruce Lee. Each blow was followed by a "hi-yah!"

Once Amber went limp, Brix stood up and dusted herself off. As she turned to walk away, Amber grabbed a pool ball and threw it at the back of Brix's head. It missed her by inches. Brix spun around, picked the colored hair girl up off the floor, and bent her over the pool table.

"You wanna play bitch? Let's play then," Brix shouted and chopped Amber in the middle of her back. Amber howled and Brix pulled her bikini bottoms down to her knees. Brix grabbed a pool stick and broke it in half over her knee. "Mobb shit bitch," Brix said as she shoved the broken stick up Amber's ass. People grimaced, laughed, and stood around in awe at the sight. Amber's scream was so loud that it could be heard in *front* of the house. Brix pushed and jammed the pool stick further into Amber's anus and people stared in shock. Nobody dared intervene or even record the scene on their phones cuz they knew Brix was ***NOT*** to be played with.

Gutter stared with his mouth open... stunned! His dick was hard as a motherfucker, witnessing this sexy ass white girl go straight gangsta on a bitch! He knew right then and there that he was gonna *wife* ol' girl.

Brix had one hand on the pool stick and a handful of Amber's hair in the other as she smashed her face into the pool table repeatedly. The white and black zebra striped felt turned red. Brix yanked the stick out of Amber's ass and threw it on the table. Then she picked up the other half with the fat handle on the end and shoved it back in, causing Amber to cry out in pain as blood seeped out of her puckered hole.

Brix leaned down and whispered into Amber's ear. "From now on, leave me the fuck alone bitch. And if you snitch on me, I'll have *YOUR* head cut off too." Brix stood up and looked around the room. "Anyone, and I do mean *anyone*, mention this shit to the police... You'll all be fucking sorry." Everyone looked at the floor nervously, lumps in their throat, not saying a word because they were scared to death.

Brix, Tanya, and Gutter began to leave when Brix stopped and looked over her shoulder. "Amber, I always thought you had a stick up your ass. For goodness sake, get it outta there honey," Britney said, and laughed hard with her girl and new man joining in.

24

DRAMA

Ma Baby was walking around her crib in just a thong, smoking a fat ass blunt and loudly rapping along to 2Pac's "All Eyez On Me."

"I bet you got it twisted you don't know who to trust, so many playa hatin' niggaz trying to sound like us. Say they ready for the funk but I don't think they knowin, straight to the depths of hell is where those cowards goin!"

Carol stumbled into the living room, having been waken up by the loud music. She stood there staring at the Puerto-Rican goddess and her fat ass cheeks jiggling around like *Jell-O*. Carol's mouth watered and her pussy throbbed. But seeing as how it had been weeks since they made love, she knew trying to initiate anything was useless.

"Live the life of a thug nigga until the day I die, live the life of a boss playa, cuz even getting high...All eyes on me!" Ma Baby was all in Carol's face, throwing up Double M's now. Carol was uncomfortable and mistakenly pushed Ma Baby away and the hammer dropped.

"Bitch, who da fuck you putting your hands on?" Ma Baby shouted angrily.

"What the hell's wrong with you mami?" **WHAP!** Ma Baby slapped the shit out of Carol, leaving a red handprint across her cheek.

"Ho, who the fuck is you talking to like that? Do you know who I am bitch?"

Carol stood there with tears in her eyes, holding her face and looking like a wounded puppy. "I-I-I'm sorry. You just– "

"I just what?" Ma Baby sneered, grabbing a fist full of Carol's hair. "I run this. All this is me bitch. If you don't like it, you can get the fuck outta here. Yo punk ass would still be in that hell hole if it wasn't for me. Turkey neck would have your green ass bent over his desk on the regular. But uh-uh, not no mo. That bitch ass honky finna get his too!"

"Huh? What are you talking about Ma Baby?" Carol said in confusion.

"I'm talking about bitch ass Arnold Whiteside. You remember him? Our fat, slimy, rapist ass Warden. I'm about to pay his disgusting ass a visit. Oh yeah, pay back finna be a bitch," Ma Baby said, rubbing her palms together and smiling wickedly.

"Mami please. Leave that stuff alone. He's dead to us. There's no need– "

"You're right. He's dead alright. He was dead the day he laid his fat fingers on me. His wife, his kids. All them muthafuckaz gonna feel my wrath."

"No! You can't. Don't do nothing stupid Ma Baby. We're free. Are you *trying* to go back to prison?" Carol pleaded, grabbing Ma Baby's arm in desperation.

"Bitch, get off me! I ain't trying to hear that shit. It's on and muthafuckin' popping. Bullshit ain't nothin'," Ma Baby said, taking another hit of her blunt and blowing smoke in Carol's face. Carol reached out and stroked Ma Baby's exposed nipple.

"Did I *say* you can touch me? You do as I say. You understand?"

"I never get to touch you anymore, and you sure don't touch me. But if I was Neef– " Ma Baby stopped Carol mid-sentence and grabbed her by the throat, slamming her against the wall. She squeezed Carol's windpipe and lifted her off the ground, toes dangling in the air. With her free hand, she brought the blunt to her own lips and took deep pulls. She looked into Carol's terrified eyes.

"Keep my nigga's name out cho mouth ho. You don't know nothing about him. Shit, he can fuck me better than you *ever* could," she said and blew a gust of smoke at Carol. She released Carol's neck and the young girl fell to the ground like a dishrag. She was crying, gagging, and trying to catch her breath. Ma Baby crudely put the blunt *out* on Carol's neck, burning her with the hot cherry. Carol howled in pain.

Ma Baby laughed and walked off rapping. *"The FEDS is watching, niggaz plotting to get me. Will I survive, will I die? Come on let's picture the possibility."*

~

AFTER THE HORRIFIC CAR CRASH, there were paramedics, helicopters, ambulances, and the jaws of life had to be used on several cars. Miraculously, Julie Ainsworth was not D.O.A. Becky had thought for sure the job was done, but Rose checked up on the situation and informed her there was still loose ends to be tied up. Julie was in a coma with severe brain damage, laying up in the same hospital she worked at. And even though she'd probably be a vegetable, BBC didn't wanna take any chances of her putting two and two together and talking to them people. So they made plans to eliminate her for good this time.

Becky was to make sure she was seen gambling at all the big Casinos in Las Vegas to ensure her an airtight alibi while TLB went into stealth mode, taking care of business. One mid-afternoon, the fire alarm was pulled in St. Elizabeth hospital. The staff and administration was forced to evacuate the building. The patients who were unable to move were guarded by security personnel while rooms and hallways were checked for fire hazards.

There were two security guards on the floor Julie was housed at. A short light-skinned woman in a doctor's coat and name tag that read "Wilson M.D. "told one guard to check the next floor while she checked in on the patients. The other guard was helping a thick ass Latino nurse walk an ill patient down the stairwell.

A new TLB in training– Kitty– was executing her first contract killing. Wearing purple scrubs with butterflies on them, the 5'11" redbone crept into Julie's room, latex gloves on, and head down so the security cameras could not get a good look at her face. The frail white girl laid up with all kinds of tubes running out of her body and throat. The heart monitor beeped at a slow rate. She was on life support, but her life was about to end that day.

Kitty stood over her mark and flipped the off switch. Julie's breathing ceased as the assisted air no longer filled her lungs. Her body went completely still. Kitty looked at her watch; she only had so long before she had to get out of there. Sweat beaded her brow and her heart raced as her first official killing was completed. When she turned the machine back on, it immediately flatlined. One long constant beep filled the room as Kitty vanished. Job Complete. *Beeeeeeeeeeeeeep.*

~

WHILE JULIE WAS FLATLINING, a Tryfe Lyfe Bitch was in Patricia's office, spiking her coffee with cyanide. And while the female assassin was poisoning one of the Slinkowskis enemies, Brix was busy rolling a fat blunt laced with rat poison. Deemontay called Britney a couple of days after the party, begging for her to take him back. “Baby, I’m sorry I cheated on you with that weak ass bitch. She ain’t got *shit* on you. Never has and never will,” Deemontay told her.

“Oh yeah?” Britney said, rolling her eyes to his bullshit.

“Hell yeah ma. I miss you boo.”

“Hmpf. Funny how a bitch gotta put the smack down with a pool stick to get your attention.”

“Naw, it ain’t like that.”

“Dee. I don’t wanna hear that shit man. You dumped me and left me looking stupid. There’s no coming back from that.”

“LOOK Brit— ”

“*Brix*,” she corrected him.

“My bad. Brix. Can we just meet up and talk about this?”

“Meet up? Yeah, we can meet up if you buying something,” she told him.

“You still got three zippers for da five?”

“Mmm, for you? You can get them for 450.”

“Bet! Let’s meet up and I’ll match a B with you and we can talk then.”

“Sure Dee, whatever you say,” Brix said, disconnecting the call. She was gonna show her ex she wasn’t no fool. Brix was ***not*** the bitch you crossed.

They met at their old “fuck spot,” a country road off County E. Deemontay’s ‘94 Caprice with the new paint job and rims thanks to Amber was parked when Brix pulled up next to him in her GMC Terrain SLT. She got into his whip and pulled the three ounces out of her Peach Crown Royal bag and handed them to him.

“What the hell you doing with mittens on girl? It’s hot as a bitch,” Deemontay said, looking at the big wool gloves she had on.

"Oh, I was putting all these boxes of meat in the deep freezer for this cookout I'm throwing, and my fingers got froze. I'm just trying to warm them up," she lied.

"Oh," he said and handed her four one hundred-dollar bills and a fifty. She took her mittens off and counted the money before stuffing it in her bra.

"Here. Light this up and tell me what you wanna talk about," Brix said, handing him the poisoned blunt. He smiled like a kid in a candy store as he pulled out his Bic and fired up the B.

"Well Brit– oops, I mean, *Brix*. It's like this," he began as he inhaled the first few tokes and began coughing. "Wooooooo, this dat killa!" Brix smirked to herself, *sure is cocksucker.* "I miss you honey. We were good together. Amber's a fucking bitch," he paused and smoked some more, then offered the blunt to Brix.

"Go ahead and smoke some more. I'm good right now," she said, declining the B. Deemontay shrugged and greedily sucked more on the strawberry lit Swisher.

"I..." Deemontay dropped the blunt in his lap as he grabbed his throat and began to violently cough. Smoke shot out of his mouth, nose, and ears. His eyes bulged and turned yellow as he began wheezing.

Brix looked over at him calmly. "What's wrong Dee, cat got your tongue?" she said, smiling. Deemontay began going into cardiac arrest. His whole body thrashed like a fish out of water. His lungs shut down and he bit the tip of his tongue off. Brix looked into his eyes as her first love came to the realization that she gave him some tainted weed. That old school joint "Tainted Love" popped into his head as fear, panic, and hurt covered his body like a blanket. He began foaming at the mouth as the choking and gagging turned extreme.

Brix enjoyed watching him die a slow, painful death. In a matter of seconds, it was over. His body slumped over the steering wheel and Brix put her mittens back on. She pushed him back into the seat and took the blunt out of his lap and re-lit it. Once the cherry had a nice fiery flame on it, she dropped it on his T-shirt. She grabbed the ounces of weed she just sold him and opened the door. Brix took a book of matches out of her pocket, lit them and threw them in Deemontay's lap before closing the passenger side door. She stood outside and watched as her first ever boyfriend and lover's entire body engulfed in flames.

"Burn in hell you rotten son of a bitch," Brix said and spat on his car. By the time he was found, him and his whip was nothing but a heap of ashes. The police thought that he accidently burned himself to death after falling asleep while smoking. Brix was now a certified killer, and she didn't feel the least bit jaded about it. She got into her car and called Gutter. "Baby, I need to see you."

THE PROBLEM with cocky niggas was they thought they're untouchable. Give a muthafucka a little money and they thought they had enough power to float above and beyond any and everything. And when they got revenge on their enemies, they felt even more powerful and vindicated. But the average nigga never dotted all his I's and crossed all his t's. That's something the BBC took pride in. These were syndicate like bitches who left no stone unturned. They handled their business efficiently. The rapper couldn't *fathom* the level BBC was on.

Thinking Summer and her girls were stankin', he began moving about like nothing ever happened. He got some new bitches on deck, but he watched them like a Hawk and kept his heat on him and some extra thug niggas around all the time. What he didn't know was every Nightclub, Casino, Stripclub, and Awards show he went to, THOT Gang chicks and TLB were all around, watching his every move and making their way into his inner circle.

These were beautiful women with bodies you only seen in rap videos. Niggaz didn't suspect them to be anything other than some bad groupies trying to get the bragging rights of partying with or fucking a famous rapper and his crew.

After attending an award show at Radio City Music Hall one night, the famous rapper and his goons decided to go to Score's Stripclub on West 28th. He'd heard the number one exotic dancer on the planet– Gushy– was performing, and he had yet to see her live. From the clips he saw on WorldStar and YouTube, he knew the bitch was an animal on the stage. An animal he wanted to bang and tame!

Pulling up in bulletproof SUVs, him and his crew (over twenty deep) stormed Score's with lit blunts and plenty of ice on. They ordered thousand-dollar bottles of Hennessey XO and bottles of champagne to pour on the strippers. They were accompanied to the V.I.P. area, where strippers of all sizes and nationalities swarmed them like bees to honey.

French Montana and his Coke Boys crew were also in the V.I.P. and Gushy was giving French a spectacular show as he made it rain on the chocolate goddess. French saw the envious rapper staring at him and Gushy as she did her thing. He never liked the fake ass thug cuz he knew an imposter when he saw one. French smiled and grabbed Gushy's ass. UGK's "International Players Anthem" bumped while she swiveled and swayed seductively.

GG turned to see who French was ice grilling and smiled to herself. *Oh yeah muhfucka.* She turned her back to French and made her booty do "the wave" as she winked and blew kisses at the rapper who tried to assassinate her best friend.

Thinking she was "choosing," he smiled and opened up the small briefcase he'd brought with him. A quarter mill in fifties and hundreds neatly lined the black leather, and now it was his turn to smile. She gave him the hold up one second finger as she finished giving French Montana a show. When the song ended, she gathered up all of her money, wrapped a rubber-band around it, and walked her naked ass up out of there.

She put her money in her locker, changed into a new outfit, and called Summer.

"Girl, he's here. Round up the troops, we gonna do Plan C."

"Alright. But remember, leave that muthafucka for me!" Summer snarled.

"I gotchu ma. Love."

"Love." Summer hung up and took out a brand new Llama handgun. Then she grabbed a silencer for it and screwed it onto the barrel. After months of recuperating, physical therapy, and planning, she was finally about to get her revenge.

For weeks, Summer had been flying to every city the rapper appeared in. Every show he threw, every award show he went to, every studio he recorded at, she lurked in the shadows, watching; *waiting*. Now as she chilled in her hotel suite in New York where all the drama started at, she began shaking with rage as she cocked one in the chamber. "Nighty night fuckboy!"

GG strutted back to V.I.P. in a barely there, sparkling silver two-piece. She straddled the rapper and chatted him up while she grinded in his lap. While he got inebriated on marijuana and alcohol, she stroked his ego, among other things. She could feel his massive dick through his jeans while she gave him a lap dance. She feigned lust and excitement and he smiled.

"You like that don't cha ma? I can blow yo back out wit dis," he said, holding onto her hips while he grinded against her ass. *Naw nigga, it's yo back that's finna get blew out*, she thought to herself.

"Shit, let's go to your spot and do the damn thing then daddy. I'll tell all my dancer girls to cum... and we can all party," she said, taking his hand and "waterfalling" him. Like always, it worked like a charm.

"Bet. You know I got the mansion in Weston?" he said.

"Yeah, I saw it on Access Hollywood. That muthafucka *fat*," she said.

"Yup. Twenty-six rooms, fourteen bathrooms. That's how ballers do it baby."

"I hear you daddy," she said, licking his diamond chain. One of his drunk buddies shook up a bottle of champagne and hosed GG down with it, getting some on the rapper too. GG shrieked and the rapper snapped.

"Ho ass nigga, you got me wet dog," he yelled, tossing GG off his lap as he stood up.

"Yo son, I-I-I..." his guy stuttered and got slapped by the rapper before he could finish his apology.

"I ain't trying to hear that shit man. Damn," he said, dabbing at his wet clothes. "Now I gotta go change." He looked over at Gushy, who was wiping champagne off her pretty skin. "Shit, we finna hit the crib anyway, so you lucky muhfucka." He gave GG the address, and she said she'd round up the girls and be there as soon as the club closed.

It was four in the morning when two party buses full of women pulled up to the rapper's fancy estate. 54 bitches from TLB and THOT Gang exited the luxury buses all with purses on their arms. Every last chick was a dime. Short skirts, high heels, and coke bottle bodies. GG led the way as she rung the doorbell and was let in by a light skinned cat with gray eyes and tattoos all over his face and neck.

"Yo, shorty, you da truth ma. Fam need to put you in his next video. For real, for real," he said to GG as she and her crew entered the mansion.

The rapper and his crew lounged in the huge living room, playing Xbox One X. There were a few bitches already there that they invited over, and those women were not happy to see the bad bitches that just walked in and was taking up all the spotlight. GG did a head count. Twenty-seven men and eleven women. So, thirty-eight people had to die tonight.

The bitches that were there already turned up their noses at GG and her "stripper crew." Clearly intimidated by their expensive dresses, shoes and handbags, they knew GG and them were levels above their knockoff selves.

Blunts were lit, shots were poured, and clothes began shedding as people began branching off to various parts of the mansion. Gushy buttered the rapper up and suggested they go to his room for a "private" show. He signaled one of his boys and they went up the spiral staircase.

"What's up with him daddy? I don't do doubles," GG said, stopping outside the master bedroom.

"Aw, naw ma. We gonna one on one, he's just gonna sit out here on S," the rapper told her. That's when GG noticed the chair next to the door. The big, hulking 6'8" football player looking dude pulled a pistol out of his waistband and sat in the chair. *Shit*, GG cursed to herself as they entered the bedroom. The rapper himself pulled a .45 out of his pants and sat it on the nightstand. He plopped down on the King size bed and patted the spot next to him.

"Um, let me freshen up real quick daddy so I can give you this prime Gush-Gush," she said. He pointed towards the bathroom and she slung her booty cheeks extra hard as she slowly walked to the restroom. He was hypnotized by all her jelly!

GG turned the sink on and quickly pulled out her phone to text Summer.

Sum: **27 niggaz 11 bitches. 2 at the guard shack. 1 outside the master bedroom with heat**, she typed. Then she texted **GREENLIGHT** to several of the TLB and THOT Gang chicks scattered throughout the mansion. Knowing looks were given to crew members in the middle of blowjobs, make-out sessions, and intercourse. A few of them were getting their pussies ate and ass licked when word was sent.

By the time GG exited the bathroom in nothing but her six-inch Givenchy heels and Hermes Birkin bag, TLB and THOT Gang were putting holes in the bodies of the rapper's crew with the silencer pistols they had in their purses.

"Now *THAT'S* what I'm talkin' bout," the rapper said, licking his lips and unbuckling his belt. GG sat her purse down on the ottoman at the foot of the bed. He grabbed a remote off the nightstand and hit a couple buttons. Anthony Hamilton came blaring out of the hidden speakers as she crawled into his arms, kissing his chest and neck.

When Summer got GG's text, she was only ten minutes up the road. She calmly drove to the gated community, pulling up to the small shack in her Lamborghini Aventador. Before the first guard could exit the shack with his clipboard, she'd already had her window down enough to fit the silencer barrel of her Taurus PT92 gun. ***Pffft. Pffft.*** Two quick shots struck his neck and chest as the second guard who was halfway sleep stood up in shock.

"What the fuck?!" he exclaimed, looking down at his coworker bleeding on the floor. Summer hopped out the Lambo with a bright red wig on and a body hugging lime green catsuit painted to her curves. ***Pffft. Pffft. Pffft.*** She shot the second guard three times as he crumpled on top of the other guard. She gave them each a dome shot just to be on the safe side. She had leather gloves on and dug into her purse to pull out a half smoked blunt from a zip lock bag. She dropped it in front of the guard shack, hopped into the Lam, and cruised up to the mansion.

Inside the crib, niggas were dropping like the stock market. A Puerto Rican chick who wanted to get in on some orgy action walked in on two TLB's merking a nigga.

"Oh my God!" she screamed and made a quick dash. "Helll-llp! Their– " ***Pffft. Pffft. Pffft.*** They popped her up in the middle of the hallway. Bullets clipped the Puerto Rican girl's spine as she fell face first onto the marble floor. Her cries had been heard though, and other girls began looking around to see what was going on. This forced TLB and THOT Gang to act swiftly and kill the women before they could finish off the men. ***Pffft. Pffft. Pffft.*** The sounds of silenced bullets whizzed to and fro as targets were hit left and right. People died mid-scream, and niggas didn't even have a chance to pull their guns out. Everyone was high and drunk, so their natural reaction time was slowed.

TLB and THOT Gang walked from room to room counting bodies and putting an extra bullet into the brain of every person shot in case they were playing dead when Summer walked in. She assessed the damage. Bitches bled out in the hallways. Niggas were slumped over with their pants around their ankles. One couple was murdered mid BJ. A girl's head was blown off with the dead man's dick still in her mouth. He had one single hole in the middle of his forehead, his eyes opened, and his head against the wall. *Well, at least you went out with a bang*, Summer said to herself.

She nodded to her assassins that milled about while she walked up the stairs. The bodyguard sitting outside of the rapper's bedroom was busy Facebook scrolling when Summer walked up to him with her hands in her purse. ***Pffft. Pffft. Pffft.*** Two to the chest and one to the dome. His 300-pound frame collapsed against the door as soon as he stood up. The rapper, hearing the loud thud, reached for his pistol instantly. "Big Mike? What was dat fam? Big Mike?"

GG removed his dick from her mouth with a loud slurp. "Damn daddy, why you grabbing guns and shit? How we— "

"Shut up ho," he said, pushing her off him and getting up. He crept to the door ass naked with his .45 in hand. "Big Mike? Yo, what was that sound fam?"

"Daddy, you trippin'. It was prolly one of your guys fucking a ho in the hallway," GG said. The rapper spun around and pointed his gun at her, paranoid as fuck.

"I said shut da fuck up ho! I don't trust you bitches. That shit ain't sound right." The door opened and before he could fully turn around, ***Pffft. Pffft.*** He was shot in his leg and his right forearm. The gun flew out of his hand and he fell to one knee.

"You right fag ass nigga. Never trust a bitch," Summer said, kicking the door shut. ***Pffft.*** She shot him in his hipbone and he rolled onto his back in pain. Summer pulled the wig off and his eyes got big as tires as she stepped closer. "What's wrong fam? See a ghost?" she said, smiling.

GG got off the bed and grabbed her purse. She put on some gloves and took out blunt roaches, a fifth of half drank vodka, and a loaded nine. She began scattering evidence around the room.

"Ya see, you tried to body me. But you failed. One in the arm, one in the leg, and one in my ass. Nigga, you shot me in my ***ass.*** This my money maker muthafucka!" ***Pffft.*** She put one in his kneecap and he screamed like a bitch. "Burns don't it fuckboy? Yeah, I been laying low, watching your every move. I been on your ass this whole time and you ain't even know it. Had you been more observant, you would've known Gushy was my girl. Look at her tat, stupid."

GG stood in front of him and Summer stroked her bicep with the gun. The rapper saw the same BBC tattoo that he'd licked and kissed on Summer's arm many times before. *Fuck! I got played **again***, he quietly thought to himself.

"Yeah sucka. And all the bitches that came with her? *MY* crew. And they merked every... last...one of yo niggas. And them bird ass bitches y'all had witchu too," Summer said, standing over him. He spit blood onto her legs.

"Fuck you bitch. I ain't gonna beg you to spare my life. You gon' kill me, do it hoe. Fuck you thought this was? You gon' do it, do it bitch. Do iiiiiiiiiiiit!" he shouted.

"All you had to do was ask. My pleasure." ***Pffft. Pffft. Pffft. Pffft.*** Summer silenced her enemy forever. GG took the nine out of her purse, cocked it, and put three more bullets into his body and shot up the rest of the bedroom before dropping the gun on the floor.

Like the masterminds they were, BBC always collected blunts, bottles, Du-rags and other paraphernalia from every club and chill spot that niggas were at. So whenever "moves" were put into play, they would leave behind these clues containing various men's DNA, fingerprints, hair etc. for the police to link those dudes to the crimes. Innocent men would be charged with all kinds of heinous crimes because some genius ass bitches bagged their left-over party favors and left them somewhere they were not even at. They did that all over the mansion, leaving shit behind and using stolen guns to shoot up all the rooms to make it look like a mob of goons came into the rapper's mansion on some beef shit and shot everybody up. To make it even more believable, all the cash, jewels, and valuables were all loaded into the party buses too.

GG and Summer made sure to confiscate all of the security footage from the interior and exterior of the house before they left too. The only evidence left behind was the stuff they planted.

~

AMBER WAS NO FOOL. She knew Deemontay didn't nod off while smoking a blunt in his car like the coroner had reported. She knew what it was. Britney had killed her boyfriend and she was sure that she was next on the crazed girl's hit list. Drama was in the air.

With tears rolling down her blemish-free face, she swiped

through tons of pics of her and Deemontay on her iPhone. Their song, Ellie Goulding's "Army," played on repeat on her stereo while she sat on her bed sobbing.

"I love you baby. You were my one, my only, my all. I know that psycho cunt fucking killed you. But she'll get hers. Karmas a bitch," Amber sniveled and wiped her nose with the back of her hand. Tears fell on Deemontay's face as they rained onto the screen. "I won't leave you up there alone sweetie. If you go. *I* go." She grabbed a bottle of prescription pills and dumped a handful of them in her hands. She threw a dozen or so in her mouth and drank them down with a bottle of Jack Daniel's. She repeated this process several times until all 120 pills were ingested. On some modern day Romeo and Juliet shit, Amber seeped into an unconscious state as she sprawled across her bed and passed away.

"We both know what they say about us,
But they don't stand a chance because.
When I'm with you, when I'm with you
I'm standing with an army, I'm standing with an army."

25

MA BABY'S REVENGE

After Ma Baby's blow up with Carol, she practically moved into Neef's crib. Bitches were too much drama. Niggaz didn't nag, bitch and moan like women did. And Neef was one of the coolest, laid back niggaz she had ever met. Plus, his dick game was crazy stupid! He had a big piece of meat and knew what to do with it. She was falling in love with the second in command of Mud Money.

Trying to prove how much of a down ass bitch she was, she took him to Madison's hottest stripclub, Silk Exotic Gentleman's one evening. They got his and hers lap dances from the baddest dancers in the place! When they left, it was with a thick ass native chick that they took back to the telly and had a threesome for the ages with. Already rolling off Ex, the stripper convinced Neef and Ma Baby to join her in snorting some coke. Neef and Ma Baby knew better than to get high off the same white girl that they sold, but their minds were already altered from a combination of Molly, weed, and Patron. So, they shrugged and each snorted a line from the hundred dollar bill the stripper provided.

That first high of anything was the most intense, exhilarating feeling in the world. Addicts spent their entire lifetime "chasing that first high," not realizing they will **NEVER** be able to achieve it *ever* again. Neef and Ma Baby experienced for the first time, at the same time, why that white powder drove people to kill, steal, and destroy. They felt invincible! And to share that feeling together, that first high as a couple, made them feel even closer. They were now bonded by coke.

The FEDS were on her ass about the Stripclub Capers and drug busts. She kept spinning them, saying she was getting close to finding out who the women were. In the meantime, to tied them over, she got Neef to tell her about all of Mud Money's enemies and biggest competitors.

With all of the money and drugs the FEDS gave her, and Neef's endless supply of boy and girl, she was able to hit the streets hard! She began recruiting bitches for the new and improved Milwaukee Mami's resurrected. She set up all of Mud Money's rivals, whole blocks came under siege. Hundreds of people got indicted. Ma Baby didn't feel the least bit jaded as niggas went to jail cuz of her snake moves. The constant flow of cocaine up her nose kept her conscience numb enough to feel no guilt, no pain, and no remorse. When she told Neef she'd be in Cali for a week or so to get acquainted with her old plug, they popped some rollers and snorted an 8ball before they had marathon sex for nine hours non-stopped.

"That oughta hold you over til I get back," Ma Baby panted after they both came explosively!

THE INTERNET WAS A MOTHERFUCKER. There was no one and nothing you could not find on the good old world wide web. Using the "Darknet" web browser Tor– the underworld of the internet– Ma Baby was able to get everything she needed to extract revenge on Warden Whiteside.

When she got to Cali, she rented a car under a fake name and got a hotel in Pleasanton, the city next to Livermore, California, where Arnold Whiteside and his family lived. Ma Baby cased his crib out for a couple of days and followed him to and from work to get familiar with his schedule. On her fifth day out there, she walked up to his crib at 12:30 in the afternoon with leather gloves on and holding a bouquet of flowers. She rang the doorbell and Mrs. Janna Whiteside answered.

"Mrs. Whiteside?" Ma Baby inquired.

"Yes," the heavyset woman replied, eyeing Ma Baby and the flowers suspiciously. Minorities didn't come around their neck of the woods, so she wondered what the Latino girl wanted.

"I have a special delivery for you from a..." Ma Baby pretended to check out the blank card on the bouquet. "Arnold?"

Janna's face lit up like a Christmas tree. It wasn't like her husband of seventeen years to send her flowers. As she reached out to retrieve the bouquet, Ma Baby slid the dart gun from behind the flowers and fired off a tranquilizer dart to Mrs. Whiteside's throat. The porky woman held a hand to her neck and collapsed in the doorway. Ma Baby looked left and right to make sure she wasn't seen before dragging the fat lady into the house and closing the door behind her.

Ma Baby sat her knapsack down and went to work immediately; she searched the whole house to make sure no one else was home. They had a Russell Terrier that surprised her when she went to the basement. It started barking and attempted to lunge at her. But she came prepared with dog treats. She fed it then put it in the closet.

Ma Baby pulled the merch out of her knapsack and laid it on the floor: rope, wire, gagballs, Ginzu knife, a mini Louisville slugger, pliers, a screwdriver, and duct tape. It took some work, but she finally managed to drag the 300-pound Janna Whiteside into the master bedroom, where she stripped her ass naked and tied her to a chair before duct taping her mouth. Janna was still out like a light. Ma Baby looked at her watch; by her estimates, she had about two hours before the kids came home from school. Ma baby went into the living room to watch TV and do coke off the coffee table until they arrived.

When they walked in the door, two boys and a girl, ages thirteen, ten, and eight, Ma Baby smiled at them. "Hi guys, I'm a friend of your dad," she said, greeting them. Kids, being the naïve creatures that they were, knew no better as they sauntered up to her smiling.

"Where's mommy?" the eight-year old girl asked, holding her Sesame Street bookbag to her chest.

"Oh, she's upstairs taking a nap honey. Why don't you go and wake her up," Ma Baby said, getting off the couch. The girl ran up the stairs and Ma Baby pulled a gun on the two boys. "Make a sound you little shits, and I'll blow your fucking brains out all over this muthafucka," she snarled, her chinky eyes turning to evil slits. Both the boys peed on themselves and tears ran down their faces. Upstairs, the little girl screamed repeatedly. Ma Baby pointed to the stairs with her gun. "Move," she told the boys. They scurried ahead and their sister came to the top of the stairs screaming and crying loudly.

"Mommy's— " ***Pop! Pop! Pop!*** Ma Baby shot the girl three times. Her tiny body rolled down the stairs and landed at the bottom, twisted awkwardly on the floor. The two boys swallowed their screams and cried uncontrollably as Ma Baby put the gun to the back of the head of the thirteen-year old and told them to get their ass up those stairs.

She led them to their parents' bedroom where they saw their mom tied to a chair crying. Ma Baby tied the boys' hands behind their backs, bound their feet together, and duct taped their mouths shut. Then she placed them on the loveseat next to the King size canopy bed.

Ma Baby went back downstairs and waited on the Warden's

arrival. When she heard his car pull into the driveway, she took her position behind the door. She looked over at the dead girl's body crumpled at the foot of the stairs. Coked out of her mind, she smiled. *Revenge is the sweetest joy next to getting pussy*, she rapped to herself as the door opened.

"Honey, I'm home!" the warden announced as he entered his home.

Ma Baby stepped from behind the door. "We've been waiting for you Turkey neck," she said, putting the gun to the back of his head. His hands immediately went into the air. "Yeah, that's it you fat motherfucker, put those rapist paws in the air bitch!" Ma Baby turned on a lamp and walked in front of the Warden.

"Rivera? What the hell?"

"Shut up muthafucka. Yeah, I came back for dat ass. Your violating days are over now you crooked ass honky. I vowed that you and your family would pay for all the evil shit you did to me and the other women in Dublin. And look, your daughter has already paid for your sins." Ma Baby nodded towards the stairs. The warden looked over at his baby girl balled up on the floor in a pool of blood.

"Claire!" He made a move towards his daughter and Ma Baby hit him in the face with the butt of her gun.

"Be still muthafucka," she ordered. The warden held the bloody gash above his eyebrow as he pleaded for his life.

"Rivera please...please don't hurt me. I-I'm sorry. I didn't mean to– "

"I ain't trying to hear that shit turkey neck. Get your fat, bitch ass up the stairs. Get on some funny shit and I'll put more holes in you than a golf course!"

Warden Whiteside did as he was told. Tears slid down his doughy face as he stepped over his lifeless daughter. Once he saw his wife and boys tied up, his heart broke in a million pieces. He may be a piece of shit, but he did love his family dearly. And to think, it was because of him and his perversions that they were at the mercy of this deranged woman.

"Rivera look, I've got money. Nearly one hundred grand in the bank. And— "

"Shut the fuck up I said!" she slapped him with the pistol again. "I don't want your money turkey neck. I wanna see you *suffer*. I want your soul! Now put that gag ball on," she said, pointing towards the bed. He hesitated as he surveyed all of the "toys" she had laid out.

"Yeah, we finna have some fun man. Now do what I say, and I'll spare your wife and kids," she lied to him. He grabbed the gag ball with the leather headband on it and put it over his head. The shiny red ball made him look like a big roast pig with an apple in its mouth.

"Now strip turkey neck. Get asshole naked." Ma Baby picked up the pliers and walked over to Janna. The warden fumbled out of his clothes quickly. His mind raced a mile a minute. He had a .38 revolver in the closet. If he could just get to it.

"MMMMM!" The muffled scream of Janna filled the room as Ma Baby took the pliers and ripped one of the fat woman's meaty nipples right off her breast. Blood squirted out like a stepped on packet of ketchup.

"Get on the bed turkey neck. Now!" Ma Baby snapped, throwing the pliers down and picking up a screwdriver. She tied the warden's arms and ankles to the bed posts as he sobbed into the rubber gag ball. "No use in crying now. You wasn't crying when you was raping me was you? Yeah, that's right Janna. Your fat, sleazy husband is a serial rapist." Ma Baby said, walking back over to his wife. "Yup, the prison he works at? I was there. He called me into his office and raped me. *Repeatedly*."

Janna Whiteside shot daggers at her husband. She could sense the anger and hurt in this woman's voice.

"But I'm not the only one. He's raped dozens, if not *hundreds* of helpless inmates. But who are we? No one gives a fuck about us. We don't have any rights in there. They do whatever the hell they want to us and get away with the shit. Ain't that right turkey neck?" Ma Baby walked back to the bed and sat on it. She pulled the gag ball out of his mouth a bit. "Tell her Warden. Tell her how you fuck us bareback, nut inside of us, then make us take Plan B pills before you kick us out of your office."

"Oh God. Rivera please."

"Tell her motherfucker!"

"Ok, ok. I'm sorry. Jann it's true. I-I've had sex with the inmates—"

"Sex? You *RAPED* us muthafucka!"

"Ok. I'm sorry. You're right. I raped you. And I'm sorry—" Ma Baby stuffed the gag ball back into his mouth and looked over at his sons.

"Your daddy's a bad man," she said, lifting his heavy penis up in her leather glove-clad hands. She took the screwdriver and circled it gently around the tip of his dick. He began thrashing around, eyes wide.

"Didn't I tell your bitch ass to be still," she said, shoving the head of the screwdriver deep down his pee hole. Blood squirted out like a volcano erupting. His muffled screams bounced off the bedroom walls. Ma Baby stepped back, leaving the screwdriver halfway embedded in the warden's dick. Janna blacked out from the gruesome sight and one of the boys threw up. But because duct tape was wrapped around his head, he choked on his own vomit, swallowing the bile that tried its best to escape out of his main orifice. Some dribbled out of his nose, but the rest overloaded his esophagus and he rolled off the loveseat, choking to death on the bedroom floor.

Ma Baby slapped Janna Whiteside awake. "Wake up bitch! Don't want you to miss the finale," she said, pacing the floor.

"Warden, you ever see that movie '*The Girl With The Dragon Tattoo*'?" Ma Baby asked, grabbing the mini baseball bat. "Remember what ol' girl did to her social worker after he violated her?" she said, patting her palm with the Louisville slugger. "Well it was only right ya know? Eye for an eye and all." Ma Baby pulled a bag of coke out of her pocket and sprinkled some on the dresser. She did two fat lines and felt that rush of fireworks igniting in her brain. "Oh yeeeeeah, that hit the spot. I hope this spick pussy was worth what's about to happen. One thing you were right about Whiteside, I ***am*** a tough little cookie. But I am *not* a Latin whore," ***WAP!*** She punched Janna in her nose.

"You know, you two definitely belong together. Look at y'all. Two fat ass whales. Rolls upon rolls upon rolls. Ughh, that's disgusting," Ma Baby said, poking Janna's belly with the Louisville slugger. "Janna, I need some lube for my next act," Ma Baby said, shoving the mini bat into the warden's wife's pussy. The woman howled and tears poured down her face as Ma Baby jammed it in and out about fifteen times. When she removed it, the wooden bat was drenched in blood. "Perfect," Ma Baby smiled and walked over to the bed. She freed one of the warden's feet from the posts and lifted his leg in the air. He knew what was coming and tried to fight her off, but he was weak and woozy from the substantial blood loss. By the time she crammed the bat into his anus, he no longer had enough strength to even cry out. She raped his ass long and hard, making sure everyone in the room could hear his organs rupturing. Blood soaked the sheets while she violated his back door for what seemed like forever. When she was done, she pulled it out of him with a sickening *fllllurp!*

"How'd it feel to be violated muthafucka?" she screamed, hitting him in the chest and stomach with the shit and blood smeared bat. She walked over to the little boy and ripped the duct tape off his face. She shoved the baseball bat down his throat, breaking several teeth in the process. His eyes bulged and Ma Baby kept pushing until half the bat went through the back of the boys' skull. He crumpled onto his side with the bat buried in his face and sticking out of his cranium.

Janna couldn't believe what she just witnessed. Her tears could fill up a swimming pool as she shook and spasmed in grief. Ma Baby went back to the bed and pulled the screwdriver out of the Warden's penis and threw it on the floor. She yanked the gag ball out and grabbed the razor wire. She wrapped it around his dick a couple of times and pulled it back and forth in a sawing motion until she severed his male organ. It was a slow torturing process and he felt every cut as the wire tore into his most prized possession. Ma Baby picked up the fat bloody sausage and jammed it in his mouth. "Suck your own dick muthafucka," she growled, putting the gag ball back in his mouth. He moaned and groaned as blood trickled down his throat. He blocked his tonsils with his tongue so that he wouldn't swallow his own penis.

Ma Baby grabbed the Ginzu knife and carved the word RAPIST into his chest and stomach. After seeing her husband dismembered and made to engulf his own penis, Janna did the same thing as her child did, threw up in her mouth and choked to death on her own vomit. Her head slumped forward, triple chins resting on her chest as her lungs filled with bile and life slowly exited her large body.

"You're gonna die a slow painful death turkey neck," Ma Baby said, pulling a small black bottle out of her pocket. "You're gonna bleed out. But remember muthafucka, you brought this shit upon yourself." Ma Baby took the top off the bottle and poured Fluoroantimonic acid all over the warden's body. His bloody wounds sizzled and foamed over like 100 Alka-Seltzers. He spasmed and shook violently in his restraints but to no avail. The stinging acid re-awakened his senses, sending signals of extreme, agonizing pain to his brain.

Ma Baby gathered up her torture tools and backtracked to make sure she left no DNA behind. She grabbed the dog out of the closet, thinking it would make a wonderful gift for Carol. Then she left Warden Whiteside to slowly die in his marital bed. *Revenge is like the sweetest joy next to getting pussy!*

26

SNAKES!!!

Keep your grass cut low so the snakes will
show...

"Damn Summer, that's some ill ass shit ma. How da fuck did you think of that?" Nacho asked.

"You remember the Larry Byrd video I was in where I was in the pet store? I was in the snake aisle and the shit came to me then," Summer told him, sitting at the Titty Table were the trusted members of TLB and THOT Gang. BBC was holding an exclusive meeting at the Greenhouse and Nacho was the only male invited. Blunts of BBC bomb were passed around while they discussed their upcoming plots and shared uncovered information about Nacho's babymama.

"As y'all know, Chula and GG got Carol zooted and got her prints and DNA off a glass. We had it ran by our insiders and found out she is Carol Jerica Coleman. born October 18th, 1995.

She was born and raised in Phoenix, Arizona," Rose spoke, pointing a stick at pictures she showed on the projection screen. "She got twelve years for gun possession and conspiracy to sell military arms as a first offense. But our sources say it was her big brother Goldy that she took the case for. Now I know what chy'all thinking, why so much time for a young girl's first offense? Well, they had some heavy shit. DPMS Panther Arms Assault Rifles, M240PPG's, MP-22's, Yavuz-16's and some shit from Russia and Afghanistan that only terrorists can get they hands on. Well, they slammed her and sent her to Dublin a couple years ago. Ma Baby evidently took her under her wing and cuffed her. According to records, her case was overturned the same day as Ma Baby's. Coincidence? Fuck no!"

GG stood up and took over. "The girl is as green as a Sprite can. She and Ma Baby got into a big fight and she ran over to Chula's looking for consoling. Chula slipped her a mickey, fucked her real good, and got the young bitch to talking. She said Ma Baby got her involved in some shit that could get them both killed. She didn't say exactly *what* that something was, but we're pretty sure it's working for the FEDS."

"I couldn't believe the shit either," Nacho said. "But shit just wasn't right. The bitch popping up out the blue, asking all kinds of questions and shit. It was just too...funny style."

"But what about her and Neef? They say them two moving plenty of dope on the east side," Nymphy said.

"Yeah, she's in with Mud Money now. They setting up their competitors and robbing others for they shit," Lyza said. T-dub had proposed to "Tasha," so she had the inside scoop on all of Mud Money's activities, just as BBC planned. Lyza flashed the half million dollar engagement ring as she passed the blunt to Kitty.

"She's got a team of new bitches she's calling the new Milwaukee Mami's. A bunch of young, dumb bitches that don't know their pussy holes from their booty holes," Lyza continued. "But they ain't on shit. She got the young bitches setting niggaz up for buys and then them people swoop in and arrest muhfuckas."

"That rat bitch!" A THOT Gang chick spat.

"Most def. But don't trip. We gonna take care of this correctly. Ain't no telling if she's wired up 24/7 or just freelance snitching. Either way, we done kept our lips tight enough not to incriminate ourselves around her. She thinks we're 100% legit with the business shit now. But she ain't stupid, she's still street smart. So, we gonna ball hard and show her what corporate money looks like. The thing is, we can't keep her at ***too*** much of a distance, or she might think we're on to her," Rose said.

"Keep your friends close and your enemies closer," Summer commented. Everyone nodded in agreement.

"So, while we lure her in and learn her moves, we're gonna let her see the ones we ***want*** her to see. In the meantime, we're gonna send her and a few others our new message courtesy of Summer," Rose said, smiling.

They all discussed who was to get it, when they were to get it, and how they were to get this new method of madness that was a direct message to all that apply. Whenever a scheme was brought up that hit close to home for Nacho, he replied like a G. "Shiiiid, I don't give a fuck yo! I'm a street nigga. I'm loyal to dis shit for real for real. I'll do whatever I gotta do to show dat ho snakes are not acceptable. Breaks my heart that it's my B.M. But at the end of the day, the only thing I'm loyal to is this game. Bullshit ain't nothing," he declared.

A few women got the chills after hearing Nacho. They may have been cold-blooded killers, but even some of them couldn't imagine doing what he agreed to do to the mother of his child. It brought a new meaning to his "No Mercy" tat on his hand.

"Hey Rose, any word on getting Kanari out yet?" A THOT Gang girl asked. Kanari Yellow Diamonds was a good friend of hers who got locked up on some bullshit, and because he was on extended supervision, he had a P.O. hold on him.

"I'm trying ma. His P.O.'s supervisor is being a punk bitch cuz of the charges, but we're working on it. We did pull some strings and got him to go back to the fifth floor in MSDF tho. So, Algae gonna make sure his ass is cool," Rose said.

"You mean Sergeant Algae?" Lyza asked.

"Yup. The only cool Sergeant that I know. That nigga is A-1," Rose said.

"Yeah, a couple niggas in Mud Money who was locked up before had nothing but good things to say about him. They be like fuck every cop and C.O. except for Algae. So, he must be a good dude."

"He is. He's from the hood, but he chose to go legit which I don't blame him for. But he uplifts brothers in there and chops it up with them on some real shit. Trying to help them better themselves and giving them some G on how to stay outta that hellhole."

"That's what's up," Nacho commented.

"Yeah. Well everyone knows the plans, so if there are no further questions, let's make some shit happen y'all," Rose said, closing the meeting.

THE TLB MEMBER who failed to off Patricia Clooney was merked herself. Rose didn't like failed missions. Though technically it wasn't *her* fault that the medical manager didn't drink her poisoned coffee the day the fire alarm forced the staff to evacuate the hospital. It was just too cold by the time Patty got back in the building, so she poured the coffee out dismissively.

Becky volunteered to kill the incompetent Tryfe Lyfe Bitch for not eliminating her enemy. What the girl thought was a double job to tie up loose ends wounded up being a two to the head murder administered by Becky's .40 Cal Beretta. She pushed the ex TLB member's dead body out of the stolen LeSabre and left her laying in a grimy alley on 32nd and Burleigh.

Afterwards, Becky ditched the car and got into her E350 Benz and hit it to Appleton. Shortly after midnight, she broke into Patricia's two-bedroom townhouse with a mesh bag slung over her shoulder. Out in the boonies, they didn't believe in much security cuz it was nothing but the upper echelon around those parts. Car alarms and burglar systems? That shit was rare in those small, lily white towns. They barely locked their doors and left the keys in their running vehicles at gas stations. So, it wasn't a problem for Becky to pick the single lock at Patricia's crib. She knew the fifty-six-year old bitch would be knocked out on sleeping pills by now. The only obstacle Becky would face was Patricia's feisty Rat Terrier. Luckily, the little fuck was also fast asleep in its dog bed when Becky entered.

She pulled out her 9mm with the silver silencer on it and pumped four rounds into the 16 pound animal. After the first ***Pffft***, it barely groaned as it died instantly.

Becky carried the heavy bag up the carpeted stairs and crept into Patty's bedroom. Her chest rose and fell rhythmically as she lightly snored. The nature sounds playing on the Echo Smart Speaker on her nightstand helped Patty sleep more peacefully. Ocean waves, crickets, birds, and waterfalls filled the room, making Becky feel like she was in a forest or some shit.

Meanwhile, Patricia was dreaming that she was in a jungle. Monkey's screeched, wild birds cackled, and a loud hissing sound was so loud it felt like it was right in her eardrum...and it was. Becky dumped the eleven-foot neon green boa constrictor out of the mesh bag on Patty's bed. She learned that if a boa feels threatened, it will quickly suffocate its prey. Becky lifted Patty's head off the pillow and coiled the snake around the sleeping woman's neck. Becky began taunting and poking the dangerous reptile. Zonked out on Zolpidems and Xanax, the woman barely stirred until the compression around her throat cut off her windpipe. Her eyes shot open as she choked and reached for her neck. Patty felt the slimy, smooth, scaly skin on her fingertips and immediately removed her hands, putting them at her sides as panic set in. Becky smiled down at her foe. Patty looked into Becky's cold blue eyes and got the chills. She couldn't even scream. She wriggled and thrashed and gagged as the boa constrictor squeezed tighter and tighter due to Becky's prodding. The more Patricia fought, the louder the snake hissed. *Ssssssssss. It wasn't a dream*, she thought to herself as her life flashed before her eyes. *The bitch* ***SHOOTS*** *at people. She's freakin nuts!* Jessie's words of warning replayed in Patty's mind as she stared into the crazed woman's eyes.

The snake glowed in the dark as it made love to Patricia Clooney's neck, passionately squeezing the life out of her by the second.

"Live as a snake...die by the snake," Becky said to her right before her body went limp. The veins in Patty's forehead were purple and bulged profusely. Her eyeballs were centimeters from dangling from their sockets. Becky made sure there was no pulse before she left the bedroom. Back downstairs, she picked up the four shell casings, wrapped the dead dog up in some towels, and threw it in her mesh bag. She carried it and the dog bed out to the car with her before locking the door behind her and disappearing into the night.

ONCE BECKY PUT Britney on to the "message move," she thought it was cool as shit. That was some Mafioso stuff and she couldn't *wait* to get in on it herself. But Britney was quickly falling for Gutter. It was time to see if he was bout dat life.

"Oh my God, Gutter! Fuck me baby," Britney moaned.

"Call me daddy. Who's your daddy bitch?" Gutter growled.

"Oooh daddy. *You* are. You're my daddy! Mmmmm shit." Gutter smacked her big round white booty cheeks, making them wobble even more. *Goddamn, this bitch got the best pussy I done ever had*, he thought to himself. Britney was tight and super wet. But not the "liquidy" wet like most chicks he fucked. Brix was a CREAMY wet. Her secretions were thick like custard or gravy. And her pussy was so damn pretty, it looked like a perfectly drawn pink rose. He was in heaven whenever he was inside of her.

"Oh, yeah daddy. Fuck...me...just...like...that," Britney stuttered. She'd been watching so much porn after her and Deemontay had broken up, that she adopted porn star dialogue in her sex sessions now. And it was kind of a turn on for her. It made her get more into it. And even though Gutter was only her second lover, she knew he had some bomb ass dick. He made her orgasm EVERY SINGLE TIME they had sex. Even when they had quickies, he made her cum long and hard. He always put her in positions where he or *she* could stimulate her clit easily. And he knew how to make her squirt too. Whenever he laid her on her stomach and poked her G-spot from the back while yanking her hair by the roots, she gushed like a fire hydrant being opened! Which is exactly what she was doing at the moment.

"Dad...dyyyyyyyyyy," she screamed as he gyrated his pelvis against her ass, stroking her G-spot expertly. She squirted white gravy all over him, herself, and the bed. As soon as he felt that hot cream slather his pole, he lost it himself.

"Awww shiiiiiiiit," he howled as his body shook and convulsed, busting a big nut inside her hot, tight, white pussy. They were both covered in sweat as they panted heavily. It took a few minutes before he slid out of her, but when he finally collapsed next to her, she curled up in his arms like a little kitten.

"Daddy, you got that bomb!"

Gutter laughed. "Nah ma. ***YOU*** da one wit dat bomb. Shiiiid, if I woulda known Snow Bunnies was this damn good, I woulda been stop fucking with black hoes."

Brix chuckled and said, "Well, you know what they say. Once you go snow, you gonna want some mo!"

Now it was *his* turn to laugh. "Girl you crazy."

"Mmhm. Crazy about you! But for real though. You remember what we were talking about yesterday baby?"

He tensed up a bit before responding. "Yeeeeah."

"Well, are you down or what? Cuz I need a Ride Or Die dude by my side," Brix said.

"Shorty, I *AM* ride or die," he said defensively.

"Well, show me."

"Why I gotta show you anything?" he asked, getting upset.

"What? Well, fuck it then Gutter. You right, you ain't gotta show me shit! Just lose my number then. You da second dude I've been with. I ain't no slut bitch. I do relationships. And I may be young, but I'm about to do big things. And I'm not letting *ANYONE* stand in my way. And that includes any snitch motherfuckers trying to fuck up my money or hate on my squad," Britney said, sitting up against the headboard.

She got one of Becky's friends to get her a nice two-bedroom apartment so she could duck off and do her own thing when she wanted to. Since the police had their ranch on the radar now, it was good for Brix to have her own spot to chill at. Especially now that Britney was forming her own Snow Bunny Click that sold weed for her; they were called S.B.G.'s (Snow Bunny Gangstaz). These were the wild childs, goth bitches who cut hoes, strong Amazon athletic chicks who took no shit, and kick ass fighters she got cool with in her self-defense classes. So far, they were seven deep. Britney schooled them on the game like BBC did her, showed them hood movies, and told them the pros and cons of what they'd be getting themselves into. She did not sugarcoat the consequences that came along with playing the game. Death and incarceration were real outcomes if one did not be careful. But she earned their trust and her inner leader was growing by the day. Everyone wants something to be a part of. Especially the outsiders, loners, and black sheep. All qualities Brix looked for in a click member.

"Why you acting like that Brix? I am down for you. I'm moving up here for you ain't I?" Gutter whined. While Gutter told her he was a D-boy, the truth was, he hit a major lick ten months ago. He and two of his boys robbed a bank in Tennessee and got away with 1.5 million. After splitting it three ways, Gutter spent $150,000 on his grille, $200,000 on other jewels, bought him a souped up Denali and some nice clothes and had ten geez left to his name. One of his guys got killed by the police when they came to raid his crib looking for the stolen money. Gutter was paranoid that them people knew he was in on the bank heist too, so he left his grandma's house in the middle of the night and came to Wisconsin.

He called his OG on the way, letting her know he was coming to visit. He'd been there ever since. And then he met Britney. And for the first time in his twenty years, he fell in love. He wanted to wife the young white girl who was wise beyond her 17 years. He never sold drugs. He used to rob old ladies at the gas station for studio money. He never killed nobody. He did live in the projects, but he never really did no *REAL* dirt besides the bank robbery.

Now here this white chick was, talking about killing some muthafuckas and leaving behind some snakes to send a message. *Who the fuck was he fucking with?* He was hella intrigued, but he was also scared. He saw the bitch shove pool sticks in her enemies! What else was this young, wild teenager capable of he wondered?

But if he didn't go along with her, he knew she'd dump his ass and keep it moving without hesitation. She was rich and heavy in the game. He wanted to get his feet wet in the dope game to add some authenticity to his "trap music." Damn near broke and not wanting to go back to Stevens Point to live with his moms and her weird ass honky sugar daddy, he looked at Brix.

"Fuck it ma, I'm witchu. Let's do dis," he said.

She wrapped her arms around his neck and kissed him. "You sure? Cuz ain't no turning back once we do this," she said.

He looked into her big pretty eyes. "Yeah. I'm sure babygirl."

"Ohhhh, daddy, thank you. I love you baby," she beamed.

"I love you too ma," he told her for the first time ever. "You crazy girl you!" They both laughed and rolled around on the bed kissing and touching.

CHULA BECAME Carol's best friend. After the fight Carol and Ma Baby had, they'd barely seen one another. Special Agent Bradshaw drove down on Carol and asked her if she knew anything about the Warden Whiteside murder.

"What? How the hell would I know? What happened, did some bitches in Dubhouse shank him or something?" Carol said, eyes wide.

"No. Someone went into his home, tortured, and killed his whole family. And for good measure, they cut his cock off and shoved it in his mouth!" Bradshaw yelled.

Carol shuddered. "Holy shit. That's fucked up. He musta pissed someone off really bad for that to happen. But no, I never had no beef with him."

"What about Ma Baby?"

"Nah, she was grateful to him for getting her out," Carol lied.

"You better not be lying to me Coleman."

"I'm not. Jeez, aren't we giving y'all what chy'all want?"

"***YOU***, ain't giving us shit. Rivera's the one setting up all of the dealers and shit. What the fuck do you do?"

"I help."

"Sure you do Coleman. Get us something on those Strip-club Capers," he said and left the house the FEDS bought for her and Ma Baby. Had they really listened in and reviewed the 24-hour surveillance within that house, they would have heard Ma Baby's threat of paying the Warden a visit and getting even with his rapist ass. But somehow it went unheard. They *did* however see when GG came over that first time. Once they found out she was a stripper, they'd been on the lookout for her, but she was hard to locate.

Stressed from the federally badgering her, she ran over to Chula's and got Superman high! After an intense 69 session, Carol threw it out there.

"Chu, you remember when them chicks hit all those strip-clubs in the state?"

Chula looked out the corner of her eye and hesitated. "It was on the news a while back. Why?"

"Shit, I just thought you might know who pulled that off," Carol commented.

"Why the hell would *I* know?" Chula asked, raising one eyebrow at Carol.

"I don't know. You a hood bitch and I– "

"Why you asking anyway? You da police or something?" Chula asked, already knowing that she was.

"Naw girl. I just...well, I was just thinking about pulling a caper myself and I want some bitches like *that* on my team."

"Oh, do you now?"

"Yeah," Carol responded.

Chula grabbed her phone and made a call. When she hung up, she turned to Carol. "I know some bitches..."

An hour later, Carol was bloody and battered in the back of a Dodge Caravan with a black bag tied over her head. She was brought to an abandoned warehouse on the south side of Milwaukee. Once she was sat in a chair, the bag came off and before her stood Summer, Becky, GG, Rose, Chula, Nadia, Quintasia, and Lyza.

"We know who you is bitch. What we *don't* know is, who are you working for and how much do you know?" GG said.

"GG, I don't know what you're– " Quintasia punched Carol in the mouth so hard, she fell out of the chair. Nadia, the tall Russian, quickly scooped her up and sat her back in the chair.

"Now let's try this again. Your case was overturned on the same day as Ma Baby's according to records, so what's the biz? Y'all roll over on somebody or what? Y'all rat on us?" Rose asked the frightened mulatto girl.

"No. No! The FEDS...they..."

"They what?" GG screamed in her face.

"Look, they don't know anything. I swear to God," Carol cried.

"This ho think it's a game. You're gonna talk to us bitch. One way or another," Becky said, grabbing an oily bicycle chain and twirling it above her head before whipping Carol all over her body with it. Bones cracked, teeth flew from her face, and blood seeped from wounds before Becky got tired and threw the chain on the floor. Everyone looked at the pretty white girl who was breathing heavily and flushed pink. Her swollen nipples were bursting through her blouse.

"Talk bitch. *NOW!* Or I swear on everything I love..." Becky ordered. Carol was never cut out for the street life. She was a fragile, square girl who was easily manipulated, and used for other's gain. And when any kind of confrontation came her way, she folded like fresh laundry.

"Ok, ok. The FEDS came to Dublin asking Ma Baby about the Stripclub Capers. They said she was so famous on the streets, that they'd let her out if she could find out who pulled it off. She didn't want to do it at all. But they threatened her with a life bid cuz this chick Ratchet Ronda got shanked and they needed a scapegoat to pin it on. So, they were gonna frame Ma Baby if she didn't help them. She wasn't going, but then they brought up her mom and daughter and— "

"She folded," Rose said.

"Yeah. She agreed to cooperate and work for them but only if they let me out with her. I was supposed to be her partner in crime, set up some drug dealers, find out who did the Stripclub Capers, and keep the feds in the loop on who was doing what in the streets. But once she got with Neef and started doing coke, she pretty much said fuck me! It's just been her and him doing their thing. Robbing niggaz, setting up bogus deals with marked money, all kinds of shiesty shit. She's got her new crew doing most of that shit, but I don't have nothing to do with it, I swear. You gotta believe me. Chula, baby, I'm sorry. I love you mami," Carol whined, looking her Puerto-Rican lover in the eye.

Chula spat in Carol's face. "Love? Bitch please. And don't *sorry* me hoe. You finna be *REAL* sorry in a minute. We knew you was a rat from the get go. And do you know what we do to rats?" Chula asked, pulling out a pink .380 and aiming it at Carol's head.

"Please, no! I swear— "

"So, the FEDS aren't on to us then?" GG asked.

"What? No, why would they... wait. Y'all were the ones that?..."

"Yup. We the Bad Bitchez Click. Any motherfucking criminal activity in the state of Wisconsin, you bets believe we got a hand in. And that includes them Stripclub moves. We Bad Boss Chicks," Rose said, walking up to Carol. "But never in a million years would we have thought that Ma Baby would be a snake. Guess it really ain't no more loyalty in da game nowadays. But she's about to feel the wrath now. We're gonna send her a heartfelt message...courtesy of *you*." Rose gave the head nod and Lyza came up from behind and strangled Carol with a coax cable chord.

She thrashed and twitched for a couple of minutes before she finally faded to black. Once Carol stopped moving, she was stripped naked and a live gerbil was stuffed up her asshole and a dead rat inside her pussy. A bull snake was then shoved up her ass to feast on the live Gerbil, and a rat snake (ironically) was put up her pussy to devour the dead rodent in her womb.

Ever since Ma Baby slaughtered the Whiteside family, her mental state was in complete disarray. She never killed a child before, and now she had the blood of *three* of them on her hands. Innocent kids the same age as her daughter. Ma Baby had trouble sleeping after those gruesome murders. She had frequent nightmares and woke up in cold sweats almost every hour, on the hour. Even her daydreams were haunted by mutilated kids crying out for mercy. In her dreams, she kept seeing the little girl that she shot, laying at the foot of the stairs; but she had Anita's face. "Mommy, why'd you kill me?" the corpse groaned. That's when Ma Baby would bolt upright, sweating, crying, shaking, and breathing heavily.

She was awakened by the same dream nightly. On this particular night, she padded barefoot into the kitchen to down a couple shots of Patron and do some lines of coke. It's like the drugs and alcohol were the only things that kept the nightmares and monsters away. Ma Baby heard a bunch of sirens in the near distance. She was at Neef's crib in Franklin, a suburban town on the outskirts of Milwaukee county. Looking out the living room window, Ma Baby saw dozens of flashing lights up the block. Police cars, fire trucks, and ambulances sat at the end of the Cul-De-Sac. Ma Baby slipped on a robe and slippers and went outside to see what was going on.

There was a crowd milling about at the intersection, looking up at the sky. Something was hanging from a street-light. From a distance, it looked like a kangaroo because there was a long tail hanging down. But the closer Ma Baby got towards the intersection, the clearer the image became. Stunned pedestrians whispered and made comments in shock. Ma Baby's mouth dropped as the realization hit her. She gagged and threw up on an old lady standing in front of her.

"Hey!" The gray-haired lady howled as vomit dripped from her hair and clothes. Ma Baby emptied the rest of the contents in her stomach on the cold cement before wiping her mouth with the back of her hand. Through teary eyes, she looked up at the sky with the rest of the nosey rubberneckers. Forty feet in the air, Carol dangled ass naked from a streetlight. A noose around her neck, a dead rat stuffed in her mouth, and the tails of two snakes hung out of her ass and vagina. Her battered body swayed left to right in the cool nights breeze. No one had seen anything like it before. Not even Ma Baby, who walked back to Neef's crib numb and in a daze.

Greg Wombek, Todd Borland, Whitney Shloof, and a couple of other kids who were envious of Britney fucked up by running their mouths about how they felt towards Brix-Brit. She, Gutter, and Tanya went on a reptile rampage.

Gutter usually held their victims at gunpoint while Brix-Brit or Tanya recorded the footage on pre-paid smart phones of the live killing that they dubbed "hashtag trunked." They filled each victim's trunk with seven or eight poisonous snakes before walking them to their car, opening the trunk, and making them get inside where they'd be bitten and choked until they died.

Snakes are already one of the most feared things on the planet. So, imagine being locked in a small space with several of those slimy ass, scaly creatures while they slithered all over your body. The sound of eerie hissing overpowered the fear and panic of each victim while he or she screamed. Many getting their tongues bitten mid-scream as they thumped and banged on the trunk of their own cars like four 15" subwoofers. Eventually, the trunk stopped rattling once the snakes did their job on the human snakes. Brix and her accomplices posted the complete footage from beginning to end on all of the major social media websites. **#TRUNKED** became an internet phenomenon for those fixated on grotesque imagery.

The snake killings brought Brix and Gutter closer together and sealed the S.B.G'z bond in loyalty. A couple of the girls were brought into the mix to see how "down" they were, and they passed with flying colors. The message was clear to all who even thought of crossing BBC or S.B.G. If you live by being a snake, you'd ***DIE*** by the snake!

"Listen here Rivera. You got your fucking partner killed somehow. Who the fuck would do this sick ass shit?" Agent Christine Holis shouted. They were at the house Ma Baby shared with Carol. Her and Agent Bradshaw were sweating Ma Baby for answers.

"I don't fucking know. I've shielded her from all this dirt I'm doing for y'all. She hasn't had to get her hands dirty. But when I fucking find out— "

"Fuck all of that! SOMEBODY knows about her. Or you. Or both. That was a direct message catered for you. Outside of your drug dealing boyfriend's house at that," Agent Holis said.

"Listen bitch. Keep my man outta this. He– "

"Rivera, stop it! We don't want Janeef anyway. We want his man Terrance and their Mexican Cartel connections. But this shit is hitting close to home. We're gonna have to put 24-hour surveillance on you," Bradshaw said.

"Surveillance? Hell naw. Let me do me like I been doing. I ain't worried about nobody running up on me. Don't none of these bitches or niggas want any smoke with me!" Ma Baby yelled. She stood up and paced her living room floor, arms flailing wildly. "Fuck all these bitch ass muthafuckas out here man. Ain't none of 'em on shit. Kill ***my*** bitch and get away with it? Hell naw, fuck that!"

"Calm down you coke whore," Agent Holis interjected.

"Coke whore? Your sister's a junkie whore, you prissy white bitch," Ma baby shot back.

"You fucking cunt!" Agent Holis reached out but Bradshaw got in between the two women before they could claw each other's eyes out.

"Goddamnit you two! Enough with this catfighting shit. We are trying to get to the bottom of all these snake killings. From here to Appleton, motherfuckers are getting snaked and we need to find the connection."

"Wait, what? What connection? Appleton? What the fuck are y'all talking about?" Ma Baby asked. The agents informed her of the Patricia Clooney murder, the hashtag trunked videos, and all the other snake related homicides that have been happening lately. So immersed in the streets, she hadn't heard about this shit until she saw Carol with the snakes hanging from her most intimate orifices.

Ma Baby sat in silence, stunned. She listened to them and watched the clips on an iPad they showed her of teens getting into their trunks. The wheels began turning in her head. "You say all this started in Appleton?" she asked. The agents nodded.

She only knew one person from up those ways. "I might have something for y'all," Ma Baby said.

~

NOT ALL FRUIT is good for the soul. Cherries and berries are of no nutritional value to you, so steer clear at all costs.

"What the fuck does that mean?" Becky said out loud. Confused by her horoscope, she fed her poodle Dior before grabbing her purse and leaving. Rose told Becky that she wanted her to keep Ma Baby on her hip for the day to see what was on her brain after the Carol killing. Since Ma Baby called Rose and said Neef's guy Dirty Sprite wanted to chop it up with a white bitch, Rose told her Becky would double date with her.

Becky decided to pull out the AMG Benz that BBC got her as an initiation present. She bumped rap music and crunched numbers in her head as she headed down to the Mil. Since the J-Twins' murder, her clientele had tripled. The only other motherfuckers selling pills up north was Pill Mobb, and BBC was slowly working on them. They'd be out of the way real soon. In the meantime, she was counting cash by the duffle bag. *Weekly*. Now that she was plugged with a never-ending supply of pharmaceuticals, she was able to pump out a mass amount of product with no delay. The two for $50 deal on every pill imaginable caused an influx in usage and new pill poppers.

Becky got in on the plan Rose spoke of about sending girls to school for various professions that was a thing of genius that would benefit BBC in the future. Chicks her little sister knew who had graduated or were on their way to graduating were being enrolled in all the top universities across the country in numerous fields: law, medicine, social work, engineering, accounting, and much more. They scouted the most passionate individuals, befriended them, and agreed to bankroll their education. The eager young girls gratefully accepted, not knowing they would be called upon for favors sometime in the future once they were in a position to help. They were also lavished with all kinds of gifts. Expensive clothes, jewelry, and tech gadgets. Anyone being lavished with presents would naturally succumb to the charms of the giver. It brought down walls. Becky won over a lot of loyal followers because of her gracious actions. She became the most popular benefactor in the Snow Bunny community.

Becky disliked Ma Baby from the moment she met her at Summer's place months ago. She knew something wasn't right about the bitch, and the information that BBC uncovered proved her intuitions correct. The snake ass Latina made Becky's skin crawl, and she hated that she had to be the one to roll with her on the double date. But since Mud Money was one of their marks, everyone thought it wouldn't hurt to get one of their boys wrapped around Becky's white finger. And by keeping Ma Baby close, they were killing two birds with one stone.

Ma Baby was waiting outside her home when Becky pulled up. The batman doors rose in the air and Ma Baby slid into the luxury Mercedes.

"Hey mami. You ready to roll?" Ma Baby beamed.

Becky rolled her eyes but played along. "Yeah, where are we headed?" Becky asked, putting the car in drive.

"We gonna meet them at the domes, then they gonna take us out to eat somewhere."

"Oh, alright," Becky replied.

"Yeah, I told Dirty Sprite all about chu and he's geeked as fuck to meet you."

"Hmpf. So, why they call him Dirty Sprite anyway?" Becky asked.

"Cuz, he be leaning hard. And he mixes his shit only with Sprite," Ma Baby told her.

"Oh."

"You lean?" Ma Baby asked.

"Who me? Nah. I tried it before, but it just had me stuck. I'm a pothead. Maybe a lil Molly every now and then... on special occasions."

"Well, he cool peoples. Got plenty bread too. But from the looks of it, you rolling in your own loot girl. Whatchu moving?" Ma Baby asked, admiring the plush interior.

Becky almost burst out laughing. *This rat bitch really has no shame does she?* "Tanning beds, ma. In case you haven't heard, my family owns a lucrative tanning salon chain."

"Must be doing pretty good to afford a whip like this. And you blinging pretty hard too." Becky didn't answer her. Instead, she chose to pop her bubblegum loudly. Becky put on Ralo's hottest album as the Benz glided on the interstate.

Ma Baby pulled a blunt and lighter out of her purse and was about to spark up when Becky stopped her. "Uh-uh ma. Ain't no smoking in my car."

"What? I thought you said you chiefed."

"I do, but not in my ride. Shit, a bitch get pulled over and the police smell weed? That's cause for them to search my shit," Becky schooled her.

"Girl, you trippin'. You legit ain't chu? What they gon' find if you're not doing nothing?"

"That isn't the point Ma Baby. I don't like the police touching my shit. And I'm not trying to have any reason for them to fuck with my shit."

"Huhn. Alright then. I still don't see what the big deal is tho. You a white woman anyway. The police will let your ass get away with murder," Ma Baby said. Becky didn't even respond to her comment.

"You know what Becky? It's a lot of muthafuckas getting away with murder nowadays. You heard about my homegirl right?"

"Yeah, I'm sorry about that. You must be devastated," Becky

said, glancing over at Ma Baby. Her chinky eyes turned into squinty slits.

"Same shit that happened to my boo is the same shit that's been going on in Appleton. Snake related deaths. You think that's a coincidence Becky?"

"Huh? Are you trying to say something Ma Baby?"

"Nah, not really. But you're from Appleton right?"

"Yeah. So?" Becky said, becoming agitated. She wanted to shoot the rat bitch in her face then and there but refrained herself.

"A lot of shit has been going down up there in your lily-white town. Some *crazy* ass shit. I know one thing tho, I'm gonna find out who did that shit to Carol. And then, I'm gonna do the same thing to every... single...person...they love. And that's on everything that ***I*** love!"

Becky swallowed hard and wrestled with her thoughts. She had her Glock in her purse and could easily push this snake bitch's wig back, but she was sure the alphabet boys were probably lurking in the near distance. She kept checking her rearview for inconspicuous looking cars.

I know some niggas that's wit me ain't wit me
So I will not never put them in my bidness.
Fuck whoever ain't wit me, tell em stay out my bidness,
Fuck whoever ain't wit me, tell em stay out my bidness,
I know some niggas that's wit me ain't wit me
So I will not never put them in my bidness
I know some niggas that's wit me ain't wit me
So I will not never put them in my bidness.

BECKY RAPPED along to Ralo's heartfelt declarations as she censored herself at the N-word parts. They rode listening to the music for a while. Then Ma Baby turned the music down.

"Look, my bad Becky for getting in my feelings. Me and

Carol were close. But I'm working on healing tho." Becky patted Ma Baby's hand in good nature. "Hey, can you swing by the liquor store before we get to the Domes? Gotta get some top shelf drank to turn up with. Let me text my Boo and see what kind they want," Ma Baby said, grabbing her iPhone and began to text.

Becky stopped at a liquor store on South 27th. When they pulled into the parking lot Ma Baby patted her pockets and pretended to look through her purse.

"Shit! Girl, I forgot my license at the crib. It's probably in my car. Damn, can you go in and get the liquor?" Ma Baby asked.

Irritated, Becky huffed and opened the door. "I guess. What am I grabbing?" Ma Baby handed her two one-hundred dollar bills and told her what to get. While Becky was in the store, Ma Baby pulled a bag out of her purse and dumped the contents underneath Becky's seat. Then she lit up a blunt and puffed big clouds of smoke all over the car. She was finishing up a text when Becky got back into the Benz.

"What the fuck is your freaking problem? Didn't I say *NO* smoking in my car?" Becky snatched the blunt out of Ma Baby's hand and put it out in the ashtray. Becky threw the bottles of alcohol in the back and pulled out of the parking lot with the windows down. She grabbed a bottle of perfume from the glove compartment and spritzed the citrus-y vanilla scent in the air.

Ma Baby grabbed the blunt out of the ashtray and slid it into her cleavage. Seeing as how all she was wearing was a lace push-up bra under a skintight leather jacket, all of her business was on full display. "You need to take a chill pill mami. It ain't that serious. You need some good dick and weed," Ma Baby said, fanning the heavily fragranced air and laughed. No sooner than she said that, a squad car got behind them and flicked its lights. Becky cursed under her breath and pulled over.

Cherries and berries are of no nutritional value to you, so steer clear at all costs.

"Motherfucking cocksucker!" Becky shouted, looking over at Ma Baby.

"What?" Ma Baby said, fidgeting. The cop walked up to the car asking for license, registration, and proof of insurance.

"Sure officer, is there a problem?" Becky asked.

"Ma'am, just give me what I asked for. You ladies been drinking today?" the cop asked, bending down and sticking his face in the driver's window to peer at the passenger.

"No sir," they both said in unison.

"How about smoking? I smell marijuana."

"No officer, that's just my new perfume," Ma Baby said, leaning over Becky's lap.

"Uh-huh. Is that why you have what appears to be a blunt in your bra ma'am?" Becky and Ma Baby looked down at her titties at the same time. The half smoked blunt stood proud and tall between her butter Rican cleavage.

"I'm gonna need both of you to step outside the vehicle," the policeman said, unholstering his gun. Just then, two more squad cars arrived on the scene. Becky shot daggers at Ma Baby. This was no coincidence. She ***never*** got pulled over. The policeman said because he not only smelled marijuana, but also seen a blunt out in the open, it gave him probable cause to search Becky's car.

"Nice vehicle too. How much this set you back?" another cop asked, Becky was tight lipped and fuming mad.

The police sat Becky and Ma Baby in the back of separate squad cars. It didn't take long for one to walk up to Becky holding a bag of prescription pill bottles full of ecstasy, Oxycontin, Percocet 30's, and Xanax. Over 300 pills in all. They also found 2 ounces of Heroin and 4 and a half ounces of crack cocaine.

"Soooo, do you know anything about this stuff that we found under your seat Ms. Slinkowski?"

Becky's heart dropped like she was on a rollercoaster. Her

mouth was dry and for the first time ever, she was actually scared. "Wh-what? I never seen any of that shit before. And what do you mean under *MY* seat?"

"Looks like we have a big-time dealer on our hands boys," another officer walked up and said. "You're in big trouble Rebecca. But maybe we can help you..." Becky closed her eyes as anger, rage, and the strongest of all, hatred, replaced her fear.

That snake bitch set me up! She fussed to herself.

TO BE CONTINUED....

ABOUT THE AUTHOR

Perk Thirty is a multi-faceted writer from Milwaukee, Wisconsin. His passion for books, poetry, screenplays, and music, fuels his creativity in all of those art forms. While "Bad Boss Chicks" is his first official release, there are many more Perk Thirty novels to come.

Through his words, Perk Thirty aspires to take readers on a vivid journey, bringing them out of their current world and into an exciting, entertaining one, if only for a brief time.

For those wishing to discuss Perk Thirty's characters or have special requests, you may write:

Perk Thirty
P.O. Box 1954
Eau Claire, WI 54703

Or you can contact him via Facebook: Perkthirty

Made in the USA
Monee, IL
04 September 2020